DESTINATION
2020
WHITE HOUSE

AUTHOR'S NOTE

This is a work of fiction. The names, characters, and incidents are fictional and imaginary, except for some of the events that happened during World War II, which are described from the author's personal experiences or documented reports. If there are any inaccuracies, they should be considered fictional additions. Any references to real events, businesses, organizations, media, and locales are intended only to help give the story a sense of reality. Prediction of future events is derived from the imagination of the author.

Published in 1999 by
Newmark Publishing Company
South Windsor, Connecticut 06074

Phone or fax (860) 282-7265

Book design by Irving Perkins Associates, Inc.

Manufactured in the United States of America
10 9 8 7 6 5 4 3 2 1

Library of Congress Cataloging in Publication Data
98-6844
Grant, Pete
Destination 2020 White House
1. Night carrier flying
2. Women flying jets
3. Military and Congressional politics
4. First Woman President of the United States
ISBN 0-938539-53-1

DESTINATION
2020
WHITE HOUSE

PETE GRANT

ACKNOWLEDGEMENTS

I wish to thank the following people for their help in the preparation of this manuscript: Dina Friedman, Matt Sawyer, Barbara Harding, and Kimberly Kozlowski. For technical help: Captain F. Richard Whalen, U.S.N. Ret; first Skipper of the Aegis Cruiser, U.S.S. Mobile Bay, the military administrative staff at the Naval Academy, the Air Boss of the U.S.S. Harry Truman CVN-75, and numerous Navy pilots of World War II vintage, and actively flying Navy carrier fighter pilots.

DEDICATION

This book is dedicated to Judy Sharp, my executive secretary for over thirty years. She served first as my medical secretary and then as a copy editor and executive for Newmark Publishing. She was diagnosed with advanced ovarian cancer while this manuscript was being written, and has succumbed to the disease. She will be deeply missed by all those who have known her and loved her.

* Part of the proceeds from this book will be donated for basic Ovarian Cancer Research.

EPIGRAPH

He shall cover thee with his feathers, and under his
wings shalt thou trust: his truth shall be thy shield and
buckler.

Thou shalt not be afraid for the terror by night; nor for
the arrow that flieth by day; nor for the pestilence that
walketh in darkness; nor for the destruction that
wasteth at noonday.

A thousand shall fall at thy side, and ten thousand at
thy right hand; but it shall not come nigh thee.

Psalm 91:4-7

PROLOGUE

U.S.S. HARRY TRUMAN CVN75
JULY 20, 2002

Lieutenant Commander Kelli Fitzgerald climbed up the ladder of her F-51 Cobra jet and stepped into the cockpit. She was getting ready to fly her plane at night off the flight deck of the supercarrier U.S.S. Harry Truman CVN75. Kelli was the skipper of Strike Fighter Squadron VFA-263, on a shakedown cruise to requalify her pilots for overseas assignment.

It was a dangerous night for flying . . . black as the ace of spades with heavy cloud cover that made visibility impossible. As she looked up towards the sky, everything was one big black glob. Vertigo would be a problem and her flight instruments would be vital for her survival. Kelli glanced at the dimly lit heads-up display (HUD) instrument panel that cast a blue-green glow over the cockpit, put on her helmet and connected the plug to her radio. She could hear the constant chatter of the Air Boss seated high above the carrier's deck, as he directed all the action on and about the flight deck.

As bad as the weather was, it was an ideal night for retraining Navy jet carrier pilots for night carrier landings. The top Navy brass were aboard watching, so the pressure was on. The Air Boss had made it clear in preflight that he did not want any fuck-ups on his flight deck. He expected a stellar performance.

Kelli settled into her cockpit and could feel a brisk wind coming across the flight deck as the carrier's nuclear powered engines, in preparation for launch, wound up a notch. For a moment she felt awed by the massive power of the floating air base. She turned up the light on her instrument panel and quickly checked out the plane's warning, caution, adversary, and indicator lights. They were okay. Her crew chief plugged in her G suit, and she fastened the leg straps, lap belt, and shoulder straps that locked her into the seat and ejection unit.

She checked the position of the bailout handle between her legs. Once pulled, pyrotechnic charges would blow off the canopy and rocket motors would ignite. She'd be shot up 350 feet. A gyro stabilizer would keep the unit upright. Hopefully the parachute would open, and a ballistic spreader would make sure that it stayed open. If the parachute didn't open, she'd be like a Roman candle dropping out of the sky to her death.

Her crew chief rotated his orange lighted wands in a circle, the signal to start the F-51's engine. She checked her throttle adjustment, pushed the rudder brakes down, and hit the starter switch. There was a high whining sound, a cough, and then a puff of exhaust as the jet engines started.

The chocks were removed from under her plane and then, with his wands, the crew chief directed her up the carrier deck. As she got close to the catapult, she taxied her plane up close to the metal shield, the jet blast deflector that protected the flight deck personnel from the take-off blast of the jet engines. She pressed the switch to extend the plane's folded wings and felt them lock in place. She could hear the roar of the other jet engines ahead of her as they came to full power and were thrust one by one out into the night sky. Her eyes darted about the cockpit gauges in front of her. Kelli went over her check-off list and inspected the plane's control functions. She moved the control stick around and pushed the rudder control pedals. The shield dropped down as she taxied into position for take-off and adjusted her wing flaps. Finally, she reached the catapult.

The crew hooked the plane's belly onto the steam-activated tract. The launch officer started to swing his lighted wand in fast circles, telling her to increase the r.p.m.s to full military rated thrust to power up the engines for the launch. She flashed her wing lights when she was ready. The steam catapult engaged, and the F-51 accelerated from 0 to 170 knots in just 200 feet.

It took three seconds for her plane to travel down the catapult shuttle tract that launched her skyward. Below the flight deck, at the end of the tract, a large heavy piston slammed into a water brake; the dissipation of energy was so great that it shook the entire ship. After the plane got over the edge of the carrier, Kelli pulled back on the control stick and nudged her throttles all the way to full military power. She watched her flight instruments on the H.U.D. intensely. There was a deep roar as the additional fuel shot into the jet engines activating the afterburner, giving the plane an added jolt of energy. Because there were so many split-second decisions to be made, Kelli felt like a one-armed paperhanger as she used the controls to raise the landing gear, pulled back on the stick, and raised the flaps. Her r.p.m.s reached full power as she soared into the dark sky. She was flying completely on instruments.

On her VHF radio, she heard the Air Boss tell her to fly out to the Marshal stack and orbit at 9,000 feet.

"Roger," she replied as she shot upward to the designated altitude.

The Cobra jet Kelli was flying had the most sophisticated Pulse-Doppler radar equipment in the world. It could penetrate any kind of weather and could see surface vessels and aircraft at distances up to 200 nautical miles. The radar could spot approaching targets long before the F-51 could be detected, if it could be visualized at all. The plane had been constructed with highly sophisticated technological materials and devices to defeat enemy sensors. It was the newest sophisticated upgraded fighter plane.

Even with the Cobra's ability to search deep into the night, carrier landings (known as traps) after dark are difficult because you cannot see what is happening on the flight deck. There is no horizon, no lights on the ground to refer to, just a big mass of black ocean and sky with no depth perception. In order to land safely, you have to rely on sophisticated computer instrumentation in the plane and at the super carrier base. The pilot's flying ability is tested to the zenith at night because critical adjustments often have to be made just before touch down. The visible ceiling might be a few hundred feet, and the pilot has to land a plane within 200 feet on the back of the deck, using a hook on the tail of the plane to catch a wire. The deck can be rising and falling 20 feet or more and if the ship hits a wave or a swell, it can roll from side to side. Once hooked, the plane decelerates from about 150 knots to zero in seconds. Throughout naval history night traps have had a well-deserved reputation as ass-tighteners and are considered the most difficult challenge for a pilot.

Kelli was proud of her flying ability, yet every time she attempted a night trap, it still scared the shit out of her. Because of the piss poor weather, her anticipation and anxiety increased as she went over the steps in her mind that she had to precisely accomplish to insure a safe landing. Finally the "approach controller" guided her plane giving her vectors until she was about eight miles from the ship to prepare for landing. Kelli had pulled back on the throttles to get down to 1200 feet. Her jet would be landing on the angled deck nine degrees to the left from the center line. That meant that she would have to fly her jet slightly to the right of the moving Air Base in order to come into the groove accurately. She was on I.L.S. instruments now, making constant flight control changes for proper alignment. She was also receiving verbal commands from the final controller who was using radar data displays in the C.A.T.T.C. of the carrier.

At three miles out, Kelli centered the needles on her cross pointer indicator of the I.L.S. equipment. Because of the shitty weather, she still couldn't see the carrier's deck. She checked her landing gear, flaps, and hook instruments. Her plane was barreling towards the 'boat' as her altitude over the water decreased.

Kelli's plane broke out of the bad weather at about three-quarters of a mile. She saw the meatball on the left side of the flight deck and the vertical lights indicating the center line.

The plane's glide path is marked by a mirror, a fresnel lens embedded in the middle of the flight deck and a bright light. The pilot watches the deck-mounted light called the "meatball" that determines the plane's position in reference to the moving flight deck. If the meatball is in the center, surrounded by green lights for contrast, the pilot is on the proper glide path. Red lights aligned vertically by the meatball and flashed to indicate a wave-off, which means that the plane is not in a safe position to land. The L.S.O. operates the red wave-off lights.

Kelli picked up the meatball, notifying the L.S.O. that she had it in sight.

"Tiger Lady One, ball, 6.2," she said, identifying herself by call sign and the amount of fuel in the tank (6200 lbs.).

"Roger, ball," acknowledged the L.S.O., Bill Pearce. "Little right for lineup."

Kelli made the adjustment and lowered her wing flaps slightly and then watched the luminous amber meatball on the port side of the deck. Her plane was perfectly aligned, slightly below the row of green lights. By pulling back on the stick, she nudged the meatball up to the top edge of center, so she could see it move better. As her plane rapidly approached the flight deck, she controlled the stick with her right hand, the throttle with her left hand, and her feet moved the rudders. Her glide slope was perfect and her plane was on the center line strobe light. To get it exactly right was harder than trying to fine tune a Steinway for opening night at Carnegie Hall.

Bill Pearce got on his mike. "Clear deck. Wire gear set, Cobra. Right for line up."

As her plane thundered toward the back of the carrier's deck, the meatball drifted to the left of the center line. She made a quick stick and rudder adjustment as the deck came up rapidly. She felt the wheels hit the deck and pushed the throttle forward in case she missed a wire and had to take off again (a bolter). The tail hook engaged as her body was thrust against the straps. The plane bounced around and came to a sudden stop. She pulled the throttle back to idle.

With her heart pounding in her chest, Kelli heard Pearce give his assessment of her landing that is recorded. "Pitching deck, good adjustment, OK #3 wire." A few words on which a lot of adrenaline was spent.

And Kelli was far from finished. She taxied her plane up to the catapult and was launched again into the black sky.

Lieutenant Brian Fox was not having as good a night. He had made two touch and go passes that the L.S.O. did not like, and in addition was waved off twice with the hook down. Each time he got eight miles from the ship the Air Operations Center's final controller had taken over, and Fox announced when his plane's computer was locked on the carrier's automatic landing system. The weather had gotten worse, and Fox did not like giving total control to the computer. If he was going to fly into the black ocean and die, he wanted to have control of the plane in his own hands. He was afraid to use the computer controlled landing. Now, on his fifth try, he'd lost his nerve. As Pearce tried to sugar-talk the pilot in, along with his I.L.S. the Air Boss in the tower was beginning to lose his cool. Fox was causing a back-up in the landing circle which was fucking up his flight deck. The Air Boss told Pearce to send him to a "bingo field," referring to a safer landing site about 250 sea miles away.

"Not yet!" he replied.

L.S.O. Pearce didn't want that. Once they landed at the bingo field, some pilots lost their confidence completely and could never land safely aboard at night again. "Fox, how's your fuel?" he asked.

"2.4," he replied—meaning 2.4 thousand pounds. "Maybe enough to get to a bingo field."

"Forget the bingo field. Go up and refuel on the tanker."

"Roger."

Fox was pissed as he climbed up to 10,000 feet to find the tanker. Five passes without a successful trap was not something to be proud of. It would be on his permanent flight records. Refueling at night when it's completely black is also a bitch too. You feel like you are blindfolded trying to hang your hat on a spike. The big difference is your life is at stake and sometimes the tanker pilot's. The fuel hook-up has to be perfect. You're inches away from a total disaster if you can't see. The tanker has a fifty foot hose that extends out of the tail with a drogue basket at the end. It is a funnel-shaped device that the fighter aircraft with its pointed fuel connector has to hook onto for refueling. There are red lights at the end of the basket to help you locate it, but it ain't easy to see. Your own plane's spotlights are also used. A green light goes on when it's hooked up properly, and the air speed of both planes has to be almost identical to hook up safely. It is like a crap-shoot—a mid-air collision waiting to happen in bad weather.

Fox had frequently refueled in the daytime but had limited experience in refueling at night. His flying was rusty. His last tour of duty was as a flight instructor at Pensacola and refueling a Cobra at night was not part of that program. As he sat in the cockpit, he could feel his heart pounding in his chest. He knew he had to forget about his failure to make the night trap, pull himself together and concentrate, but he was having trouble seeing anything in the darkness. He was losing his cool.

When he got sight of the tanker on his Doppler radar, he announced his presence.

"H.T. tanker, this is Fox Tiger Ten. I have you in sight. What is your air speed?"

"190 knots."

"Roger. I'm approaching your tail. I think I see the drogue basket light."

"Fox, I have you in sight. Slow down your air speed. You're coming in too fast."

Fox put his speed brakes on and slid by the tanker's right wing. He missed the basket. His left wing almost hit the right wing of the tanker, the wing lights almost touching.

"Holy shit! I almost hit him! I can't see a fucking thing!"

"For Christ's sake. Watch what you're doing," shouted Joe, the tanker pilot.

"Sorry," replied Fox, meekly. "I'm trying my best!"

"Well, it ain't good enough! Wake up! We'll both be real sorry if you do that again."

Fox was right on the edge. He had a cramp in his stomach and was sweating profusely. He knew he was running out of fuel.

After two unsuccessful tries which were dangerously close, he pulled himself together and slowly eased up on what he thought was the drogue basket. It was bobbing and weaving, and the turbulence in the air, which he couldn't see at night, wasn't helping. Finally, he hooked the plane's nose into the basket and connected and pushed it in about 5 feet ... the green light went on.

"Christ! I finally did it! Hallelujah!" he shouted.

Within a few minutes he took on 5,000 pounds of additional fuel. As he broke away, he gave a huge sigh of relief. At least now he had a shot to get back aboard.

He had enough fuel to make more passes at that elusive flight deck.

"H.T. Base. This is Fox Tiger Ten. Have refueled successfully."

"Roger, Fox. You may enter the holding pattern at Marshal Angels 10."

He would again be using his second option, a carrier controlled approach responding to verbal commands from a controller using radar data displayed in the C.A.T.T.C. and radar data transmitted to the plane. At three miles out at 1200 feet, he centered the needles on his cross pointer indicator.

He finally saw the meatball. It was on amber, but he was settling too rapidly. His sink rate was too fast.

Pearce saw him break out of the clouds at about 1500 yards. He heard him announce the ball.

"Tiger Ten. Ball 6.4."

"Fox, easy as you go, add ... a little power."

Fox's plane finally hit the deck.

Pearce thought for a moment that Fox might actually have a successful trap, but he kept his thumb on the pickle switch, tickling it nervously in case he had to order Fox to abort the landing. The Cobra came in fast, but as it cleared the ramp and set down, the deck pitched and Fox overcompensated. Pearce saw the wings tilt too far to the left relative to the deck and shouted, "Take it up, take it up, bolter! Bolter! Bolter!" As he hollered the Cobra's left wheel crashed into the deck and snapped off.

The flight deck crew dove right and left, seeking cover in the deep grooves on the side of the carrier's deck. When the Cobra's left wingtip hit the deck, it sent a wave of sparks into the air, and made a god awful screeching sound as it broke off. The main fuselage and cockpit headed like a bullet for the water in front of the carrier. Fox pulled his ejection seat handle and the pyrotechnic charges and rocket motors ignited, lighting up the sky and launching him straight up into the air. Luckily, the parachute opened in front of the carrier, and he rapidly descended into the water.

"Craft and pilot overboard! I repeat, craft and pilot overboard," Pearce shouted with an urgent calm familiar to pilots. "Let's get him."

The bullhorn announced the crash. Flood lights went on all over the place. The Air Sea Rescue helicopter, with its propeller spinning, searched the dark ocean for the pilot behind the carrier. Huge floodlights on the undersurface of the helicopter frantically scanned the water. The rolling sea and waves made the search difficult, but they finally found him bobbing around like a cork. The helicopter put a man in the water to assist in his rescue.

One half hour later, Lieutenant Fox, cold, soaked, slightly injured, and feeling embarrassed and dejected, was pulled from the water. Sixty million dollars of taxpayer money was down the drain.

When the Air Boss witnessed the Cobra crash, he got on the squawk box right away. "This is H.T. Base. All Tiger planes are to hold position until further notice."

He was debating sending them all to a bingo field. He told the planes low on fuel to gas up on the tanker. Since Kelli was the fighter squadron Commander, he contacted her directly on his VHF radio.

"Tiger One, this is the Air Boss. We lost a Cobra, but got the pilot. Aerology informs us that we have a front moving in, and I'm not out to prove to the brass here that we're crazy."

"H.T. Base, this is Tiger One. I'll come down and take a look."

"Okay, Tiger One. Cleared to approach. Cleared for fly-by."

Kelli used her instruments and Doppler radar (an instrument approach) to get into the groove and about half-a-mile from the stern she picked up the meatball. It wasn't going to be easy getting aboard unless she used a computer controlled landing. For a moment she thought of all the training she'd been through to get here, all the inspections, tests, dawn patrols, classes, and Navy bullshit. And now, tonight, the boys from the top were assembled, checking out the Navy's finest. They just saw one pilot take a dive, and now the female slick-chick was coming down for a look. She knew all eyes were on her. "Fuck it!" she hollered. "If I land this plane, it's because I know I can, not because they think I can't."

"Tiger One. This is H.T. Base. What does it look like up there?"

"H.T. Base, this is Tiger One. It looks shitty. But I'll give it a try on my next pass." "Roger, Tiger One."

Kelli circled the carrier, picked up the ship on her Doppler radar, and then made an I.L.S. approach to the flight deck, starting eight miles out and lowering to 1500 feet. Pearce could hear her whining jet engines get louder as she approached the deck. He couldn't see the plane because of the cloud cover and darkness. However, her I.L.S. approach and glide path was perfect. Suddenly, she broke out.

"Tiger One, slow down."

"Roger, cutting speed," she replied.

At 300 yards she cut back slightly on her throttle and got a quick glance at the meatball. It looked okay to her.

"Easy as you go," Pearce said. Her landing approach looked good to him.

"Roger."

Kelli hit the deck hard, which came up at her too quickly as the ship hit a swell, and missed the third arresting wire. The nose wheel hit like a rock, and she heard the fuselage crack. The plane bounced to the left, rolling over off the port side. It spanked the water, started to flip over on its back and then settled. She reached for her ejection seat handle but couldn't find it as her left shoulder crushed into the instrument panel. Her head snapped sideways behind her shoulder, and then she blacked out.

As she came to, she was aware of warm blood running into her eyes and cold water pouring in on her feet. Luckily, the heavy jet engines in the back of the plane kept the nose up in the water. She had to act quickly because the plane would sink rapidly. She fumbled for the handle to release the canopy with her left hand and screamed out at the pain in her shoulder. She reached across with her right hand, groping under the brine for the canopy handle. She found it, pulled with all her strength, and the canopy finally opened. The water was at her feet as the nose of the plane slowly dipped below the surface of the sea. Water filled the cockpit.

She had to get out of that cockpit in a hurry. She started hyperventilating, not out of panic, but to flood her blood with oxygen in case she needed more time under water to get free of the Cobra. Then she remembered what she had been taught. She unstrapped her legs and seat belt, pulled herself up and out of the cockpit, and entered the cold black water, feeling the tow of the Cobra tug at her feet, as if it secretly wanted her to accompany it to the ocean floor.

When the plane went off the port side of the carrier, the captain on the ship's bridge hollered out to the helmsman, for the second time in an hour, "Right hard rudder." That turned the carrier's bow away from Kelli in the water. Then he hollered, "Shift your rudder."

That reversed the ship's course so the stern would swing away from her. She now had the best chance to avoid being sucked under the water by the carrier's four huge screw propellers.

Sirens sounded and search lights went on again around the carrier. The Air-sea Rescue helicopter, hovering off the port side, finally saw Kelli treading water with one arm, struggling to stay afloat. They put a swimmer in the water to rescue her.

The Air Boss sent the rest of the airborne planes to a bingo field. He was not taking any more chances.

As they hoisted Kelli aboard, the Vice Admiral on the bridge looking on said to the ship's Captain, "Who is that?"

"Lieutenant Commander Fitzgerald, the Strike Fighter Skipper."

"That's one hell of a pilot," said the Admiral, "trying to land his plane on this deck in this horrible weather. He's got balls made of solid brass."

"It's a woman, sir! It's Kelli Fitzgerald."

"A woman? I can't believe it. What's her moniker?"

"Tiger Lady"

"That name certainly fits her! She's got to be some kind of a super woman."

"She is." replied the ship's Captain.

I

JULY 4, 1970
KELLI GROWING UP

Kelli Armstrong Fitzgerald was born on July 4, 1970, at Baptist Hospital in Jacksonville, Florida, a breech baby delivered by Caesarean section, weighing 8 lbs. 4 oz. She was given her middle name, Armstrong, after astronaut Neal Armstrong. Her father was a Navy carrier pilot stationed at Jacksonville Naval Air Station, and her mother was a former Chief Petty Officer. Her parents had met at Pensacola, Florida, during training. They fell in love and conceived Kelli on a weekend pass the night they were married.

Kelli grew up a Navy brat, following her dad around the world, as he was transferred from one base to another. When she was six years old, her father returned to Pensacola as a flight instructor. Kelli often played in the sandbox behind her home on the base and watched the Navy's planes that flew overhead. She also watched the small birds flying around in her backyard with their flapping wings, but those big planes in the sky were different.

"How come the wings of your plane don't flap like the birds?"

"That's an interesting question," he remarked, as he looked at his daughter, impressed at how smart she was. "Someday, they might have movable wings, but right now they don't. People can't fly like birds . . . it's too complicated to duplicate."

"If it can't flap its wings," she asked, "then how does your plane fly?"

"With wings to create lift and a big engine with tremendous power and thrust to get the plane into the air. To keep the plane moving, you need to overcome the resistance of the air, called drag. The airplane engines do that too! The wings and tail have controls that guide the plane and tell it which way to go."

"Clear as mud," replied Kell."

Her dad laughed. "It is. And it's getting more complicated every day."

The urge to fly, the *need* to fly, ran through her family, something she became aware of as she got older and became close to her grandfather, a former Navy torpedo bomber pilot during World War II. He had volunteered for one of the navy's first night carrier air groups (Night Air Group 53) and had landed safely at night on ten different carriers during World War II. She loved to hear his war stories about when he participated in the first night carrier air raids over Tokyo aboard the U.S.S. Saratoga and participated in the air support at Iwo Jima. He was on the Saratoga when the ship was hit by seven kamikazes at Iwo and almost sunk.

Most of the naval air stations her father was stationed at were on the coastline of the U.S. . . . Jacksonville, San Diego, Alameda, Oceana, so Kelli was introduced to swimming at an early age. She loved it and was good at it.

When Kelli was 12, her father was assigned to an air group flying out of the San Diego Naval Air Station. She attended public schools there, swam in the outdoor pool, and could race with the best of the boys. One of the women swimming instructors saw her and asked her to swim the 200–meter freestyle as fast as she could. When she looked at the stopwatch, she was impressed. Kelli was promptly given an instructor to improve her skills, and she won the state high school championship in the 200 meter freestyle when she was a freshman.

The one man in her life, her father, was not always around, since he went out to sea six months at a time with carrier air groups. Her grandfather would fill the void in his absence, attending her swim meets, talking about life and flying. He noted, though it did not happen often, that Kelli hated to lose.

Because she was a girl and may need to protect herself, her grandfather suggested she enroll in a weight lifting program as well as take Karate lessons. She finally earned the black belt, making her an expert in the art of self defense. During this time, he also saw the pilot inside of her taking shape.

Kelli continued to bug her grandfather about learning how to fly.

"Grandfather, how old were you when you started flying?"

"Nineteen. I was a freshman in college when Pearl Harbor was attacked by the Japanese. All able bodied men were drafted to join the armed forces. I didn't want to go into the infantry to do hand-to-hand combat, so I enlisted in the Naval Air Corps."

"How long did it take you to learn to fly?"

"I had to solo after eight hours of instruction, or I'd be washed out."

"That's not very long."

"That's because the government needed lots of pilots in a hurry. They needed to know early on whether you could fly. Training a military pilot is an expensive proposition."

"Grandfather, would you take me up and teach me how to fly? Mom told me that you still fly once in awhile."

"I'll have to think about that."

Finally, he convinced her parents that it would be safe for her to fly. In the air her grandfather saw Kelli's true passion for flying come forth. He arranged for Kelli's flying instructions and also taught her himself. She quickly soloed and often flew with her grandfather.

As Kelli grew older, she became a stunning redhead, five feet seven with a pretty figure, a swimmer's broad shoulders, and a thin waist. Her achievements in swimming continued to improve and when she was a junior in high school, she broke the United States' world record for women in the 200 meter free-style swimming meet in Los Angeles.

A short time later, she was invited with a group of outstanding high school athletes to meet the President at the White House. When she went up to shake his hand, he remarked, "That was an outstanding accomplishment, young lady. What are your plans after you finish high school?"

"I am going to go to college and become a pilot."

"Good for you," he replied. "Where do you plan to apply?"

"The Air Force Academy or the Naval Academy."

"If you have trouble getting accepted, give me a call. I might be able to help. We need leaders like you whenever we can get them."

Despite the fact that her heart was in the clouds, Kelli ended up with good grades and was sought by many of the top colleges in the country. Harvard, Yale, Brown, Duke, University of Michigan, University of California at Berkeley, and Stanford, all offered her free rides. But her final choices were between the Air Force Academy and the Naval Academy.

She decided to choose the Naval Academy because it seemed to offer more opportunity for women. Wendy B. Laurence, class of 1981, was selected by NASA as the first female naval aviator to train as an astronaut.

In the summer of 1988 Kelli checked in, received a name tag, alpha numbers, and an assignment to a Company. She had to stand in a long line to have her red hair cut. It took years to grow and three minutes to cut. She was then fitted for uniforms and issued "white works" and "Dixie cups," the uniform of a plebe. Her eyesight was tested, blood was drawn and shots given. She was taught how to stand in formation and how to salute properly. The plebes formed up in the Colonade connecting Bancroft and Dahlgren Halls, marched into Tecumseh Court, took the oath of office, and became midshipmen fourth class. She was then given a plebe bible, "Reef Points," that she would have to memorize.

Reveille was at 0500 every morning, and thirty minutes later she was at the athletic field for pull-ups, push-ups, and sit-ups. Kelli thought she was in great shape because of her swimming and jogging in high school, but she was wrong. The concentrated physical demands on her body at the academy were overwhelming. She had to pass personal physical readiness tests every semester and was timed doing push-ups and curl-ups.

Part of her indoctrination was learning how to stow her locker and how to wear and keep her twenty uniforms in top condition. She constantly did close-order drill and was taught how to handle pistols and rifles. The best part of her summer was learning the basics of seamanship, navigation, and signaling. All midshipmen have to learn how to tie knots, splice a line, and row a boat.

She was not allowed to forget that she had joined the Navy. In Bancroft Hall, which housed the fourth class regiment, walls are bulkheads, stairs are ladders, floors are decks, and bathrooms are heads.

Since "Mother Bee" is considered a ship, the midshipmen must fulfill shipboard duties. They have to wear their caps, salute superiors, wear uniforms, and stand watch. "Mother Bee" helps prepare future officers to become leaders and assume command … this is in contrast to civilian universities. Only ten to fifteen percent of the Naval Academy midshipmen were female, and there were rigid rules concerning fraternization between sexes, particularly between the upper classmen and the plebes. Dating within the company was prohibited and upper classmen were not allowed to date members of the fourth class at any time. The upper class midshipmen could only touch fourth class midshipmen for legitimate training purposes, such as correcting or adjusting the uniform, drill and rifle positions, or holding feet for sit-ups.

When the upper classmen returned in the fall, inspection became a daily chore. Everything had to pass muster. Kelli learned to dress and stow her gear perfectly. Her uniforms had to be clean and there could be no dust on her cap visors. Her shoes had to shine like a mirror; even the crows on her hat buttons had to stand at attention.

When her room and its contents were inspected, she stood at attention while an upper classman administered the "white glove test". Kelli learned how to brace up— chin in and chest out.

"Shoulders back! Suck in your gut!"

"Yes, sir."

She didn't think she could suck her gut in anymore than it was.

"Suck your gut in better, midshipman! You can do better than that!"

"Yes, sir!" she replied as she took a deep breath and held it. It was frustrating at times, but she knew she had to go through the same routine as the men to graduate.

At the Naval Academy, the academic curriculum places an emphasis on science and engineering. The grades achieved are your own because of the honor code that prevails. This holds every midshipman accountable for their every action. Midshipmen are persons of integrity; they do not lie, cheat, or steal.

Kelli's social life during plebe year was nonexistent . . . the code is clear. Whenever midshipmen of the opposite sex were in a room together in Bancroft Hall, "Mother Bee" was watching. The overhead lights had to be on, and the door could not be locked from the inside. It could be locked at night after taps. Sexual misconduct (including sexual acts and sexually motivated nudity) was a separation offense. Kelli wanted to graduate and become a Navy carrier pilot. If it meant doing without, she would abide by the rules.

Later on, after plebe year, there was fraternizing off campus . . . the academy had no control over that. Upper classmen were allowed to leave the yard after their last class on Saturday and expected to return Sunday evening by 1830. The first classmen could leave Friday evening and had unlimited weekends.

Kelli finished in the top five percent of her class in her plebe year. Fifteen percent of her class did not make it.

Every day, Kelli worked hard and put her best effort forward. Her leadership qualities were recognized early on by the Academy's staff.

The midshipmen's chain of command, which is fashioned after the Academy's executive department, is headed by the Brigade Commander. When Kelli became a first classman (Firstie), she was appointed the Brigade Commander during the spring semester.

Finally, the week for graduation and commissioning ceremonies arrived. A full dress parade before distinguished visitors took place. All the cadets assembled on the parade field and the entire Brigade of cadets passed in review. There were over four thousand cadets in two regiments, six battalions, and thirty-six companies.

Leading the parade was the Brigade staff and leading that staff was Brigade Commander Kelli Fitzgerald. As they marched by the reviewing stand, she hollered . . . "Eyes . . . Right!" All the officers in the reviewing stand stood up and saluted.

The President gave the commencement address at graduation and when Kelli went up to the podium to receive her diploma, he recognized her.

"Aren't you the young lady who set the record in swimming?"

"Yes, sir" she replied.

"You said you'd become a midshipman and here you are, the Brigade Commander."

"Yes, sir."

"All right, what's next?" he asked.

"I'm going to be a pilot, sir."

"Somehow I don't doubt you. If you were a little bit older, I'd worry about my job. Good luck to you!"

GOLD WINGS

After graduating as Brigade Commander, Kelli was asked by the Secretary of the Navy if she would be willing to go on tour and be interviewed on the early morning TV and evening talk shows. He told her that it would help the navy recruit women. She thought about it and accepted. It would give her an opportunity to relax from the four years of rigid discipline of the Naval Academy. For six weeks she traveled around the country, talking to the media.

On the last day of her tour, just before she was to start flight training at the Naval Air Station in Pensacola, she was invited to be on a talk show in Dallas with Mark Palmer, the new quarterback for the football team.

The moderator introduced Palmer as a graduate of Stanford University, an all-American football player in college, an academic all-American with a 3.8 GPA, and the most eligible bachelor in town. Mark gave an excellent talk. Then the narrator introduced Kelli.

"I'm what you call a Navy brat," she said as she smiled at the audience. "My father and grandfather were Navy pilots. I'm very proud of them. You might call them my role models. Becoming Brigade Commander at a male bastion such as the Naval Academy wasn't easy. It was an exhausting physical and mental challenge. I had to compete with the men on an equal basis."

When she finished her speech, Mark approached her and asked her to have dinner with him.

"I have to catch a plane to Pensacola in five hours," she said.

"Then that's a yes, right? As long as we enjoy the unrivaled cuisine of DFW airport."

"I'm game if you are."

"Let's go."

In the cab to DFW they talked about the show. "Wasn't television wild, with all those people covered with makeup?"

"That's one benefit of my job," he said. "The only makeup is two grease smears under my eyes."

"Why do football players do that?" asked Kelli.

"To reduce the sun's reflection in their eyes and to look tough."

"Really? I thought football players are tough."

"Many are," he said.

"What about you?" She was feeling her way along. It had been a while since she flirted. She almost expected a barracks commanding officer to explode from the front seat, yelling at her to drop, do 40, and clean out the head.

"What about me?" he said. "You mean, am I tough?"

"Yes." She held his gaze.

"When I have to be. Which is often. But it's better to be smart and alert, and know the play book. Playing hurt is part of it. But knowing your script back-to-front going in, and being in shape, keeps you from having to be tough. There," he said. "how did that sound?"

"Pretty polished," said Kelli. "Most men don't talk straight up like that."

"Oh, yeah? How do most men talk?" he asked. They were close in the cab's backseat. DFW was approaching, but neither was in a hurry anymore. They were both beginning to relax.

"Well," said Kelli, "most of the men I deal with don't talk, they scream orders, like 'get on your knees and give me 40!'"

He laughed. "Sounds tough."

"It can be."

"Are you?"

"Am I what? Tough?"

"Yes."

"Sometimes, if I have to be. But if I understand being a pilot, it's better to be smart and alert and know your plane inside out, and be in shape. That keeps you from having to be tough. There," she said, still looking at him. "How did that sound?"

"Familiar," he said.

The setting for dinner in the dining room at DFW was not exactly the best scene for a special date. But it turned out much better than either of them anticipated. Mark ordered a bottle of Chardonnay, and after pouring wine into each of their glasses, he raised his glass to Kelli in a toast.

"Here's to the beginning of a beautiful new relationship."

She looked him in the eyes and liked what she saw.

"I'll drink to that."

"You've got a beautiful smile."

"Thank you. Yours isn't so bad either."

Their conversation was light at first, but as they talked, it achieved a greater depth. They had a mutual exchange of concepts and thoughts that did not conflict. It was obvious that they were enjoying each others' company. The food they ate was immaterial. It could have been Hungarian goulash or a fast food hamburger.

Kelli's flight was delayed an hour, so they had extra time together. She took her jacket off as they finished the bottle of wine. Her blouse couldn't hide any of her physical attributes, and she noticed that Mark was pleasantly distracted and had difficulty keeping his eyes off her.

"Where does this go?" he said.

"My very thought," said Kelli. "I don't know."

"Then let's leave it be," he said. "Stay in touch, but don't overdo it. I've got a career ahead of me, getting knocked on my ass and being chased all over a field by psychopathic linebackers. You're going to fly jets."

"Right now," she said, "I'd rather go back to the lounge with you and make some really bad decisions."

"Yeah. Oh, yeah?" he said. "But if you ever want to fly jets, you gotta get on with that one first."

"Okay, Palmer." It seemed okay to call him that.

"All right, Kelli. Watch your back. I think we'll be seeing each other again."

"I hope so," she replied. She came closer to him, and he gently took her in his arms and kissed her.

Pensacola, Florida was the first stop for would-be modern Naval aviators and Naval flight officers. It is also the home of the Navy's "Blue Angels" who were now flying the F/A-18 Hornets.

As Kelli approached the base, she thought of how far she had come. Her grandfather had been a freshman in college when Pearl Harbor was attacked, and he volunteered for the V5 Naval Air Cadet program. He did not have as much college training as she had. Now, just to get to Pensacola, she had to finish in the top ten percent of her class and had to be a computer whiz to fly some of the new high tech fighter-bomber planes.

First, she underwent three months of preflight training: military drilling, flight academics, aerodynamics, navigation, engine mechanics, and lots of swimming, with a water survival course. In one test, she had to jump off a 35-foot tower, and in another, she was dumped into a pool upside down in a simulated cockpit, 'DILBERT DUNKER', and had to escape. She also learned how the pilot's ejection seat worked. She was placed in what looked like a regular airplane cockpit and was strapped into the seat with her legs, abdomen and shoulders tightly holding her in place. There was a canopy over her head, and she wore a regular pilot's helmet. She was told that she had to activate the ejection seat herself by pulling the handle between her legs. She finally got up enough nerve and suddenly she felt like she was being kicked in her rear end by a mule. Her breath was taken away when the rocket motors ignited, and she was shot up on the tract. She also had to learn how to parachute into the ocean and how to be lifted out of the water by a helicopter hoist.

She was shown how her judgment could get screwed up and lead her astray when her equilibrium was upset or her body was deprived of oxygen. She was rapidly whirled around in a mechanical device. This can happen in high speed flight drawing Gs. She was also placed in a hyperbaric chamber, and her body was deprived of oxygen, making her hypoxic. This could happen at high altitudes if she didn't use her oxygen mask.

Her primary flight training took place at Whiting Field in Pensacola. It was similar to what they called E-Base in her grandfather's day. The E stood for elimination. Here she got her first taste of flying in a fully acrobatic agile turbo-prop plane, and underwent check flights by instructors to determine her ability to fly.

The first day she went down to the hangar and was fitted for a

G suit and helmet. She checked the flight board to see who her instructor was, Lieutenant Bill Orr.

On her first flight she was taught how to call the tower for take off and landing instructions, and once her instructor got the plane in the air, she was allowed to work the control stick and rudders. She had no trouble flying the plane because of her previous flight experience, except that the turbo-prop plane had more power than the one she was used to.

After twelve instructional flights, she soloed. When a rookie pilot solos, the instructor usually takes a scissors and cuts the pilot's necktie, the first step out of the nest. Since Kelli didn't wear a necktie, her flight instructor cut the kerchief she wore wrapped around her neck.

The challenges then began in earnest. She started flying a two-seater trainer jet and was taught stalls and spins, and acrobatics—lazy eights, chendelles, loops, slow rolls, and eventually air combat maneuvering. She also experienced the pulling of Gs in a fast tight turn for the first time and felt the G suit inflate, compressing the blood vessels in her legs and abdomen. In a fast turn, the gravitational pull of her blood goes from her brain to her feet, and in the old days before the use of G suits, would cause the pilot to black out. Compression tubes in her flight suit help prevent that from happening. It was a new eerie sensation for her.

Kelli knew her future depended on how well she did in primary flight training. Confidence was critical; you had to walk the walk. She was as aggressive and intimidating to her fellow student pilots as they were to her. All of the grades were posted next to your social security number. Kelli was determined to get into jet fighter training to become a carrier pilot, the dream of all the flight cadets. Those who did not make it were assigned to advanced training in multiengine, reconnaissance, or carrier support. Most ended up in helicopters. Not bad, but not the same as flying those hot jets.

Whiting Field was similar to the E-Base that her grandfather went through flying the biplane Stearmen (The Yellow Peril) during World War II. Fifty percent of the cadets were washed out then, and some are still washed out today. Kelli had to take check-flights as she advanced in the different stages of her flying, and the check-flights got progressively more difficult. Not all the check-pilots were happy about women flying combat aircraft. Unfortunately, Kelli ran into one gruff, tough check-pilot, Lieutenant Alex Rothenberger better known as "Rotten Burger" because of his reputation for washing out a lot of cadets.

Kelli's heart skipped a beat when she saw his name next to hers on the flight board. "God! I hope I can please him," she thought, as she said a little prayer.

She waited for Lieutenant Rothenberger on the flight line next to her plane and saluted as he approached.

"So you're the woman who wants to be a carrier pilot?" he remarked.

"That's right!" she replied.

"Why?" he asked.

"Because I like flying and my father and grandfather were navy carrier pilots."

"That ain't gonna help you one bit with me for passing your check flight! Either you can fly or you can't!"

He looked her straight in the eye and added, "Get in the cockpit."

"Yes, Sir!" she replied.

"Call the tower for the runway being used and get clearance for take-off. Then take the plane up to 6000 feet."

"Yes, Sir!"

"Show me what your instructors taught you about acrobatics. Do a barrel-roll followed by a slow-roll."

A barrel-roll is rolling the plane through 360 degrees while the aircraft traces a circle. In the slow-roll, the nose of the plane is rotated 360 degrees on a point rather than around a circle. If the pilot is able to do these maneuvers without a mistake, it means that he's really wired into the aircraft. It is the "piece de la resistance." The slow-roll employs the function of each flight control in the rolling attitude. The elevators and rudders exchange functions and the movements of the controls must be exaggerated in order to execute a slow-roll smoothly.

Kelli pointed the plane's nose down, pushed the throttle forward, and did a beautiful 360 degree barrel-roll followed by a slow-roll. She felt that she had done both procedures perfectly. To her surprise Rothenberger hollered at her, "Repeat the slow-roll."

"Christ! What did I do wrong?" Kelli muttered under her breath.

She repeated the slow-roll maintaining the plane's nose on a point and rotating 360 degrees.

"That's enough!" he shouted. "Take me back to the base."

When they got back to the line, they got out of the plane and Lieutenant Rothenberger pointed his thumb down—signifying a down-check.

Kelli couldn't believe it. Her entire future flashed in front of her. What had she done wrong? Tears were in her eyes. There must be something wrong. She stood next to the plane . . . dumbfounded. She tried to catch up with Rothenberger to ask him what she did wrong as he walked up to the flight board to mark it down. When he got to the board, he hesitated for a minute and wrote an up-check. He turned around with a smirk on his face and then a smile before he said, "That's the best slow-roll by a cadet that I've seen in a long time. That's why I had you repeat it. I didn't think that a beautiful woman like you could fly as good as a man. I'm a believer now. Good luck to you!"

As he walked away, Kelli was pissed off. Why that bastard! I'd like to kick him in the ass. He was playing with my emotions because I am a woman.

At the end of primary flight training, the day arrived for the student pilots to be listed alphabetically in the Commandant's office with their orders and future assignments. Kelli was afraid that she wouldn't be assigned to jet carrier duty because she was a woman. She had matched and beaten the best of the men; this would tell how the Navy dealt with women.

At the Commandant's office, she crowded up to the list, thankful that if she was listed, her name would be near the top. Aaron. Addison. Appleby. Barnes.

"God darn it! I got helicopters. Shit!" said Barnes swearing loudly.

Kelli knew Barnes, and thought he was a pretty sharp cadet. His reaction only increased her anxiety as she edged closer to the bulletin board.

Caldwell, Desmond . . . Emery . . . Erskine . . . Fitzgerald.

She stepped away from the pack and leaned her head against the wall, heart beating, face flushed. She went back to look again, just to be sure.

She would be going to Kingsville, Texas for jet training. It was south of Corpus Christi, buried in the flat desert sand, not far from the Gulf of Mexico. A perfect location for cutting your teeth in a jet plane.

There she did formation flying, advanced instrument flying, air-to-air gunnery, and made her first carrier landings in the T-45 Goshawks jets. Landing on a bobbing deck and catching a wire with a tail hook, and feeling the jolt of deceleration from 130 to zero knots for the first time, gave her palpitations that almost overwhelmed her. It also eliminated quite a few cadet pilots. They either lost their nerve or reconsidered their goals.

She completed her advanced jet flight training and qualified for her Navy gold wings, finishing in the top five percent of her class. When she got her orders, she was assigned to Strike Fighter training. Her father and grandfather flew in for the ceremony, and Vice Admiral Eric Fletcher did the presentation. It isn't every day that a woman gets Navy gold pilot wings, so the ceremony made national television.

The next day she received a dozen red roses with a card. "Stay alert at all times. Congratulations, Mark."

Why didn't he call or come to see me, she asked herself?

She called her mother that evening.

"Mother, I received a dozen red roses from Mark Palmer."

"Who's Mark Palmer?"

"He's the quarterback for the Dallas football team."

"Tell me another one."

"I'm not kidding. We met when I was on that Navy tour."

"I hope you behaved yourself, Kelli."

"I did."

"Did you sleep with him?"

"Oh, Mom. We didn't even have time for a beer."

"Good. Football players are trouble."

"This one's different."

"How so?" In matters of men, her mother was a tough analyst, and Kelli had trouble hiding her emotions from her. She thought for a minute and then replied.

"He's smart. He's . . . I don't know . . . he's there. When we spoke, he didn't try to impress me, and he wasn't impressed with himself. He seemed like he understood what I'm trying to do. Probably because he's trying to accomplish something similar."

"You mean running a football team?"

"Yes. I have a feeling there's more to it than you and I think."

THE LADY INVADES THE READY ROOM

After completing her advanced flight school training, Kelli received orders to report to Cecil Naval Air Station in Jacksonville, Florida, to be checked out in the Navy's top jet aircraft—the F-14 Tomcat and the F/A-18 Hornet.

Before flying those "hot jets", she had to requalify in the hyperbaric pressure chamber, water survival and ejection seat use in case of a crash, and night vision training. She also completed several hours in simulated ground cockpit trainers.

On her first flight a check pilot sat in the cockpit behind her, making sure she didn't foul up the $40 million dollar jet. Kelli was apprehensive before take-off, but once she got the Tomcat into the air and tried various aerial maneuvers, she regained her confidence and enjoyed flying it.

Checking out in the Hornet was a bigger problem and more difficult than the Tomcat. It was a one-seater strike fighter-bomber built for air-to-air (fighter against fighter) and air-to-ground (strike) capabilities, possessing complicated computerization and a reputation as the best fighter in the world.

Kelli had to go back to school and learn everything about it before she would be allowed to fly it. She used computer assisted instruction in simulated trainers on the ground. Finally the day arrived for taking the Hornet into the air. She had memorized all the instruments and their location, checked the weather, operating area and communication frequencies, and reviewed all the required memory items with her flight instructor . . . engine failure, ejection procedures, etc. Her instructor answered all her questions, and then she climbed the boarding ladder to her F/A-18 Hornet. Once she was snugly seated in her cockpit and anchored in her ejection seat, she taxied her plane out to the runway. She was excited, her heart was pounding, and she was in a cold sweat anticipating the take off. At the end of the runway, she received clearance and remembered what a Marine captain had told her, "Just release the brakes, shove the throttle all the way forward, and then holler 'shit' and take off."

The power in the Hornet was obvious as it took off like a rocket. When the plane reached ten thousand feet, she put it through its paces: aerial aerobatics, vertical climbs, high G vertical turns, and a short run at full throttle. Its maneuverability in the transonic speed range was unbelievable. It could turn and change direction rapidly. It flew like a dream.

50 YEARS OF NAVAL AVIATION PROGRESS

Kelli frequently called her grandfather about the progress she was making in flying, and sometimes her grandfather would ask questions about her experiences. You could tell that flying was still in his blood, but the aging process had caught up with him. They compared notes, and her grandfather was amazed about the progress the navy had made in carrier operations. However, he noted that some of the pilot training methods used during World War II were still being used today. The pilots still had to practice field carrier landings and had to hit a spot on a runway of 200 feet every time before they were allowed to attempt a real carrier landing.

Today, the pilots do a computer controlled I.L.S. landing on a canted flight deck with a power-on approach using a complicated system of mirrors (fresnel lens) to check the landing angle. There is an elaborate "meatball" for the pilot to watch that guides him as he attempts to catch a wire using a "touch and go" technique. If he misses a wire, he applies full power and goes around again (a bolter).

CATAPULTS — TAKEOFFS

During World War II the catapult used hydraulic power to help thrust the plane off the flight deck. The tract that was used was 200 feet in length. The hydraulic catapult had limited strength and sometimes had difficulty getting the heavier planes, when fully loaded with bombs, into the air—particularly the TBM-3 that weighed 18,000 lbs.

The British navy developed steam activated catapults which were much more powerful and were placed on our newer U.S. carriers. They were needed because of the increased size and weight of the jets. Fully loaded, some weighed over 60,000 lbs.

The hydraulic catapults would occasionally fail during World War II, and it was a major disaster. Today, with the steam catapults, a bad shot is quite rare; however, it can happen. The plane can have an engine flame-out, lose a generator, have other mechanical problems, or the weight for the shot can be miscalculated.

Kelli's grandfather told her about a catapult shot on one of the torpedo bombers that he was asked to fly off the Japanese coast during World War II. Sometimes the TBM-3 planes were shot up in combat but returned to the carrier and were repaired at sea for further use. Her grandfather was assigned one of these planes for a searchline mission. The Mags dropped off too much before takeoff, so he downed the plane. He was given the plane again, and he downed it a second time. He was accused by the air operations officer of being chicken and afraid to fly it.

"That plane is not safe to fly," he said.

The next day the plane was given to the executive officer to fly. It was hooked up to the hydraulic catapult and activated. As it went down the track, the plane's engine cut out before it reached the end of the bow and was literally thrown into the ocean in front of the carrier. The plane and pilot were almost chewed up by the carrier's screw propellers.

Eventually Kelli was assigned to do field carrier landings at an outlying field in preparation for landing on an aircraft carrier. Every day, under L.S.O. (Landing Signal Officer) control, she tried to hit a 200 foot spot on the runway. When she was able to hit the designated landing area every time, she received clearance to attempt day carrier landings out at sea.

She flew out to the supercarrier U.S.S. America (CVN-69). It would be her first experience landing a combat jet on the deck of a floating air base.

When she got over the ship, she was told to orbit at Marshal at ten thousand feet. Kelli finally received orders to descend and enter the landing circle. She eased back on the throttle, and the Hornet started losing altitude down to 1200 feet.

Kelli was nervous as she called the ball and turned her plane into the groove. "Ball 623, Hornet 7.6."

"Roger, 623. Cleared for landing."

Kelli realized that trying to land on a floating air base with a canted deck, that was moving and rolling from side to side, was a hell of a lot different than trying to hit a spot on a stationary runway. She had to line up her plane perfectly in a controlled power-on "touch and go" attempt to catch the third arresting wire on the flight deck.

Luckily she caught the third wire. She felt the arresting gear grab, jolting her body back against the cockpit seat. She quickly pulled the throttle back to idle and taxied her plane up to the catapult.

Kelli eventually made 30 successful day traps during the next two weeks.

II

NIGHT CARRIER LANDINGS

During World War II, most of the navy's sea and air battles took place in the daytime, and the carrier became the most important ship in the Task Force. However, the carriers were most vulnerable to night attacks by enemy planes, so a method of protection had to be developed. Navy pilots were unable to fly off and land on carriers at night. A series of unpredictable events during the war demonstrated the urgent need to develop this capability. A small group of pioneer navy carrier pilots volunteered to try to learn how to do this. Kelli's grandfather was one of them. He flew with VTN-43, VTN-53, and VTN-63 during World War II . . . his moniker was "P.G."

FIRST NIGHT CARRIER INTERCEPT
LIEUTENANT — COMMANDER BUTCH O'HARE
NOVEMBER 26, 1943

Out in the Pacific war combat zone, Japanese aircraft snoopers were causing havoc to the American fleets at night. They would drop parachute flares to light up the U.S. Task Forces, and the carrier commanders had to rely on anti-aircraft guns to try to shoot them down after dark. Aboard the Big E (Enterprise) was Air Group Six under the command of LT.CDR Butch O'Hare. He decided to organize night fighter teams, using the F6F-3 (Hellcats) and torpedo bombers (TBF-1C). They would be guided in the air by ASB radar carried by the TBFs.

The Enterprise was in the Gilberts on November 26, 1943. In the evening the Japanese made a determined torpedo attack on the Enterprise Task Group, lighting up the ships with parachute flares. O'Hare and Lieut. (j.g.) Skon were in the air with Hellcats, and Lieut. Comdr. John Phillips was in a TBF. They were waiting for the Japanese intruders. The plan was for Phillips in the TBF, with the better equipped radar (ASB), to direct the fighters onto the hostile Japanese bombers and shoot them down. Unfortunately, it didn't work out that way. Phillips picked up the Japanese planes with his radar and torched a Betty with his forward-firing 50 calibers, and five minutes later splashed another—the first radar directed night intercepts for carrier aviation. The intercepts were done with a TBF, not a fighter plane, and were recorded in the C.I.C. Center of the Enterprise.

Phillips called for a rendezvous with the fighters and when they started to join up, his turret gunner abruptly opened fire, thinking that an enemy plane was getting on his tail. It is not known for sure, but evidence indicated that Butch O'Hare's Hellcat was the target.

His fighter glided down out of sight and was never seen again. Unfortunately, the widely respected CAG Butch O'Hare[1] was lost.

This incident demonstrated to the Navy brass that night intercepts were possible, and more night fighter pilots should be trained. Also, a better method of plane identification at night had to be invented.

THE PACIFIC NIGHT FLYING EXPERIENCE
PHILLIPINE SEA BATTLE, JUNE 19–20, 1944

Along the winding road back to Tokyo were the Marianas Islands. They figured importantly in the U.S. Naval strategic plans in the

---

[1] Chicago's Airport is named after Lieutenant Commander Edward Butch O'Hare. He received the Congressional Medal of Honor for bravery in action.

central Pacific. It would be necessary to control the Marianas to drive off the Japanese and take back the Phillipines.

The invasion of the Marianas, with Saipan as the first target, was set for June 15, 1944.

Late in the afternoon of June 19, Admiral Mitscher, leading the American carrier group Task Force 58, was looking for the Japanese Mobile Fleet under the direction of Japanese Admiral Ozawa. He sent search planes out looking for the enemy.

Lieutenant Nelson was flying on a search line in his torpedo bomber late in the day, found the Mobile Fleet, and reported back to Task Force 58. Unfortunately, he announced the wrong longitude and latitude. Actually the Japanese fleet was 60 miles further away than initially described. The closest enemy vessels were at least 275 miles from Task Force 58—almost out of the range of the carrier's planes.

Admiral Mitscher decided to take a big gamble. He signaled his carriers to prepare to launch a "deck load strike." He wanted to destroy the Japanese Navy once and for all. He wasn't happy about his decision because he knew that the aircraft would have to be recovered after dark, and a great number of planes and pilots would be lost. The big problem was that the pilots were not trained in night carrier landings.

Just before sundown, the pilots sighted the Japanese fleet and in uncoordinated attacks dove on the enemy ships. They were very successful. Quite a few Japanese carriers and destroyers were sunk. Darkness came quickly, and the American planes were a long way from their floating home bases. The returning planes started running out of fuel at different distances from the fleet; some made water landings together before it got too dark.

Most of the planes that hadn't ditched began to arrive at 2015. It was pitch black, and the pilots did not know where or how to land. Mitscher ordered Task Force 58 to turn on all their lights. Searchlights were pointed straight up in the air, and star shells were fired. Utter mayhem developed. Some pilots made passes at cruisers and destroyers; others made as many as six passes before getting aboard the carriers. Some ran out of fuel and spun into the water while a few landed on top of each other and the planes caught fire or blew up. When they did land on a carrier, many crash-landed because it was a completely new experience. Most ended up in the water. Blinking waterproof flashlights, pinned on the pilot's life vests, covered the ocean surface, and screeching whistles helped to locate a few of the pilots.

The night sea battle against the Japanese was won by Vice Admiral Mitscher's pilots with only 18 Helicats and Avengers lost. The long flight back and attempted night recovery, however, was disastrous. One hundred planes were lost in deck crashes and ditching, as well as 16 pilots and 35 crewmen. The message was clear . . . all navy pilots would have to learn how to land their aircraft at night on the carriers.

ATLANTIC OCEAN "HUNTER-KILLERS" AND "NIGHT OWLS"

All through 1943 and 1944 the conflict in Europe raged and the war effort in Europe was supported by the enormous capacity of the United States to manufacture new weapons in large quantities. However, delivering those weapons often posed a problem. The Merchant Fleet was frequently confronted by the highly successful German Submarine Fleet operating in the Atlantic. Hundreds of thousands of tons of Allied cargo needed for the build-up in Europe were sunk by German U-boats.

Admiral Ponitz, in charge of the German U-boat fleet, had cleverly placed his U-boats in an area known as the Mid-Atlantic Gap. This was the area where the submarines could operate beyond the range of land-based aircraft. Here, free from the threat of American planes, the U-boats roamed at will, searching out and destroying ships. They could safely surface at night to recharge their batteries. The biggest stumbling block facing the United States Navy was developing a way to prevent German submarines from operating at night.

The United States Navy ComAirLant, stationed in Norfolk,

realized that a new type of aircraft carrier was needed to close this Mid-Atlantic Gap problem. They decided to try the escort carrier (CVE) . . . the "Kaiser Coffins". This was a small carrier that had a composite squadron of 28 aircraft aboard, each plane manned by a trained carrier pilot. The TBF-TBM Avenger was to be the main backbone of the new anti-submarine attack force. By adding extra fuel tanks to the bombay, the plane's operational range was increased to almost 1,500 miles.

Initially the pilot, with his radar operator, took off at sundown and remained in the air all night searching for German submarines. If the plane's radar picked up a sub, the pilot contacted destroyers on the surface and guided them toward the enemy. The extra fuel tanks in the Avenger's bombays allowed the planes to stay keyed in on the target until contact was made, and then they returned to the ship at sunrise to make a daylight landing.

Because of the rough seas in the North Atlantic and losses in the past, when pilots had attempted to land on carriers at night, no one conducted routine night operations early in the war. Planes consistently went up at sunset and returned at sunrise, but they never tried to land on board ship at night.

Captain Dan Gallery, the commanding officer of the escort carrier U.S.S. Guadalcanal, wanted to try night patrols with fully armed TBF-TBM Avengers. The planes were now equipped with 8 MK rockets on the wings and aerial depth charges.

The development of night-flying demanded some adjustments. For example, blue-gray surface paint over a gray camouflage worked well for daytime flights but clearly failed for night operations. To reduce chances of detection, midnight blue replaced the gray on the night torpedo bombers.

Flame-dampening devices covered the plane's exhaust to obscure any light emitted by the engine. The cockpit lights were changed to red to improve the pilots' vision. Special edge lights, visible only from the air, outlined the sides of the carrier's deck. Primitive radar (ASB) was developed to search the surface of the ocean. A bubble apparatus was placed on the wing of the TBFs and a radar operator was in the belly of the plane.

Once this was accomplished, full-time Atlantic night carrier operations were initiated by Captain Gallery on CVE-60 (Guadalcanal) in April 1944.

To train carrier pilots for night-flying, he first sent them up at sundown to try landing at dusk. He then sent them up when there was a full moon. Later, as their skills in night-carrier landings improved, they flew in the worst weather and the blackest of nights. A few accidents befell pilots and escalated the risks for the flight deck crew as well; whirling propellers at night could cut a man in two or take off a head or an arm. The Navy pilots soon mastered the difficult technique of making night landings with the loss of some pilots, while the ship's crewmen learned how to launch and land planes safely.

Captain Gallery launched relays of dusk-to-dawn Avengers. VC-58 sank two German U-boats in the first three nights of nocturnal anti-sub patrols, showing how valuable round-the-clock air operations were.

INDEPENDENCE CVL-22
FIRST NIGHT CARRIER AIR GROUP
VFN-41 VTN-41 — AUGUST 1944

In August of 1944, the first night carrier division was formed in Hawaii, with the Saratoga (CV-3) and Ranger (CV-4) employed for night flight training. Barber's Point on Oahu was designated an advanced night training center.

On August 16, the carrier Independence (CVL-22) sailed with 19 F6F-5s and 14 F6F-5Ns and 9 TBM-IDs. VFN-41 and VTN-41 were established to squadron status. This was the navy's first night carrier air group to head out to the Pacific. The fighters flew dawn-to-dusk CAPs and the TBF Avengers did anti-sub and search patrols at night in front of the fleet.

In September 1944, in the Phillipines, two VFN-41 pilots chased a Japanese bomber (enemy snooper) and splashed it near the task force just after dawn. The air group's first night intercept was accomplished. The night air group then took part in the Battle of Leyte Gulf and proved to be very valuable. The VTN group found VADM, Takeo Kurita's Japanese surface force. The torpedo bombers (Avengers) also found VADM Ozawa's carriers northeast of Luzon.

VFN-41s pilots shot down 46 enemy aircraft (27 at night) with the loss of eight aviators. Night Air Group 41 had an exceptional record when you consider that the CVL carrier's deck (Independence), which the carrier pilots had to land on at night, was only 70 feet wide.

NAVAL AIR STATION
NORFOLK, VIRGINIA
MAY 1944

Kelli's grandfather was in the replacement pilot pool at the Naval Air Station in Norfolk, Virginia. He had to muster at the hanger every day waiting to receive orders for active flight duty with Air Groups that were being formed. He was a trained torpedo bomber pilot.

The pilots were hanging around, putting in flight time in the morning, drinking plantation punch and martinis in the afternoon, and chasing the Norfolk girls at night. They were not a happy bunch; they were pilots who liked to fly and be on the edge.

After three weeks without orders, one morning in May, 1944, a bulletin was posted in the hangar requesting replacement pilot volunteers for night duty flying off the jeep carriers in the Atlantic. The Navy was particularly interested in torpedo bomber pilots.

The next day at muster, the air operations officer, Commander John Barett, addressed the group:

"Gentlemen, as you know, we're having trouble with the German subs in the Mid Atlantic Gap. Too many merchant ships are being sunk. Captain Gallery on the Guadalcanal and the Skipper of the Block Island need trained night torpedo bomber pilots who have the skill and guts to land their planes on the jeep carriers at night. They've lost a few and need replacements. We want eight pilots to volunteer."

The next day there was another bulletin posted in the hangar with a deadline of seven days for volunteering, or pilots would be assigned.

Lieutenant-Commander Nick "Bullet" Carlson, one of the senior pilots, saw the bulletin first. He hollered out to the group. "Which one of you hot-rod pilots wants to join the suicide squad?"

"What do ya mean?" asked Lieut. (j.g.) Tom Egan.

"This bulletin announces a great opportunity for the mentally incompetent. The Navy wants volunteers to become night carrier pilots on those Kaiser Coffin CVEs or they'll be assigned."

"I've already thought about that. They've gotta be kidding," said Jiggs Jordan, a seasoned combat pilot. "It's hard enough trying to land in the daytime on those miniature floating air bases called jeep carriers ... trying to hit the deck at night will be a crap shoot."

"It's right here in black and white," replied Carlson. "The Navy wants you to become night carrier pilots. They're offering 100 percent hazardous pay if you sign up."

"That's so you can buy a fancy coffin," said Jiggs. "I've been in the Navy long enough to know that you don't volunteer for anything."

"Why do you think the Navy's doing this?" asked Egan.

"They want 24 hour CAP coverage over the fleet ... that's why!" said Carlson.

"The top Navy brass is dreaming," said Jiggs. "There's no way that anyone in his right mind will risk his life trying to land on a postage stamp at night."

"Hell! You can't see anything ... they don't light up the deck ... you don't know which way the deck's going ... up at you or away ... and then you've got the roll of the waves. Some of those jeep carriers only weigh 7,000 tons. Your plane's flying at 130 knots, and you've got to catch one of four arresting wires in a space of 200 feet. The flight deck is only 65 feet wide. Who are they kidding? It's hard enough doing it in the daytime. What's the Navy trying to do ... kill off more Navy pilots!"

"Look at the bulletin. The Navy's serious about this. You may not have a choice!" said Egan. "We could be assigned."

"I feel that those jeep carriers are too small for night landings! The flight deck has to be bigger and wider!" said Carlson. "The wing span of the TBF is almost as wide as the flight deck."

"Do they think we're crazy and stupid?" asked Ensign Kevin Moxley.

"I think they want to get those German subs recharging their batteries at night in the Gap," said Jiggs.

"You're probably right," said Carlson. "So you sacrifice a bunch of crazy Navy pilots to sink a German sub."

"You knew we are all expendable, didn't you?" replied Moxley.

That evening, eight of the young pilots went to a bar in Norfolk and discussed the issue of night carrier landings over a few boiler-makers and shots of straight whiskey.

Kelli's grandfather was in the group.

"What do ya think we ought to do about flying at night off those jeep carriers?" he asked. "Who's going to volunteer? Raise your hands." There was silence . . . no one raised their hand.

"Flying off is OK. It's trying to land on the bouncing deck at night that'll scare the shit out of you," said Egan. "It's a controlled crash, and you'd better know how to survive. It's like a roll of the dice. When you take a cut, either you catch a wire or you're over the side."

Kevin Moxley spoke up. "The good part is if you can hack it, you'll get a double paycheck and you'll have lots of money to raise hell with before you die. You'll die with a smile on your face."

Jack Zippert, a Lieutenant who had flown in combat off the U.S.S Block Island in the Atlantic, spoke up. "There's one good thing about the deal. The chances of getting shot at in the Atlantic are slim . . . there are no Jap or German warships out there.

But landing on those small jeep carriers that are bouncing around can kill you just as fast. You can't see the fucking deck at night. You got to be lucky to survive. You're shark meat out there. The North Atlantic ocean can be hell."

"What have we got to lose?" asked Egan.

"Just your life," replied Carlson.

"I'm bored hanging around this fucking hangar," said Moxley. "At least we'd be flying! We're pilots aren't we? We're supposed to be able to handle being on the edge!"

"I'm for giving it a shot!" said P.G. "It's better than sitting on our asses contemplating our navels."

The next day they signed up as replacement pilots for the jeep carriers. They were given an intensive training course in night flying for six weeks at an outlying naval air station and did some practice night flying on the CVE (U.S.S. Solomons) off the coast of Norfolk. They quickly realized that it was not going to be a picnic. The jeep carriers were converted freighters with a flight deck 500 feet long, had a narrow deck (65 feet), and very light tonnage. The ship bounced around on the surface of the ocean like a feather doing a fancy dance most of the time. It was up and down, sideways, every which way, and rolled with the swells, creating a big challenge to the skills of the pilots.

VTN-43 VTN-53
AUGUST 1944

Just before the eight pilots were to be shipped out to the Atlantic, they received orders to proceed to Quonset Point, Rhode Island and report to the commanding officer of torpedo-squadron VTN—43, Lieutenant-Commander Jim Taylor. The eight pilots would eventually be the nucleus of VTN-53 that would fly off the U.S.S. Saratoga (CVN-3).

After checking in at Quonset N.A.S., P.G. and the pilots had ground school orientation for a week, and then they began intensive instrument flying instruction using the Link trainers under a hood. They were also put on special diets concentrated in Vitamin A to help improve their night vision. They ate carrots until they came out of their ears and wore red goggles to adapt their eyes before getting into the cockpits at night.

Cross country flying at night, using a buddy system of two planes flying in a loose formation, was one of the first things taught. Using your radio to help home in on other naval air stations was helpful in promoting this method of navigation. Later, going out on search lines for 300 miles, flying 100 feet above the ocean on the radio altimeter, and then returning to base in weather that was socked in, made the pilot appreciate the need for instrument flying capabilities.

They would land their planes at Quonset Point Naval Air Station doing an instrument landing. Quonset was the first air base to have I.L.S. capability in the U.S.A. Another part of night training was teaching the pilot to land a plane at night in a 200 foot space on the end of a runway. This was practiced at Charlestown, N.A.S. and Westerly, N.A.S. The technique for landing on the 200 foot length of runway was similar to what the pilots would have to do on a carrier, except that the carrier would be a moving target.

It was a complete power-off landing trying to catch one of four arresting wires elevated above the carrier's flight deck. If you missed and were lucky, you hit a steel barrier beyond the four wires . . . the propeller would be entangled in the large steel wires.

One of the early problems the pilots faced was vertigo. It was not understood and was a killer. The pilot becomes disoriented in the air. It is a dizzying sensation of tilting in the plane when actually the plane is flying perfectly level. Sometimes at night, it is so dark that there is no horizon to tell you if your wings are level, and the pilot can become mesmerized by the taillight of another plane or a single light out in the darkness.

A strange aircraft accident happened one night when the torpedo bombers were practicing formation flying out of Quonset Point. The lead pilot noted that one of his wingmen left the formation without explanation. His moniker was "Jigger". The torpedo squadron's call signal was "Beaver". The lead pilot called the straggler.

"Beaver Six. This is Beaver One. Do you read me?"

"Roger, Beaver One."

"Jigger, what the hell are you doing leaving the formation?"

"Beaver One. I haven't left the formation! I'm right on your tail. I'm following your taillight."

"Beaver Six. You are like hell. You're flying too low. Go on your instruments. Check your air speed, radio altimeter, and artificial horizon. Pull up! Do you read me? Pull up or you're gonna crash!"

There was no answer.

About five minutes later there was a massive explosion on the ground, lighting up the sky.

Jigger's plane had hit a truck on a four lane highway. He was mesmerized by the white taillights on the truck. He had become hypnotized and had lost all sense of balance; he thought he was still flying at a high altitude. When the wreckage was examined, it was determined that Jigger may have forgotten to turn his artificial horizon instrument on in his cockpit before take-off, and he hadn't watched his altimeter and air speed indicator. He was not watching his instruments. There was no way he would have been able to tell what position his plane was flying in space. Vertigo had killed him.

NIGHT TARGET FIXATION

At Quonset Point, Kelli's grandfather flew the TBM-3N which was a specially equipped plane for night attacks. It was faster and had an AN-APS-4 radar pod carried under the starboard wing for air and surface visualization. The gunnery equipment was the state of the art. The torpedo bombers were no longer dropping 2000 lb. torpedoes on the Japanese ships because they weren't accurate; they'd porpoise and had to be dropped at 100 feet above the water. The planes were easily shot out of the air. MK rockets and 350 lb. depth charges were being used in the Atlantic to knock out the German subs. Glide and skip bombing using four 500 lb. general purpose bombs were used in the Pacific against the Japanese ships. The attack was started at 10,000 feet with a 45 degree dive to an altitude of 500 feet or lower. The pilots released the bombs as they leveled off and the bombs were spaced 75 feet apart, guaranteeing hits from a stick of four bombs. The technique worked great in the daytime but was less than perfect at night. Usually the enemy would light themselves up with anti-aircraft fire . . . parachute flares would be used by the TBM pilots.

Vision and vertigo played a role in night bombing because there were no reference points for orientation. The pilot had no depth perception . . . the sky and the ocean looked the same . . . black . . . instruments had to be used to tell where you were and at what altitude.

VTN-53 practiced dive and glide bombing off the New England coast, first in the daytime and then at night. A lighted sled would be towed by a destroyer. The pilot approached the target and went into a dive. He pointed the nose of the plane at the target, then opened the bombay door, and the bombardier used a sighting window at the rear of the bombay to release the bombs at 500 feet. The pilot had to watch his altimeter, so he had enough altitude left to level out without flying into the ocean. As he pulled out of a high speed dive, he would black out, becoming unconscious. When the blood returned to his brain, he went back on instruments in order not to get vertigo and spin in.

Near the end of their training on one of their blackest nights, six planes took off from Quonset Point Naval Air Station and rendezvoused out in the North Atlantic with a destroyer towing a sled. Everything was going poorly, and the pilots were missing the target. The bombs of one plane came close to hitting the destroyer. The skipper of the destroyer hollered at the plane section . . . code name was "Bulldog".

"Bulldog section, we're going to start firing our guns at you if you drop those bombs any closer."

Lieutenant Jones, the flight leader, responded: "The weather's piss poor. Maybe we should call it off tonight."

"If you can't hit the target and drop any more of your bombs close to us, we'll shoot you out of the sky."

"We'll try one more run," replied Lieutenant Jones. "Bulldog section, hit the fucking target or we'll send you all back to training school."

On the next run, the planes individually peeled off and some good hits were made by five of the torpedo bombers. The pilots got down closer to the target but were putting themselves at greater risk; some of the planes pulled out awfully close to the ocean floor. P.G. had hit the target along with his flying buddy, Moxley.

Unfortunately, a tragedy occurred on the next pass. The last torpedo bomber to dive on the target had a rookie Ensign called Peabody. He didn't want to be shown up by the other pilots. He hit the target but flew too low and went into the ocean like a submarine, killing all three occupants of the plane. It was called 'target fixation' . . . just another problem a torpedo bomber pilot faced with vertigo at night.

After an intense eight weeks of night training, a jeep carrier, the U.S.S. Block Island, pulled up alongside Quonset Point, and the pilots were sent back out into the Atlantic to practice night carrier takeoffs and landings (traps).

"Here we go again. The shit has hit the fan," remarked Moxley.

"You should be an expert by now," remarked one of the new rookies.

"Listen, Sonny," replied Mox. "No one ever becomes a real expert in landing on those jeep carriers at night. If they say they are, you can call them a fucking liar and you can quote me!"

"I'd rather be in your shoes than mine," said Ensign Tom Locke. "You're experienced."

"Not really," said Mox. "Most navy pilots feel the term 'scared shitless' originated with the first night carrier pilots, because just before launch, all the body sphincters get as tight as a drum. You can't get a popcorn fart out if you want to. If you can … you've had an accident. Once you get your plane off the deck, you go on instruments immediately, watching the artificial horizon, air speed, and altimeter, keeping the nose up at full power and getting wheels up as fast as possible so you don't drag them in the water. You also have to remember to raise the flaps. When you get up into that vast black sky, as you look around disoriented in space and can't recognize anything, you ultimately ask yourself, 'What the fuck am I doing up here?'"

"What do you do then?" asked Locke.

"You realize that you're in deep shit and you have to get out of it. You look around, you can't even see the ship, and you panic a little more. The pilot can't see the flight deck because the lights along the 200 foot landing area can only be seen as the plane flies into the groove."

"I'm not even sure I want to try it," said Locke.

"Sure you will," said Mox. "It's the ultimate challenge—better than riding on the biggest roller coaster without a safety belt, and where else can you put your life on the line every time you land your plane? Eventually you'll find the carrier. You'll open your canopy, pull your goggles over your eyes to prevent eye damage, and enter the landing circle. You hope that your tailhook won't drag in the ocean as it's impossible to see the L.S.O. from a distance until the plane gets about 300 yards from the back of the flight deck."

"Anything else?"

"Yes, there's something that is most important."

"What's that?"

"Say a prayer to God and ask Him to let you get aboard safely."

"Thanks Mox. You're a big help! You've given me great confidence!"

L.S.O.s

Bull sessions amongst the pilots, L.S.O.s and air operations officers took place whenever a bad accident occurred. Everyone was in a learning curve when it came to flying at night, and sometimes the discussions got heated. The pilots were the key to the success or failure concerning landing safely at night. They were putting their lives on the line every time. They were a dedicated group with a lot of moxie. The L.S.O.s respected these guys.

One evening, the executive officer of VTN-53 was having trouble getting aboard the U.S.S. Block Island. The weather was as black as a "witch's tit" and both the pilot and the L.S.O. were at each other's throat. The sea was rough and the jeep carrier was in no mood to accept any aircraft . . . it was a "fickle lady". The swells and waves were high, and the L.S.O. was not about to have the exec take a swim in the ocean. The X.O. was waved off five consecutive times and almost hit the bridge on one of the wave-offs.

"For Christ's sake! What's wrong down there, Hooker," (the L.S.O.s moniker), he hollered.

"You're not in a safe position to land."

"You better get me aboard soon, or I won't have any gas in this fucking plane."

"You're coming in too fast, Sir! Do you have your flaps down?"

"Yes, you little shit!" he replied. "I'm having trouble seeing you, though. I can't see your arm signals. You look like a midget."

"Try slowing it down next time."

The L.S.O. was just as frustrated as the pilot. He could hardly see the plane until it was right on top of him. He could hear the thundering engine coming at him each time but couldn't see him.

Finally, as the X.O.'s torpedo bomber got into the groove, it looked like the plane was going to hit the fantail. The plane was coming right at the L.S.O.

"Why that bastard is trying to kill me," remarked the L.S.O. He hollered, "Waveoff!", frantically waving his lighted paddles and jumping into a steel net below the flight deck. He was sure that the plane was going to crash. A big wave hit the bow of the little "Kaiser Coffin", forcing the bow up and the back of the flight deck down. The plane's front wheels hit with a crunch just over the edge of the flight deck at the first wire and . . . the plane bounced skyward, missing all the arresting wires and missing the steel barrier. Luckily, the tailhook grabbed the top steel wire of the barrier and the front wheels pancaked and broke on the deck. The big bomber was stopped in its tracks.

When the X.O. got out of the plane, he saw what happened.

"Holy shit!" he replied. "I sure was lucky on that one!"

When the pilots got together in the bull session about that incident, it was decided the L.S.O. had to be lit up better . . . he really was a midget . . . you couldn't see him at night. Thereafter Christmas tree lights were placed on the arms and legs of the L.S.O.

NIGHT FLYING AT N.A.S. BARBER'S POINT, HAWAII
ADVANCED NIGHT TRAINING CENTER

Prior to going into combat, the night air groups did their final night training at the Naval Air Station at Barber's Point in Hawaii. They were now flying the latest planes that they would be flying in combat and were putting the final touches on their preparedness. They had lost one pilot coming out to Hawaii on the U.S.S. Bataan, practicing night landings, so a rookie fill-in pilot "Jigs" Jensen was added to the torpedo bomber squadron.

Kelli's grandfather was assigned the job of flying lead on a section of six planes attempting to get into formation at night off Barber's Point. They were going to do some night target practice with live bombs and rockets.

Most of the planes had fit into their slots well. There was still the green rookie Ensign named "Jigs" Jensen who had to fly into the number six slot. He was coming in too fast and started to overshoot, so he threw his right wing up to slow down his speed.

Kelli's grandfather saw what was happening. He hollered at the rookie Ensign, "For Christ's sake, Jensen. What the fuck are you doing? Dive and get the hell out of here before you kill us all."

Jensen dove his plane and just missed hitting the plane in the number five slot. They both came close to being killed in a mid-air collision.

Jensen came back on his VHF radio, "I'm sorry, Sir. I guess I tried to fly into the formation too fast."

"Slide into the slot, slowly. Don't put your fucking wing up . . . you'll be blind sided. If you keep screwing up, you're going to be a bottle cap floating on the ocean. Watch what the fuck you're doing, you stupid asshole! If you don't, you'll kill one of your fly-ing buddies. Do it right! Don't fuck up again! Do you understand?"

"Yes, Sir!"

A few minutes later, a female controller's voice came on the VHF radio from Barber's Point tower. She had heard the conversation and broke into the radio transmission.

"Plane using that foul language, identify yourself . . . report your flight number and call signal."

Kelli's grandfather responded, "Lady, we may be fucked up up here, but we're not that fucked up."

KELLI'S FIRST NIGHT CARRIER LANDINGS

Kelli had green cat eyes just like her grandfather . . . both were 20/15 and her depth perception was incredible. She took vitamin A sup-plements and frequently ate carrots, so she had sufficient visual pur-ple on her retina to see well at night. Her athleticism and reaction time in flying her plane was as good as any. Yet all this meant noth-ing when trying to land a jet aircraft on a floating Air Base at night. The vast ocean and the sky blended as one big black blob of dark-ness . . . her vision and depth perception were useless. To compli-cate matters, if a front with dense cloud cover came in, it was worse . . . it was like trying to find a keyhole blindfolded.

Vertigo and disorientation in space was still a problem and didn't help the situation. You could be flying upside down, and if you were going fast enough, you wouldn't know it unless you referred to your instruments, believed them, and made a correction. Sometimes you had to put the plane on automatic pilot to relax and get straight-ened out.

A catapult launch at night still was a total instrument take-off. Your plane was being thrown like a slingshot into one big black ink well of homogeneous sky and ocean.

Being able to control the stress of night carrier flying and keeping your cool was absolutely necessary to land the aircraft safely. Luck was also a factor.

Night carrier qualifications were different from her grandfather's, but there were some similarities. It still was an ass tightener and considered the "coup de grace" if you didn't do it right . . . one small miscalculation and you were dead.

The planes had gotten much bigger and faster since World War II. However, the plane still had a hook on its tail, and the pilot had to snag an arresting wire in the space of 200 feet in order to land safely.

The flight deck had gotten longer (750 feet), and the Air Base had gotten much wider. It grew from 65 feet wide (CVE) to 251 feet wide at its widest point. The ship had nuclear power, so that its propulsion could exceed 30 knots, and its height from waterline to mast was 20 stores high. The flight deck had a canted deck nine degrees off to its left, and the technique of landing was a power on "touch and go" method.

The pilots flying these jets are different than the older pioneer pilots. As children they grew up using computers and playing combat video games. The H.U.D (heads up display screen) in the cockpit is one massive computer screen and you better know how to read it or you could end up being a "fireball."

On the port side of the back of the "boat" was a lighted meatball where the L.S.O. stood. He radioed instructions for the final approach before touch down and determined whether the plane was in the proper glide slope to land.

Kelli was orbiting her F/A-18 Hornet at "Marshal", a designated holding pattern 20–30 miles away from the carrier, and the planes were stacked at different altitudes to avoid air collisions. Kelli's call signal was Bearcat Seven.

When visibility was poor, there were options that the pilots could use to land. The carrier had a Combat Air Traffic Control Center (C.A.T.T.C.). In the worst scenario, if the visibility was zero and the pilot could not land the plane himself, the C.A.T.T.C.'s computers could link up with the Hornet's computers and control the plane completely until "touch down" on the carrier's flight deck. Most pilots did not like this method of hands-off control because the computers were not infallible, and a malfunction could occur. Each pilot wanted to be the captain of his own destiny when he flew into the ocean.

The majority of Navy carrier pilots preferred the I.L.S. instrument approach for landing in bad weather and at night. The C.A.T.T.C. Center's computers and the plane's I.L.S. instruments would be used by the pilot as the plane began its descent to determine the proper glide slope and altitude for a safe landing. This was what Kelli would be using for her first night carrier qualifications. She would have to hit the deck properly for two or three "touch and go's" and then the L.S.O. would tell her that she could put the hook down.

Three air traffic controllers would help Kelli guide her F/A-18 Hornet to land safely. The Marshal Controller, about 30 miles away from the carrier, called Kelli.

"Bearcat Seven, go to a holding pattern at Angels 5 and await instructions."

After a few minutes with the sweat increasing under her helmet and in her underwear, she heard from the second controller.

"Bearcat Seven, you can start your descent from Angels 5."

"Roger," she replied.

Kelli cut back on her throttles and her plane dropped down to 1200 feet. When her plane was four to six miles out, the final controller took over.

She changed her I.L.S. cross pointer designation to a landing configuration. At approximately three miles out, she centered her needles in the plane's I.L.S. instrument and began her descent. Her altitude and glide path was set right in front of her on her H.U.D.

"Bearcat Seven, your altitude is high and fast. Cut back on your speed."

"Roger," she replied. She was responding to verbal commands from the controller using radar data displayed in the Combat Air Traffic Control Center.

Kelli's nerves were on edge and she was scared; she had to be focused and everything had to be perfect. Her sphincters were tight . . . her grandfather was right . . . it still was an ass-tightener.

At three-quarters of a mile, the L.S.O. took over. She called the ball.

"Bearcat Seven, Ball, 4.2."

"Looks good," said the L.S.O.

Her Hornet was rapidly approaching the flight deck and the meatball was right in the center. The Hornet hit the deck right at the third wire. She applied full power and took off. She made three "touch and go's" before she got the OK to put the hook down.

Kelli made five successful night traps. As she approached the flight deck, her heart was pounding rapidly and felt like it was in her throat.

Each time that she had a successful trap, she had a total release of her emotions . . . she felt completely exhausted and had said a prayer before landing. That night she was one of the lucky ones . . . one of the other pilots had to eject on landing and was lost.

Upon completion of her stay at Jacksonville, Kelli received orders to proceed to Strike-Fighter Squadron VFA-153, The "Black Diamonds" stationed in Norfolk, Virginia. VFA-153 was assigned to the U.S.S. Nimitz, one of the biggest supercarriers cruising off shore. The "Black Diamonds" went on a shakedown cruise for six weeks. Near the end of the six weeks, the Secretary of the Navy and the Chief of the Navy, Admiral Vincent Russell, came aboard to observe them in action. The ship's crew and fighter squadron received top grades from the brass and was ordered to the Mediterranean. The United States was finally organizing an armed response to the reports of genocide that had been in the news for months.

A new dimension was added to Kelli's life. There was an enemy out there who someday may try to blow her out of the sky. That thought had never entered her mind. Her obsession and desire to be a Navy carrier pilot like her father and grandfather obscured the risk of mortal combat.

III

U.S.S. NIMITZ

Kelli was told that the U.S.S. Nimitz would have a six month deployment in the Mediterranean and Middle East if everything went according to schedule. The "Black Diamond" fighter squadron left Oceana Naval Base outside Norfolk and flew out to sea to land aboard. Vice Admiral Henry Mercer, Commander of Carrier Strike Force Seven was aboard along with Captain Fred Anderson, the skipper of the carrier. Both were former Navy carrier pilots.

The U.S.S. Nimitz was the centerpiece of the group with Aegis cruisers and missile firing destroyers along side. There were about fifteen to twenty ships in the carrier strike group, yet not all were on the surface. There were a few nuclear powered submarines that would join the group en route.

The Air Wing on board was made up of super specialist planes and pilots for specific jobs. The planes flew twenty-four hours a day whether the weather was good or bad. Overhead there was an advanced E-2C Hawkeye warning and control plane with electronic gear that was the state-of-the-art and an EA-6B Prowler aircraft for electronic eavesdropping and signal jamming.

Most of the planes were F-14 Tomcats and F/A-18 Hornets for CAP and attack missions, along with their KA-36 Sky Warrior tankers and A-6 bombers. Helicopters on board were used for air-sea rescue and there were special planes used for anti-submarine control.

As Kelli orbited above the carrier strike force, she was amazed by the awesome formidable armada below her. The flight deck was about five acres in size, and there were over 6,000 personnel aboard the U.S.S. Nimitz.

Other women were aboard ship, but Kelli was the only fighter pilot. Her hair was chopped off so she could put on her flight helmet easier, and she wore the same light weight khaki jumpsuit as the rest of the pilots. There was no way she could hide the fact that she was a woman because she was well endowed, and her curves were in the right places. Most of her time was spent flying, in the ready room playing cards, or in the sack. She also watched TV via satellite or listened to the radio.

Sometimes the Air Operations Officer would assign the pilots to special missions, and two planes flew together. Kelli was usually assigned to fly on the wing of the fighter skipper, Commander Mike Jessee.

SEXUAL HARASSMENT

Not all of the pilots were friendly on board ship. With some of the pilots and personnel, she knew there was a problem. They resented her intrusion into the male bastion of Navy carrier pilots. She'd experienced it before, but on land she could walk away. Now she had to put up with the deep-rooted contempt towards women held by some members of the Navy. It was more noticeable and volatile in the Naval Air Corps and in particular with some of the young carrier pilots. At sea she had nowhere to go.

Part of this attitude could be due to the Tailhook scandal, but that was just the tip of the iceberg. What happened there by a group of young drunken Navy carrier pilots exposed a conduct that was demeaning to all women. It had a profound effect in raising the awareness of the nation to the problems of sexual harassment in the U.S. Armed Forces.

Unfortunately, the Tailhook convention in Las Vegas attracted "groupies" and "bimbos" from all around the country. Many were party girls trying to snag a Navy pilot and were well versed in the art of making love . . . whatever happened was not a new experience. Older Navy pilots were there to see their buddies. The young Navy pilots got out of hand.

When a group of women were forced to pass through a gauntlet of men who molested them, it demonstrated a complete breakdown in the principle of the chain of command. Senior officers who were present could have immediately stopped the debacle, and that would have been the end of it. They chose to ignore what was happening, and as a result, some of the top young and older high ranking Navy pilots paid the price—dismissal from the service for some and the inability to go up in rank for others because of a reprimand.

Kelli's grandfather and father were proud members of that Tailhook organization. It was an exclusive group. Members had to be able to land a plane several times on a carrier's deck to become eligible. They were mad that a few young Navy carrier pilots had tarnished the respected image of all Navy pilots who had fought bravely in the past. Ironically, Kelli could now join the Tailhook organization.

Kelli occasionally flew in a six plane section and got to know the men better than the rest. Three were married and were perfect gentlemen. The three bachelors did not hesitate to confront her in the ready room and ask her for a date and weren't very subtle about it.

"You don't know what you're missing, Kelli," said one. "I'm the biggest and best stallion in the Navy. I can thrill you beyond comprehension."

"Keep your pistol in your holster," replied Kelli, "before you shoot yourself in the foot."

"Come on, Kelli. Be a sport. We could make beautiful music together."

"It takes two to tango, Mr. Stallion, and I don't want to tango with you."

"Fuck you!" he replied and walked away.

Fortunately for Kelli, the fighter squadron skipper Mike Jessee was snoozing in the back of the ready room and heard the conversation. The next day that pilot was reassigned to another section.

There were times when Kelli was confronted in a different manner. She was coming down one of the hatchways on a ladder when a young Navy pilot waited for her at the bottom. He purposely bumped into her and brushed against her breasts. She was about to hit him with a Karate chop but thought better of it.

"Pardon me, Mademoiselle," he said. "I thought you were built right in some places, but now I know!"

"If you try that again, you'll get a knee in your balls," she replied. "Why didn't you apologize for bumping me?"

"Because I don't believe women should be flying jet airplanes in the Naval Air Corps."

"Oh, that's it! Your ego has been crushed because a woman can do what you're doing. Listen here, Buster. I'm going to do it better than you do until I make sure you eat crow!"

The Ensign shook his head in disbelief and walked off.

The harassment continued by the young Navy pilots, and she was surprised when it went to a higher level. Kelli was an Ensign nugget until she finished her first cruise, and all the navy pilots felt that she was fair game. She was an attractive single jet pilot.

On overseas deployment, fighter and bombing skills had to be maintained, so there were frequent practice sessions. After completing a bombing mission with some of the EA-6B Prowlers, the skipper of the bomber pilots, Lieutenant-Commander Scott Watson, stopped her on the flight deck.

"Ensign Fitzgerald, I'd like to see you in my office after you are debriefed."

"What's that all about?" thought Kelli. The bombing run had gone well. Watson was a sharp skipper, six footer with excellent pilot skills.

She saluted when she got into his office.

"Be seated, Ensign. I want to talk to you about a personal matter. I don't want you to feel I'm being forward. It will have nothing to do with your promotional status in the Air Group."

"I don't understand," replied Kelli.

"You've probably heard the scuttlebutt in the squadron that I'm separated from my wife."

"I haven't," replied Kelli.

"Well, it's true. We're getting a divorce."

"I'm sorry to hear that," said Kelli.

"I find that you are an attractive, intelligent woman. When we hit one of the foreign ports for R&R, I'd like to spend some time with you."

"Would you define what you mean by that."

"I mean just what it implies. We both are healthy individuals and have hormones. I'd really like to get together with you."

"I feel complimented by your invitation."

"That means you'll accept. Right?"

"Not at all. I am an Ensign, and I'm primarily interested in improving my flight skills right now. Sex is on the lowest level of my ladder."

"I could really help your career," he said.

"Not by having an affair with me. I suggest you get counseling and make up with your wife. When I get serious with anyone, it will not be with anyone who has been married before. Besides, I have someone in mind back in the States."

"You're making a big mistake, Kelli."

"No, you're making a big mistake, Commander. I'm not interested in being a 'weekend lover'."

With that remark, she saluted and left.

One day after landing her plane behind Mike Jessee's, she noted that the Commander was waiting for her when she walked towards the bridge.

"Kelli, I'd like to see you in my office. I want to talk to you."

"Not again," thought Kelli. "What's this all about?" She felt her flying was okay, but she didn't know why the secret meeting. She started to get apprehensive.

She saluted when she got into his office.

"Be seated, Kelli. I've noticed that some of the younger pilots have been bugging you in the ready room. Have you had any harassment by our pilots?"

"Not any that I can't handle," she replied.

"That's not what I asked," said the Commander. "I want to hear about it and by whom, if there has been any."

"I've had some remarks that haven't been appropriate, but I don't think I should make any issues about them."

"Well, if there is any attempt at direct contact or something that you wish to talk to me about, the door to my office is always open. Incidentally, you're doing a great job."

"Thank you, Commander." She saluted and left.

"There's a Commander I respect," she remarked.

While the U.S.S. Nimitz was cruising in the Mediterranean, the Middle East was becoming a hot spot again. Saddam Hussein dispatched 40,000 troops to exploit the ongoing war between the Kurds and northern Iraq. In response, the President dispatched the carrier U.S.S. Vinson and its strike carrier force to the Persian Gulf and told Saddam to stop. When he didn't, the President ordered the Navy's strike force to fire cruise missiles on Iraq's S.A.M. air defenses in Tallil, Nasiriya, Kut, and Iskandariya. He also extended the no-fly zone an additional sixty miles to the 33rd parallel.

The U.S.S. Nimitz received orders to join the U.S.S. Vinson. The United States was not interested in getting into another major land war with Saddam. All they wanted to do was to contain him. The no-fly zone was designed to protect the oil fields of Kuwait and Saudi Arabia.

Things had changed since Desert Storm. Some of the S.A.M.-6 sites were mobile and difficult to detect. First the pilots had to fly photo reconnaissance missions, and once the data was analyzed, strike aircraft could take over the job of destruction.

A few of the pilots were on their first squadron assignment, and like Kelli, they had honed their flying skills without any real sense of air combat. They were apprehensive.

Once the "Black Diamonds" fighter squadron arrived, they immediately participated in the action over Iraq. The flights took place at a much higher altitude to avoid Iraq surface to air missiles, and the planes had B.V.R. (beyond visual range) capability for firing their missiles.

The Iraqi pilots had a healthy respect for the American aircraft and pilots. They were flying Russian-made MIGs, and whenever they detected the radar signal on their electronic countermeasures equipment, they would bug out, turn tail, and run.

On one of the flights in the air corridor, Kelli noticed two Iraqi MIGs on her HUD. "Tally ho, two bandits, 90 miles, vector 170 degrees."

"Put a lock on them," said Commander Jessee. "Let's go get em."

"Roger," she replied, as she pushed her throttle full forward.

"We'll box them in," said Jessee.

Kelli noticed that the enemy planes made a rapid turn away from the area adding full power, turning tail and getting out of there as fast as they could. Kelli and Jessee had them within their gun sights and could have easily destroyed them. She was elated that the plane she was flying appeared to be much faster and better than the Iraqi's.

Kelli and Commander Jessee used up quite a bit of fuel in the encounter, so the planes needed aerial refueling before returning to the carrier. Kelli refueled first with no problem and flew nearby to wait for Commander Jessee to approach the tanker and refuel.

"I got a compressor failure," she heard him say over the headset, surprised his voice was so calm. Then his voice exploded, "Flame out! Flame out!" Both his jet engines lost power. Kelli saw his plane start to dive like a broken elevator to the ground.

"MAY DAY!" he hollered.

Kelli threw her stick forward and followed his plane down. At 10,000 feet Jessee was able to restart one of his engines and pulled up to level out. The two planes were still over Iraq territory heading towards Kuwait.

"Looking good, Commander," Kelli said. "How's your heart rate?"

"About 200. But it's coming down." Suddenly, in both cockpits a short, staccato alarm sounded, indicating they were being fired upon. "Scratch that," said Jessee. "We got S.A.M.s on our ass. Pull up and break right." Both planes shot skyward to 25,000 feet, splitting up and out. The S.A.M.s lost their trail. Back in formation, Kelli got on her mike.

"What's the bad news?" she said. "How's your fuel?"

"Lousy. But this place is too hot to refuel. Let's get over the water."

"Roger. I'll call for a tanker to meet us over the Red Sea. It will be safer over there if you have to eject."

"Thanks," he replied.

A KAD-10 tanker met them en route, and Jessee was able to refuel.

The following week, the executive officer, Lieutenant Commander Leo Andrews, had trouble landing his plane at night after CAP. The weather had gotten nasty, and he had received three wave-offs. The Air Boss and the L.S.O. were as frustrated as Leo because there was no bingo field to send him to unless he flew over Iraqi territory to Saudi Arabia. They sent him up to angels twenty (20,000 feet) to refuel, which delayed things even further. The strike carrier group had been warned about suicide one-man subs (Kamikazes) which the enemy had in the area.

Leo was a seasoned carrier pilot. That wasn't what worried the Air Boss or the L.S.O. The flight deck was a place where accidents took place. A plane could crash and start a fireball, a flight deck crewman could be blown overboard by a jet engine blast, or an arresting wire could snap and take off someone's head.

The L.S.O. and the Air Boss were working overtime because of the piss-poor weather. There were more wave-offs, more refueling, and more accidents. The tailhooks were sending up showers of sparks as the successful planes slammed down on the deck and caught the arresting wires.

Leo called the ball as he came out of the black sky heading towards the flight deck. He had used an I.L.S. approach, and he was coming into the groove a little fast.

"Right for line-up," said the L.S.O.

The Air Boss was watching from atop the bridge, and it was hard for him to see the plane clearly. It looked like the plane was drifting to the left. Leo made an adjustment, picking the left wing up and cutting back on the throttle. The L.S.O. gave him the cut. It looked like he was overshooting the third wire but snagged the number four wire. Then the wire snapped, and the hook disengaged. He had cut his engine back to idle. It was dark, so it was difficult to see completely what happened. A scream from a deckhand could be heard above the roar of the jet engines . . . a flight deck crewman had been hit. Leo applied the brakes, but it looked like they didn't grab. The plane dropped over the front of the carrier but the ejection seat was not activated.

On the bridge, the helmsman made a sharp starboard move away from the plane. Sirens sounded, and the bullhorn announced, "Man overboard."

Helicopters, with their bright lights, tried to find Leo and the plane. They searched the area all night long . . . to no avail. Some scraps of metal from the plane and pieces of cushion were picked up by a destroyer, but no body was found. Leo was gone and would no longer be a part of the fighter pilot's daily routine. A memorial service was held, and Leo's family was informed of the tragedy.

That night and the next day, the planes were back flying off and over the strike carrier group. The surviving pilots were doing their jobs. Most were fatalists. They felt, 'There but for the grace of God, go I.'

GREELEY

After five months without a break, the constant stress of the combat conditions and the frustrations of a difficult, busy work load every day and night was beginning to take its toll on the pilots. The weather had been bad, which didn't help, and the death of Leo, the executive officer of the fighter squadron, was disturbing everyone. Even on the bridge, it was becoming noticeable. Captain Anderson mentioned it to Vice Admiral Mercer.

"The pilots are getting uptight, Admiral. I hope we get our replacement strike carrier group on time."

"I'll call Washington and check it out if you'd like," he replied.

"No. We'll do what they want us to do. It shouldn't be too much longer. I wonder which supercarrier is going to replace us."

"I believe it's the Constellation," said Admiral Mercer. "That's not for publication, however."

"I understand," replied Anderson.

Jack Ewing, was promoted to Lieutenant Commander and became the new executive officer to replace Leo. Two replacement pilots flew in to join the squadron. One of them was a full Lieutenant named George Greeley.

Unfortunately, he became entranced by the fact that a good looking woman was flying with the "boys." He wasn't very subtle about his thoughts. When he first saw Kelli in her flight suit in the ready room, he said in a loud voice so all the pilots could hear, "How come this fighter squadron rates a doll like that young lady?"

Kelli blushed when he said that and hoped that would be the last of his remarks.

"Thanks for the compliment," she said.

"My pleasure," he replied.

Later he tried to monopolize Kelli's relaxation time in the ready room, trying to break into the acey-deucy game she was playing with another pilot. Kelli was insulted, but because he was senior to her, she had to grin and bear it. In the ward room, when they ate dinner, he always made a point of sitting near her. Greeley was overbearing, so Kelli tried to avoid him. She felt he was crude and not someone she wanted to be part of her life. He was a P.I.T.A . . . a pain in the ass.

One day, after she had just finished a flight and was leaving the flight deck, he grabbed her by the arm and spun her around almost knocking her down.

"Kelli, I want to talk to you. I think you're a pretty woman, and I'd like to get to know you better. I think we could hit it off."

She pulled her arm away and gave him a dirty look, "I'm not interested, Lieutenant. Find someone else!"

"So, I'm not good enough for you?"

"I didn't say that! I said I wasn't interested. You're not my type. Leave me alone! Get lost!"

Greeley's face and neck got red as a beet, and his blood pressure boiled. His ego had been deflated by this pip-squeak Ensign, and he didn't like it. He grabbed her arm again, spun her around, and put his fist in her face.

"You're a fucking stupid broad! You're lucky I don't punch that pretty face of yours and break your jaw."

"Try it, and you'll regret it for the rest of your life. I'll kick you in your nuts, and your balls won't ever function again. On top of that, your Navy career will be finished!"

"If it weren't for my Navy career and the fact that I love to fly, I'd do it right now. You're one broad I'd call a real bitch."

"Too much for you to handle," said Kelli, as she smiled, broke his grip and walked off.

That wasn't the end of it. Greeley continued to follow Kelli around, stalking her and looking her up and down at every chance, muttering, "Mm, mm, mm," to himself and to anyone within earshot. Most of the other flyers thought it funny. They laughed and called him Greeley, or "Big Dog".

He continued to bother her in the ready room, and Kelli was getting mad. He was a horrible nuisance that she couldn't get rid of. She had had it!

"I think I'm finally getting to you, Kelli," he said, with a big grin.

"That's what you think. If I were a man, I'd punch you in the nose, and you'd know what I really think of you."

Bill Patten, one of the young Ensign pilots, who was six feet tall and weighed 220 pounds, heard the whole conversation and stood up to face Greeley.

"Lay off! Leave the lady alone!" he shouted.

"Ensign, you better watch your remarks, or you won't be flying planes around here very long."

"There's enough people in this room who know what you're doing. You're the one who could be in trouble."

"Thanks, Bill," said Kelli. "Greeley's been out to sea too long. He's the one who can't take it. I'll handle my own problems."

The next week, walking out of the wardroom, Big Dog actually whistled as Kelli walked by. How original, she thought, and kept walking. He followed her as she went to the ready room and then put on a show for everyone in sight. She waited until a couple dozen flyers were looking at him. She spun around, fast enough to be nose-to-nose with Greeley.

"Tell me something, Greeley," she said. "Do I owe you money?"

He came up short. "What?"

"Money. Do I owe you money?"

"No."

"Then stop staring at me. Haven't you seen a woman before? Hit the head, and do yourself and me a favor. I'm sure you can handle that much responsibility." She spun, walked away, leaving him there with a stunned, stupid look on his face. Kelli had humiliated him, and all the pilots in the ready room laughed.

"Lay off, Greeley," the fighter squadron skipper growled, "or you'll have to deal with me."

"I was just having a little fun, Sir!"

"Not in my book," responded Jessee. "Keep your trap shut!"

Greeley was red in the face and hot under the collar. He was a full Lieutenant, and although he was outranked, he wasn't going to let it die.

"We can't let these broads take over the Navy, Sir."

"They're not taking over the Navy, Greeley. And she's not a broad. She's a woman and an excellent pilot. Lay off and forget about it."

Greeley walked out of the ready room visibly disturbed.

Greeley wasn't through. On board ship there was no place to hide, and he ran into Kelli on the flight deck and in the ready room.

He was mad, and somehow he had to get even. His ego had been shattered, and he noticed the senior pilots were keeping their distance from him. He was also worried about how the incident might affect his Navy career, and flying was what he wanted most. Commander Jessee would be making out his fitness report.

Kelli felt better that Jessee was aware of her problem. She couldn't fight Greeley's harassment alone.

Finally, the U.S.S. Nimitz pulled ashore at Naples, Italy for a little R&R.

The first evening ashore, Kelli accompanied two of the ship's senior officers to an exclusive Italian restaurant.

After the meal, the officers had tickets for the opera. Kelli left them at the restaurant's exit, which was in a back alley, and walked down the narrow isolated street to hail a cab back to the ship. Suddenly, out of the darkness a man appeared, with what looked like a hood over his head, and threw a punch at her face. She ducked but felt a hard blow to her chest that took the wind out of her and knocked her to the ground. It was dark, and she couldn't see the assailant's face, but knew she had to get out of that alley or fight back if she wanted to survive. As she started to get up, the assailant tried to kick her. She grabbed his foot and twisted, lifting it up towards the sky and throwing him off balance. When she started to run, she felt him grab her leg, almost knocking her down. Then she remembered what her grandfather had told her. When you're out weighed by a big assailant, you have to hit him in a vital area, such as right between his legs with your foot or knee—get him in the balls, but don't miss. It will cripple a male faster than any other blow. As he got up, she kicked her foot right between his legs and heard him gasp as he doubled up and fell to the ground. He grabbed her leg as she tried to go by him, again knocking her off her feet.

"You bastard! I'll kill you for that," he said as he struggled to his feet. She rolled to get away from him, but he still blocked her exit from the alleyway. He ran towards her, throwing a right upper cut. She quickly turned her back, grabbed his right arm, and in a crouch using all her strength, threw him over her shoulders. When his body hit the ground, there was a big grunt and then a thud-like sound as his head slid along the cobblestone sidewalk and hit the side of the brick building. Suddenly everything was silent.

Kelli ran as fast as she could out of the alleyway and wasn't about to look back . . . she had to get out of there. Her hair was in disarray, her khaki uniform was dirty, and she had a pain in her left shoulder, but other than that, she had survived.

She hailed a cab. "Pier 41, U.S.S. Nimitz," she hollered as she slammed the door shut, exhausted.

"You all right, lady?" asked the cab driver.

"I'm okay. I fell down on the cobblestones."

When she got to the ship, she paused and saluted the Marine sentry at the end of the gangplank, signed the log, and then saluted the bridge. She went to her room and washed up. Later, she decided not to report what had happened. It might cause her more trouble than it was worth. Nobody would believe her story anyway.

The next morning, the pieces to the puzzle fell into place. Greeley did not report back to the ship. The report said he had been found unconscious in an alleyway by a group of Italian peasants. He was in a Naples hospital with a fractured skull.

Later that week, in the ward room, Kelli found out that neurosurgeons had to put burr holes in his skull to decompress his swollen brain. He was in a coma and desperately ill. It would be a long time before he flew again—maybe never.

Kelli decided that she had to forget what happened. If it was Greeley and he had used a knife, she would be dead. Whoever it was, obviously meant to hurt and possibly kill her. She would say nothing, but she knew she never really would forget it.

Kelli continued to impress everyone with her flying ability, including her fellow pilots, the Air Boss, and her Air Group Commander. She had flown well in the most difficult weather with

Commander Jessee, and she had received high marks for her tactical judgments in Iraq. Near the end of her overseas deployment, she was told to report to Jim Johnson, the Air Group Commander.

"Ensign Fitzgerald, you have done an outstanding job flying with my Air Group on the Nimitz."

"Thank you, Captain Johnson."

"The L.S.O. tells me that you have the best record for hitting the #3 wire, both day and night and in bad weather. Your flying ability has been flawless. You were cool under fire in the no-fly zone in Iraq. When we were flying at night with those unexpected fog banks, you still landed your jet on a dime. Your record is quite impressive. Because of that, I'm recommending you for early promotion to Lieutenant Junior Grade."

Kelli's eyes said it all.

"There's something else I have to tell you. You and Scott are competing for the #1 spot in our fighter squadron. Originally, we were advised that upon completion of this tour of duty, one of you would be given the opportunity to go to Miramar Naval Base in California, the Navy's Top Gun School.

"But, as you know, I'm a former graduate of that school and one of my pilots, Commander Bob Clark, is the chief pilot there. He's the Top Gun. I have contacted him, and have recommended that he take both of you. You will both report to Miramar after you finish your thirty day leave in the States. What do you have to say about that?"

"I don't know what to say."

"Then don't say anything. By the way, do you have a moniker?"

Kelli blushed. "I'm not sure. Some call me 'Tiger Lady'."

"Why?"

"Because a dirt bag flyer was dogging me, and I publicly emasculated him."

"Where is he now?"

"I don't know."

"Some men are intimidated by aggressive women."

"I don't think I'm that aggressive," replied Kelli.

"Maybe you are and maybe you aren't," said Johnson. "But remember this, a good fighter pilot has to be aggressive. As for your call sign, don't worry, by the time you finish Miramar, you'll have a moniker that'll follow you around for your entire Navy career."

When Kelli got back to the States, she spent most of the time with her family, including her grandfather, who was getting older and was in failing health.

She told him about her orders to Top Gun School at Miramar. He was visibly impressed, but also thought she might be getting too cocky. She still had a lot to learn about flying. The new high tech equipment and fast planes were putting tremendous demands on her body and mental capacity. He was worried about her physical stamina.

"Do you really think you should go there at this stage in your career?" he asked.

"Why not?" she replied.

"You're going to have to be on your toes every minute. It's extremely risky and fatiguing."

"I realize that. A Navy carrier pilot can't be a wimp."

"You'll be flying with and against the best. They're all very aggressive."

"I know. But they haven't flown against me! I'm going there to learn. I'm still in the learning curve. I'll put my wings against anyone's."

"If you go there with that attitude, you'll do well."

"It's the only attitude I've got."

IV

U.S. NAVAL AIR STATION, MIRAMAR, CALIFORNIA

Kelli checked into the Naval Air Station at Miramar and was assigned to the BOQ (bachelor officers' quarters). In the lobby of the BOQ was a board that listed the names of the new training class. She was the only woman. Muster was at 0700 in hangar A at the airfield.

When Commander Robert Clark, the CO of Top Gun arrived, the class stood at attention. At six feet and 190 lbs., he was typical of the Top Gun physique. He had that intense look of a Top Gun pilot—focused eyes that missed nothing.

"At ease. Be seated.

"I don't plan to inflate your egos, but if you look at your fellow pilots next to you, you are seeing what the Navy considers the top one percent of Navy carrier fighter pilots. You are, what we call, the elite of the elite. When you complete your training here, you are expected to return to other Navy commands to teach, and by example, demonstrate the latest techniques in fighter aircraft tactics.

"You will spend five weeks here flying with and against Top Gun instructors and fellow students. You will learn all about tactical sorties, one-on-one fights, section fights with more than one aircraft, six-plane night attacks, and multi-plane strikes. The staff instructors will grade you on a weekly basis, and your grades will be posted.

Your future orders and assignments are to be given out on a competitive basis upon completion of your training. The number one individual or "Top Gun" gets first choice for future orders. He can remain as a Top Gun instructor or select any one of the other billets. This will give you an incentive and motive to do your best. You are and will continue to be trained in air-to-air combat. At Miramar you will fly state-of-the-art fighter planes. The last two weeks of your training, you will be flying the F-37, a new jet fighter. I have flown that plane, and I can assure you that you have an exciting new experience in store for you.

"There is one thing that I want all of you to remember. A Top Gun pilot is the best pilot in the world. But first and foremost, he is a safe pilot. You will be doing high G turns and knife edge passes with split second timing. It is the world's most dangerous job. If you stay in the Navy for any length of time as a carrier pilot, you have a twenty-five percent chance, exclusive of combat, of being killed. The best Navy fighter pilot is the aggressive pilot, who is focused, and attacks and kills the enemy to survive. He has to have the killer instinct. That's what we try to develop. Most true champions have that killer instinct: Ali, Bird, Jordan, Montana, Nicklaus. The only difference is if you fuck up in the air, you're dead. If I feel you are unsafe and can't keep up, you will be dropped from the program. Do you understand?"

There was a quiet, "Yes, Sir."

"Let's hear it loud and clear!"

"Yes, Sir!"

"That's better!"

Kelli thought, some things never change.

"The training class will be divided into two sections." Clark continued, "The first section will have ground school in the morning and fly in the afternoon. The second section will fly in the morning and have ground school in the afternoon."

"The two sections will eventually compete against each other. In the final week of training, there will be a Top Gun selected from each section, and they will fly against each other in a one-on-one competition. The best two out of three dog fights wins the Top Gun designation."

"Your first week will consist primarily of ground school instructions and indoctrination by senior Top Gun instructors. I know that you are all itching to get into the air to fly, but that will come soon enough."

"Just one more thing. If any of you have any gripes or problems during your stay here, my office is open at all times. Are there any questions?" Silence. Kelli looked at the blank faces of her classmates. She wanted to ask a question, but already she felt conspicuous enough.

"Since there are no questions, you are to line up in the back of the hangar at Station B to be fitted for new G suits and special helmets. Ground school instruction will start at 0700. Lieutenant Fitzgerald, I would like to see you in my office after you get your G suit and helmet. Class dismissed."

Kelli followed the crowd to the line, picking up shreds of conversation in front and behind her. But no one spoke to her, and there was something about the way the men turned away from her that made her uneasy. She wondered why the commander had asked to see her. Kelli entered Commander Clark's office and saluted.

"At ease, Lieutenant. I'm sure you are aware of the fact that you're one of the first female fighter pilots to be selected for training at Miramar."

"Yes, Sir, I am."

"When your boss, Captain Johnson, called me, I was reluctant to accept you for Top Gun school. He reassured me that you could handle it. I hope he's right."

"I know I can handle it."

"That's not the whole problem."

"I don't understand, Sir."

"In training here, you will eventually fly one on one against your fellow pilots and will be graded on your performance. This school has been a male stronghold for many years. To be invaded by an intelligent, aggressive woman who is also attractive, can present unpredictable problems."

"I understand that," replied Kelli. "But I'm not here to offend anyone or disrupt anything. I'm not looking for sex. I don't plan to create any problems."

"A fighter pilot's job is to create problems. The best fighter pilots have excellent eyesight, three-dimensional intelligence, and a physical endurance to stand high Gs. If you fit into that category, you'd have to be a super woman."

"I don't consider myself a super woman, but I'm prepared for this. And anyone who flies with me, knows I'll give my best effort. Anyone who flies against me will find out what I'm made of."

"If you beat those guys out there, I'm not so sure they can live with that defeat."

"That's their problem, isn't it?"

"That's correct. Since you are one of the first woman here, I hope you won't object to a close monitoring of your skills."

"What does that entail?"

"More frequent physical exams and evaluations."

"If that's the price I have to pay to stay here, I'll do it."

"If you have any sexual harassment problems with any of the pilots, you're to report to me immediately. Do you understand?"

"Yes, I do."

"Thanks for your cooperation. Good luck, Lieutenant."

Lieutenant Commander George Spencer, the Executive Officer of Top Gun, gave the first indoctrination lecture to the new class, which was about the historical development of the various fighter planes and the various armaments they carried.

"Gentlemen," he said. By now Kelli was used to being put in that category. "Believe it or not, air-to-air combat with fighter planes has not changed since World War I when the 'Red Baron' shot down eighty enemy planes using plane-mounted machine guns. We still use guns in aerial combat for close-up shots because they cannot be jammed electronically like missiles.

"With the passage of time—World War II, the Korean War, Vietnam, and Desert Storm—the speed of the aircraft has accelerated tremendously, and sophisticated weaponry has entered the aerial combat arena.

"Most of you are aware of the weapons that we use to destroy fighter planes in the air. The side winder, which works by tracking the heat emissions generated by the burning of the jet's fuel, was one of the first of these weapons developed. At first, you had to get behind the enemy to get a kill. But the side winder, which is still in use today, has been improved. The latest one has a seeker head. You lock on the enemy and shoot.

"The sparrow, one of the world's most successful radar-guided air-to-air missile, was introduced after the side winder. However, it had a limited range and could only track one target. Now, radar guided missiles have also been improved. They have many new search modes that can chase elusive enemy targets up to a hundred miles away. The new Phoenix missile has a launch range to target that can exceed one hundred miles and track numerous targets. The missile carries its own radar, which turns on in the final stages of flight to lock onto the target. It has electronic counter measure capability to prevent jamming, and can actually hone in on the jamming aircraft.

"As the weaponry to destroy the fighter plane has improved, sophisticated counter measures to protect the pilot have been developed. Some of you know how tight it gets when a missile starts tracking your plane, and you have to use counter measures and astute flying techniques to survive. I've had that experience, and I assure you that it will scare the shit out of you. We will teach you how a missile can be avoided if the fighter pilot responds properly with the best evasive action.

"If you get involved with multiple planes in a big air battle, identifying your fellow pilots or the enemy can also be a serious problem. During World War II, the Marianas Turkey Shoot is an example of what can happen when three-hundred planes get involved in a massive air battle. Back then, the planes were much slower and were painted with distinctive colors on the nose and tail to identify them. The pilot had to recognize the enemy's plane. Identification wasn't easy, but it was necessary before shooting.

"Identification friend or foe, or IFF equipment, came into being during World War II and saved many a friendly pilot's life. If you didn't have your IFF on at all times, you got shot out of the air. In weeks to come, you will learn every aspect of what it means to be a 21st century fighter pilot and what it takes to be the best."

The Top Gun instructors flew adversary programs against the trainees, usually with different aircraft to simulate third-world fighter tactics.

On the ground there were tactical air training systems that reclaim data from the training flights. Pods on the wingtips had recorders that taped everything the plane was doing. The instructors debriefed each flight when the pilots returned to base.

The first three weeks of Kelli's training was learning basics of air-to-air combat and various innovative techniques used to defeat the enemy. She quickly learned it wasn't always the fastest plane that won the fight. The turning rate was very important, and the plane's and pilot's ability to control the aircraft properly was what counted. If you could change your heading and bring your guns to bear on the other guy first, you had a kill. Speed brakes, taking high Gs, and being at the zenith of your alertness was most important.

In her first one-on-one dogfight, zig-zagging all over the sky with vertical climbs and numerous attempts to get an advantage over her opponent, she lost the fight, was so exhausted that she got the shakes in the air, and was afraid she wouldn't be able to land her plane safely. She finally calmed down and set the jet down safely on the runway.

She walked to the hangar and "Spike" Martin, her opponent, was waiting for her. Kelli was utterly exhausted.

"No fucking woman is going to beat me!" he said, and walked away.

Kelli was upset and depressed because of the defeat as well as Martin's remarks. Lieutenant Johnson, an instructor, explained her mistakes in her first encounter, and when he got through said, "Kelli, don't let one air fight at Top Gun school get you down! Remember you're flying against the best pilots in the Navy, and you're one of the best! They're not going to win them all!"

Kelli decided not to let her emotions get the best of her. She was determined to do better and spent time with Lieutenant Johnson trying to gain insight into how to win. He gave her constructive ideas to use in a fight, and they paid off. She got a direct hit on her drone expendable target and won her next three dog fights. The pilots who she beat seemed to accept her presence better than "Spike". Commander Clark met up with her coming out of the hangar.

"I hear you're doing a good job, Lieutenant."

"Thank you, Sir."

"Do you have any complaints?"

"Just a small one. I'd like to have a lock put on one of the heads in the hangar."

"Has there been a problem?"

"No, but I'd like a little privacy once in awhile."

"I think we can arrange that. I understand that your call sign is sticking . . . 'Tiger Lady'. . . is that correct?"

"That's right."

"Our Top Gun instructors tell me that moniker fits you."

"It sure as hell doesn't fit anyone else here," she replied as she smiled and left.

The Top Gun training intensified. Kelli spent more and more time in the air learning fighter tactics, and she began to realize the importance of her eyesight and manual dexterity. Air-to-air combat is a three-dimensional arena, and when an enemy plane is flying towards you at high speed, you have to try to picture what the pilot's next move will be and how you can counteract it. She had to do it quickly. Most fights ended up with a kill within thirty to fifty seconds of the initial contact.

She also learned that you need to be flexible in your reactions against an adversary's moves in the air. You have to mix up your tactics to be unpredictable. But you can't be foolish. Your life is at stake.

A good fighter pilot, like a boxer, has to have a knock-out punch. Navy fighter pilots are not afraid of death. They accept the high risk that comes with the job.

Kelli was beginning to think like the rest of the pilots. She was becoming a fatalist. Navy carrier pilots were on the "edge" all the time. You couldn't let your mind interfere with your actions. She had seen death when Leo, the executive officer of the Black Diamonds, was killed. It wasn't messy; it was quick.

If you get shot out of the sky in an air fight or by a missile, when your plane blows up, there's little pain. If you have to die, that's the way to do it. One thing she didn't want to happen was to burn up in a fireball on the flight deck.

Kelli decided that to win an aerial dog fight she had to have a perfect plan of attack. She was now in the aerial arena where she was being watched by her peers and tested to the edge of her ability. If she could continue to perform and win the dog fights, she would be accepted and be part of the elite team. If she lost, it was a kill, and there would be no tomorrow. The Top Gun pilots would say she didn't belong. They weren't using real ammunition, but in terms of her career it meant the same.

After four weeks of flying, Kelli was second in her section and was scheduled to fight the number one pilot the following day.

She went to the "Winners Circle", a local pub with video games and fighter memorabilia, where the Top Gun pilots hung out. It was "guys' turf", but she figured that shouldn't stop her.

Her opponent, "Slick" Barnett, was already sitting at the pub bar with a beer. Scott was there with Duke Soester, and they waved her over. She joined them at their table and ordered a Coke.

Slick walked over to their table. "So you're the Tiger Lady I'll be flying against tomorrow. You don't look like a tiger."

"You don't look so slick!" she replied. "I'm a human being just like you." The other pilots in the room laughed.

"You've beaten a couple of my buddies. That's why I plan to even the score tomorrow."

"I like your attitude. It looks like we'll have a good match. Let me buy you a couple of shots." More laughter. Kelli was controlling the dialogue.

"Tigers are strong. Are you?"

"When I pounce, you'll find out."

Scott and Duke smiled at her remark.

"Tigers," Slick said, "are just about extinct. I guess I'm going to have to teach you a lesson tomorrow. I'll add you to that list."

"We'll see," replied Kelli.

The next day was clear and sunny. As the air corridor was cleared and ground air control got ready, Commander Clark spoke to Kelli and Slick about the rules of engagement. The fight had to take place within a designated air circle of seventy miles. The initial altitude and entry point would be designated and monitored under ground control radar. The planes were equipped with special cameras in pods on the wingtips and a lock-on radar that could measure the distance between them. The fight would be a guns-only angle fight. The cameras would eventually determine the winner.

THE DOG FIGHT

The pilots had been told that they could not exceed 450 knots on "heads-on" approach until they saw each other. Doppler radar had to be turned off. Once the first to sight the other announced "tally ho," any speed was possible.

As Kelli taxied into position for takeoff, she looked over at Slick. He winked. She cleared for takeoff and gunned the plane down the runway, throttle full forward, feeling the twin engines thunder. Pressed against her seat, she leveled out at the designated altitude, banked around, and began her approach, straining for visual contact.

Kelli saw Slick first and announced, "Tally ho, one bogey."

Both planes came at each other at equal altitude and speed. Kelli immediately put on full afterburner in order to climb to get an advantage, then made a hard right turn. As Slick's plane got closer, she reversed her turn and began an aggressive nose-low level turn on his plane. Slick countered with a hard turn of his own, right up towards her angle of attack. Kelli continued her nose-low turn trying to get a lock. Slick reversed his turn to again set up a nose-to-nose battle.

The two planes screamed head-on towards each other. Hell, Kelli thought, he actually wants to play chicken. She pushed the throttle forward as his plane expanded in her range of vision. Chicken was stupid, she thought, so why not be smart?

Within one mile, at 600 knots, Kelli broke low and away, afterburners blazing as she pulled back, whipping the nose up and to the left, pulling Gs that flattened her into the seat—a vertical yo-yo procedure. As she soared upward, she smiled. Slick, anticipating her move, had pulled up into a rolling scissors. She turned wide of him and got his plane in her cross hairs, activating the photography gun for a kill. Ground control confirmed the kill, and Kelli won the fight. The whole thing was over in thirty seconds.

When she got her plane on the ground, her entire section of Top Gun pilots cheered. The other pilots were silent. Slick came up to her.

"I'm a believer," he said, and walked away.

TOP GUN SHOOTOUT

Because she won her section of the training class, Kelli would be in the shootout for the Top Gun designation. Her next opponent was

"Bullseye" Jones. He had won all his dog fights with unpredictable maneuvers. The other pilots said he did not think like any other pilot; his moves didn't make sense. He would be formidable.

Kelli was uptight about the shootout and almost wished she had not gotten into this position. She noted too, that the pilots did not seem as friendly since she beat Slick. She had successfully invaded their domain, and she felt uneasy. She figured they didn't like the idea of a woman competing for the number one spot.

The night before the shootout, she decided to go to the Winner's Circle again to relax and have a beer. Bullseye Jones was already at the bar drinking either gin or ice water, shooting the breeze with the pilots in his section.

"How do you plan to beat the Tiger Lady?" asked one of his buddies.

"How do you beat anybody? You out-think them, out-react them, and out-perform them. She's no different than you or me."

"She's a woman, for God's sake," said Hannibal, a flyer who'd been beaten by Kelli.

"No," said Bullseye. "That's your mistake. She's a pilot. Don't make her into anything else."

"She's a sharp, aggressive pilot," said Lieutenant Adams, one of the Top Gun instructors. "I've flown against her, and she knows what she's doing."

"Sure she does," replied Bullseye. "But she doesn't know what I'm doing. No one does. That's how I fly. And that's how I win. I stay out of my opponent's head and in my own."

"You may be right," said Adams, "but the instructors at this flight school feel it's going to be an even fight."

"Of course it is," said Jones slowly, measuring his remarks. "Why does everyone want to make it into boy versus girl? Man, I'm a professional. So is she. We left that crap behind us in the school yard."

Kelli joined Scott and Duke Soester at their table.

"Bullseye says this 'Battle of the Genders' stuff is bullshit. He says you're both pros," said Scott, "and let the better pilot win."

"I don't even know him, and I already like him. Have you got any ideas how I might outsmart him?"

"Keep your cool," replied Duke. "For every action, there's a counter-reaction."

"How did he beat you?" asked Kelli.

"He suddenly shut one of his jets off to get behind me, and he got me in his crossbars."

"Wow!" said Kelli. "I'm going to have my hands full!"

Kelli had difficulty sleeping that night. What would it be like if she got to be the Top Gun? She worried about that. She would like to be number one, but is it better to be number two and still have the respect of her colleagues? She felt she could beat Bullseye ... but should she? Would her actions affect her career in the Navy? She kept tossing and turning. She could not relax, and knew she had to get some sleep so she would be alert to fly the next day. She finally slipped into an uneasy sleep with a lot of unanswered questions on her mind.

The next morning, Tiger Lady and Bullseye met with Commander Clark. They entered the room together and saluted the Commander. He acknowledged their salutes.

"Be seated. I want to congratulate you both for winning your sections. That, in itself, is a big achievement. The instructors here are proud of you both. As you know, you will be competing in the best two out of three engagements. You will be flying the new F-37s, and because of the increased speed and maneuverability of the planes, the circle of engagement has been increased to 100 miles. Are there any questions?"

"Is there an altitude restriction?" asked Bullseye.

"No, there is not. Although this will be a guns-only fight that starts at 10,000 feet; missile tactic shooting at a long distance will not come into play. Your Doppler radar will be on. Your guns will have photography distance and time attachments, and a kill will occur only if your radar lock is within 1500 feet of the target. The cameras will tell the final story."

"This means you can't shoot down your bandit 50 miles away with a missile just because you see a blip on your radar screen. Each shot will register in the central intelligence center, and I will be monitoring the screen. It has to be a perfect hit to register. If it is, we'll notify you on VHF radio. Then you're to return to base and land your aircraft. Are there any more questions?"

"If there is a question about the kill, what happens?" asked Kelli.

"There will be an E-6C reconnaissance plane flying above you at thirty thousand feet recording the event from the air. Their video of the action will help determine the final decision if necessary."

"What about safety instructions?" asked Kelli.

"I'm glad you asked that. If I know you two, you'll be going nose to nose. When you get real close, the plane coming out of the sun banks to the right, and the plane coming into the sun banks to the left. There can be no variations. It's to be a fair fight, and we don't want any mid-air collision."

"If we feel you're getting dangerous up there, we'll cancel the fight. The first fight will be in the morning at 1000. Then there'll be a lunch break. The second engagement is at 1500. Good luck to you both."

FIRST DOG FIGHT

In the first fight Kelli and Bullseye approached the 100–mile encounter circle at 10,000 feet at a speed of 500 knots. The opposing fighters approached nose to nose. They both started a flat scissors maneuver, sliding back and forth. Each pilot turned toward the other in an attempt to get positioned behind. Because their planes' turning radius and speed were about the same, three scissors maneuvers were done with no advantage to either one.

Kelli decided to do a high yo-yo procedure again with her wings level. She did a quarter plane roll and pulled up out of Bullseye's plane of turn. As she climbed up, he made a sharp left turn, and she rolled over towards his tail. She was in a good position to shoot at a short range but didn't lock on. She felt that her plane's nose was too high on Bullseye's, so she held back. Bullseye dived away, gaining separation.

He climbed his plane to gain altitude and came back nose to nose again at high speed. Just before they flew opposite each other, Kelli put on her speed brakes and chopped her throttle. Slick anticipated her move and chopped his throttle also, to prevent overrunning her plane. He skidded to Kelli's right and half rolled to his left . . . wings vertical. Kelli turned sharply to the left. Bullseye pulled his stick hard back, working the rudder pedals and whirled around, cutting inside the radius of her aircraft. He had the Tiger Lady right in his gun sights and pulled the trigger . . . it was a kill.

Air Plot called on the VHF radio. "That's a kill. Return to base."

Kelli couldn't eat her lunch. She was upset with herself for not activating the pistol grip early on when she had Bullseye's plane in her cross hairs. Okay, that's done, she said. Move on. She took a cool shower to collect her thoughts and decided to take a short nap. The dog fight had used up quite a bit of her energy, so she had little trouble failing asleep. She set the alarm to give herself an extra thirty minutes to get out to the airfield. When she awoke, she ate a couple of Snickers candy bars and hurried over, feeling confident again.

SECOND DOG FIGHT

Tiger Lady and Bullseye started the second fight at 14,000 feet. Each entered the 100-mile fighting circle at the same speed. But there was one difference this time. Once they got into the circle, they added whatever power they wanted, but could not exceed an altitude of 40,000 feet. Each pulled their stick back and climbed their plane for altitude advantage and then dove, approaching each other head-on at high speed.

Once they met, they immediately pulled back on their control sticks and went straight up in a vertical climb. Since they both had similar turn rates, the speed of their aircraft determined the turn radius—the slower plane would have a smaller turning radius. Bullseye knew this. He had not flown as high as Kelli, so he had the slower aircraft, and because the planes were close enough, he was able to get on her tail. He locked on and hung on. Kelli, inside her cockpit, went into a frenzy, turning left and right, throttling up and down. Bullseye stayed on her tail and squeezed the photo guns. The fight was over. Bullseye was the "Top Gun."

That night at the Winner's Circle, with the tension over, the flyers turned out in force to drink.

Bullseye came over to Kelli's table. "Mind if I sit?" Kelli gestured with her beer. He sat.

"In that first fight you had me right in your gun sight and didn't fire. Why didn't you?"

"It wasn't a clean shot. It was a judgment call. I would have had you with a missile."

"I know," he replied. "And I'm not condescending, but I need to say this: Not every shot is going to be clean. If I was a MIG, and you had a chance to punch some holes in me, you'd shoot, wouldn't you?"

"Yes," said Kelli.

"I think we're trained to be perfect," said Jones, sitting back and pressing his hands against his eyes. She realized he was tired, too. "We think in terms of ideal reactions, but what we're doing is not a precise science. There are accidents, miscalculations. All that's intangible."

"Point well taken. And well said."

"Anyway, I need to say one more thing."

"Shoot."

"We've both heard a lot of static leading up to this fight. You're a woman; I'm a man. But don't ever think that I underestimate you. I know how good you are. And don't think that if things went your way today, I wouldn't be sitting here saying what I'm saying now. I fly how I live. Straight up."

"I believe you," said Kelli.

"One more thing," said Bullseye. "I think you're one hell of a pilot. I would certainly want you on my side in a dogfight."

The next day, Kelli received a call to report to Commander Clark's office.

"Kelli, I looked at the video of your encounters with Bullseye. The Top Gun instructors feel it was a tie. You easily won that first fight but didn't fire. Why?"

"Because I wanted to be sure of the kill. If I could have fired my missiles, I would have."

"You were within 1000 feet," replied Clark. "We feel there should be another fight to declare the real Top Gun."

"I can't accept that," replied Kelli. "Bullseye won, and he's the Top Gun. I will not be a poor loser!"

"So be it," said Clark.

"Thanks," she replied.

"Just one more thing, Kelli. You are being promoted to full Lieutenant."

V

MARK PALMER

After completing her training at Miramar, Kelli got to pick her next assignment. She chose a new Fleet Replacement Squadron (FRS) that was forming at Oceana Naval Air Station and became the Executive Officer of the strike fighters. Prior to reporting for duty, she had two weeks off to visit her family in San Diego. Her first night there, Mark Palmer called.

"Kelli, there's a character on the phone by the name of Mark Palmer who wants to talk to you. You don't know anyone by that name, do you? Do you want me to hang up?"

"No, don't hang up," she replied, with a smile. "He's the football player."

"Ah, yes," her mother said. "The football player." Kelli took the phone.

"Hello, Palmer. It's been a while."

"Yes. I've been busy getting my body racked while you've been busy flying jets."

"What happened?"

"I took a hit last Sunday and fractured my left leg. I'm out for the rest of the season. I'd like to see you."

"I've got two weeks before reporting to Oceana Naval Air Station in Virginia," she replied. "I'd like to see you, too."

"I'll fly out."

"No. You're crippled, remember? Besides, flying out here as the injured quarterback seeing his Navy concubine would draw some attention, wouldn't it?"

"Concubine?" he asked. "I've never had a concubine in my life . . . much less an officer."

Kelli wanted to say that Hawaii was only five hours away by jet, but she didn't want to sound too eager. So she said, "Okay, you name it."

"How about San Francisco or Hawaii? I'll meet you wherever you want. I'll even come out to your home in San Diego."

That last statement really shocked Kelli. He knew her family was there, and if he wanted to meet her parents, he really might be serious. Her heart started to beat a little faster. She knew she'd be sacked by a quarterback. Spending a week with him would be a big commitment. She was hesitant. But if anything was going to jell between them, she had to cooperate and try to make it happen. She decided to bite the bullet.

"Okay, Palmer, my heart is pounding, but I'm used to it. I'll meet you in San Francisco in uniform."

"United Airlines ticket counter, San Francisco Airport around noon tomorrow."

"I'll be there."

Kelli didn't know what was going to happen, but there were distinct possibilities. Accepting a rendezvous with a handsome single aggressive quarterback was an obvious commitment. She would be ready, willing, and able. She remembered his face and that one kiss. He'd be on crutches and easy to recognize.

Wardrobe was easy: dress whites. She was upset because there was not enough time to get her hair done. She'd have to rely on her natural curls. She called and obtained a plane reservation.

When she got into the San Francisco airport, there was a tall handsome man with a cast on his left leg, leaning on crutches. He had a big smile on his face as she approached. He saluted. She saluted back.

"I'd like to start our relationship where we left off," he said. He reached around her with his right arm and pulled her to him. She didn't resist the kiss. There was that sensation again, a tingling that reached all the way down to her toes. He held the kiss for a long time, and tried to change position and wrap his arms tighter around her. It didn't work. He started to fall over his crutches, but Kelli caught him before he fell.

"You protect me better than my linemen."

"I don't have their muscles or their build."

"I'm glad to hear that. I like yours better!"

"Well, Palmer, you're the tour director. What do you have planned?"

"Hawaii. It's five hours away. Or we can stay in San Francisco at the St. Francis and see the city. My leg may be a problem, though."

"I'm for going to Hawaii. The weather will be warmer."

"The plane leaves in four hours. I already have the tickets."

"What if I didn't want to go?"

"Then I would have to convince you that denying a disabled person his one wish would be inhumane. We have three hours to sit and talk, have lunch, or take a cab around the city. I want to hear about Miramar."

"Miramar was intense," replied Kelli. "But I don't want to talk about myself. I want to hear about you. I don't even know how you broke your leg."

"I got hit by Karl Dikavitch, a three-hundred pound defensive tackle from Pittsburgh. My leg buckled, and I knew I was hurt. An MRI showed a fracture of my left tibia with a ruptured blood vessel in the muscle."

Kelli took it all in. He was playing it light, but she knew his career was in jeopardy.

"Being stoic, are we?" she asked.

"What else is there? Ranting doesn't help and worrying about losing my job isn't going to make me heal. It sucks. It happened, and it's over. We're here now, so let's enjoy being together while we can."

"Okay."

"Let's do you. Tell me about jets."

"It's been incredible. Flying feels so natural to me. It's not just what I do, it's who I am," Kelli smiled at herself. She never spoke about her job. Her green eyes lowered.

"You're embarrassed."

"Palmer, I live in a world where everyone is so busy being superhuman that talking about feelings isn't even a blip on the radar screen."

"Me, too."

"So if we're going to spend time together, let's agree that it's okay to talk not just about getting sacked or shot at, but how it feels, too. We barely know each other."

"Yes," he said, "but I understand that Hawaii tends to bring people together."

"So do banana daiquiris. Let's get some."

The three hours at the San Francisco Airport and the several tropical beverages passed quickly. Her luggage was transferred to the Hawaiian flight, and they had a light lunch in the dining area. She noticed that Mark's left leg was pretty much immobilized by the cast. She wondered about that.

"How long will you have to wear your cast and use the crutches?"

"As long as I have to. My season's over right now. I won't be playing anymore this year."

"It must be painful."

"Not too."

"Can you sleep okay?"

"With you next to me? No."

After the plane landed in Hawaii, they took a commuter flight to Maui and checked into the Hotel Royale Hawaiian. The three room suite Mark had reserved had a beautiful view of the Pacific Ocean, and the beach was right outside their front door. One room had a king sized bed and another a queen sized bed. The third room was a living room with a small dining area.

"Lots of room," he said. "It's your choice. Pick whichever room you like."

She brought her gear to the room with the queen-size bed,

dropped it on the floor, and went into the larger bedroom where he was doing the same.

"Palmer, I don't know if we should sleep together yet, that's all."

"Kelli, listen, don't sweat it, okay? Let's agree that what happens happens."

"You mean, don't force it."

"Exactly."

"You're the quarterback. You call the signals."

"And you're the pilot. So you call the Ball."

"The Ball? How do you know about the Ball?"

"I read."

"A little learning is a dangerous thing."

"So is an F-14, if what I read is accurate. Are they hard to fly?"

"It was a new experience. Just like this."

Kelli went into her bedroom, changed into a skin tight bikini, and put on a white terry cloth cover up. She waited in the living room for Mark.

He came out wearing a snug-fitting suit that showed off his magnificent physique. It left very little to her imagination.

"I'll say it again, Kelli. You're very pretty."

"You don't look so bad yourself," she said, "except for that cast." She bit her lip. "I'm sorry."

"I understand. Don't worry about it."

The ocean waves and surf splashed against the volcanic rocks. No one was around as they walked along the beach beneath the palm trees. Kelli felt completely relaxed, the way she might feel if she was on her honeymoon, except that their physical relationship had not been consummated. She wondered about that and how soon Mark might attempt to break down that barrier. That cast on his leg could be a problem.

After their walk, they stretched out together on the blanket. Mark's eyes could not help but notice how pretty she was. Her red hair glistened in the sunlight, and she obviously was quite happy and relaxed in this Hawaiian setting and new adventure.

Mark opened a cooler and took out two glasses that he filled with daiquiris. He passed a glass to Kelli.

"Here's to the beginning of a beautiful relationship," he said as he tapped his glass against hers.

"I'll drink to that," she replied.

They spent the rest of the day on the beach talking and drinking daiquiris. Kelli looked beautiful in her skin tight black bikini. Her athletic slender body was elegantly displayed. Her long slender legs, beautiful buttocks, and full breasts left little to his imagination. Kelli noticed how Mark watched every movement she made. His eyes told it all. Her heart seemed to beat faster in anticipation.

The afternoon went by too quickly. At dusk, their arms around each other, Kelli helped Mark limp along without crutches. They went back to their suite, slightly sunburned and drowsy.

Together they made their way into his room, flopped on the bed, and let it happen. They were tentative at first, touching each other apprehensively. But the longing was there, working its way to the surface. Their skin was salty and sweet from suntan lotion. She felt him trying to hold back and be delicate.

But her own anticipation was uncontrollable.

He removed her bikini and let it fall to the floor. She untied his shorts and worked them over his cast. "Hell," he said, trying to lift his leg. She giggled, got them off, and stood naked at the side of the bed, looking at him, "Wow," she said. "So this is a quarterback."

"Get over here," he said as he rolled toward her and grabbed her arm.

"Wait, let me," she said, straddling him. They worked at each other slowly, knowing it was a matter of time . . . of moments . . . but relaxing into it, letting it happen. His hands gently palpated her breasts as her nipples firmed up. He then lowered his large hands behind her back and placed them around her buttocks, pulling her body tighter on his. Kelli responded, rotating her hips, the passion continuing to rise until they both became overwhelmed, and let themselves surrender to it.

Afterwards, he picked up the phone. "Champagne for Suite 101. What kind? I'm a football player. I have no idea. But I do have money, so you choose, okay? Two bottles of the best. And two glasses."

He turned to her, still in bed. "Maybe it's corny," he said, "but it seems like the right drink for us."

"Why?"

"Why champagne? Because we're celebrating. Because it's what you drink when you win the Super Bowl, or launch a ship."

"That's not a good comparison, Palmer! This is not about winning. It's about love."

They both laughed.

"Palmer, I'm scared."

"You're scared? Why?"

"Because it's so good, and it's happening faster than maybe I'm comfortable with."

"Sounds funny coming from someone who flies at Mach 2."

"This is different, and you know it."

"Okay, yes, I feel it, too. But why worry? Let's use the time we have. One week together is better than any alternative I can think of. Let's just relax, let things happen, no need to use force."

She smiled. "Sometimes I might want to use force on you."

"That's different," he said. "if you're up to it, I'm ready again right now." He pulled her over to him.

They were more relaxed now. Her mouth quickly found his. She had no trouble mounting him as he arched his back, no trouble working together to an overwhelming, exhausting climax.

Kelli had dreamed about what it might be like to make love to Mark. Her dreams had come true.

Day two was day one all over again. They never left the hotel. Near dawn of day three, Kelli's beeper went off. "Damn it," she said when she read the number. The phone call was short. Military communication usually is.

"You're to return to your base immediately. Use military transport and top priority if necessary. Contact Barber's Point Naval Air Station."

She hung up and only then started to cry.

She packed while he slept. When she kissed his forehead, he stirred. "You ditching me, Lieutenant?"

"Yes, I'm afraid so."

"No shit. Just when we are starting to get to know each other." He smiled weakly.

"It's the Navy. They say jump, and I say, 'with or without a parachute?' It's an occupational hazard."

"Bye. See you around."

"Hey, don't be like that," she said.

"Sorry. I'm let down. You're the pilot, and I'm the crippled jock."

"Not forever. When do I see you again?"

"It's your call. When you get settled, you can reach me in Dallas."

She took a cab to the airport, a shuttle to Oahu, and caught a Navy transport at Barber's Point at 8:45 A.M. back to the mainland. It was the first time she hated the Navy.

EXECUTIVE OFFICER, FIGHTER SQUADRON

On the Navy transport, Kelli called her Strike Fighter Skipper, Lieutenant Commander Steve Vardo. She was angry and wanted to know why her leave had been shortened. She had forgotten about the time zone change, and didn't realize it was 4:00 A.M. in Virginia.

"Commander Vardo, here."

"This is Lieutenant Kelli Fitzgerald, what's going on? Why the hurry-up call?"

"The Mid East is heating up again, Kelli," Vardo explained sleepily, "and COMAIRLANT is going to expedite our new Replacement Air Group. They're knocking out some of our rookie pilots and replacing them with more experienced pilots."

"Fine. But why all this rush?"

"Vice Admiral Johnson is meeting with us in three days. You and

I will be briefing him about the F-28. You know the plane, and we've got to be prepared for the top brass. That transport you're on has a fax. You'll receive some written material within an hour to start reviewing. The Navy owes you some R&R time in the future."

"How comforting."

An hour later Kelli received a top secret outline of the current political situation in the Middle East. Iran and Iraq were stirring the pot. Nothing new. Afghanistan was now in the geopolitical arena training terrorists in a religious 'jiad' against all Americans.

They were stockpiling sophisticated arms and missiles. The Chinese, the report said, had gotten the plans for some of America's best fighter planes and had made some copies for export. Iran and Afghanistan, which had been behind a lot of recent terrorist activity, were storing these planes in underground hangars. Fortunately, they did not have enough trained pilots to man the aircraft. They also did not have the satellites needed for global positioning of the guided missiles, although the Chinese were rapidly placing satellites into orbit that might be used for that purpose.

To counteract all this, the Navy's carrier attack strike force needed to increase their forward presence in the Red Sea and Mediterranean, which meant she would be going on another six-month overseas tour. It also looked like U.S. political and military judgment might have been wrong in focusing too much on Saddam. Iran and Afghanistan had joined the opposition. The whole region was in geopolitical play.

But Kelli's biggest worry at the moment was Mark Palmer. The new man in her life she had to leave in haste, and it meant that her romance would be on the back burner for six whole months. She was infuriated.

As Executive Officer of the strike fighter squadron, her responsibilities increased. She would be briefing the Admiral about the new advanced fighter, the F-28. It was a two-seater that could fly at speeds greater than Mach 3 and fly higher than most aircraft. Kelli had flown the F-28 several times and liked the way it flew. It had a tight turning radius, tremendous power and speed, and was safer than the F-14, F-16, or F-18.

The briefing for Admiral Johnson went very well. He was pleasantly surprised that the Executive Officer of the fighter squadron was a woman and commented about it.

"Nice job. Welcome aboard."

"Thank you!" she replied.

Admiral Johnson reported that Carrier Air Wing 259 would have a short shakedown cruise of four weeks on the U.S.S. Stennis and would then be heading for the Red Sea under Rear Admiral Jack Cronin.

As the Executive Officer of the strike fighter squadron, Kelli was the main instructor for the new fighter pilots. The shakedown cruise went by quickly without any problems. The U.S.S. Stennis and its carrier strike force then headed for the Middle East. The Mobile Bay was the lead Aegis cruiser in the force, and all the ships were connected electronically. They were capable of inflicting massive damage to any enemy.

When the Stennis came on station, 24 hour CAP (Combat Air Patrol) was placed over the strike carrier group. Soon the CAP duties became routine, although at night the flying got hairy and dangerous when the weather socked in.

Kelli had plenty of time to relax in the pilot's ready room. Sometimes she would just day dream and fantasize about Palmer. She relived her memories, but with a tinge of worries because she had not heard from him. He had not answered her letters or the messages she left on his answering machine. She hoped he didn't think she was a one-night stand.

The weather wasn't always good, and one black night the sea was so rough that the L.S.O. was having difficulty getting the CAP fighter group safely back aboard. Kelli was in the air, the last to be cleared to come down to the landing circle.

She made two passes and received mandatory wave-offs. She hated wave-offs. It was an affront to her skills as a pilot.

Because she was the executive officer of the fighter squadron, she felt that she had a little clout, so she called the L.S.O. She wanted to know what was going on. Skip Foster was the L.S.O. on duty.

"Skip, this is Jaguar 2, what's up? Why the two wave-offs?"

Skip was a little bit disturbed by the challenge and gave her a curt reply.

"Jaguar 2, this is S.T. Base. You were too hot in the first pass, and in the second pass the deck wasn't clear."

"Roger, S.T. Base." Kelli was relieved by his remarks. She had to be patient and wait for clearance as she orbited over the strike Force at Marshal.

After another five minutes of using up her fuel, the Air Boss gave her clearance to enter the landing circle.

Kelli let down to 1200 feet and turned into the groove, making an instrument approach to the flight deck.

The L.S.O. could hear the shrill whine of her jet engines as she got closer but couldn't see her plane. Kelli broke out of the clouds at about 500 yards and got a quick glimpse of the meatball and beep lights lining the flight deck. She felt that she was coming in too fast, so she cut back on the throttle. The L.S.O. did not give her a wave-off, and the plane caught the #3 wire. It was a rough, fast landing as the plane jerked backwards when the tail hook engaged. She quickly put on full power in case she had to do a bolter. Suddenly, she felt something snap in the back of the plane as it rolled down the deck.

"Shit!" she hollered and pushed the throttle to the fire wall. She didn't know what it was, but she knew she was in big trouble and had to get her plane back into the air. As it went over the bow, the plane dropped below the flight deck and skimmed the water.

The hook man, who releases the tail hook after the plane lands, noticed that the plane's metal tail hook was lying on the flight deck. It had been torn off the back of her aircraft. He immediately notified the L.S.O. who notified the Air Boss and called Kelli.

"Jaguar Two, this is S.T. Base. You lost your tail hook on that last pass. You're to climb to 17,000 feet and rendezvous with the tanker. Standby for instructions."

Kelli's heart slammed in her chest. Usually when this happens, the pilot's plane is fueled up and vectored to a bingo field a few hundred miles away. Right now they didn't have any bingo fields. Saudi Arabia was the nearest land, and she would have to fly over Iraq to get there. She could eject, and bail out over the task force, hoping that one of the ships would pick her up. But between darkness and bad weather, they'd never find her. There was one other option; since her plane didn't have a tail hook to catch an arresting wire, the carrier could string a barricade net twenty feet across the flight deck, which if it holds, would prevent the plane from going overboard. But to go for this, she'd have to stay in the air until daylight.

Captain Keating, the Operations Officer, called her on VHF radio and asked her what she wanted to do.

Kelli chose the barricade landing on the carrier's deck in the daylight. The crash crew would be ready for her, and if she went over the side, she had a better chance of being picked up. She would keep her plane in the air and wait for the sun to come up. This carrier landing would be difficult. It would be like the way her grandfather landed his plane on a carrier during World War II. She wouldn't be flying her plane onto the deck trying to catch a wire—her plane's tailhook was gone. She couldn't do a bolter. Her plane's landing had to be perfect. She would have to cut the power completely and hope that the barrier stopped her plane. It was a one-shot deal.

Kelli realized it would be a long night, and she'd have to stay awake. Her legs were cramping, and she was getting a queasy feeling in the pit of her stomach. She finished the coffee in her thermos, refueled her aircraft, and talked with the tanker pilot.

"Nice night for flying," he offered.

"Just peachy."

"How you holding up?"

"Oh, fine. Could you pipe over some scrambled eggs with that fuel?"

"Sorry, the cook's on his break right now. Anyway, the Navy seems to place more emphasis on feeding planes instead of pilots."

"I'm going to talk to the brass about that when I get out of this mess."

"Right on. Just land that bird, and I'll buy you a steak dinner."

Dawn comes early at 15000 feet, particularly if there's cloud cover below. Kelli contacted the carrier and requested permission to come aboard. She was told to continue orbiting for another hour. Luck was with her because the ceiling lifted, and visibility increased.

"Jaguar One. How're you feeling?"

"Like I'm ready to put my feet on that deck. I'd like to do a fly-by first."

"Jaguar One, permission granted."

She did an I.L.S. approach, used her Doppler radar to pick up the carrier, and broke out of the clouds at 600 yards.

On the fly-by, she noted that all the planes had been cleared from the flight deck. After flying back up to Angels 5 at Marshall, she let down to 1200 feet.

"This is what it's all about," she muttered, as she directed her plane into the bullseye of her I.L.S. gear. The rear of the carrier lay ahead, somewhere in the fog. "I've got to put this plane down like a feather."

Five seconds from the trap, she caught a glimpse of the flight deck and saw the meatball.

The L.S.O. tried to sugar talk her aboard. "Jaguar One, you're right on. Slight left ... doing good."

As the plane got to the edge of the stern, he hollered, "Cut!"

Kelli pulled the throttle back to cut power, her plane without the tail hook hit the deck soft and smooth as a pussycat, and bounced forward. The nose of the plane hit the center of the barricade and skidded to rest in the center of the deck. There was very little damage.

"Thank God!" exclaimed Kelli.

The skipper got on the bullhorn. You could hear it over the cheers of the deck crew.

"Job well done, Lieutenant! We're all proud of you! Good landing!"

During the next three months, the Mid East confrontations

cooled off with the American show of force in the area. Kelli was looking forward to returning to the States. She still hadn't received any response from Mark. God damn it! Why didn't he call her?

The answer came too quickly. One evening when she was sitting in the ready room watching television via satellite from the States, there was a program on about the lives of professional athletes. It showed Mark Palmer with a beautiful blonde socialite who was the daughter of a prominent Texas oil millionaire. They were engaged to be married. Kelli felt as if she had been kicked in the stomach.

VI

KELLI UNDER FIRE

When the U.S.S. Stennis returned to Norfolk, Virginia, Air Group 259 was detached, and Kelli received orders to Patuxant River, Maryland, to be a test pilot for the F-51, a new combined fighter and attack bomber. It was shoreline duty not far from Washington, D.C. Her new job was a complete change of pace, low key with not much flying. But every time she did fly, she took new risks, testing new and unknown equipment designed for the 21st Century.

Aircraft design had changed dramatically even during the short time Kelli had been with the Navy. Pilots first tested new aircraft on the West Coast in the desert, where there'd be plenty of flat ground to land in case of an engine flame-out.

Only the Navy's best became test pilots. Most of the aircraft corporations had their own test pilots. The planes were now designed with the use of computers, and the design studies could almost match what happened in the air. The maneuverability in the transonic age was the most important in a combat fighter. Most jet fighters had two engines, and the planes ability to fly on one engine was a necessity.

The undercarriage of Navy planes had to be strong because of the potential damage that could occur when the planes caught a wire on the flight deck. The visibility in the cockpit also had to be perfect, and there could be no flaws in the sophisticated computerization that was necessary for early detection, counter measures, and accurate gunnery controls.

The Congress had to give final approval before millions of dollars were spent in the production of fighters for the 21st century.

At the age of 32, Kelli was promoted to Lieutenant Commander. She received orders to form a new strike fighter squadron for the supercarrier, the U.S.S. Harry Truman. The fighter pilots would be flying the F-51.

The Far East had undergone dramatic changes. Japan's economic power was waning and was threatened by a modernized, industrialized China. As China's economy improved, its military presence became more noticeable.

China's balance of trade with the United States was overwhelming. Because of China's large population base and cheap labor market, they could make products much cheaper. China was undercutting Japan and affecting its economic stability. They were very good at making inexpensive copies of everything and then dumping them on the world market. This was disruptive to most countries and led to economic chaos in some of the smaller countries.

However, Taiwan, an island about 100 miles from the Chinese mainland, was still a political sticking point. It had been originally occupied by the Chinese though the Dutch, Portuguese, and Japanese had each occupied and controlled the island at one time. As a result of the Sino-Japanese War of 1894–5, Taiwan was put under Japanese sovereignty until the Japanese defeat in World War II. In 1950, Chiang Kai Shek and the Chinese Nationalists took over Taiwan and declared its independence. However, mainland China never recognized its independence.

While the U.S.S. Harry Truman was enjoying its R&R at Yokasuka Naval Base in Tokyo, the Chinese decided to challenge Washington again about Taiwan. A group of Chinese warships surrounded the island and began firing missiles in what Beijing called "war games". The U.S.S. Harry Truman and the carrier strike attack force received orders to head for Taiwan immediately with missile cruisers, frigates, submarines, and supply ships. As the carrier strike force got closer to Taiwan, the tension aboard ship increased. They were entering a potential combat zone, and everyone was afraid that something unpredictable would happen. Communications between China and the U.S. worsened in response to the "chess match". China threatened to retaliate against U.S. cities.

Nevertheless, the U.S. launched jet fighters and bombers to show the Chinese that America fully intended to defend Taiwan. The Air Boss was kept extremely busy with as many as 40 or 50 aircraft "on the roof" at one time. The pilots and planes were in a protective mode, but if they had to fight, they were ready.

Everyone hoped the diplomats and military in Beijing and Washington did not fuck up. Both sides had explicit emergency instructions in case of major confrontation, military battle, or missile exchange. The Navy's new E-9C Hawkeye planes were kept on station above the task force, so its Doppler radar and electronic equipment could keep track of all movement around the force.

The pilots were given explicit instructions not to engage the Chinese. However, they had permission to fire or retaliate if their plane was fired upon.

The next morning, the CAG, Captain King, called all the pilots together in the ready room. The Chinese pilots over Taiwan were getting more aggressive, and one of their pilots had fired his cannons at a Tiger fighter plane and missed. The pilot who was shot at said that the Chinese pilot had separated and disappeared, heading for the Chinese mainland.

Because of that incident, Captain John King felt that he had to make it clear what the Tiger pilots' reaction should be if they were confronted.

"I'm sure you all realize that the Chinese pilots are trying to create an incident. If you can safely retreat without being shot down, you're to do so."

"What if they get a lock on your plane, and your HUD lights up?" asked one of the pilots.

"Use your chaff flares; take evasive action and separate."

"What if they fire at you?"

"That's a different matter. If your craft and life are threatened, you may respond with any force deemed necessary."

Kelli did not like that. It meant that if two or three Chinese fighter planes fired missiles, you would not know which direction to take evasive action. It was a no-win situation.

"What if a Chinese frigate fires S.A.M.s at you?" she asked.

"Evade maneuvers only. But we don't believe they'll do that. That's a major confrontation, and our submarines and Aegis cruisers will handle it. We have informed the Chinese government that if they invade the air space over our carrier strike force within one-hundred miles, they do so at their own risk. What we're telling you is use your head. Check with Base before making any drastic moves. Are there any more questions? If not, let's get airborne, fly smart, and fly safe."

If the Chinese pilots were forcing the issue, it would be difficult not to respond, Kelli thought. She had confidence in her Doppler radar but did not know whether the Chinese pilots had the same or better instrumentation. Her Phoenix and the new Starlight missiles were the state-of-art and could handle multiple targets. She had adequate armament, but she did not want to take on the entire Chinese air force.

Three days later, Kelli drew the night milk run patrol, flying CAP between 0300 and 0700. The weather was so bad she could barely find her plane. A heavy rain pelted the flight deck. The plane captain wasn't optimistic about the weather when she climbed into the cockpit of her F-51.

"Bad night, tonight," he remarked.

"Been there, done that," said Kelli.

"You'll be all right."

"I know I will," Kelli held up her thumb.

It was a night to frazzle your nerves, pitch black skies and no horizon to orient yourself in space. Because of the horrible weather, it was time-consuming recovering the planes. The L.S.O. was having a lot of trouble because the planes broke out of the clouds only a short distance from the back of the flight deck; the pilots could not see the meatball until they were right on top of it. The fresnel lens and cameras on the flight deck were useless. All the landings were I.L.S., instead of the planes landing one by one right after each other. There were so many bolters that the planes kept filling up the landing circle. Many of them had to go up to the tanker to get refueled more than once, which wasn't easy in bad weather. The air boss and L.S.O. were earning their keep.

Just before Kelli got off the number two catapult, she saw a plane go over the side and heard the L.S.O. call the Air-sea Rescue helicopter. When the radio reported no success in finding him, a second helicopter was launched. As soon as Kelli got in the air, the weather worsened, and she put her plane on automatic pilot. Her global positioning system told her where she was, but everything else was fucked up.

Because of her senior pilot status, she flew the CAP in front of the strike force and finally broke out of the bad weather at angels twenty. Soon she was in a majestic sky, covered with beautiful bright stars.

Thirty minutes before completing her flight, the Air Boss called her on her VHF radio and told her to refuel. "Tiger One, this is H.T. Base. You're to refuel on one of the tankers in preparation for landing. We'll give you the vectors and help you lock on."

After she refueled, the beauty of the night was disappearing as the sun came up, and the silence was abruptly violated by her VHF squawk box.

"Tiger One, this is H.T. Base. We have an unidentified bogey at Angels 25, vector 130 degrees, 110 miles. He's getting too close to the air corridor over our strike force. You're to investigate, but not splash."

"Roger, H.T. Base." Kelli made a right bank and headed toward the intruder. She looked at her panel, but her HUD showed two bogeys, not one.

"H.T. Base, this is Tiger One. I have two bogeys on my screen."

"Tiger One, this is H.T. Base. Tiger Three will join you shortly."

She decided to arm her missiles just in case and to get up above the bogeys. The heels of her hands hit the throttle knobs as the jet afterburners lit up, and she went at transonic speed to 630 knots. "Tally ho, two bandits," she announced as she spotted the two enemy planes above the clouds.

The Chinese fighter planes turned their noses toward her. She couldn't believe it. They were coming after her.

She reported in to H.T. Base. "Two bogeys approaching at high speed looking like they want some."

"Tiger One, this is H.T. Base. Pull away! Do not engage! Do not fight!"

Just as Base responded with their orders, one of the Chinese fighters fired at her. She could see the tracers; they were very close. This meant that she could respond. The other plane did a scissors maneuver to try to get on her tail. They both started firing their front cannons.

Kelli made a sharp left vertical turn—a modified yo-yo maneuver—and snapped on the tail of the closest one that had shot at her. She got his plane in her sights. Not a perfect shot. She pressed her pistol grip and remembered what Jones had said: 'It's not a perfect world—take the shot.' She did. The plane shuddered as she squeezed the trigger, and the bogey blew up in front of her eyes. She pulled up sharply to avoid the debris, and saw the flare of the enemy's ejector seat shoot away to her right.

Her HUD lit up. She saw that her radar warning device was on, telling her of a radar lock on her plane.

"Shit!" she hollered, then pulled back on her control stick and made a tight vertical turn. The second bandit was on her tail. He fired his missiles. Kelli hit her electromagnetic countermeasures and released a bolus of metal tinsel out into the air. The missile went for the bolus and detonated, the explosion threw her plane over on its back, and the edge of the bolus explosion knocked the tip of her left wing off. The F-51 went into a rotating nose dive, upside down, picking up speed. Instead of pulling the control stick back, Kelli pushed it forward. She kept the nose up and added full power. It helped. The horizontal stabilizers began to take over. Slowly the plane was heading down. She moved the control stick to try to get the right aileron to stop the roll, but the plane continued to lose altitude because of the missing left wing tip. The horizontal stabilizers were also damaged.

Meanwhile, a CAP Tiger fighter bagged the Chinese bandit with his starlight missile, and the plane burst into a fireball that lit up the sky. Five F-51 Tigers of fighter squadron 63 scrambled from the carrier and came on station.

Kelli kept the afterburners on to get some stability to her aircraft. But she was screaming seaward, heading for the deep six, going too fast to use the ejection seat. Her radio crackled. "Tiger One, pull up!"

"MAY DAY! MAY DAY!" she shouted. "I'm hit."

She managed to get the plane to stop rotating by dropping her wheels and speed flaps, but it was still going too fast for ejection. She waited until the plane's cockpit was straight up, then hollered, "Shit," and pulled the ejection seat lever between her legs. The curtain came over her face to protect her from the flash of the ignition, and the vernier rockets ignited. The two metal bars on the ejection seat broke through the plane's canopy as the seat shot 350 feet up into the sky.

The explosion took her breath away and almost knocked her out. One of the pieces of the broken canopy hit her on the head and neck area, slicing through her flight suit cutting her neck. She could feel the wetness of her blood on her skin and was in a free fall, but conscious. Suddenly she felt a hard jerk on her parachute harness as the drogue chute opened above her, and the personal parachute deployed. "Shit, I'm hurt," she screamed as the harness grabbed her left shoulder. Then the metal ejection seat automatically dropped away.

It didn't take long before she hit the water, and the weight of her body took her beneath the surface. She felt a burning in her left shoulder as the salt water hit the open cut. Then her life raft automatically inflated. Kelli swam with one arm, splashing through the cold brine. She grabbed for the side of the raft and pulled. Feeling like she weighed a ton, she hauled her left leg up, over, and pulled again with her right arm. The pain in her left shoulder made her focus. "Hyaaaah!" she screamed in frustration, in agony, and then in relief as she fell into the raft.

She managed to stop the bleeding from her neck wound with continuous pressure and located the small hand-held radio and infrared strobe homing device attached to her life raft. She decided not to activate it in case the Chinese Navy was close by. Where the hell was the Air-sea Rescue? What were they waiting for?

She knew that the Chinese warships in the area would like to capture her. Another thought that entered her mind was that she had seen the Chinese pilot eject. Could he be floating around nearby and want to finish the fight? She pulled her .45, checked the clip, and locked it back into place.

She couldn't see anything on the horizon; all she could hear was the gentle splashing of the waves against the side of her life raft. Fortunately, there weren't any big waves. It was eerie to be soaking wet bobbing around alone in the life raft. She had stopped the bleeding, but the pain in her shoulder was getting worse, frazzling her already shaken nerves. She fought the urge to cry.

As she sat there in the life raft, she remembered what her grandfather had told her. "Sometimes when the situation looks impossible, it will be a fight to the finish. Never give up!"

ABOARD THE CHINESE NUCLEAR MISSILE CRUISER BEIJING ONE

On the missile cruiser Beijing One, Admiral Lu Chiang, was the commander of the Chinese Naval Task Force that had surrounded Taiwan.

He sat in the CIC directing the action of the two Chinese pilots.

"Tell Lieutenant Lee to fire his cannon at the American."

Chu, the Chinese air plot commander, looked at his superior. "Admiral, do you intend to start a war?"

"No. The Americans won't fight over a small island like Taiwan."

"You seem to be sure of that."

"As sure as I am of our weaponry and pilots. Do as I say."

The order was given and Lieutenant Lee fired. The Chinese air combat center let out a big cheer. But within seconds the American had maneuvered behind the Chinese Zinto fighter plane and shot it down, leaving the Chinese CIC in stunned silence as the plane disappeared from the air plot screen.

The mood improved as the second Chinese fighter soared behind Kelli's plane and fired his heat seeking missiles. "Splash, one American pig pilot," the pilot announced over the radio. They could see the explosion when the missile hit the chaff, but the U.S. plane did not go off the screen for a while and another big cheer went up in the Chinese air command center, but it was short-lived, as a Tiger plane arrived on the scene and within seconds, the pilot shot down the second Chinese fighter.

" I can't believe this. What happened?" asked Admiral Chiang.

"The Americans have excellent planes, pilots and missiles," said Captain Riping who was in charge of the air combat center. "Should we call in more planes from the mainland?"

The Admiral listened for any insolence, but found none.

"No. Send a frigate out to pick up their downed pilot. I'd like to interrogate him. The pilot is not to be killed."

ABOARD THE U.S.S. TRUMAN
COMBAT INTELLIGENCE CENTER
AIR PLOT

Commander Brett Clancy, who was in charge of air plot, put a mark on the board where Kelli's plane was thought to have entered the ocean. The global positioning system was accurate. He called his Air Boss, Bill Pearce.

"Bill, send your copter out to where Commander Fitzgerald's plane went down. It's possible that those two Chinese pilots ejected and could be in the water near her. There's a Chinese frigate about seventy-five miles away from her, and he's steaming in her direction at 25 knots. We've vectored five of our CAP planes to get there pronto and orbit over the area. We might have to fly cover for the chopper and discourage that frigate from getting too close."

Captain Bill Fuller was watching the action on his screen in his Aegis cruiser. He received a call from the CIC command center on the Truman.

"Captain Fuller, this is Captain Carey on H.T. Base. You're to detach from our strike force, and launch your helicopter on vector 170–90 miles to assist Air-sea Rescue. We have a downed pilot."

"Roger, H.T. Base." He then ordered the helmsman. "Right full rudder—full power—vector 170 degrees."

Captain Fuller wondered why they were sending his ship out to aid in the rescue. He really wasn't worried because the weaponry he carried aboard could take on an Army and Navy if it had to. He was about seventy miles away from where Kelli had splashed down, and it would take him more than an hour to get there. The screen in his control center told it all. Six planes up in CAP would be over Kelli in minutes, and the carrier was launching over twenty fighters and bombers in case the Chinese Navy made a miscalculation.

Admiral Cronin did not like what he saw.

That Chinese Frigate was entering the zone that had been declared out of bounds and obviously was out to pick up their two downed pilots, if they were in the water. They'd love to get their hands on Kelli. Admiral Cronin was in the control center when she shot down the first Chinese plane and almost got away from the second. The command officers and enlisted men had let out a big cheer in the C.I.C. when she splashed the Chinese pilot. Cronin was not about to let that Chinese Frigate get their hands on her.

"Who's in charge of the CAP section flying cover over Kelli?" he asked.

"Lieutenant Commander Mark James," was the reply.

"We've got to change the direction of that Chinese Frigate. Tell them to get their ass out of the restricted zone, or we'll blow them out of the water."

The message was sent, but the Chinese Frigate chose to ignore it.

"Have Commander James fire a few missiles in front of the frigate."

"They may blow his plane out of the sky," said the Air Plot Officer.

"If they do, we'll blow their tin can Navy to Timbukto. Send the order."

"Yes, Sir."

Commander James fired two missiles in front of the Chinese Frigate.

The frigate made a sharp turn and backed off. The loss of two pilots in the water would be a lot better than losing their frigate. They proceeded to change course and left the area.

As the sun got brighter, Kelli recognized her CAP fighter planes overhead. Her neck had stopped bleeding, but she'd been opened up. She activated her radio and infrared strobe. Parachute float lights and powdered green sea dye were dropped by one of the planes to mark her location. Off in the distance, she saw what looked like another rubber life raft. It looked like one of the Chinese pilots had ejected successfully.

The Chinese fleet and pilots would be racing to pick up their pilot, and her fighter group overhead would be keeping an eye on her.

Suddenly a periscope came up through the water 100 feet away from her and circled her life raft.

"Oh, my God!" she muttered.

The sub split the surface. Kelli stared at the partially visible mass. Its massive hull created huge swells that heaved her raft up and down. From the deck of the sub, a raft was launched with two seamen on board.

Kelli looked for a flag or insignia but saw none. She drew her .45 and flicked off the safety.

A voice hollered out, "Are you all right?"

"Who won the NBA Championship last year?" she hollered back.

"Milwaukee. Allen was MVP," shouted the seaman.

"Thank God." She waved them on. Alongside her raft, one of the seamen helped her over while the other held the raft steady.

She boarded the submarine, and they quickly submerged. They took her to sickbay and laid her down. The doctor, a woman, quickly dismissed the men who brought Kelli in. She was soaked and bloodied from the injured shoulder and was still holding onto her sidearm. Gently, the doctor took it from her hand, set the safety, and put her hand on Kelli's forehead. Kelli cried briefly, then regained her composure and said, "I need a good strong drink."

"I think that can be arranged," replied the doctor.

VII

THE BLUE ANGELS

After the shoot-out off the coast of Taiwan, Kelli and the other Tiger fighter pilot who was involved received AIR medals. The presentation was not publicized.

The Chinese Task Force withdrew from the area around Taiwan. The United States knew China would suffer a loss of face if the truth was told about the encounter.

Diplomacy finally prevailed. The Chinese government asked that the subject of control of Taiwan be discussed at the United Nations General Assembly. Six weeks later, the U.S.S. Harry Truman was relieved by the carrier U.S.S. America and received orders to return home to San Diego.

One month later, Kelli was promoted to full Commander and was given a vacation.

Away from flight duty, Kelli finally had time to reflect on what had happened. She could have died during the shoot-out, and being so close to that reality had changed her and made her wonder what she really wanted. She was a Commander in the U.S. Naval Air Corps. Her career was on fire, but her life was dragging. Jets, jets, jets. Orders, orders, orders. Duty, duty, duty. She loved flying, but would she survive it? Sure, jets were bigger and faster, but so were short and long range missiles. Somehow it no longer seemed to be enough.

She still thought of Palmer, still felt the sting of his abandonment. She always thought she'd get married, and here she was past

30. No sense in dwelling on it. She'd be better off wondering what her next job would be. A few weeks later, Secretary of the Navy, Henry Anderson, called her to Washington, D.C.

"Young lady, you're not what the Navy's built on, but your professionalism and leadership qualities are outstanding, and I believe you will be one of the first women to become a Captain in the Naval Air Corps." Kelli saw he had all the characteristics of a politician: tall, 50s, brown hair cut short, a hawkish bearing, and a way of speaking that did not invite controversy.

"Thank you, Mr. Secretary."

"You are due for new orders, and I asked you to come here today to discuss them. One choice you have is to go to Command School in Newport, Rhode Island, in preparation for becoming a captain on a supercarrier. The other is for you to take over command of the Blue Angels."

Kelli was stunned and never expected anything like this. She'd joined the Navy to become a pilot and had seen all it could show: getting shot out of the sky, bailing out at night, sitting in a rubber life raft in the Pacific Ocean, becoming the skipper of a fighter squadron. She didn't want to just sit on the bridge of a carrier, even if it did have prestige.

Before she could respond, the Secretary spoke up.

"Kelli, consider the Blue Angels. You have all the credentials. Your past experience with the fighter strike squadrons suggests you can handle the job. The Blue Angels is the most important unit that helps sell Naval aviation. The six top Navy pilots do difficult precision acrobatics with their planes in front of thousands of people."

Kelli reflected for a moment and smiled. She had evaluated the Navy Secretary perfectly. He really was a shrewd politician. She was a woman, and if she took the job, he would get all the credit. She wondered if he would clarify his motive.

Secretary Anderson continued, "It will help the Naval Air Corps restore its image regarding women. However, I want to caution you. You'll be the only woman on the team. It might be awkward."

"Why will it be awkward?"

"Because the Blue Angels flight team eats, sleeps, flies, and works out together. You have to remain in top physical condition to fly with them. There could be some problems."

"Only if they're created," she replied, "and I don't plan to create them."

"It's not as simple as you may think. It's a physically demanding job. You have to be able to maneuver freely at high speeds, so you won't be able to wear a G. Suit—that puts an extra strain on your body. You'll pull Gs in that aircraft you've never felt before."

"Mr. Secretary . . ."

"That's not all," he continued, as he cut her off. "Your rudder pedals will be all the way up, putting an extra strain on your legs. There is also a spring on the control stick that requires 45 lbs. of pull during the 45 minutes of the air shows."

"Mr. Secretary, you suggest the job, and then imply I may not have the tools to handle it. I'll say this once - I can."

"So I have your commitment?"

"Indeed you do." There was a big smile on the Navy Secretary's face.

Kelli received orders to proceed to the Naval Airfield in El Centro, California, for winter training with the Blue Angels. She would be there for three months, flying twice a day, in a more advanced model of the F-51.

She asked that the boss and members of last year's Blue Angels team stay on for an extra two weeks, so she could have a few indoctrination flights with them—an elementary type of flight lesson, but with a wider base formation. After flying with them for a week, she asked Lieutenant Commander Lloyd Parker, the #4 slot pilot in the Diamond Formation, to stay on for an extra year as a Blue Angel pilot. The #4 slot pilot has the most difficult job because of the air turbulence, flying behind and below the other three planes. He is also considered the training pilot because he can see what the other three pilots are doing ahead of him. He is the only one who can tell if the wingmen are out of position.

All Blue Angel pilots are selected after consultation with the team they replace. They have to be top carrier pilots and have at least 1500 to 2500 hours in the air. When the Blue Angels first started in 1946, the pilots were bachelors because of the risks involved. Kelli did not insist on that requirement, just as long as they knew how to fly properly. She did not want any Blue Angel midair collisions on the evening news.

She got the Navy to transfer Ken Scott, her former wingman, to fly the #2 slot on her right wing. The #3 slot on her left wing was Bill "Bullseye" Jones, who flew with her at Top Gun school. The #5 and #6 slots were considered the solo pilots, and when they joined up with the Diamond Formation, they were called the Delta Formation. The #5 slot was filled by Lt. George Dunbar, and the #6 slot was filled by Jack Andrus, a Marine Captain.

She called her grandfather and told him what she was doing. He was amazed . . . he couldn't believe it. Being her grandfather, he worried about her and told her to be careful. He also told her he had flown with one of the early Blue Angels command pilots, Lieutenant Commander Bob Clark. Her grandfather had flown with VTN-53, and Bob Clark had been the executive officer of the fighter squadron that bombed Hammamatsu Airfield around Tokyo during World War II.

Training to become a Blue Angel pilot was a terrific challenge. In the beginning of training, the pilots flew together, at first wide apart and high in the air. As they gained more confidence and improved their balance in the sets of acrobatic maneuvers, they flew closer together and closer to the ground. There were usually six planes in the air at a time (Delta Formation). The planes can fly at two-to-three times the speed of sound, but usually fly between 350–550 knots when doing acrobatics. The pilots had to be comfortable flying upside down. The main formation flown was the Diamond Formation which involved one to four planes flying wing tip to wing tip with 36 inches in between. The #5 and #6

slots were for the solo pilots, who joined up in the Delta Formation and performed aerial acrobatics separate from the Diamond
Formation.

Their first air show was at Lambert Field in St. Louis. Kelli held
a briefing, going through the exact order of each maneuver, and reviewing safety details, aircraft limitations, and everyday procedures.
The air corridor was cleared, so there would be no mid-air collisions. Then, Kelli's plane led the Blue Angels to the runway.

"Lambert Field, this is Blue Angels' Tiger Lady. Request taxi and
take-off instructions."

"Tiger Lady, you are cleared to taxi to runway 12 and take off
when ready."

Once the planes were lined up, they took off together. Kelli used
her hands-off radio attached to her helmet to direct the flight. Each
time she announced what she was doing in her plane, the other pilots had to respond instantaneously.

"High performance flight to a split S."

"Smoke on."

"Burners ready now."

"Rolling out."

"Come left."

"Smoke off."

"Easing power. Easing more power."

"Wings level."

"Left echelon flat pass."

"Now, right forty-five."

"Smoke on."

"Now left . . . forty-five."

"Add afterburners."

"Rolling out."

"Come right."

"Tuck over roll."

"Hit it."

Everything was done visually and exactly. There was no such
thing in the air as "not exactly." "Not exactly" meant certain death.
Flying with the Blue Angels was utterly unforgiving. The bond be-

tween the pilots on the team had to be absolute. They had to think together, link together, and know what the other pilots were thinking from moment to moment in a split-second sequence.

This was the Blue Angels' first show with a woman pilot leading the stunt team. The precision flying over the sell-out crowd at Lambert Field was perfect.

Kelli finished the Blue Angels' stunt show with one of her favorite maneuvers.

The six planes flew high above the crowd in a tight Delta formation. Then the six aircraft separated in a vertical break heading in different directions with their white exhaust streamers on. The planes then came together at the air show center in a dramatic six-plane cross. It looked like they were going to have a mid-air collision as the spectators held their breath.

After the planes landed, each pilot stood by their planes to sign autographs and answer questions for the children and adults attending the show. Kelli, appearing in her flight suit, was interviewed for national and local television. She was asked a very familiar question by one of the TV interviewers.

"How did you do it? How did you get to be one of the top pilots in the Navy?"

Before she could answer, a man behind her stepped forward.

"She did it because she's the best! That's why! She demonstrates that the Navy no longer has a gender problem when it comes to Navy pilots."

"Who are you?" the man was asked abruptly.

"I'm Henry Anderson, the Secretary of the Navy. I'm here to watch the show."

"Oh!" replied the questioner. "Thanks for your remarks! If you don't mind, I want to hear the Commander's response."

"It wasn't easy," said Kelli. "But because I loved flying, I was motivated to do anything to become a pilot. I put my best effort forward every time."

"Have you had any harassment in the service?"

"There was some, but I was able to overcome it," she responded, as she glanced at the Navy Secretary. He looked apprehensive about what she might answer. That evening, at a local restaurant, he told her that she had handled herself well with the press.

"Thank you, Mr. Secretary."

Kelli would have liked to elaborate on the harassment question but felt that it was better judgment not to embellish her remarks. Secretary Anderson had arranged for numerous photographers and television personnel to be present. He was out to get as much publicity for the Navy and for himself. He had numerous pictures taken with Kelli. His actions confirmed her impressions; he certainly was a real aggressive politician!

The Blue Angels' next show in Los Angeles was one of their biggest.

Kelli decided she wanted to try a different maneuver to end the show, a Double Barvel with four planes involved. Both the lead and slot aircraft fly past the spectators upside down while the two wingmen fly straight up level in the Diamond Formation. They practiced the maneuver high in the air and then continued to lower their altitude as their confidence built up. They finally decided to try it. Kelli didn't mind flying upside down doing the Barvel in her aircraft because the jets had so much power.

The stunt team took off together and put on a spectacular exhibition of precision flying. Everything went well as they got set to do the Double Barvel for the first time. The pilots were excited about showing off their new trick.

Unfortunately, things did not work out the way they planned. The number three wingman suddenly lost power, and his plane dropped down out of position, close to the ground as his plane was going past the grandstand. Fortunately, Kelli in the lead plane, did not fly down as low to the ground as she had planned because it was their first try with the new stunt. The slot pilot flying upside down saw the #3 plane drop below his. He was smart enough to use his rudders and ailerons to slide away out of the formation and roll over into a vertical climb. What happened could have been a mid-air collision in the making and scared the shit out of all four pilots. The audience thought that what had happened was part of the air show and cheered and hollered. They didn't realize that they almost saw a massive mid-air collision.

"That's it," screamed Kelli on her VHF. "We were lucky on that one! Let's call it quits."

In the briefing that followed, everyone pointed a finger at "Bullseye Jones", the experienced Navy pilot in the #3 slot.

"What happened?" asked Kelli.

"My plane's engines sputtered, and I briefly lost power. I thought I was going to crash. I lost about 100 feet of altitude and thought I had a flame-out. I didn't really know what was happening. It scared the shit out of me. If it was a car, I'd say it was water in the gas tank, a fuel line problem, or someone adding water to the fuel tank. Something could have gone wrong in the engine. I was lucky and thank God for that. The engines sputtered just for a second or two and then caught, so I didn't hit one of you guys. When I got on the ground, I downed the plane. The mechanics are going to have the engine manufacturers check it out and also check the fuel for water. They said they'd replace the engine if necessary."

"That's scary," said Kelli. "I'm glad I started this stunt higher than normal. We can't let this happen again! We're due for a month off. I'll have the manufacturers check out all the planes before we fly them again. Maybe, we'll have to tighten security around the planes. That's something that we didn't count on—equipment failure, cheap fuel, or sabotage!"

After the show, she was asked to speak to a large group of young women at the Century Hotel in Los Angeles on a panel with two other women. The topic was "Success and Acceptance: Facing Challenges as a Female Professional." One of the speakers was Senator Jane Farber from California, the other was the president of a woman's college. The conference was covered by TV and other media. The audience, naturally, wanted to know how she had overcome sexual harassment.

"Day by day," said Kelli. "It's the only way. You draw limits on what you'll take and how you'll respond to things you find unacceptable. It's like rebounding in basketball. If you go after every ball every time, you'll be too exhausted to snag the ones that are really your responsibility." There was a round of appreciative laughter.

Senator Jane Faber suggested that she ought to go into politics.

"I'd rather flame out at 30,000 feet," said Kelli. The Senator laughed. "Besides," she added, "I don't enjoy the limelight that much."

"Yes, you do," said the Senator. "We don't have to dance around it. You like being in front, and the front women like you are fighting for equal opportunities and respect. Think about it."

FT. WORTH/DALLAS ADVENTURE

The next assignment for Kelli's Blue Angels' team was at the Fort Worth-Dallas Airport. The air show, featuring Kelli Fitzgerald, the Tiger Lady, and the Blue Angels, drew more than 80,000 spectators.

After the show ended, the pilots, as usual, stood by their planes, posing, answering questions, and signing autographs. After Kelli signed about fifty program books, someone stuck a book under her face, "Remember me, Commander Fitzgerald?"

She'd recognize his voice anywhere—Mark Palmer.

"The quarterback, right?"

"That's right, but I'm not playing as much. I've been injured a few times."

"Me too."

"How about dinner?"

"I don't think that would be a good idea. You're married ... remember?"

"Incorrect, Lieutenant."

"Commander!"

"Sorry, Commander. I'm not married. That girl was interested in being seen with me more than in anything else. When I was put on the injured list, she lost interest."

"Okay, Palmer, dinner it is."

"Do you have a curfew?"

"That depends," she said, as she smiled again, looking into his eyes.

"On what?"

"On whether we're still friends." The crowd had thinned out, and they were alone.

"Well, I guess we'll have to find that out."

"Okay, but you should know now that I'm going to be reassigned."

"Not that again!"

"Hey, Palmer! It happens. Haven't you ever been traded?"

"No.

"Well, use your brain. It happens."

"Okay. Listen, I'm sorry. First things first. Dinner tonight?"

"Sure."

"What are you hungry for?"

"I'm used to Navy chow. Anything would be great. You pick."

The valet brought his new Mercedes convertible around, and Mark held the door as she got in. They drove to an Italian place called Arturo's.

Halfway through a bottle of Chianti, they eased into being together again. But Kelli still felt wary. She remembered the unanswered letters and messages, and the shock of seeing Palmer on the arm of that blonde while she was busy getting shot at over the Gulf.

"The last time I saw you," he said, "you were bolting out of our suite."

"And the last time I saw you," said Kelli, turning her wine glass in her hand, "you were bopping around with some bleached bimbo on national television."

"I told you, Kelli, that was a mistake."

"It's not that easy."

"It could be. Or we can find out how complicated it is, right here, right now!" She looked up, hearing the edge in his voice. It was the first time she recognized that he was pissed and hurt.

"Okay," she said. "Duty called. I had to go. I'm sorry. I expected you to understand, and maybe that was asking a lot."

"You also expected me to become a priest, apparently."

"No. But I won't deny you hurt me. I was a long way from home. I thought we shared something beautiful in Hawaii; I was beginning to fall in love with you. You were special, and you also seemed to be happy. I had forgotten that you were a star quarterback, and women were just playthings. Yet after what you did by not returning my phone calls, and getting engaged to a blonde bombshell, I felt that was the last straw. Most intelligent women wouldn't give you the time of day or a second chance; they'd tell you to get lost."

"Okay, hold up. I think I see where this is going, and I don't want to go there. You left. That hurt. But I didn't start seeing her to hurt you back. I did it because I was lonely, bored, all of that male stuff. You're back. We're together. Now let's get drunk and forgive each other." He raised his glass. After a moment, so did Kelli.

At Arturo's they spent the night together talking, drinking wine, and letting the conversation drift this way and that. She heard about his life as a pro athlete: the pressure, the scrutiny, the fans, coaches, players, the travel. The pain. She related to it silently, knowing he'd end up saying, "You understand, don't you?" She did. Flying in the Navy involved pressure, constant scrutiny, competition, pain, travel, you name it. They drew closer.

"Tell me about your career," she said.

"Right now it's about rehab," he said. "I'm almost 100 percent again, and my contract is up."

"Any other team interested in a slightly used quarterback?"

"Kansas City is."

"Ugh."

"Ugh? They're 12 and 4 this year."

"The city is less than, shall we say, glamorous."

"Agreed. But San Diego has been calling my agent twice a week." Mark sat up straighter. "Yeah, I know," he said. "You have family there. I love it there, too."

"Hmmn."

"Hmmn is right. But it's too soon to tell. Drink."

"I'm beginning to feel very relaxed," Kelli said.

"Me, too." They drank. The restaurant had emptied, and their check lay on the table. "Let's go," said Kelli, reaching for the bill. He put his hand over it.

"Not so fast. You may be more successful, but I still make more money."

"No argument from me, Palmer."

He drove back to his condo, a classic Dallas high-rise. The top was down in the Mercedes, and Kelli felt the wind in her hair. She felt reckless. Ah, the wonderful hazards of Chianti. He gunned the coupe along the straight blacktop toward Dallas. The speed was intoxicating, the night air refreshing, and there was a sense that something wild was approaching. She felt the Navy fall away from her thoughts, the discipline, the order, the regulations. The wind rushed through her blouse and lifted her skirt. She shuddered, not with cold, but with anticipation. Palmer was focused on driving as the wind blew his hair back, and his eyes searched the night and the road ahead. She had seen him play on television, but now, this close, she saw the look of being locked into what he was doing to the exclusion of everything else. "My God!" she thought, "He could have been a pilot."

They entered his building, and as he walked with her to the elevator, he waved at the night concierge. "How you doin, Charlie," he said. The clerk waved back.

"Just fine, Mr. Palmer."

Inside the elevator, he pressed the Penthouse button, entered a code on a keypad on the wall, and started to say, 'Mr. Palmer,' ... but he got no further. She crushed her body to his, reaching up with her mouth, her body rising into his chest, letting it go.

"No cast this time," he said, and grabbed her waist, lifting her easily and putting her back against the wall. Their mouths exploring, getting the feeling going again as they searched each other, hands on muscle, straining. He told her what he was going to do to her. She gasped; somehow there was not enough air in the elevator.

The doors opened to his penthouse. He carried her in, still holding her aloft, as they entered the bedroom, and Kelli, tearing at his shirt, feeling him hard against her, thought, "What the hell am I doing in the Navy?"

It was different this time. They both made love with complete abandon. Those beautiful dreams she had about being close and intimate with Mark were now being fulfilled. There was no cast on his leg this time, so he took the lead. Their bodies became one as their rhythmic love-making reached a crescendo of passion that overwhelmed them both. Just before they fell asleep as the sun was coming up, she rolled over and said, "Mark, I now know why you're the best quarterback in the world. I love you! You were worth waiting for."

They spent the next week in Dallas. He continued rehab. She continued thinking about the Navy. They had breakfast together and took turns making dinner, although he was the better cook. They slept together, actually sleeping, waking up, talking about the news, sports, politics. She caught herself in moments of what she'd always thought of as trite—kissing her man goodbye, and telling him to have a great day. Three years ago it would have made her sick to her stomach. Now she felt natural with it; a different uniform she had grown into.

What was happening in Dallas was a reversal of what her motivation and life had been all about—flying was her life completely, and she didn't let anything interfere with it. Suddenly, Mark had come back into her life, and she had another love—a handsome man with whom she wanted to share her life. Fortunately, she had a month off waiting for reassignment. She wondered what the Navy Secretary was planning for her future, and she had reservations about whether she should stay in the Navy. She was totally confused and had lots of unanswered questions on her mind. As she was making love to Mark, she thought that someday they might want children. That would not fit easily into her Navy flying career. She also wondered what the Navy Secretary would do if she suddenly resigned. At the air show in St. Louis, he had suggested that she might want to spend some time in Washington on her next assignment to enhance her career. Whose career was going to be enhanced? Hers or his?

The one thing that she did know was that she was happier now than she had every been before!

She didn't miss flying but knew that her transition into becoming a housewife might be difficult. Hell, she didn't even know how to cook. She also needed a complete new wardrobe since practically all of her clothes were uniforms or flight suits. She had been a grease monkey too long.

Kelli decided to bite the bullet. She told him that she was considering resigning from the Navy. He tried to contain his enthusiasm.

"Is that what you want?"

"You're what I want. I'm through being careful. What I need to know is, are we going to make a go of it?"

"Yes.

"Are you sure?"

"Do I sound sure?" She looked at him. He had that look. Nothing else was on his mind.

"If I were in a dogfight right now," she said, "my HUD would indicate you had your weapons system locked on me."

"Don't evade me. I say we're together. What do you say?"

"Yes."

"Good. Because San Diego is serious about signing me. I say we go to San Diego, live by the beach, and settle in."

"It sounds like a plan to me," said Kelli.

Two weeks later, Kelli sent an overnight letter to the Secretary of the Navy stating that she was going to get married and asked permission to resign from the Navy. It didn't take long to get a response. The Secretary called her on the phone the next day.

"Kelli, I'm going to be in your area in three days. I'd like to have lunch with you and discuss your decision. I don't want you to do something that you might regret for the rest of your life."

"I don't plan to change my decision," said Kelli. "I'm in love!"

"Yes, I know. It's not about that. We'll talk!" he replied.

The Secretary was obviously disturbed about her resigning from the Navy but was not concerned about her getting married.

"We'll have lunch at the Hotel Del Coronado," he told her.

Kelli started to cry when she finished the call.

She told Mark about the lunch date.

"Do you want me to give you support and go with you?"

"I don't think so, Mark. I feel that I can go one-on-one with him. I'm not going to let him interfere with my decision."

"Stick to your guns."

"I plan to, Mark. I've taken a big chunk out of my life for the Navy. I almost got killed when I was shot down in the Pacific. The Navy owes me big time!"

Kelli put on her uniform and met Secretary Anderson at the hotel. He had a couple of cocktails and then got right to the point.

"Kelli, you've had a tremendous career in the Navy, and you've helped the Navy a great deal. I want you to reconsider your resignation. I'm willing to work things out for your benefit, which includes giving you a three-month sabbatical if you stay with us. You could get married and have a honeymoon. It would also give you time to work things out and get acquainted with your mate."

"I love to fly, Mr. Secretary, but right now I don't miss it."

"I can understand that. I was young once and in love, and my mind wasn't completely rational at all times."

"I know exactly what I'm doing," replied Kelli curtly. "Flying jets off carriers is not the best thing to do if you're married."

"I know. But flying's in your blood, and you're really good at it. We can keep you ashore and away from dangerous flying if you wish," replied the Secretary. "Don't make any hasty decisions. There are two prospective billets that I want to tell you about."

"I'm really not interested, but I'll listen."

"We have two attractive openings for you in Washington, D.C. President Bill Gray needs a naval aide, and his Chief of Staff called me. Your name was suggested for the job because the President has never had a senior woman of your stature in that position. However, you would be exposed to big time politics, wearing your ribbons on your dress uniform and expected to attend White House functions. I believe it will enhance your future in the Navy.

"The other opening is also quite interesting. Admiral Jack Perkins, who is now the head of the Joint Chiefs of Staff, is looking for an intelligent Navy officer to be on his staff acting as a liaison between his office and the Congress. In that position you may be asked to testify or to aid Admiral Perkins when he has to testify before Congress. He has looked at your record, and you are on the top of his list."

Kelli looked at him with a puzzled expression.

"When I accepted your invitation for lunch, I was determined that I would not be swayed by anything that was offered to me. What you have done has really, and I apologize for the term, screwed up my brain."

"That was not my intent, Kelli. The Navy wants you to stay in. You still have almost three years on your contract."

"I like the three-month sabbatical. It would give me a chance to try and work things out in my own mind and with Mark. I know I don't want to work as a presidential aide. I don't like the principles that President Gray stands for. We would not get along, and I would be very unhappy.

"The opportunity to work for the Joint Chiefs of Staff with Admiral Perkins intrigues me. I've heard him talk, and I have the utmost respect for him. Testifying before Congress might be difficult, but I think I could handle that. At one time when I saw what the President and Congress was doing with the military budget, I was furious!"

"You just have one more week of your leave, Kelli. What's your answer?"

"I can't give you an answer right now. I'm going to have a full-time partner very soon. I have to discuss this with Mark Palmer."

"Call me . . . as soon as you know."

Mark was hopping mad when Kelli broached the possibility of going to Washington D.C.

"Kelli, you said you would not listen to any propositions. What made you change your mind?"

"Because it isn't easy for me to get out of the Navy. That's why! I've got to go back in one week, and serve out my time. I accepted a bonus and signed up with the Navy for three additional years. When you got involved with that bimbo, what did you expect? I thought you were married and out of my life. I still loved to fly, and there was nothing in my life to challenge that love until you came back into the picture. Unless I agree with one of the Secretary's propositions, I'm back in the Navy. I've got three years to go. He promised me a three-month sabbatical if I wouldn't resign. My new billet would be in Washington, D.C. for two years."

"That Navy of yours sucks!" said Mark.

"I know," said Kelli, as she started to cry. "I want to get married to you and have a honeymoon."

"Please don't cry, Kelli. I understand. I agree, but I don't like it. Your fucking Navy screwed me up again!"

"You screwed yourself up," said Kelli. "That screwed me up!"

Kelli called Secretary Anderson. One week later, Kelli and Mark were quietly married in Mexico City, telling their families beforehand and explaining that they would all meet as soon as it could be arranged. They bought a beautiful home near the ocean in San Diego and a large apartment on Connecticut Avenue in Washington, D.C.

During the three-month sabbatical, she felt like she was on a constant honeymoon. She didn't even think about flying. She was so much in love with Mark. He obviously had met his match in Kelli, for she kept up with him stride for stride.

One night, after an exhausting evening of love-making, she laid beside him, smiled, and looked him in the eyes. "Mark, it took a champion quarterback to subdue me."

"And it took a beautiful Navy Commander jet pilot to lasso me and bring me to my senses. I love you, Kelli."

2004

VIII

WASHINGTON, D.C.

It was cherry blossom time when Kelli reported to Navy BuPers in Washington, D.C. for her orders. Because it was springtime, Mark was not tied up with football, so they had fun purchasing furniture and setting up their penthouse apartment on Connecticut Avenue. It was a nice section of D.C. with excellent restaurants, hotels and apartment buildings. They had decided to live in the city where most of the action was, and Kelli would commute to the Pentagon in Arlington.

Mark was aware of the fact that Kelli was excited about her upcoming job working with Admiral Jack Perkins, the Chairman of the Joint Chiefs.

"Kelli, you're like a little kid going into the candy store for the first time. I can't believe how excited you are about this new job. In fact, I'm a little bit jealous."

"I am excited, Mark, because I'm the first woman to hold this position. I feel I have a responsibility to do a good job!"

"I'm not worried about your doing a good job. You'll wow them! Just you wait and see."

"You're prejudiced," replied Kelli. "I hope you're right."

Kelli checked into the BuPers the next day to be fingerprinted and photographed. Voice recognition disks were also taken. She was then given a special badge with her photograph and special code, to be used for entering specific top-secret areas of the Pentagon.

The following day, Kelli checked into Admiral Perkins office in the Navy's Executive Corridor where she noticed solid oak doors modeled after old ship captains' doors.

Kelli was introduced to Admiral Perkins staff by his Chief of Staff, Rear Admiral Zachary Keen and was then ushered into Perkins' office. She saluted him, as he stood up.

"At ease. I'm pleased to have you on my staff, Commander Palmer."

"Thank you," she replied.

"If you're half of what I've been told you are, I'll be pleased with your contributions. I've heard you're quite a pilot, and I understand that the moniker you picked up at Top Gun school has stuck with you. I believe it's 'Tiger Lady'. Is that right?"

"That's right!"

"Hm. That tells me something about you . . . to get where you have gotten, you would have had to be a tiger. We need people like you in this office and in this Navy."

"Thank you, Admiral."

"You'll soon find out that some of the fights that we get involved with in the service are quite vicious. I'm going to start you right out with an important project and an introduction to military politics.

"The Navy is in the process of selecting new Admirals, and President Gray has sent us a memorandum as to how he wants the Navy to do this. As you know, President Gray is the Commander-in-Chief of all of the Armed Forces, and when he talks, we listen.

"You'll be an observer over at BuPers, where Admiral George Davis and a selection committee of twelve senior Admirals will be discussing the merits of the candidates. You're to listen and to keep me informed about any unusual developments. Do you have any questions?"

"None, right now," replied Kelli.

"Here's some written material for you to read and a letter of introduction to Admiral Davis. Just one more thing. You're to have your own office, right over there, next to me. You'll be in an educational mode for awhile, meeting Congressional members and high ranking officers from all branches of the service. You're to go over to BuPers tomorrow morning and check in with Admiral Davis' staff."

Kelli noticed that there were few women on the Admiral's staff; most were enlisted personnel and low-ranked Ensigns and Lieutenants. She was the only Commander with pilot's wings on her chest and ribbons to emblazon her uniform. It was apparent that the Secretary of the Navy had thrust her into the inner sanctum of high-ranking naval officers who were all males. She felt it was going to be interesting as to how they reacted to her presence.

After cordial greetings from the staff, Kelli retreated to her new office which had her name on the door and underneath it read: Military and Congressional Liaison . . . at least she knew what her job was supposed to be . . . only time would tell what it really was.

The big walnut desk that the Navy gave her was impressive, so she decided to sit back in her leather chair and relax. What she was now doing was a far cry from flying jets off carriers. She wondered about that and whether she would get bored. After sitting there for a while, she started to peruse the documents that Admiral Perkins had given her. The folder was quite thick, and there was a copy of a letter with the President's seal right in the front signed by President Gray. She slowly read the letter:

"Thirty new Rear Admirals are to be selected out of one-hundred candidates who have been rated by seniority. They are considered the best candidates to be promoted.

"It is my feeling that there should be more black, Hispanic, and Asian American citizens in this high leadership rank. It may mean that some qualified white candidates will be passed over in order to develop more diversity in our Navy's senior officer ranks. I hope that the Admiral's selection board will consider my wishes when they make their selections."

Kelli was quite perturbed when she read that letter. The President was obviously advocating quotas, and she didn't like that.

Besides, there was no mention of any women candidates being considered. She felt that there must be at least one woman who should be on that list.

Kelli arrived early the next morning at the Navy's BuPers Building in Arlington, Virginia and presented her credentials to a Lieutenant Commander Frank Johnson, who was on the administrative staff of the Admiral's board. Admiral Perkins had given her a letter to give to Admiral Davis. She proffered the letter to Commander Johnson, and he went into Admiral Davis' office to give it to him.

Admiral Davis came out to greet her and told her that there was one important rule that she had to abide by. She could listen in but not participate in the board's discussions.

"I understand that," replied Kelli. "I'm just to be an observer."

"We'll be having a board meeting in about an hour, Commander. You're welcome to join us."

Kelli entered the boardroom fifteen minutes ahead of time and was told to sit by the recorder. Admiral Davis would be sitting at the head of the long walnut table, and each Admiral on the selection board had a name plate in front of where they were to sit. She was told that they were seated according to seniority in rank.

The Navy certainly had its rules, thought Kelli, even here in the inner sanctum of its leaders. The junior admirals down at the end of the long table arrived early and before taking their place, were introduced to Kelli. There were a few full Admirals, but most were Vice-Admirals.

One of the senior Admirals looked her over and said, "What are you doing here, young lady, in this selection boardroom?"

"I'm just an observer," she replied.

"I thought these meetings were confidential!"

"They are!" replied Kelli. "I'm a member of Admiral Perkins' staff."

"Oh!" he said and then sat down.

Admiral Davis entered the boardroom last, and they all stood up.

"Be seated, gentlemen. As you know, we have already selected fifteen candidates whose names will be passed on to the Senate and President for approval. We have not selected any blacks or Hispanics in that group. It looks like we are going to have to bypass some qualified Captains to get that diversity that the President wants. Before we start going through some of the files in front of you, are there any questions or discussions about this?"

One of the senior Admirals, Scott Fletcher spoke up. "George, we don't have any senior Captains in that diversity category that qualify to be a Rear Admiral. The President is putting politics into the military selection process so he can be re-elected."

Admiral Davis turned to the recorder, "Strike that from the minutes. Everyone in this room knows that, Scott. None of us approve of quotas. We should always take the best candidate for the job. That's not the real world, and you know it! When you look through those files in front of you, every one of the candidates has a letter or letters from their Senator or Representatives, praising them to high heaven. I'm sure you have a special candidate you want. Our job is not an easy job, and we can't keep everyone happy."

Vice-Admiral Dick Flanagan spoke up. "I've looked through those files of one hundred candidates, and there are only two blacks, two Hispanics, and one Asian up for consideration. They're all at the bottom end of the list. How are we going to look those other captains in the face when we pass them over? Just look in this room, there's not a black, Hispanic, or Asian on this committee."

"Well," said Admiral Davis, "the faces of the Navy are changing, and it's our job to make sure that it happens!"

"Why don't we just look at the files of those blacks, Hispanics, and that one Asian captain?" said Admiral Robert Clark. "Maybe we could select at least one candidate out of that group."

"That's a good idea," replied Admiral Davis as most of the junior Admirals nodded their heads in agreement. "We'll start with looking at the files of the highest ranking black in that group, Captain Jefferson Mobley. He's number 81."

At the end of the room, a picture of Captain Mobley was projected on a screen and his complete service record, letters of recommendations, and fitness reports were shown. Most of his duty had been served as a line officer, and his highest command was as a Destroyer Division Captain. However, he had one questionable black mark on his record: he hadn't seen combat and had to appear before a review board because of a complaint of a woman officer under his command. The complaint was sexual harassment which was resolved when the woman resigned from the Navy and withdrew her charge.

Kelli's ears perked up when she heard about the sexual harassment charge.

"At least one or two of you gentlemen know this candidate," said Admiral Davis. "Would any of you care to comment?"

Vice Admiral Metcalf spoke up and said that Mobley had been under his command.

"What do you have to say about him?" asked Davis.

"Average officer, compulsive, always afraid he was going to make a mistake. Complete gentlemen, however."

"Would you want him under your command again?"

"No, you wouldn't want him in a sea battle with you. He would be indecisive. Incidentally, that sexual harassment case came up under my command."

"What happened?" asked Davis.

"The woman was a beautiful black Ensign who had graduated from the Academy. She accused him of sexual harassment. I believe that she was telling the truth, but when she realized that his career might be in jeopardy, she backed off and stated that she had lied."

"Did she receive a dishonorable discharge?"

"No. The Secretary of the Navy's office intervened. The publicity would have been horrible. Believe it or not, she is now a senior TV commentator on a 6 o'clock TV news program in New York City."

"Well, what do you think, gentlemen?" asked Admiral Davis.

Metcalf spoke up. "I don't worry about that sexual harassment nonsense. We're going to see a lot more of that in the future. I don't like the fact that he's indecisive. When you're in a command situation, you've got to be able to make up your mind! He'd be putting the rest of the people under his command at risk."

"We could put him in a maintenance or ordinance command.

There are some Rear Admirals in that category," said Admiral Flanagan. "He wouldn't have to make any combat decisions. That would be one way of appeasing President Gray."

"That may answer the problem, but it wouldn't be the best thing to do for the Navy," said Clark, one of the Full Admirals.

"I'm not happy about it, however, we've got to do it or the Navy's in trouble. The Navy needs the President's support! Let's take him!" said Admiral Davis. They took a vote with only one dissension.

Kelli was disturbed that evening when she thought about what had transpired in that selection boardroom. She liked the idea about considering blacks, Hispanics, and Asians for flag positions but wasn't sure that the rules should be changed for advancement. She also didn't like the idea that there was no mention of any women being considered. At lunch later that week, with the Chief of Staff, Rear Admiral Zachary Keen, she mentioned what had happened and wondered whether there were any women in the flag rank.

"I don't know. Not any that I know of," he replied. "I'm sure there are no jet pilots! Maybe that's something you can shoot for."

"I'm not interested," replied Kelli.

One week later, Kelli was asked to step into Admiral Perkins' office.

"Kelli, I want you to attend a Senate Committee hearing with me tomorrow. Senator Walter Lawrence is chairing a meeting of the Senate Armed Forces Committee to discuss an Appropriations Bill for service personnel which raises their salaries and housing allowances overseas. He is also going to discuss the inequality of gaining promotions in the enlisted and officers' ranks. We want to be ready for him, at least from the Navy's point of view."

SENATE ARMED FORCES COMMITTEE MEETING

The Chairman of the committee, Senator Walter Lawrence from Virginia, tapped the gavel and called the meeting to order.

"The purpose of this meeting is to discuss the Navy's request for increased funds for salaries for naval personnel and also increased allowance for overseas housing. We are also to discuss discrimination in the Armed Forces in regards to promotion in the enlisted and officer ranks. Admiral Jack Perkins, the Chairman of the Joint Chiefs of the Armed Forces will be our first witness."

Admiral Perkins was sworn in and then asked the first question by Senator Lawrence.

"Admiral Perkins, has there been discrimination in the Armed Forces in regards to promotions?"

"I believe there has in the past. The Navy has made great strides forward in correcting that problem. We are a Navy in transition. For over two hundred years, the combat force of the Navy was all male. Today, we have women serving in every capacity on board our ships. This young lady sitting next to me is a prime example of the opportunities that women can achieve."

Senator Lawrence interrupted, "Why don't you introduce that young naval officer?"

"Kelli, why don't you stand up."

Kelli stood up. Her bright glistening red hair stood out against the dress whites that she wore. Her chest displayed her gold Navy wings and the brightly colored ribbons of achievement.

"This is Commander Kelli Palmer. She is a former Top Gun Pilot, who has been the skipper of a carrier fighter squadron."

"My! That's quite an accomplishment, young lady. Admiral Perkins, our committee may want to question her later on."

"I'm sure she will be amenable to that."

"Has there been any discrimination because of color or race?" asked Lawrence.

"We're solving that problem also," replied Perkins.

"Our Admiral Selection Board has recently selected a black, Captain Jefferson Mobley. He will become a Rear Admiral. Once the Senate and President approve, he'll be joining the ranks of the flag officers."

"That's commendable and quite interesting," replied Lawrence.

Senator Richard Slossberg from Minnesota interrupted, "What about enlisted personnel? Are they getting a fair shake?"

"It's not that easy because of the cultural change in the Navy's personnel makeup. Some of the senior enlisted personnel are not happy about some of the changes. We now have blacks, Hispanics, and Asian men and women competing for the same job. The Navy, however, is reemphasizing our tradition of strong character and ethical behavior. Harassment and sexual problems now exist because of the blending of our Navy's make-up, but we are coping with it and making progress."

"Admiral Perkins, I'd like to change the subject and take up another issue. Do you feel that the government should be paying our military personnel better?"

"Definitely! I'll give you an example. We have spent millions of dollars in training our pilots. In their ranks, we are losing some of our best senior pilots because of income factors. They can get jobs with the airlines, without the hazardous risks of military flying off of carriers. This also applies to specialized enlisted airplane maintenance personnel. We have to address that issue promptly! I also feel that our government has to increase the pay allotment for overseas housing. The military personnel will not want to travel and stay overseas because they are at risk by terrorists. This also applies to Marine and Army personnel."

"I don't believe that you have to convince me, Admiral Perkins. You have to convince the Senators sitting on this podium."

"I know," said Perkins. "Just visualize that one of your sons or daughters are in the military service defending our country. What would you want for them?"

Senator Lawrence hit his gavel. "With that statement by Admiral Perkins, we'll adjourn the morning session."

LA COLLINE
LUNCH WITH THE SENATORS

Admiral Perkins escorted Kelli to a luncheon engagement at the La Colline Restaurant on the Senate side of the Capital. La Colline was a French restaurant with high-backed leather booths and excellent food.

A small select group of six was invited to the luncheon, four Senators including Lawrence from the majority party and Bill Morgan from the minority. Perkins had arranged the meeting to introduce Kelli to the group of politicians.

Kelli had a glass of Chardonnay wine which helped her to relax. The others had martinis. The usual questions were asked. "Where are you from? How did you learn to fly? What are your plans for the future?"

She gave short answers to those questions.

Admiral Perkins informed the group that she was a Top Gun Navy pilot who had been decorated for bravery. Some unexpected questions were finally asked by Senator Lawrence.

"Did you have any sexual harassment in the service, Commander? You're not under oath here in this restaurant."

Before she could answer, Admiral Perkins intervened. "This is a friendly luncheon, Senator. I'm not sure that I want Commander Palmer to answer that question."

"I'll answer it, Admiral," said Kelli. Before the Admiral could stop her she replied. "Not anything that I couldn't handle."

"That's good enough for me," replied Lawrence. "Would you be willing to answer that question under oath in our committee meeting tomorrow?"

"Certainly!" replied Kelli.

When Kelli got back to her office with Admiral Perkins, he told her that he wanted to talk to her. "What did you think about that Armed Forces Committee meeting and the luncheon you went to?"

"It was very nice, Admiral Perkins, however, I felt that the Navy used me to promote their cause."

"That's military politics dealing with Congressional politics, Kelli. If you like the Navy, and I'm sure you do, you'll help it stay afloat."

"I realize that, Admiral."

IX

TRAGEDY AT MIRAMAR

"Kelli, this is Admiral Perkins on the phone. There's been a horrible tragedy out at the Miramar Naval Air Station in California. I want you to fly out there with me in a couple of hours. We've got to find out what happened. I've notified the air base at Patuxant River. They'll have a two-seater F-51 jet ready for our use. I'll get some flight time in. You trained out there, that's why I'm asking you to go."

"What is this all about?" asked Kelli.

"I'll tell you about it when I pick you up."

"What was that phone call all about?"

"It was Admiral Perkins on the phone."

"That old geezer Admiral calling you at this hour—4:00 A.M. Is there something you want to tell me?"

"You're jealous. How nice!" replied Kelli.

"Not really," replied Mark. "I've seen him! He may have a lot of gold stripes on his sleeve, but I'll guarantee you that he didn't get those for sex."

Kelli laughed and then looked serious. "Mark, you're not going to like what I tell you. I'm flying the Admiral out to Miramar, California this morning, and he says we'll be there for four days. Something big has happened. I'm picking up a jet at Patuxant River."

"You've got to be kidding me?" replied Mark. "We were going to a big White House function tomorrow night."

"This is top priority. I'm still in the Navy, remember?"

"It still sucks!" said Mark. "The sooner you get out of that fucking Navy, the better I'll like it!"

"I'm going to have to pack a few things," said Kelli, "including my flight suit."

"Do what you want. I'm not happy!" replied Mark. "That Navy of yours really knows how to screw things up."

Kelli hardly had time to pack. Admiral Perkins' limo picked her up exactly at 0600. When she got in, he remarked, "Sorry about this."

"Admiral, it wasn't easy convincing my husband that the Navy had an emergency. What's this all about?"

"Believe it or not, early last evening around 0900, someone using a large Navy armored truck, drove down the flight line at Miramar Naval Air Station and destroyed fifteen of our top fighter aircraft."

"Did they blow themselves up?"

"No, but they started some fires. It was a professional job. It happened on a Sunday night when nobody was around. The heavy armored truck hit the back of the planes destroying the tail assemblies and jet engines. The planes are worthless."

"Did they catch the bums?"

"No. They mustered all the officers and men at the base, and three men are unaccounted for. That could mean nothing!"

"Why are you going out there?"

"The Secretary of the Navy, Henry Anderson, called me and said that two of the planes that were destroyed were the latest top of the line secret jets. It could have been sabotage. The estimated damage cost is over $600 million."

"How could they get on the base to do that?"

"We hire a lot of civilians who work at our Navy bases. They all are checked out closely. Sometimes the system fails.

"I'm sure that the Senate Armed Forces Committee is going to have a hearing about this. The Secretary suggested that you go out there too, since you have been through that program and are part of the Congressional liason team."

"Admiral Perkins, Secretary Anderson is not helping my marriage!"

"Kelli, I'll make sure you get some time off when things settle down."

When Kelli and the Admiral arrived at Patuxant River, they changed into flight suits and went to the flight line. The plane captain greeted them. Kelli wondered whether she'd be sitting in the front or back cockpit.

"You sit in front, Kelli. You're the pilot."

"Okay!" she replied and was relieved. Admiral Perkins wore thick-rimmed glasses and was approaching sixty—most of his flying days were over.

Kelli climbed into the cockpit, and the plane captain helped her hook into her ejection seat and G-suit. She called the tower for taxi instructions and checked her inter cockpit radio connections.

"All set, Admiral?"

"All set, Commander. Let'er rip!"

After getting clearance at the end of the runway, Kelli pushed the throttle forward and quickly climbed to 36,000 feet.

"How soon do you want to get out there?" she asked.

"Let's see what this plane can do," he replied.

Kelli slowly pushed the throttle forward and watched her speed accelerate rapidly. She refueled enroute and in a very short period of time, she was calling the tower at Miramar Air Force Base for landing instructions. The sun was just coming up as she set the plane down on the runway as soft as a feather.

"Nice landing," said Admiral Perkins.

Kelli felt exhilarated! She hadn't been flying much, and she didn't realize how much she missed it. After she taxied the jet back to the tower and hangar area, she couldn't believe what she saw. Parts of planes and engines were strewn all over the surface of one runway and hangar. The area had been cordoned off and military police were everywhere. It looked like a bomb had detonated in the middle.

When Kelli cut the jets engines, the reception committee was commensurate with the Admiral's rank, and it looked like Kelli was going to be lost in the shuffle until Admiral Perkins hollered.

"Over here, Kelli. I want you to attend the meeting with me."

That's great, thought Kelli. At least she wasn't going to be a glorified chauffeur for the Admiral.

There were quite a few high-ranking officers in the hangar area where the meeting was going to be held. Military police and armed service personnel isolated the room for the interrogation of the personnel involved.

Naval legal officers, F.B.I. and C.I.A. officials were also present. Local and national media were trying to crash the gates but were refused entry. The military wanted to investigate its own debacle quickly to make sure any press releases were accurate. No photographs were allowed.

Captain Ralph Strong, the Commandant at Miramar Naval Air Station, quickly assembled pertinent personnel to present the known facts to Admiral Perkins. The on-call duty officer and enlisted personnel who were suppose to be guarding the planes were also present.

Lieutenant-Commander Bill Wood, the on-call duty officer was asked to describe what happened. He looked quite nervous because he realized that the disaster had occurred on his watch, and it could mean the end of his naval career.

"At 0900, I received a call from First Class Seaman George Foote on the flight line. He said, 'Commander Wood, we've had a horrible accident up here. Someone in a big truck went down the flight line hitting lots of planes, starting fires, and everything's out of control.' I called for fire trucks and personnel, but there aren't enough available. I'm having trouble locating some of the personnel."

"What did you do then?"

"I sounded General Quarters and called Captain Strong."

"What did he tell you to do?"

"To call the Marine barracks to close down the base. No one was to come in or go off the base. I also sent a jeep over to his home to pick him up."

"Captain Strong, why don't you describe what you saw and what you did."

"It was a black Sunday night, but there were enough fires going to light up the flight line. Most of the damaged planes were not loaded, but we weren't sure, so putting out the fires was one of the top priorities. The second was to shut down the base to find out whoever was responsible. I told Marine Colonel Jack Webster to get more marines even if they had to fly them in."

"Who do you think did this dastardly act?" asked Admiral Perkins.

"We don't know!"

"What do you know?"

"We've found the abandoned armored truck near the fence at the end of the runway and a fresh pre-dug tunnel to crawl under the electrified fence. We're trying to get fingerprints off the truck right now, but we've been unsuccessful. A rubber glove was found on the floorboards. There were some special night vision glasses also found. When they drove the truck down the flight line, no lights were on, and that made it more difficult to find anything until daylight."

"Have you found out anything else?"

"We've mustered all the personnel who live and work on the base. All are present and accounted for, except for three people: a maintenance officer, a Chief Petty Officer on leave from the flight line, and a Seaman First Class from the Tower Administrative Staff. We're trying to contact them at the present time. All three have legitimate leaves-of-absence."

"What's your estimated cost of damage?"

"There were fifteen F-51 fighter aircraft destroyed at approximately 60 million dollars each and two experimental SX-7s that cost quite a lot more. Total cost is over 600 million dollars."

"I'll ask you again. Do you have any clues as to who is responsible for this mess?"

"We don't know. Whoever it was, accomplished what they wanted to do."

"How did they get access to that big armored truck? How did they get the keys?"

"The keys are kept locked up in the truck office. None of them are missing. Someone might have made a duplicate."

"Do we have guard dogs patrolling the fences around this base?"

"Yes, we do. The escape tunnel they dug was wide enough, so it wasn't detected. The dogs and guards walked right over the top of them."

"This looks like a well planned terrorist act. It's an obvious professional job. We've got to find the culprits responsible for this! Our big job will be to try and explain this to the public and the media. The Senate Armed Forces Committee and the appropriations committee are going to ask a lot of questions," remarked Perkins, "but we don't have the answers."

Secretary of the Navy Anderson's plane arrived at the base that afternoon. He met with Admiral Perkins and the skipper of the base, Captain Strong. A Marine Lieutenant Colonel in charge of security at the base was also present.

Howard Anderson was furious. What had happened was poor timing. The Secretary of Defense had resigned, and he was one of the candidates up for consideration. He would really like to have that job. The news media and TV wanted answers, and from what he had heard, there were none. It was not going to be easy to explain to the public what had happened.

"Captain Strong, how could you allow this to happen at your base?"

"I refuse to answer that until we have all the facts. I'm as much disturbed as you are."

"We have to give out a press release. We have to say something. The President wants some answers also. We're in deep shit," said Anderson.

"What do you plan to do?" asked Perkins.

"I think we have to tell the President everything, but as for the press, we have to stall. Tell them, 'Because of security reasons, very little information can be released at this time.'"

"I don't think that will suffice," said Strong. "They are already interviewing the civilian workers from the base on television, and they're talking."

"They should be squelched," said Anderson. "This could be a terrorist act by a foreign country. If it is, they'll be reading those headlines and watching the TV. We have to watch what we say."

"The two of us could go on TV together," said Perkins.

"No," replied Anderson. "Since this is a military disaster, you should explain what happened to the public."

Perkins had a smile on his face. He fully understood what the Secretary was up to.

"Okay, but my remarks are going to be brief. I agree with Captain Strong. We need more facts."

MARK'S ATTITUDE

That evening, Kelli called Mark in Washington, D.C.

"I was worried about you, Kelli. You didn't call after you got out there, and then I remembered, you're in the Navy, right?"

"Right," replied Kelli.

"It's hard for me to understand the Navy; they keep trying to screw us up. I've never been in the service, but believe me, I do believe that Navy term, 'SNAFU' (Situation Normal All Fucked Up). I wish the Navy would get their act together."

"I don't like being away from you, anymore than you do. I'll be back as soon as I can."

"The football season is ready to start, and that isn't going to help matters. I'll be commuting all over the country to get to see you," replied Mark.

"I know. That's poor planning."

"I play half of the games in San Diego. I wonder if the Navy will let you commute out there on weekends."

"If there's nothing cooking, I'll be there. Although, I don't think I'll enjoy seeing you get beaten up by some three-hundred pound psychopaths."

"How long are you going to be out there now on the West Coast?"

"Until they have some idea about what happened."

"What's going on out there at that Navy air base, anyway?"

"Nothing that I can tell you about."

"The papers out here in the East say that there's been a big accident, and the Navy's trying to cover it up. Is that true?"

"I can't answer that, Mark."

"Why not? I'm your husband."

"I know, but I received specific instructions not to talk to anyone about what I see or hear."

"The media and the public are screaming for information."

"Well, tomorrow, the Navy's going to have a press conference. My boss will be on television to answer questions. Try to catch it."

The Navy set up a press room in one of the dining halls at the base. Radio, TV, and West Coast journalists were present in force—the *L.A. Times*, *San Francisco Chronicle*, *Seattle Times*, and other representatives from the *Chicago Sun Times*, *New York Times*, and *Washington Post*.

It was decided that Admiral Perkins would make an opening statement and Captain Strong would try to answer questions.

"Early last evening, someone drove a heavy truck down the flight line at Miramar and destroyed some aircraft by hitting the planes and starting numerous fires. We have no information who was responsible for this dastardly act. A comprehensive military investigation is under way, and as soon as we get pertinent information, we will inform the public and the media. Captain Ralph Strong, the Commandant of the base will try to answer your questions."

Ed McQueen of the *L.A. Times* asked the first question. "How many planes were destroyed, and can we take some photographs of the damage?"

"Not yet," said Captain Strong. "We don't know the exact number of planes destroyed because some were totally wiped out by fire."

"Photographs will not be released for security reasons," interjected Perkins.

Tom Porter of the *San Francisco Chronicle* stood up, "Did personnel on this base do this?"

"We don't know who did this," replied Strong.

"What's the approximate cost damage?"

"That's not known at the present time. All the facts aren't in yet."

Marjorie Johnson of the *St. Louis Post Dispatch* raised her hand, "Was this a terrorist act?"

"That possibility does exist," replied Perkins.

"Has the F.B.I. or C.I.A. been called in?"

"Yes. The military and local and State Police are also cooperating in the investigation."

Pierce Baker from the *New York Times* made a comment, "We're not getting very much information about a major military disaster. Can't we get more facts?"

Perkins spoke up. "The Navy has to be very careful and candid about releasing information about this incident. As soon as we get more information, you'll receive it. That will be all for today."

During the next week, very little new information was obtained.

Admiral Perkins flew back to Washington, D.C. with the Secretary of the Navy to answer numerous questions that the Congressmen were asking. He was replaced by Vice Admiral Victor Marshall. Kelli had to remain at Miramar to see what developed . . . she was upset. The Navy finally released photographs of the debacle, and there was an uproar in Congress when the estimated cost damage was announced. An all points search bulletin was put out for the missing military personnel when they didn't return. After three weeks, Kelli returned to Washington, D.C. Mark was happy to see her, but in the morning he told her that he had to fly out to San Diego on the following Wednesday for football practice. The regular football season would be starting around Labor Day.

"Who's leaving who?" asked Kelli.

"Don't give me that!" replied Mark.

"I'm just giving you some of your own medicine," said Kelli.

"If we're going to make this marriage work, we both have to understand that there are two careers involved here."

"I realize that," replied Kelli. "I'm willing to work on it, if you are."

"Of course I am," said Mark.

"Then we won't bitch about it, if one of us has to leave suddenly," replied Kelli.

A week later, Kelli was called into Admiral Perkins' office.

"Kelli, Henry Anderson has called for a strategy session in his office tomorrow. Three or four key players have been asked to attend. The Senate hasn't voted on the Appropriations Bill and the Navy wants more money to replace those valuable planes that were lost. It doesn't look like we're going to get it."

"That's horrible," replied Kelli. "Doesn't the Congress realize how important those planes are to maintain a strong posture in the defense of our country?"

"It's not that simple. When you ask for a large sum of money that you haven't planned on, it's impossible for the Senate to change it's mind. Unfortunately, the Senate is going to vote on the Appropriations Bill in about three weeks."

"How much of an increase are they asking for?"

"Six hundred million dollars."

"That's a lot of dough!" remarked Kelli.

HENRY ANDERSON
SECRETARY OF THE NAVY
PENTAGON

Kelli was the most junior of junior officers to be invited to attend the strategy session in the Secretary of the Navy's office. She was asked to attend because she was on the Congressional Liaison Committee. With all that flag rank around, she felt out of place. It was the first time for Kelli to meet the C.N.O. and Vice-Chairmen of the Navy, and she was flustered.

When they came into the room, Kelli stood up and saluted.

The C.N.O. responded, "It's not necessary to do anymore saluting in these offices, Commander. We know why you're here. You're part of the team now!"

Part of what team, thought Kelli. Just what was in store for her? The Vice-Chairman, Admiral Alex Morrison, wore gold Navy pilot's wings. He sat next to her, was most cordial, and he actually helped her to relax. When Henry Anderson came into the room, it didn't take him very long to come right to the point.

"Gentlemen," as he nodded to Kelli, "we have a serious problem on our hands. Right in the middle of the Senate Armed Forces Committee discussions about increasing naval appropriations, a disaster has hit us, and we look like a bunch of idiots. The destruction of planes at Miramar Naval Air Station cost us over 600 million dollars, and who knows how much more it's going to cost us as our image deteriorates further. In some way we have to change that in a hurry."

"How do you plan to do that in three weeks time?" asked Perkins.

"That's the problem. In order to get additional funds, we need the Senate Armed Forces Committee to recommend our request for the increased amount. We have to become lobbyists and convince them of its importance."

"It's not going to be easy," said Anderson. "There are two senators on the Armed Forces Committee who have flatly stated that they are vehemently opposed to any increased funds. One of them is the senior senator, Jane Farber from California. I think she's a pacifist. In some way, we've got to get her to change her mind."

"How are we going to do that?'

"You're all probably wondering why Commander Palmer is sitting in this room. She's also a California native."

"Kelli, we want you to request a visit with Senator Jane Farber. We'll arrange for a photo session of candids, and perhaps get a journalist from California to interview you two for back home consumption. We'll get TV coverage. I'm sure she'll go for that! In that interview, we'll want you to repeat your feelings about how we need those Navy funds and how important they are for the state of California. Some of our largest aircraft companies are out there, and Farber's received large sums of soft money from them for her campaign."

Kelli was shocked by what she heard—she would be a lobbyist—Anderson had thrown a curve ball at her without prior discussion.

"Kelli, would you do that for us?"

Kelli felt her face getting beet red in front of all the high-ranking officers. Anderson had confirmed her thoughts about him. There was no doubt that he was a shrewd politician, and he was pulling out all stops.

The members in the room looked at her in anticipation of her reply.

"What can I say?". . . She hesitated and then said, "Of course I will, if it will help the Navy."

"Thanks, Kelli!" said Anderson, with a smile on his face. "We'll set up the meeting for you, and I'll be in touch. You're excused."

After Kelli left the room, the Chief of Naval Operations, Peters, made a comment, "I'm really impressed with Commander Palmer. The Navy met the mixed gender issue head on with that one. She obviously has leadership qualities. Someday, I wouldn't be surprised if she made the flag rank."

"My department has had an eye on her for a long time," said Anderson. "She has really been helpful in gender integration."

"She's quite a pilot too! She flew me out to California in an F-51," said Perkins.

"Let's hope she can change Senator Farber's mind about increased appropriations."

Senator Walter Lawrence told Perkins that President Gray had called him and was opposed to giving more money to the Navy. After all, it was the Navy's lack of tight security that had allowed that disaster at Miramar. With the President involved, threatening to veto the Appropriations Bill, there was a new wrinkle to obtaining the funds. Admiral Perkins asked Senator Lawrence to delay the committee meeting for a few days in order for the Navy to prepare its case. The request was granted.

Secretary Anderson set up the meeting between Kelli and Senator Jane Farber. Farber eagerly agreed to the meeting because it was near the end of her fourth term, and she was anxious to obtain publicity for her re-election. Members of the West Coast Press, and the TV stations from California were present. Kelli was pleasantly surprised when they met just before going on camera with their joint interview.

"I believe we've met before," remarked Senator Farber.

"How so?" asked Kelli.

"We were on a panel together in Los Angeles at the Century Hotel quite a few years ago."

"That's right!" replied Kelli. "I remember now."

"You took the limelight away from me at that time. Are you still flying jets?"

"Yes, I am," replied Kelli, "but not as often."

"Are you still in California?"

"Yes. I have a home in San Diego. I'm stationed in Washington, D.C."

"I understand that both of us are going to be interviewed by members of the Washington press and the California press. Let's get on with it. Let the TV cameras roll."

Jim Black, from the *L.A. Times* was the moderator. "I wonder if you would comment about the Navy's tragedy at Miramar Naval Air Base in California, Senator."

"I agree it was a tragedy, but I feel that the Navy was derelict in not having tight security at that base. Perhaps Commander Palmer would like to comment."

"What happened at Miramar was a cleverly orchestrated act of violence that cost the Navy dearly. Until the facts are in, responsibility is indeterminate. It could be terrorists. The issue is how are we going to replace the planes that are vital for this nations defense?"

"Would you care to comment on that statement, Senator?"

"Yes, I would! The world around us is at peace right now. We don't need more planes and armaments. The money to replace those planes will cost millions."

Todd Phillips from the *San Francisco Examiner* was next. "Commander, why should those few planes that were destroyed be replaced?"

"Because some of those planes were experimental hi-tech planes. In order to prevent wars, you have to speak from a position of power with the strongest and best weapons available. They must be replaced. The Navy needs those funds, and I hope that Senator Farber will support the Navy's request."

"Senator Farber are you going to support increased funds to replace those planes at Miramar?"

"I'm not sure! I'll have to think about it."

The next week, Senator Jane Farber voted against giving added funds to the Navy. President Gray publicly announced in his press conference that he would veto any appropriations bill that included any added funds. Kelli was upset by Senator Farber's actions. She had worked hard to convince her to support the Navy. It was a nice try, but it didn't work. Kelli's only remark was, "Politicians stink!" She was mad. It was the first time that she had failed to accomplish something that she really wanted to do.

MIRAMAR INCIDENT INVESTIGATION

Two weeks after the Senate Armed Forces Committee refused to increase the funding for the Navy, there was some breaking news out at Miramar Naval Air Station. Two college students, scuba diving on a lake about 110 miles north of Miramar, found an abandoned truck 40 feet beneath the surface of the water. There were three bodies inside, and although they were slightly decomposed, they were the missing naval officer and enlisted men. Their bodies were riddled with bullet holes, and all three throats were cut.

Dental and DNA tests confirmed their identity. Rubber gloves and night vision apparatus were also found in the truck. Fifty-thousand dollars in hundred dollar bills were found in a canvas bag. It was a paltry sum compared to the large costly damage they had done to the Navy planes. The F.B.I. got involved, and they were sure that the two men had driven the big truck that destroyed the planes, and the third waited in the getaway vehicle. They obviously had been paid off, and then bumped off, and put into a watery grave.

There was a new wrinkle on those who committed the crime. It looked more and more like a terrorist plot to destroy valuable American aircraft equipment. It was an inside job working with an outside source. Had the three Navy men committed the crime for money, or were they misinformed patriots? Who were the perpetrators behind it all?

The F.B.I. starting back-tracking, looking into the backgrounds of the gentlemen, and they came up with some interesting findings.

The three men all came from the northwestern states and had worked together at the Oceana Naval Air Station in Virginia. None of them were married, and there was some question about their sexual preferences. Lieutenant Keith Norman had worked as an administrative assistant in aircraft maintenance and had graduated from the University of California at Berkeley with an engineering degree, before going into the Navy. In college, he was active with a political action group.

Neil Wright, a recently promoted Chief Petty Officer, came from a Navy family. His father was a retired Navy commander who had come up from the ranks. His son had had no contact with his family for the past three years. His father had wanted him to go to the Naval Academy, and he had refused, causing a family conflict.

Harold Eliot was a First Class Aviation Mechanic who had been in the Navy for four years and was up for promotion.

There was one common denominator that was found amongst the three. They had vacationed together and had traveled outside the country on different occasions. One recent trip they had taken together was to Pakistan and Afghanistan. This suggested that another country was involved in the destruction of the aircraft.

Naval Intelligence, the F.B.I., and C.I.A. decided that no information would be released to the media or public about the discovery of the bodies. One thing that did happen was that security at all military installations was reassessed and improved.

X

TWO BIG CAREERS
IN ONE FAMILY

Commuting back and forth to San Diego when she could, and commuting to Washington, D.C. when Mark could, was not conducive to a healthy marriage. There were times when Kelli couldn't make the connection because of pressing Navy business, and there were times during the football season when it was impossible for Mark to go to Washington, D.C. The best time to be together was when Mark was in the off season from football, and he could spend all of his time in D.C. Sometimes that didn't work either because the Navy would assign Kelli to be out of state on special projects.

Mark was paid big bucks to join the San Diego Football team, and when they moved, he signed a lucrative contract for three years at $30 million. However, there was a performance clause in his contract.

Because he had had a broken leg, the owner was not willing to take a chance on his health. Mark still had a strong throwing arm, and his passing ability was excellent. Running out of the pocket was his problem because of his previous leg injury. The first year as quarterback for San Diego, the team made the playoffs, and he had to play additional games. Kelli was pissed off about that and told him about it.

"How much longer are you going to let those psychopathic jocks chase you around the football field to see how many bones of yours that they can break? I don't want a cripple for a husband!"

"Get off my back, Kelli!" he replied.

"It looks like all the teams get into the playoff."

"Whadyah mean?"

"Well, there aren't too many teams that don't get in."

"Are you saying you wished that I didn't make the playoffs?"

"It woulda been nice for us."

"I play to win—all the time. Just like you, remember?"

"I know. That's a big part of our problem."

"My contract's only for three years. You never know what's going to happen in football," said Mark.

"I've only got two years left in my contract with the Navy."

"I'd like to have a family," said Mark.

"I wish I could start right now," said Kelli.

"That ain't gonna happen. I can just see you, pregnant, walking behind Admiral Perkins and appearing with him before Congress. I think that would really hit all the news media. One thing I don't like is you're still flying!"

"I enjoy flying. It gets me out of the military political arena. Flying above the clouds in the blue sky is a great tranquilizer for me."

"It's a risky tranquilizer."

"I'm not doing any formation flying or landing on carriers anymore. The runways are big and long. It's much safer."

"Accidents can happen when you least expect it," replied Mark.

"Well, that's just like the football field, isn't it?"

"So we're going to play tit for tat, right?"

"No. I don't want to argue with you because I love you. I understand we don't have an ideal situation and wish it could be better."

It hadn't been easy for Mark Palmer. When Kelli first went to Washington, it was bearable. Kelli commuted around the country to wherever San Diego was playing. It was fun at first, staying in different hotels around the country during the football season. He kept his job as the starting quarterback and remained reasonably healthy. San Diego beefed up its offensive line with some good trades, and it made a huge difference. At 35, he wasn't as mobile and needed to stay in the pocket more. Whenever he rolled out on a broken play, exposed, the crowd and his coaches held their breath.

During the football season, life for Palmer in San Diego without Kelli felt like being in limbo. He missed his wife and most of all, some sense of normalcy. Most days he practiced, worked out late with the trainers, got something to eat with a couple of other players he was friendly with, and went home to a dark house. If the team traveled anywhere near D.C., he tried to fly in to see Kelli, even for a few hours. Otherwise, he was alone.

He couldn't bitch because the money was good. They had a beautiful home in San Diego and a new fashionable condo in Georgetown which they had just purchased. He was a hero in San Diego, the one place in the country where he was regarded as more than Mr. Kelli Fitzgerald Palmer.

The situation got progressively worse as the time spent away from each other increased. Their two jobs were conflicting, and working at the opposite ends of the country didn't help.

They both kept making excuses about missed meetings. Mark played a terrific game in the playoffs against Chicago and San Diego won, extending their season.

Kelli was unable to get to the game, so Mark got mad. She gave Mark a lengthy explanation why she couldn't make it. She had to attend a special function for the NATO Naval Commanders at the White House. Because Mark couldn't go with her, she went anyway and got lots of attention because she was alone.

In the second playoff game, Mark was injured, and he was back on crutches again—no broken bones, but severe soft tissue injury. He was put in the hospital for a couple of days, and Kelli couldn't get away to see him on the coast.

"I suppose I have to get killed in order for you to come out to see me."

"You didn't have a life-threatening situation," said Kelli.

"No, but our marriage does," he replied.

"Don't say that!" she screamed.

Their marriage was better for awhile until the fall when Mark had to return to the West Coast to practice for the football season. He began to commute from the West Coast, and it just wasn't working. Kelli had to continue with occasional weekend flying to maintain her flight skills, and this added to their problem.

One weekend Mark arrived in a bitchy mood and told Kelli that she had to choose between flying and staying in the Navy or quitting the Navy to preserve their marriage.

There was some mutual name calling and on Sunday evening things got hot. They were sitting at the kitchen table discussing their problem when they said things that they both regretted. Finally, Mark blew his stack. He picked up his coffee cup and threw it against the wall, breaking the cup and spilling coffee all over the wallpaper . . . just missing Kelli.

"Why are you throwing things at me?"

"I'm mad because our marriage isn't what I expected!"

"That cup could have hit me!"

"I wasn't throwing it at you. Remember, I'm a quarterback."

"You're an older quarterback. That cup almost hit me!"

"Thanks," said Mark.

"I didn't mean it that way."

"Two big careers and two big egos like we've got, are bound to clash. I love you, but I don't like what's happening," said Kelli.

"Neither do I. We've got quite a few years left ahead of us. I think I want to spend it with you, but not like this. How do you feel?"

"I feel the same way," she said as she started to cry. "I'd like to have a baby."

"We better stop thinking about it, and do something about it!" said Mark. "You're getting older."

"Touche! We're even now! I'm not too old to have a baby."

"We've got to change our game plan," said Mark.

"You're the quarterback, what should we do?"

"Either you have to change your career, or I do. The fatigue factor is setting in for me. I'm having trouble getting out of the pocket, and my bones are brittle. I don't want to get killed!"

"I'm also having trouble flying those new jets, and I'm beginning to lose my confidence. My risk factor has increased. I don't fly often enough to be safe."

"We're in deep shit."

"Either you're going to quit the Navy or I'm quitting football. We're both in high-risk professions. I'm running out of gas trying to stay ahead of the opponents tackles, and you could run out of gas in one of those jets."

"It won't be easy getting out of the Navy," said Kelli. "I got a bonus and signed a contract for three years."

"You can try, can't you?"

"I'll give it a try. I'll talk to the Secretary of the Navy."

Henry Anderson would have no part of Kelli quitting the Navy. He knew that she was a shining star in the Navy's ranks, particularly when the Navy was trying to complete the transition to the integration of the women into the ranks.

"Kelli, you don't realize how important you are to the Navy. I wish I had ten commanders just like you! It is a shock to me that you want to get out of the Navy. You're in the top group to make captain one of these days. There's no limit to how far you can go. You could become a flag officer."

"You don't understand, Mr. Secretary. My marriage is extremely important to me. I'm losing it, and I don't want to get a divorce!"

"If that's your problem, we'll have to seriously talk about how to keep you and your husband happy."

"It's right on the edge right now. Our careers are clashing."

"I don't understand," said Anderson.

"We have a marriage in absentia. We are unable to get together when he's playing football from August to January. I'm in D.C., and he's in San Diego. That's our worst time. It's a big problem!"

"Let me think about it, and I'll get back to you."

Secretary Anderson called Kelli one week later.

"Kelli, I have a solution."

"What is it?"

"From August to January 1st, you will spend one week a month in San Diego . . . give us the dates for when your husband's football team will be in town. You can get your monthly flight time in at the San Diego Naval Air Station."

"That's a lot better than I have now. I hope it works."

Kelli told Mark about Anderson's proposition. He was cool to the plan. He wanted her out.

"The Navy still sucks!" he said.

"It's better than nothing. I can get my flight hours in out here and watch you play football. I'm willing to give it a try if you are."

"What can I say? If we have to do it, I'll get the dates for you."

Getting together one week out of every month during the football season was better for their marriage. They had more time to talk about their future. Mark was having trouble keeping up with the younger football players, and the team had hired a young back-up quarterback who was getting more playing time. The handwriting was beginning to be written on the wall for his career.

Kelli went to all of his football games when she was in town. She hated to see him tackled by 300 pound psychopaths and didn't like it when he was slow in getting up after being sacked. After the game, she saw all those bruises on his body when he took a shower.

After two successful seasons with San Diego, passing for better than 1500 yards, and tying a couple of old records, his age started to show. He was 37. They got into the playoffs, and he was getting sacked too often and pounded too frequently. "You guys up front aren't blocking and tackling well enough," he shouted at the linesmen in the huddle after being sacked twice in a row.

"If you could run out of the pocket, you wouldn't get sacked," said Jones, the offensive tackle.

That did it. On the next play, Palmer ran out of the pocket and was sacked by Steamboat Pulaski, the 270 lb. middle linebacker for the Jets. The pass was intercepted, and the defensive back ran for a touchdown. It was the deciding touchdown in the game. Palmer couldn't get up after being hit and was carried off the field. He had rebroken his left leg, and his career was over. He was depressed . . .

but he was happy. He'd be back with Kelli all the time now. Kelli was happy too.

During a week when she was in San Diego, Kelli tried to do too much. She attended two big parties with Mark, and they had a party of their own that went into the wee hours of the morning. She had to get her flight time in, so the next day she went out to the San Diego Naval Air Station. She put the jet through its paces and probably tried to do too much with a lot of G's on her body. She had difficulty landing the plane and when she got out, she felt whoosy and got sick to her stomach. She remembered that she had forgotten the rule about no alcohol for twelve hours before flying and had had two martinis the night before. She had never been sick after flying and felt "shitty". She called Mark and told him that she was going to the E.R. on the base to see a Navy doctor.

"What's the matter?" he asked.

"I don't know. I've had the dry heaves. It could be something I ate or drank last night."

"Do you want me to come pick you up?"

"No. I'll be all right."

Mark was waiting for her when she got home.

"I hope the doctor grounded you. You look horrible! You're in no condition to be flying."

"He did! There's something more important than that."

Mark's jaw dropped. "Do you have something serious?"

"Yes! Today I had a damaged nose wheel when I landed the jet, and I almost cracked up. It scared the hell out of me! The maintenance is not as good as it used to be. I've decided to resign from the Navy."

"That's a surprise, but that's great!" he said.

"I have something else to tell you."

"Is it good news or bad news?"

"Good news! I've been feeling sick in the morning for a few weeks and didn't realize what it was. We're going to have a baby. I'm pregnant!"

"Kelli, that's great!"

He took her into his arms and gave her a big kiss. "Are you sure?"

"The doctor is sure, and so am I. I don't want anything to happen to that baby!" said Kelli.

"Well, that's it! Now you're really grounded."

When Kelli announced to Anderson that she was pregnant, he conceded defeat in trying to keep her in the Navy. If she lost her baby while flying, she'd have grounds for a large lawsuit. Besides, G suits don't fit well on pregnant females. He did convince her of her value to the Navy, and she agreed to join the Naval Air Reserves in the future.

Eight months later, she gave birth to a beautiful 7 lb, 12 oz. red-headed girl. They named her Kelli Anne and called her Anne. One year later, she gave birth to a boy. He was named Mark Paul II, and he would be called Paul.

2008

XI

DOMESTIC BLISS
SAN DIEGO

Taking care of a red-headed daughter and a chunky son who never seemed to get enough food to be satisfied kept Kelli busy. Money was no problem, so they had a full-time nanny. Living with a member of the opposite sex full-time required quite a few adjustments. There were times when their marriage jelled and other times when their aggressive egos clashed. It was hard for Kelli to adjust to the fact that she wasn't the boss anymore. She was used to giving orders and expecting them to be carried out. Mark was a successful quarterback who called the signals and expected his team to comply. If he took a beating and was sacked, he knew how to holler to get his point across.

There were times when Kelli had difficulty in adjusting and was bored about being a housewife. There were also times when her red-headed Irish temper broke out of her shell . . . like a load of dynamite.

It wasn't long before Kelli decided that she didn't like what was happening in the political arena in San Diego. There was a massive influx of illegal immigrants coming into the state causing big headaches for the educational and health systems. There was a general deterioration of the public schools. Kelli graduated from public schools, and she wanted her children to go to public schools, so she became an activist for monitoring and improving the schools. She opposed the voucher system that allowed parents to use public money to send their children to private schools. This undermined the public school system. She felt that some of the schools had horrible teachers. She wanted all teachers to take a written exam every five years in the courses they taught, to be sure that what they were teaching was current and correct. The teacher's union fought her constantly on this issue. One evening she had a battle royal with Mark about the subject.

"Why are you so vehement about improving our public schools, Kelli?"

"Because I believe that all children should have an equal opportunity to get a good education. That's why!"

"Our kids are gonna go to private school," replied Mark.

"Not if I have anything to say about it," she replied. "The diversity in the public school system is necessary for understanding what life is all about at a young age."

"Forget about diversity! Come off of it," said Mark. "Public schools are full of drugs, have poor teachers, and in the inner city, are full of crime. Things have changed since you went to school."

"Then they should be changed back."

"You're talking like a politician."

"I'm thinking about becoming active in politics . . . at least at the local level."

"I thought you were looking bored the other day. As long as it doesn't interfere with our lifestyle and will benefit the kids, go ahead."

"Thanks, Mark! However, it might mean a new career."

"I know," he replied.

Kelli's opinions and thoughts were similar to the Democrats in San Diego, so she went to the party's boss and asked how she could help. He told her to get involved with the local town council and to run for office, which she did. She started to write articles for the editorial pages of the local newspapers about education and was invited to speak to several community groups on the subject. Then she got a paid staff position with the Public Education Coalition whose goal was to arouse voter interest. She started a television campaign, so that the public was better informed, and she participated in numerous debates which began to give her a following.

One year later, when she was approached about running for Congress, she seriously considered it. She was good at this stuff and felt she could help. However, she was hesitant about discussing it with Mark. She finally got up her nerve.

"What do you think about my running for Congress?"

"Consider it carefully. We have two children that we have to think about."

"That's why I would like to run. I don't like what I see on the horizon for our children."

"It would be a full commitment. Congressional seats aren't always available. I'm no longer playing football."

"If I read you correct . . . you're saying I should go for it."

"Yes."

SAN DIEGO, CALIFORNIA
ELECTION DAY
NOVEMBER 2010

Kelli Palmer ran for Congress and won, beating the incumbent by a narrow margin. She and Mark decided to keep their home in San Diego, and they purchased another condo in Georgetown.

After she was sworn in, the Speaker of the House put her on the Appropriations Committee and the Armed Forces Committee and within a week, she received numerous phone calls from lobbyists, fellow congressmen, constituents from her district, and a surprise call from the new Secretary of the Navy, John Bolton.

"I'd like to have lunch with you soon, Congresswoman," he said. "I'd like you to re-establish your relationship with the Navy."

"Thanks. As soon as things quiet down, I'll call."

Kelli called two weeks later.

"The Navy is proud that you're on the Armed Forces Committee, Commander Palmer. I hope you don't mind my calling you that. We'd like you to rejoin the Navy Reserve."

"Why should I do that?" asked Kelli.

"You've had an outstanding career in the active Navy and by joining the Naval Air Corps Reserve, you will eventually become a four striper—one of the few women pilots to become a Navy Captain."

"If I have to fly, I'd be placing myself at risk. I have two children," replied Kelli.

"We would make sure that there was no risk involved," replied the Secretary.

"I'll do it. I'll join the Reserve."

The Navy knew what they were doing. Kelli became a vocal active supporter of the Armed Forces and fought any Congressional attempt to downsizing.

She was invited to speak around the country to businessmen and women's groups. It wasn't long before she was invited to speak to the National Press Club in Washington, D.C.

She was introduced by Bill Brown, of the *Washington Times*, the senior member of the Washington press. His historical review of her background was awesome. The audience was visibly impressed. He asked the first question. It was about terrorism.

"Why do you think that we have so much terrorism going on in this world?"

"Terrorism isn't anything new. It has advanced as any systemic disease advances through society if it is left unchecked. Its purpose is terror. In the absence of a vigilant response, it becomes successful. The perpetrators must be found and punished, or it will continue. The punishment must be severe, or it will be repeated. This country is based on freedom and freedom of expression. Terrorism destroys freedom. Government must therefore destroy terror."

Her speech was shown on national TV in the evening, where she was described as a hawkish young Democrat with an agenda concerning national security issues.

Not all the feedback was good. The newspapers said that she could create a false fear and insecurity within the populace that would not be good for morale.

Illinois Senator, Bill Sheridan, from her own party called her. "Kelli, I think you should concentrate on doing a better job for your own constituents at home. Stick with domestic issues. Forget about speaking out on national issues."

"I don't understand, Senator. I thought I was elected by my constituents to fight for what I thought was right."

"You sounded more like you were running for national office."

"Well, I'm not! I'm happy being a California Representative!"

The next day, Kelli called Senator Jack Thompson, the Majority Leader, and told him what happened. She didn't mention any names.

"Ignore it, Kelli. Now that you're in Congress, many people are going to try to influence your thinking and how you present yourself. Your vote on critical issues are important. Sometimes you won't understand their motives. He's probably just jealous because of the publicity you're getting. We need more women like you speaking up on national issues. Speak your mind and your conscience, but understand that you'll ruffle some feathers along the way."

"Thanks for your support," replied Kelli.

Kelli continued her work in Congress, getting elected twice to the House.

She spoke up frequently on national issues and women's rights and became a member of the House Ethics Committee and the House Appropriations Committee. She also continued on the Armed Forces Committee.

Kelli was not afraid of a fight if she felt strongly about an issue and was constantly in the news because of her active participation in the debates on the House floor.

One day, she had a showdown with the Chairman of the House Appropriation Committee about allocating funds for a national missile defense system around the United States. The Chairman decided not to take the issue up for discussion in the committee. It had been on the agenda.

Kelli would have no part of that and spoke up, "Mr. Chairman, because of increased terrorism around the world and proliferation of missile production, I believe that it is paramount that we consider and vote in this committee on the issue of whether we should allocate funds for a national missile defense system!"

"Forget it! The world is at peace, Kelli. I have talked to General Jonathan Walker, the chairman of the Joint Chiefs, and he told me that we do have a few S.A.M. (surface-to-air) missile sites around Washington, D.C. and a Defense Artillery Center. He told me that we'll never have to use them. The world's leaders realize that if we start throwing missiles at each other, we all could be destroyed. It would be an unnecessary expense."

"I disagree. Russia, China, Iran, Iraq, and North Korea have long-range capability right now, putting all of our cities at risk. Pakistan and India have exploded nuclear bombs."

"How accurate are Iran and Iraq's bombs?"

"I think they could be very accurate. They're getting technological help from Russia, China, and who knows? . . . some of our own tech companies."

"That's a worst case scenario!" replied the chairman.

"You're not being realistic," said Kelli.

"There could be an unknown element out there that we may have to deal with. Some country could throw a missile at New York City tomorrow, and we'd have a million casualties. I want a vote by this committee to see how each member stands on the issue."

"Not now!" replied the Chairman, as he slammed the gavel down.

The next day, Kelli received a phone call from the senior Senator from California, Senator Jane Farber, a member of her own party.

"Kelli, I think that you should lay off pushing the issue of a missile defense system for this country. The cost would be prohibitive, and it won't work. Our own state of California would suffer if we divert funds for a national defensive missile system. The C.I.A. says it's not needed."

"I disagree, Senator. It will take quite a few years to install a system. It would be a valuable deterrent and create jobs in California."

"If you insist on this, I'm going to oppose you publicly in the news media and that includes California."

"Thanks a lot," replied Kelli. "I thought you were a member of my party."

"Not on this issue," she replied. "I totally disagree!"

A BLOODY FIGHT
JUNE, 15, 2013
ST. FRANCIS HOTEL
SAN FRANCISCO, CALIFORNIA

One week later, Senator Jane Farber gave a talk at the St. Francis Hotel in San Francisco to the League of Women Voters. The place was mobbed . . . there were over 1,500 women in attendance. When she got on the podium, she said, "I've decided to change the topic that I was scheduled to talk about. My topic today is titled "Fiscal Responsibility in High Office".

"All of you in the audience realize that without a strict budget in the home, for food, clothing, cars, health care, mortgages, and future college expenses . . . the debts begin to rise and soon there is no real disposable income. Credit cards are sometimes used to postpone debts and as the amount increases, the anxiety increases, and soon the family is in big financial trouble.

"Well, the government has to have fiscal responsibility just like the household. We have fixed expenditures in the government such as Medicare, Medicaid, Social Security, Veterans' benefits, a military budget for the Army, the Army Air Force, Marines, and the Navy. All involved personnel who have to be paid and costly sophisticated weapons, tanks, airplanes and ships. Some ships cost over a billion dollars and some jets cost 70 million dollars for just one plane. Your taxes have to pay for all this equipment and personnel. Also, around the world, there are numerous I.C.B.M.s in their silos, and if launched, the civilization as it exists today would be destroyed.

"What all this means, is that there is very little disposable money left from your tax dollars for improving education for the children; doing research for cancer and other diseases; controlling drugs or improving our transportation systems . . . and numerous other worthy projects that are left in the lurch.

"Why am I bringing this up to this group? I'll tell you why! We have congressmen and women, and one is from my home state of California, who want to spend billions or trillions of dollars to construct a national missile defensive system which will probably be obsolete once it is put in place. Quite a few years ago, President Reagan was convinced that the only way to protect American cities from a missile attack was to erect a protective umbrella of satellite-based defense systems that could shoot down incoming missiles (a Star Wars concept). The cost was prohibitive, and it wouldn't work. The enemy could throw up thousands of cheap decoys with the attacking missiles, and our defensive missiles wouldn't know which one to shoot down. How can you protect all our cities from a missile attack? It's impossible! Who knows what sophisticated weaponry will be developed in the future?

"I want all of you to become activists, write your congressmen, and tell them that there are better ways to spend your tax dollars. As your Senator, I urge you to do this. I'll stop talking now and will take questions."

Kathy Jones from the *Los Angeles Times*, raised her hand. "Would you care to tell us who that Congress woman from California is?"

"I think you all know who she is. Just read the Congressional record."

Edith Callahan from the *San Francisco Chronicle* asked the next question. "Should we be worried about a missile attack on our country?"

"Not at all. We have the best sophisticated weaponry in the

world. If we were attacked, the country attacking us would be destroyed."

"What about terrorists shooting missiles at us?"

"They'd get the same treatment. Their country would be destroyed."

"I'd like a follow-up. Wouldn't that destroy all life on the earth?"

"It won't happen," replied Senator Farber.

Less than thirty minutes after Senator Farber sat down Kelli received a phone call from a journalist from a San Diego TV station who was at the meeting.

Kelli couldn't believe what she was told. She was hopping mad.

The next morning the speech, in its entirety, was in the *San Francisco Chronicle* and on the editorial page was an article supporting Farber's remarks. Kelli was livid. Senator Jane Farber was the same lady who advised her to get into politics when she was a Navy pilot. She was now doing everything in her power to try to throw her out.

Kelli called Senator Jack Thompson, the Majority Leader of the party.

"Jack, you've probably heard about the speech that Senator Farber made in San Francisco last night. Do we let members of our own party castigate each other on television?"

"That's freedom of speech," said Jack. "I told you that not everyone would agree with what you said."

"I remember," replied Kelli, "but she's trying to destroy me in my Congressional district."

"I suggest that you think about it, Kelli. Don't make an emotional reply. You're gonna have to come up with an answer, however."

Not all the news media agreed with Senator Farber's remarks. The *Los Angeles Times* and the *Sacramento BEE* supported Kelli's stand on the issue and felt that there should be more discussion and debate. They agreed that the cost was prohibitive, but that didn't answer the question of need. After all, at one time China had threatened to throw a missile or two at Los Angeles or San Francisco if we prevented them from taking over Taiwan. Also somebody had to deal with the terrorists.

Kelli decided to call for a strategy session with some of her political pros who had helped her win in her district. The meeting was to be held in San Diego at the private home of one of her avid supporters, the owner of the San Diego professional football team, Don Parsons. Kelli also invited three financial supporters from the airframe and aircraft engine companies based in California. Others invited to attend were a political columnist from the *Los Angeles Times,* Bill Black, and a former political analyst and friend from San Francisco, Sara Connors, as well as Barbara Bond from the *Sacramento BEE.*

A catered dinner was served, and the discussion got under way with Kelli asking the questions.

"The reason I've called this meeting is because I've been told through the grapevine that Senator Farber has asked a wealthy millionaire friend of hers to oppose me for reelection next year. You also know that Farber's up for reelection in the Senate, and she's trying to make political hay. I'm so mad about her comments in San Francisco last week that I can't think straight. She's obviously out to get me, and I don't understand why. I'm interested in your comments and suggestions."

Bill Black, a senior editor of the *L.A. Times,* spoke up. "I read Kathy Jones' article in the *San Francisco Chronicle.* She made some well researched points about missile defense. Senator Farber is appealing to the pacifists and peace-loving element, and there are probably more of those than hawks. They hate war. Most women are not hawks . . . you're a rarity. She's trying to get women to support her and vote for her, since she's not doing well in the polls. I've been thinking about what she's up to, Kelli. This might be the right time for you to challenge her . . . go for her Senate seat. This may be why she's out to get you . . . eliminate the opposition before it gets started. I believe that you could beat her and dethrone her because she's not popular. She's an iconoclast."

"You did come out pretty strong on missile defense in that Armed Forces Committee meeting, Kelli," said Sara Connors. "Maybe you should tone that down."

"That's the way I feel. There's so much fighting, ethnic cleansing, religious wars, Middle East turmoil, terrorists, and new countries with nuclear bombs . . . there's a powder keg out there waiting to blow!"

"Maybe a defensive missile system is not a popular theme for you to pursue at this time because it could be extremely expensive," said Barbara Bond of the *Sacramento BEE*.

"You can't always support popular issues in the Congress," Kelli replied.

"Maybe you should drop the issue," said Connors.

Jack Townsend, executive Vice President of one of the largest aircraft plants in California, spoke up. "I disagree! We in the aircraft industry would like to get rid of Senator Farber. She keeps blocking funds for the military, unrealistically. She's a thorn in our side. If I had my way, I'd like to see you run against her in the Senate primary. She's been in the Senate too long. Besides, she gets most of her campaign money from out-of-state lobbyists and not from the California voters. I wish Congress would declare that illegal!"

"I agree with Jack," said Bill Black. "Jane Farber is losing her popularity. She's 72 years old, and sometimes I think that she's not with it anymore."

"You'll have a bloody fight on your hands if you oppose her. Farber's already throwing dirt out at you. She probably suspects that you might run against her," said Connors, "and she's loaded with campaign finance funds."

"I wasn't thinking about running for the Senate when I called this meeting. I thought I'd be fighting for my Representative seat. Your comments are a complete surprise. Senator Farber's made me so mad that I can't think straight! If I thought I had a chance and could raise enough money, I'd challenge her, and I'd go for it. She's playing real dirty."

"I think that we could raise a lot of money to get Farber out of the Senate," said Jack Townsend.

"Will you run?" asked Bill Black. "That's the best way to respond to her attack."

Kelli hesitated for awhile and then said, "Yes. If we can raise the money."

"Good! I'll help set up a political advisory committee. You'll eventually have to file for that primary. Are you going to resign from the House of Representatives?"

"No. Not for a while. I'll need national exposure to get to Senator Farber. The bloody fight that one of you referred to is really going to get bloodier!"

Kelli's political advisory committee decided that she should start speaking around the state to various groups for more visibility. One month later, an announcement would be made to the press of her intentions. Once the cat was out of the bag, an all out drive for financial support would be made. The machinery to gain political support would then be put in place.

PRESS CONFERENCE
WHITE HOUSE
NOVEMBER 20, 2013

Senator Farber got an unexpected boost from President Diamond. He announced during a press conference, that he wanted to slash billions of dollars from the Armed Forces budget and reduce the number of personnel on active duty. He felt that terrorism was not a big issue. To show that it was a bipartisan plan, he allowed the press to take pictures of him with members from both parties. Senator Farber was standing next to the President.

When Kelli saw the photographs in all the newspapers, she was really upset. She couldn't let the President's announcement go unchallenged. She requested and got the floor of the House. She addressed the chairperson and the assembly.

*   *   *

"I must rise in the House of Representatives of this great country of ours, to object to President Diamond's suggestion that we slash the Armed Forces funds and reduce the number of personnel on active duty. There are increasing regional conflicts developing around the world, new countries developing nuclear bombs, and increasing activity of terrorists groups. If we don't stand up against what's happening, who will? We should be increasing our armed forces and increasing our vigilance. Our current defense system is useless if a terrorist decides to blow up a building or a bridge or to fire a missile at one of our major cities. Such an attack could come from anywhere at anytime. I realize that it will be difficult to make a defensive missile system that works and will take years to develop. I feel that for every offense there is a defense. If we get our best scientists working on this project, we should be able to come up with some answers. The sooner we start, the sooner we'll succeed. I'm proposing a bill with Republican Senator Preston Adams to establish a missile defense system for our country. The argument that China or Russia will consider this bill an act of provocation is hogwash. China could have their own missile defense system already, and we wouldn't know about it. Russia can't afford it but would like to have it. With due respect, this constitutes a denial of reality. I urge you to listen closely to those who have served in our Armed Forces."

When Kelli sat down, people in the audience stood up and cheered as she walked out of the chamber . . . the media was waiting for her.

Sarah Johnson of the *New York Times* stuck a microphone in front of her and asked, "Congresswoman Palmer, why are you so concerned?"

"Because I've spent a long time in the military service, and President Diamond has not! It's like the Old West . . . when the Indians are circling the wagons, you never know where the next arrow is coming from. You have to equal the playing field."

President Diamond was enraged when he heard about Kelli's remarks. Who the hell did she think she was? After all, he was the

President, and it was his job to set policies for the government. The next day, he called a press conference and alluded to her comments.

"Junior members of Congress are junior members for good reasons!" the President said, trying to hide his anger. "Some will never graduate to a senior status. Any person, even with a small brain, realizes that if we start throwing missiles at each other, we're all dead. We don't need to spend our hard earned money on expensive missile defense systems! If someone throws a missile at our country, we'll know immediately where it came from because of our global spy satellite system. Our existing multiple defenses will respond immediately and that includes terrorists.

"People elected to Congress should pause and think before they speak. The media will pick up their comments, and the public will become unduly alarmed. Another global conflict is unlikely because the weaponry, if used, would destroy the world. Each member of the Security Council around the world knows this. I recommend a peace-time defense budget for a peace-time economy. Let's use our money wisely. Just one more word of caution to junior members of Congress. Carefully select the words you use when you speak on the national pulpit!"

Kelli saw the TV coverage of President Diamond's press conference. She was furious. She was not a junior member. She had served almost four years in the House of Representatives and sat on three of the most powerful committees. She wondered if he would have said that if she had been a man.

GOING FOR BROKE

The media around the country was divided in support of Congresswoman Palmer from California and President Diamond. She was invited to appear on numerous talk shows and was asked to speak before large groups of women. She accepted as many of the invitations as she could. Not only did the people around the country soon know who she was, but the people in California did. She got some unexpected support from the members of the Armed Forces and also from the working men in the street. Instead of cutting the number of personnel in the Armed Forces, she advocated expanding the number. Retired Army Generals, Navy Admirals, and Air Force Generals came out of the woodwork to support her. She received invitations to speak at lunchtime to a large assembly of workers at the aircraft factories in California. The labor unions started to support her because they realized that there would be more jobs available if a defense missile system was built.

The general public began to focus on the issue and when she came out with the announcement that she was going to oppose Senator Farber in the primary, she received tremendous state and national publicity. However, in California, not all the publicity was favorable, and in the media there was a call for debates between the Senate primary opponents. Senator Farber was opposed to the debates, trying to shrug off Kelli as an insignificant opponent . . . not worthy of the stature of a debate. As an incumbent, Senator Farber had raised over thirty million dollars for her re-election campaign, however, most of the money was from out of state.

Kelli's political friends in the media kept pushing in a subtle way for an open forum of the issues. Whenever Senator Farber had a press conference, there was someone in the audience who asked why she wouldn't debate her opponent. It was an embarrassing question for which she didn't have a good answer. When the California political polls showed that Representative Kelli Palmer was gaining support and starting to get even with her, Farber reconsidered. She was not about to have that upstart redhead ex-Navy pilot take her job away. There were rumors in the newspapers that Senator Farber had asked for an F.B.I. check on Kelli's past. That created an uproar in the press when it turned out to be true. Farber was digging for anything that might help her defeat her opponent.

What Kelli wanted was to confront Farber before the TV cameras in a debate on the issues. She felt that she could beat her in front of the cameras. She received some unexpected help from an editorial in the *Los Angeles Times.*

"If democracy is to succeed in California, politicians should be willing to face each other and debate the issues. If they are unwilling to debate, then the public should not vote for them."

Five or six other major state newspapers came out with the same thought, and it didn't take long before Farber agreed to three debates; one in Los Angeles, one in San Francisco, and one in Sacramento.

THE FIRST DEBATE
CENTURY HOTEL
LOS ANGELES, CALIFORNIA

The Democratic Primary for the Senate seat in California had national implications. Senator Farber had been in office for twenty-three years, and the Republicans felt that she could be defeated. Governor George Allen, a young popular Republican, was going to step down and oppose her. Representative Kelli Palmer from San Diego was challenging Farber in the Democratic Primary. President Diamond let it be known that he wanted Farber to beat Kelli and made several visits to California to support her prior to the debates.

In the statewide polls, Kelli had pulled up even with Farber, and interest in the debates escalated.

The first debate was held at the Century Hotel in Los Angeles. The ballroom was set up for the debate, and questions submitted by the public were to be used. Each candidate would be given the same questions to answer. The auditorium was packed.

Marilyn Baxter, a popular TV political analyst from L.A., was the moderator. Her first question was, "Is there an immigration problem in California, and how would you handle it?"

Senator Farber was first. "That's a tough question to answer," said Farber, trying not to offend the California residents of Hispanic origin. "Our costs of educating the young and taking care of the sick and elderly immigrants, seem to be increasing. Perhaps the Federal Government could help pay for these costs. We're not going to be able to solve the problem in this state overnight. I've talked to President Diamond about this, and he's willing to help with Federal funds."

Representative Palmer: "I'm not opposed to immigration, however, I am opposed to undesirable elements getting into this country. Diversification is what made America strong. We should remember that when this country first started, all of the occupants were immigrants. The government should try to develop an orderly way, so that immigration can proceed properly and not be a burden on one state or the Federal Government. Most of these people are willing to work and are looking for a job. Proper immigrants can strengthen this country."

Moderator Marilyn Baxter: "Do you feel that our country will be attacked by missiles in the future?"

Senator Farber: "Not at all. We have too many sophisticated weapons to prevent an attack. If they shot at us, they'd be destroyed immediately. To construct a National Missile Defense System will cost trillions. How can you protect all of our big cities? The world is at peace, and our tax dollars can be spent more wisely. A vote for me will help save your tax dollars to be spent for more worthy causes."

"Representative Palmer, do you feel that we'll be attacked by missiles in the future?"

"Yes! But nobody can tell when it will happen. We don't always know what sophisticated weapons the enemy has. Because we don't know, we should be prepared to defend ourselves. With the proliferation of terrorism around the world and increasing regional conflicts, who knows when the fuse will be lit to precipitate a major war. It could also be accidental. We should be prepared to protect ourselves with a Missile Defense System."

Moderator Marilyn Baxter: "Question three: Should the President and Congressmen have physical exams every six months with the results released to the public?"

Senator Farber: "That's ridiculous! That's an invasion into my private life. That's also a prejudicial question. I'm obviously quite a few years older than my opponent, and I might add quite a bit wiser. The odds that my P.E. will show a few more physical abnor-malities than hers is evident. I oppose it."

Representative Palmer: "I have nothing to hide in regards to my health. I think that the health of the President and any Congress-man should be public knowledge, and six month physicals are a good idea. If someone is really sick, they should be out of public office. If someone has an advanced cancer, or a stroke or severe heart attack while in office, everyone suffers. The executive and legisla-tive branches still have to function. We need healthy people run-ning our government in Washington, D.C."

Moderator Marilyn Baxter: "Question four: Should there be term limits in Congress?"

Senator Farber: "I think that term limits are the most asinine idi-otic concept that has been fostered on the American people. It's probably unconstitutional. Congress would have to pass an amend-ment. It takes years to learn how the government functions in Wash-ington, D.C. Experience is necessary to make proper judgment in evaluating new bills. You learn something new each day that you're in Washington. That's why I'm a better candidate. I oppose it."

Representative Palmer: "I'm in favor of term limits . . . a total of twelve years or six terms for a member of the House of Representa-tives and three six-year terms for a Senator. There's too much of the old-boy philosophy in Congress where seniority reigns. We need new youthful ideas and concepts, so that we can compete on the world stage. Many times, the best way to have progress is to change."

The session went on for a full hour with TV coverage. It seemed as though Kelli was more spontaneous with her answers than Sen-ator Farber. However, Senator Farber was not going to give up with-out a big fight.

EXIT POLL

The major television station *WPXS* in Los Angeles decided to con-duct an exit poll as the people attending the debates came out. The exit poll was also televised. The people were randomly selected to comment about the debates. The same question was asked to everyone.

"Who do you think won the debate, and which one will be our next Senator?"

"Seven to five for the redhead," said the first man to comment. "Why?"

"She's younger, projects better, and thinks on her feet. Besides that, she's good looking!"

A woman was asked the same question: "Who do you think will be the next Senator?"

"If Farber was younger, she'd be tough and have a chance. Kelli has some good ideas though and will probably win."

A man listening to the interview broke into the conversation. "Yeh. They're like two female pit bulls going for the jugular. All candidates should have to debate the issues."

A young man walked by. "Who would you want to be your next Senator, Palmer or Farber?"

"That Kelli gal! She's seen it all, flying jets, Top Gun pilot, and that Irish temper . . . I'd hate to have a fight with her. Hell, she shot down a Chinese pilot and floated around in the Pacific for a while. She's tough. She's got my vote!"

An elderly gray-haired woman walked out and was asked the same question.

"I think Senator Farber will win! She's got all that experience and seniority in office."

The young college groups organized to try to help Kelli. They were loud, aggressive, and enthusiastic. Farber was surprised by Kelli's public support. Some of the older age retirees tried to organize to help Farber. They weren't successful, weren't as enthusiastic, and did not have the energy that the younger voters had. The generation gap between Kelli and Farber was quite evident. Farber was desperate. She decided to use some of her thirty million to increase her negative TV ads . . . it didn't work; it backfired. She was beginning to see the handwriting on the wall. You could see on her face that she was discouraged when she tried to answer questions in the debates in Sacramento and San Francisco . . . her confidence was gone, and her answers were not spontaneous. Kelli had a charisma that was infectious and overwhelming . . . she was on a roll. The media projected a landslide victory for her. President Diamond and other prominent senior senators tried to help Senator Farber. In the Democratic party's senate primary, Kelli won in a landslide. With her victory, she was able to raise large sums of money for her campaign and went on to debate Governor Allen for the senator's job.

In the debates, Governor Allen stressed that he was a conservative and that he wanted to make the government in Washington smaller and not bigger. In one of the debates he was asked, "Are you a conservative, Governor Allen?"

"Yes," he replied.

"Please define a conservative."

"A conservative is someone who is opposed to change. Someone who does not want to increase government spending. I believe in traditional values. I'm opposed to 'free loaders'. We have too many social programs that are expensive and accomplish nothing."

Kelli was asked if she was a conservative.

"Not at all," she replied.

"What are you?"

"I suppose you could say that I'm a liberal. I support change. Things are happening so rapidly in our global society that if you don't adapt rapidly to what is happening, you're lost in the shuffle."

ELECTION DAY
NOVEMBER 2014
CALIFORNIA

Because of the publicity associated with the Senate Democratic Primary, Kelli's momentum continued, and she crept ahead of Governor Allen in the polls. She finally won big. Kelli Fitzgerald Palmer was the new young senator from California.

2015

XII

AIR DEFENSE ARTILLERY CENTER HEADQUARTERS, WASHINGTON, D.C.

1:00 A.M.
JULY 4, 2015 A.D.

At 1:00 A.M., Major General Jonathan Black and three younger officers arrived at the main Air Defense Artillery Launching Center for Washington, D.C. It was not unusual to see General Black checking the armed forces defense units in the middle of the night. The military security personnel at the gate immediately recognized the familiar gold braid on the visor of his cap and the two stars on his shoulders designating his Major General status. They saluted and let him in.

All of the defensive units: Patriots, Hawks, Avengers, and the latest defensive unit, Starlite, came under Major General Black's command. He was in charge of numerous operational defense missile sites around Washington, D.C.; many of them were mobile, so a potential enemy did not know their exact location.

The control for firing the defensive missiles in Washington, D.C. is on the ground because if the AWAC radar command plane is shot out of the air, each ground defensive unit can then respond separately. A strict chain of command prevents any half-cocked unit from inadvertently starting a real war. The Pentagon has the ultimate control.

The General's car with two stars emblazoned on the bumper, drove to the main control center where there were two armed sentries outside.

Three men, dressed in green-black fatigues and carrying automatic pistols with silencers, shot the two sentries dead. Not a sound was heard.

The Major General put his identification card into the door.

Lieutenant Colonel Brown recognized Major General Black and saluted as he entered. The three men in the green-black fatigues quickly followed, shot, and killed six men in the Control Center. They kept alive the man on the main console as well as Colonel Brown because they would need them later. They quickly taped their mouths shut and tied their hands behind their back. The Command Center was secured in about thirty seconds.

The two sentry guards who were killed had their uniforms and photo ID cards removed. Two of the invaders took their places outside the entrance to the Control Center.

"Stand by to destroy the antenna screen and the connections to the electrical power plant at 2:00 A.M.," the General said. "Locate the secret codes for firing. Colonel Brown should have some keys to a locked control box around here. They're probably in his pocket."

The Colonel and the man on the console put up a struggle, but the intruders hit them with the butt of their guns and found the keys.

Now there was no way that anyone could fire defensive missiles from this site.

The General asked one of the intruders to put some static in the communications system. "Did you bring the right electronic tools for the job?"

"Yes," he replied.

"We're going to foul up the chain of command. Set up that recording of Black's voice, so we can hook into the main communications center at the Pentagon and the AWACs plane. I'll tell you when to activate it."

Frank and his assistant began to work rapidly to hook into the integrated communication lines.

At 1:45 A.M. he announced, "I think I'm all set. We probably ought to check it out. Do you have that on-call list we stole from the Pentagon?"

"We do."

"Good."

"Let me have CD number two."

Frank activated the disk and pressed the button for the lines to the Pentagon. An electronic voice recognition device cleared the disk. Although the message was automatically garbled, it was heard loud and clear at the Pentagon, with some slight static.

"This is Major General Black. This is to inform you that we will be test firing some starlight missiles at 2:30 A.M. off the shores of Maryland. This is a surprise test to make sure everyone is alert and on the ball."

"That's crazy," replied Colonel Armstrong who had heard the message at the Pentagon Control Center. "Have you cleared this with the AWACs?"

"Yes," the general proclaimed over the static.

"Check out your equipment; we're getting a lot of static over here."

"Roger."

"We've got a bunch of idiots in the armed forces," said Armstrong. "They're afraid of their own shadows."

"I agree," said Major Bennett. "However, I can understand why they're doing it. It's better to have up-tight security and to be safe, rather than to be sorry."

"I don't ever recall firing defensive missiles at night for practice around Washington, do you?" asked Armstrong.

"That's probably why they're doing it," replied Bennett. "If someone's going to try a surprise attack, the best time to do it would be when it's dark and in the early morning."

"If the Pentagon calls again, give them all the static you can," said General Black. "Now, I want you to hook into all the Patriot, Avenger, Hawk, and Starlite defensive units. You have the list."

"Put on disk number one, Frank."

Frank activated the CD. It was 2:00 A.M. Major General

Jonathan Black's voice came through. "This is Major General Black at the D.C. Defensive Command Center. This morning at 0230 we will be practicing some missile shots off the Maryland shores. This is strictly a practice session. Do not go into an alert unless you hear my voice. I repeat. This is a practice session. Do not fire your defensive missiles. That's an order!"

Because this was a most unusual order, some of the defensive units challenged the order. They tried to call back for more details. All they got was static on their lines.

THE WHITE HOUSE
1600 PENNSYLVANIA AVENUE
WASHINGTON, D.C.
2:00 A.M.
JULY   2015

At 2:00 A.M. the phone rang at the main switchboard of the White House.

"I need to talk to the President directly. It's urgent," said the caller.

"He's a very busy man. He's asleep and can't just take any phone call," said the operator. "Who's calling?"

"My name is John McKittrick," he replied. "I know that you know exactly where this call is coming from."

"State your business," said the operator, realizing that she might be dealing with a hoax call.

"My business is to give you a warning."

"Please clarify your statement," replied the operator. It was standard procedure for the White House to tape and locate all calls. The caller was dialing from St. Louis, Missouri.

"I know you know I'm calling from St. Louis," said the caller. "That won't be helpful to you. I'm going to make this statement just once. Our militia group has been broken up and dishonored by our government. We're mad as hell, so we are going to get revenge. The government is destroying freedom! The people running the government are crooks! There is a conspiracy by our elected officials to destroy our government, and we're going to do something about it. We're going to take our government back and give it to the people, just like they did in the American Revolutionary War."

By now a Secret Service Agent, who was on duty, began listening on the other end of the line with the operator. The operator was trying to get the caller to continue talking.

"Have you discussed your problem with your Congressman?" asked the operator.

"He's just like the rest of the bums. The only reason he's a Congressman is to see how much money he can make. He was a lousy school teacher before he became a Congressman, and now he's a multimillionaire. All he does is write books, raise taxes and his own salary. He doesn't listen to the wishes of the people."

"You have the option of voting him out of office if you don't like him."

"It's impossible to vote him out! The incumbents have all the money for advertising on television and radio. Some of them are so rich that they can pay for it themselves. Campaign finance controls are a laugh. Who knows where the money is coming from? It's the fox watching the chicken coop. Congress doesn't represent the people anymore. They don't listen. They don't communicate. They don't do what the people want. They're in the pockets of the big corporations. You scratch my back, I'll scratch yours. My representative is a piss-poor excuse for a Congressman. Enough of this chit-chat. When I hang up, we'll give you about twenty minutes . . . then a missile will be fired at the White House. We're really not after you! If you run real fast, you can get your ass out of there before it hits."

The operator heard a click as the caller hung up.

She'd received crackpot calls like this before, but something about this call made her particularly uneasy.

The senior security agent on call, Bill Clark, was contacted immediately. The agent who listened to the call felt it was a real threat and not a hoax—although a missile attack seemed preposterous.

"My God! What do we do now? Should we wake up the President and get him out of here if it's real? If it's a fake, I'm going to look like an asshole."

"It's better for you to look like an asshole and have the President be safe. Or would you rather have the White House blown to smithereens with the President in it?"

"Call the security agent outside the President's bedroom and tell him to knock on the door to wake him up. I need to talk to him."

President Diamond got on the phone. "What's up Bill?"

"We've received a phone call from a crazy nut who told the operator that a missile is going to be fired at the White House."

"Come on, Bill, I don't need to hear about crank calls in the middle of the night. That's nonsense! No one can do that!"

"I know, Mr. President. But I just can't trust rationality right now. It's impossible to tell if it's the real thing or not. As you know, anything can happen in this cockeyed world of ours, Mr. President. I think it might be wise for you and your wife to take the helicopter to Camp David or to the relocation center in the Blue Ridge Mountains right away!"

"That's kind of drastic, isn't it, Bill?"

"Maybe, Mr. President, but we can't take any chances. I want you out of here right now!"

"I thought I'd heard everything . . . but this one takes the cake!"

The President sighed, "I'll be right there with my wife as soon as we dress." Kathryn, his wife, was already awake. They quickly grabbed some clothes and hurried to the helicopter pad.

It was 2:09 A.M.

Colonel Al Atwood, the Marine Corps helicopter pilot, was the first to get to the Presidential Hawk Sikorsky helicopter on the pad at the White House. It was standard procedure to have a helicopter on the pad at all times when the President was in residence. The Pentagon's National Military Command Center and Andrews Air Force Base were told they might be put on red alert, and the Reagan National Airport's control towers were told that commercial planes might be diverted. Advanced night attack fighter planes, some equipped with air to air missiles and others with air to ground FUR pods, took off from Andrews Air Force Base to escort the President's helicopter. His plane was the top of the line with a VIP interior, including cabin soundproofing, and was fitted with the most advanced weather radar and upgrades of the HIRSS to afford the best possible protection against shoulder launched infrared homing missiles.

The helicopter can detect hostile electronic emissions and has radar warning receivers and jammers with chaff-flare dispensers. In order for the President to be able to keep in touch to maintain secure worldwide communications, a cabin radio operator's position is provided with extensive state-of-the-art highly sophisticated electronics, all hardened against electromagnetic pulse.

President Diamond was met at the ramp by the Chief Secret Service Agent, Jack Ross, who would be flying with him.

"What's up, Jack?" asked the President.

"We have a missile threat against the White House, Sir."

"Yes, I know. Did they notify the Air Defense units?"

"Not yet, Sir. It may be just a hoax call."

"Might be a good time to see if they're on the ball," replied the President.

"Should I tell the Pentagon Command Center what you've suggested?"

"No. Let them run their own show. Where are we headed?" asked the President.

"We can go southwest to the relocation center or to Camp David up north."

"I don't think this is anything to worry about. Let's head to Camp David."

"As you wish, Mr. President. Looks like a nice clear night. Too bad you have to lose some sleep."

"Well, I guess that goes with the job," replied the President as he and his wife hurriedly boarded the helicopter.

Colonel Atwood, the President's chief pilot, notified Andrews Air Force Base when they were airborne as they headed to Camp David.

"This is U.S. 1, now airborne. Request altitude and vector clearance for C.D."

"U.S. 1, we have you on our scope, Vector 130 at 4,000 feet. Area has been cleared of aircraft."

Colonel Atwood did not like the altitude assigned because of the potential missile threat. He called back into base.

"Request reassign lower altitude."

"Okay, 500 feet," replied base. "We'll clear the area."

Back in the helicopter, President Diamond's radio operator contacted the control center at the Pentagon.

"Has anything developed out there?"

"Not a thing," replied Colonial Armstrong, the duty officer in charge at the National Control Center in the Pentagon.

"We haven't upgraded the alert since nothing more has happened."

Colonel Atwood heard from his fighter cover overhead, F-51 night fighters. Major Skip Henderson was the lead pilot.

"U.S. 1, this is Skipjack 2. Come in please. Do you read me?"

"Roger, Skipjack."

Due to the slow speed of the helicopter, all the planes were moving along at only two-hundred miles per hour headed northwest towards Maryland and Camp David. Suddenly, Colonel Atwood saw a fuzzy picture on his HUD Doppler radar screen. His radar-radio operator also noticed it on his second set. The picture there was fuzzy, too. The radar warning receivers lit up and started to beep. Atwood turned on his landing lights and decided to go on visual flight pattern. Something unusual was happening. It looked like someone was trying to jam his radar screen or home in on his radio or radar to fire a missile at him.

"Skipjack 2, this is U.S.1. My radar is malfunctioning. I wonder if someone has put a radar marker on my helicopter. What the hell is going on?"

"U.S. 1, this is Skipjack 2. 1 don't know. There's something wrong with my radar, too!"

*   *   *

The head fighter pilot, Major Skip Henderson, was flying cover in the general vicinity of the President's plane, when a ball of fire burst brightly just below him in the black of night.

"God damn. Someone's firing missiles at us. I think it's made a hit! It hope it isn't the helicopter. I'd better check it out.

"U.S. 1, this is Skipjack 2. Do you read me? Please respond."

There was no answer. Henderson repeated the coded call to the President's plane.

"U.S. 1. Do you read me? Are you all right?"

The silence that followed was terrifying. There was still no answer.

"Holy shit!" Henderson muttered. "I think the President's plane has been shot down! Base Control, this is Skipjack 2. The President's plane may have been shot down. U.S.1 has not answered my repeated calls. He was right below me when a missile hit! Request instructions."

"Skipjack 2, this is Base Control. Please repeat. Can you confirm. Repeat . . ."

"No," replied Skipjack 2.

"We've lost sight of the President's helicopter. It was right below us."

"We've also lost radio and radar contact."

Back at Base Control, Colonel Armstrong was sweating bullets. U.S.1 was off their radar screen too.

"We've got to know what happened to the President and his helicopter! Keep calling his radio. If he's not down, he should hear us. He has sophisticated communication equipment on that helicopter. Keep calling. We have to know if the President's plane has been shot down!"

"U.S.1, U.S.1., do you read me? This is an emergency transmission! Do you read me? This is Base Control." There was still no response.

"This country's in deep shit!" said Armstrong.

"Keep calling! Keep transmitting! Christ, what the fuck do we do now?"

"Get General Sherman in here right away! He's the senior General on call. Let him make the decisions. They're too big for me to make! Things are happening too fast. I need help! Where is he?"

"He's en route," replied one of the aides.

"God damn it! Where's the Vice President? Does anyone know? Call the White House and see if they know. He may be in charge now."

A call was placed to the White House and the on-call secret service agent replied, "The Vice President's in Boston."

"Contact him and tell him what's going on," said Armstrong. "Tell him that the President's helicopter may have been shot down. Put on extra secret servicemen to guard him!"

"Roger."

"Has U.S.1. replied yet?"

"No, Sir! Their radio is dead."

"Keep calling! Call Skipjack 2 again. See if they know anything."

"Skipjack 2, Skipjack 2, do you see U.S.1. anywhere in the air around you? You've been tailing him."

"Base Control, this is Skipjack 2. There's no helicopter up here. I'm afraid he's down!"

"Have you seen any plane's debris or fires on the ground?"

"No, Sir! Nothing."

"We've got big troubles! Atwood's not answering. The President's plane is missing and probably is blown up. We can't find the Vice President. Missiles are flying all over the place. For all we know, someone may be firing ICBM's at us already. What a disaster! Everything's fucked up . . . what can we do?"

"Have we tried the back-up transmission system?" asked Armstrong.

"Yes, Sir! No reply."

"Keep calling! God! This country's in big trouble!"

Colonel Atwood immediately pointed the nose of the helicopter down and decided to get on the deck close to the surface of the ground.

He pointed his landing lights straight downward, saw an open field, and put the helicopter on the ground.

He immediately instructed his co-pilot and navigator to turn off all the radio and radar equipment. Atwood saw a bright incandescent explosion of lights and a loud booming sound in the sky.

"What was that?" asked the President.

"It sounded like an explosion in the air overhead."

The answer came quickly over the radio.

"A ground-to-air missile has just hit one of our planes or the President's helicopter," said Skipjack 2.

He used his intercom mike and told the President, "Someone has just shot down one of our planes."

"Is there a problem?" asked the President.

"There could be," he replied.

"Oh, my God!" shouted the President. "The stupid bastards were shooting at us!"

"Could be," replied Colonel Atwood, "or our military defense units are all fucked up."

"Somebody may be trying to destroy this country," said President Diamond.

"Possibly," replied Atwood. "if that's what this is."

"I've got the electronic football that only I can activate to tell the military to retaliate and I don't know what the fuck is going on around here! Who's going to tell me what to do? I'm all by myself with only Kathryn and Jack Ross. Contact the Pentagon Control Center and see if they know what's going on. Has NORAD been alerted?"

"I'm sure the Pentagon Control Center has alerted them if they need to be," said Atwood.

"What do you think is going on, Colonel?"

"I'm in the dark just like you," he replied.

"Well, call the Pentagon and find out what the hell's going on! I'm the one guy who has to know!"

"Mr. President, I don't think we should be using our radio right now. They could be homing in on us."

"Okay," replied the President. "However, we can't wait too long."

*   *   *

Atwood did not want to make a radio transmission. He kept stalling while the President fumed.

"God damn it! Call the Base Control."

"Mr. President, we don't know whose firing those missiles and how they're controlled. They may have already located us by satellite or are using some new method of locating and firing their missiles. They could home in our radio or radar. We've got to maintain radio silence and leave our radar turned off!"

"This helicopter is supposed to have sophisticated protection against homing missiles," said the President.

"It does," said Atwood.

"Use it then!" he replied.

"We are!" replied Atwood.

"I've got to know what's going on right now! This country could be destroyed in minutes."

"I realize that," replied Atwood.

After a short period, he made a transmission to Base Control:

"Base Control. This is U.S. 1. Some missiles have been fired around us, and we believe we've had a missile fired at us. We're now on the ground. What's going on?"

"Thank God, you're safe!" said Base Control. "We thought your helicopter was hit. We don't know what's going on. It looks like a missile was fired at you from somewhere in Maryland or a sub off-shore."

"We need more information than that!" hollered the President. "If some country's firing missiles at us, we have to respond."

"U.S. 1, we're doing the best we can. We'll transmit all information as we obtain it."

There were beads of sweat on the President's forehead. He turned to Colonel Atwood and asked, "What should I do?"

"We can't do anything until we find out what's going on," he replied.

President Diamond turned to Jack Ross, his senior security agent. His hands were shaking, and he had a bewildered look on his face.

"Jack, you've got to help me."

"What can I do?" he replied.

"Try to tell me what to do!"

"We just have to wait and see what develops," said Jack. "You can't do anything if you don't know what's going on."

He turned to his wife, "Kathryn, I'm all alone. I don't know what to do. I don't have enough information to make a proper response! Everything's all fucked up!"

"Well, we won't do anything until we get more information," she replied.

"I'm scared. No human being should control the destiny of the world."

"I agree," said Kathryn.

"Why is God doing this?"

Kathryn looked at her husband. The President was shaking like a leaf. She knew she had to give him support, but before she could check her response, she blurted out, "I can think of a lot of reasons why He has allowed this to happen. Perhaps we should pray to God for His help."

"It may be too late," replied the President. "With all those missiles flying around, it could be a very short prayer."

"A short prayer is better than none! Start praying."

The President put his two hands over his face; he could have been praying or crying. He obviously was confused and visibly upset. Kathryn over heard him say in a loud voice, "God, help us. Please answer my prayer!"

The Pentagon was in complete bedlam.

"We're going into top alert," said the duty officer, Colonel Frank Armstrong. "Notify the Air Combat Center to scramble more fighters at Andrews Air Force Base and at Patuxant River, Maryland. Alert the ground Air Defense Forces for Washington.

"Has the Chairman of the Joint Chiefs been notified? Tell him someone is trying to kill the President. A missile has been fired at his helicopter, and they're still firing missiles."

"He's been called. We haven't reached him. He's out of the country," said an aide.

Marine Lt. General Mike Sherman finally showed up and quickly replaced Colonel Armstrong. He was an experienced combat General.

"Check our intelligence spy satellites and call our Air Force AWACS radar plane to get a precise read on just where that missile was fired from. Also check out all the nuclear silos around the world to see if they're uncovered in preparation for firing. We have to find out quickly if we're dealing with a domestic or an international problem. Any vital information is to be transmitted to the President immediately. Call to see if the President's still okay."

It seemed like a long time before Colonel Atwood responded and called C.I.C. Base Control back. "The President's okay. The place is swarming with state police and firemen. We're keeping the President and his wife in the helicopter in case we have to get out of here in a hurry. We're limiting all radio transmissions."

"Good. The President's still safe," said Sherman.

"C.I.C. Base, this is Skipjack 2."

"We have now confirmed that one of our fighter planes has been shot down by a ground-to-air missile. I am requesting permission to knock out the missile site because two more missiles have been fired at us."

"Hold," replied General Sherman. "That could be one of our own S.A.M. defensive units that's fucked up. Under the rules of engagement, you can respond, but first we have to find out what is going on. Do you know the direction of the missile site?"

"It looks like the missile site is somewhere along the coast of Maryland. It could be an off-shore sub that fired."

"Get me an accurate global read! Do we have one of our own mobile defensive units there?" Sherman hollered at Air Plot.

"No, Sir."

"Wait for instructions," he replied to Skipjack 2.

"Check with the spy satellites. See where they got the infrared radar reading when those missiles were fired. Get with it!"

"Sir, the spy satellites tracking room called and said the missiles were fired near the eastern shores in Maryland. They think they're from that old Air Force base that was closed."

"How could that be?" said Sherman. "We don't have any S.A.M. sites there!"

"Air plot says that's where they came from."

"Great!" said Sherman. "Get the geographical coordinates of the base. Have our air defense systems checked in?"

"No! We can't get through to the Main Air Defense Artillary Launching Center . . . all we got is static."

"How about the ground defensive units? The mobile defensive units?"

"We're having trouble with them too! We're trying to call some of them on the phone right now."

"Notify all commercial aircraft in the Washington area to get the hell out of here and go to secondary landing fields. We don't want to be shooting them out of the air."

"Yes, Sir."

"Notify the President that it's a local missile firing so far. He's to stay where he is. We'll keep in continuous contact if something else develops. Notify Lieutenant General Paul Donovan at the Quantico Marine barracks that we want him to send an armed Marine battalion up to that site in Maryland. Also notify the police in that area to approach and secure, but not enter the old air base site. They are not to let anyone leave the area.

"Tell Andrews Air Force Base to get some electronic counter measure planes up in the air pronto to jam their ground-to-air radar. We don't want any more planes shot down!. If they continue to fire missiles, we'll have to knock them out. Have Skipjack's planes stand by," he bellowed. "Have the Naval Air Station at Patuxant River launch some aircraft with MK-84 drag bombs."

By now the Pentagon's National Central Intelligence Center was slowly filling up with on-call high-ranking officers. Phones were

ringing off the wall. NORAD was on full alert. TV and radio people in Washington began to call, demanding information. The Vice
President was finally located in Boston, Massachusetts, and more
security agents were assigned to him in case something happened
to the President. The emergency broadcasting signal for radio and
TV had been put on the airways. It was almost 3:00 A.M. on the
East Coast, and everyone was sleeping—practically no one heard
the national alert. The Vice President said he didn't have an electronic football in case he needed to communicate with the military.

"Tell him we'll be in constant touch with him. If we ever get
through this, we'll have to address that issue," said Sherman.
"Someone should have thought about that before today."

"General Sherman, the Chairman of the Joint Chiefs of Staff is
on the phone."

"Where is he calling from?"

"He's at a NATO meeting in England and was informed about
the missile firing by British Intelligence. He said he's going to the
British Command Center outside London to monitor the action.
He wants to be fully advised."

"Colonel Armstrong, that's your job," said Sherman. "You take
the call and tell him it looks like a domestic terrorist attack against
the President—so far. Three missiles have been fired, and we have
one jet fighter shot down."

"General Paul Donovan from Quantico is on the line. He wants
more details about the abandoned Air Force base in Maryland. He
wants to know if you're absolutely sure that's where the missiles
came from and not from off-shore submarines."

"Let me have the phone," replied Sherman. "Paul, someone attempted to fire a missile at the President's helicopter while he was
en route to Camp David. A ground-to-air missile shot down one
of our jet fighter cover planes. The missile site is at the closed Air
Force base in Maryland. Our global satellites have confirmed this.
We need to find out who's behind this. We need information. Take
prisoners if you can."

"We're taking a couple of battalions with some armor and missile launchers to counter their fire power," said Donovan.

"Good," replied Sherman. "Proceed with caution. We'll give you air support and keep in constant communication."

"Sir, another missile has been fired. The spy satellite picked it up."

"Any direction on the missile?"

"Yes, it's headed this way—right at us or the White House."

"Christ, what's going to happen next?" shouted Sherman as he watched the command radar screen. "I hope that Air Defense Artillery Brigade knows what the fuck they're doing. They ought to be able to shoot it down."

INTERCONTINENTAL BALLISTIC MISSILE
COMMAND CENTER
IN RUSSIA
50 MILES NORTH OF MOSCOW
JULY 4, 2015 A.D.

"Our spy satellites have picked up an infrared thermal radiation blip on our screen. It's on the East Coast of the United States," Chief of Staff, Viktor Romanov, notified Marshal Vladimir Bolgansky.

"We'd better find out what that blip signifies in a hurry," he replied. "Alert our mobile Intercontinental Ballistic Group and inform the military."

"Yes, Sir," replied the Chief of Staff.

"Intensify the tracking of the U.S. nuclear submarine fleet. Do we know where they all are?"

"That's impossible!" replied Romanov.

"Either someone is attacking the U.S. with missiles, or they've had an accident at one of their nuclear plants. Just where was that blip located?"

"Not too far from Washington, D.C. It looks like it's slightly north of the city in Maryland or Delaware."

"What time is it over there?

"About 2:30 A.M., Sir."

"Monitor that area closely."

"I'm not aware of any nuclear testing grounds near Washington, D.C. Perhaps a factory blew up. Something weird might have happened. But I don't like the looks of this," said Vladimir. "What happens to them could affect all of us. Check in with our Air Command Control Center and see if they have more accurate information. Also keep them on alert and in the air."

"Yes, Sir," replied Romanov. His hands were shaking slightly, and there were beads of sweat on his forehead. "We are prepared, Marshal. We have our land-based and mobile intercontinental ballistic missiles deployed. Our submarines can launch their ICBMs once they receive the order."

"Prepared for what?" asked Marshal Bolgansky. "Destruction of all living things on this earth? The United States has their nuclear submarines surrounding our borders under the ocean. Our country would become a blob on a blotter if they fired at us."

"What do you think is going on?" asked Romanov.

"There has been a nuclear accident, or a missile has been accidentally fired from a S.A.M. installation or a submarine off the coastline. Either way, we're all in deep shit!"

Viktor nodded his head again in agreement. The sweat was pouring off of his forehead now. Though both of them had led numerous war games using computer assisted mathematical simulations, they knew this was different. Russia's electronic surveillance measures (ESMs), their detection sensors, had picked up the emission signatures of a big threat.

"Get Prime Minister Malinkov on the phone," said Marshal Bolgansky. "Immediately!"

"Yorgi, this is Marshal Bolgansky. We have a serious problem developing. Our surveillance sensors have picked up the firing of a surface-to-air missile, or there has been a nuclear accident just north of Washington, D.C. We have to call Washington and find out what's going on."

"Their Navy may just be practicing firing missiles," said Yorgi.

"Maybe they're practicing to fire missiles at us?"

"I don't think so."

"Call President Platov immediately and have him call President Diamond," said Yorgi.

Marshal Bolgansky told one of his aides to get President Platov on the phone.

"President Platov, this is Marshal Bolgansky on the phone. Our military satellites have picked up missile firings around Washington, D.C. Something big may be developing in the U.S.A. We don't know what's going on."

"What do you mean you don't know what's going on? You're the one who is suppose to be telling me what's going on, not asking me! You're the military!"

"We don't know exactly."

"That's great!" replied Platov.

"Have we accidentally fired any missiles at the United States?"

"Not yet," replied Bolgansky.

"Good! Then, what's going on? What's the big problem?"

"We don't know. Some other country may be firing at them, although we can't confirm. It could be China for all we know, or it could have come from a submarine. It could be terrorists trying to disrupt and destroy the U.S. government. It could be a nuclear accident, or possibly a domestic uprising."

"It can't be a domestic uprising, you stupid ass! Missiles have been fired!" said Platov. "Use your head! Civilians don't shoot missiles! I don't see any reason to call him. You don't have enough information yet. We'd sound like a bunch of stupid idiots! Keep me informed, if and when there are any new developments." With that comment, he hung up the phone.

Marshal Bolgansky was not happy with President Platov's responses.

"Politicians don't think like the military," he said to Viktor.

Viktor nodded his head.

"Sometimes I worry about our leaders and the stability of our government. Maybe the U.S. government is just as unstable as they think we are. When you start facing each other with nuclear bombs that can destroy civilization, the type of government you have means nothing. It's the individuals at the top, just like you and me, Viktor, who are the most important. We control the destiny of the world by our actions. The human factor is more important than all those sophisticated computerized intercontinental missiles."

Romanov nodded his head again in agreement. He was obviously agitated, disturbed, and sweating profusely.

"People wonder how you become paranoid," said Vladimir. "I worry that some demented individual might sit in our shoes."

Just then a junior officer, watching a screen in the control center, broke into their conversation. "We have another blip from that same spot on the screen. It looks like a missile heading toward Washington, D.C!"

"Viktor, get President Platov back on the phone—immediately! Something big is taking place. I think some other country with nuclear weapons is firing at Washington. It could be anyone. It could be the Arabs or Chinese or some small country with grandiose ideas. Who knows who it could be? What we have to worry about is whether they think we're firing those missiles at them and if they plan to retaliate."

"Have they opened their silos?"

"Yes, they have."

"President Platov must talk to President Diamond immediately! He's got to tell him that we are not firing missiles at the United States."

"Will they believe us?" asked Viktor. "When the Japanese hit Pearl Harbor on a Sunday morning, the Japanese Ambassador to the United States was talking peace in Washington, D.C."

"They've got to believe us! I'm sure their own spy satellites know that none of those missiles were fired from Russia. By now they should know that they were fired within their own boundaries or by an enemy submarine off shore."

"But how do they know that we didn't fire them?"

"Da, da," said Viktor.

"Do we have any of our submarines off the coast in that area?"

"I don't know," he replied.

"We'd better find out in a hurry. If we do, we'd better get them the hell out of there as fast as possible."

The junior officer, Colonel Slobov, broke into the conversation. "That missile heading towards Washington hit some big building. It could have been the White House!"

"If the President was in that White House, he's gone!" said Vladimir.

"President Platov's on the phone," said one of the aides.

Vladimir Bolgansky got on the phone. "Our spy satellites tell us missiles have been fired in Maryland, and another missile has just been fired at the White House. It may have been destroyed. You'd better try to contact President Diamond on the phone right away."

"That's ridiculous! If he was in the White House, he's dead!"

INTERCONTINENTAL BALLISTIC MISSILE
COMMAND CENTER IN CHINA
100 MILES SOUTH OF BEIJING
JULY 4, 2015 A.D.

General Li Chen, the duty officer in charge, saw the infrared thermal emissions in the U.S.A. He notified Lieutenant General Zeng Ping.

"It looks like the Americans have had an accident in a nuclear plant."

"I don't think there's a nuclear plant in that area," replied Chen. "It could be a submarine off the shore firing a missile at something."

"Why would they fire a missile in Maryland at the White House—unless the missile misfired and went off course? Are the Russians or someone else starting an attack on America?"

"We're all in trouble if they are," said Chen.

"What do we do if they start firing intercontinental nuclear missiles at each other or if one of them starts firing at us?"

"We'll have to notify our people to take shelter."

"How are you going to notify the entire population, including all the peasants?"

"I don't know."

"Where can you find a safe shelter for a billion people?"

"That's the problem," replied Chen. "There's no place to hide from a nuclear bomb."

"We'd better notify the Prime Minister."

"Prime Minister Zaido, this is General Chen. Missiles are being fired on the coast of America. Someone might be starting a war."

"Nothing we can do about that. Maybe it's terrorists from the Far East. They've got submarines now," said Zaido.

"I'm sure if they got that close to the U.S. shoreline, they'd be followed by American nuclear subs," said Chen. "They'd be knocked out of the water."

"What do you want me to do?" asked the Prime Minister.

"We have to find out who shot that missile. Call Russia and see if they're involved?"

"They wouldn't tell us," said Zaido.

"We'd better call the Americans. I'll call the Pentagon," said Chen."

General Chen made a call on his emergency red phone to the Pentagon C.I.C. A military aide picked it up.

"What's going on in your country? Missiles are being fired all over the place, and it looks like one has shot a plane down."

The phone was given to Colonel Armstrong. "General, we don't know what's going on yet. We do not know who fired the missiles. As soon as we find out, we'll notify you."

"I called to tell you that we did not fire those missiles," said Chen. "We don't want you firing at us!"

"Thank you! We're glad to know that!" said Armstrong, as he hung up the phone.

Back in the weapons control center outside Beijing, General Li Chen saw another missile firing on the scope. A missile was headed for Washington, D.C. He couldn't believe it.

"This looks like war. The question is, what should we do? What should our response be? Whose side are we on?"

"Call the Russians. I hope they're not stupid enough to start a nuclear war," said General Ping.

General Chen contacted the Russians on the video phone. General Romanov took the call.

"General Romanov, this is General Chen. I'm sure you've seen on your global satellites those missiles that were fired from Maryland towards Washington, D.C. To be frank, we don't know what's going on over there. Do you?"

"Russia has gone into a national alert," said Romanov. "We're not firing those missiles. Are you?"

"No, and we don't have any submarines in the area. We've been contacting our intelligence units around the world, and we're not getting any answers. We don't know who's behind this."

"I hope some stupid ass isn't trying to start a war because if they are, they could accidentally destroy the world! The fuse has been lit."

General Sherman watched the missile on the screen heading straight for Washington, D.C. and the White House. He waited for the Washington, D.C. Defense Center to intercept it . . . but there was no response.

"Call them and find out what the hell's going on." said Sherman. "They're suppose to be shooting at those missiles."

"There's still static on the line," said Armstrong.

"Something's drastically wrong!" remarked Sherman.

Finally, he saw a smaller missile on the screen, probably an Avenger or Hawk going for but missing the cruise missile. The missile continued and kept heading for Washington, D.C. It was traveling so fast that they knew that they couldn't respond. They were helpless. A tremendous explosion rattled and broke some of the windows in the Pentagon. The cruise missile hit a building near the Pentagon.

"Holy shit!" shouted Sherman. "Call that air defense brigade and ask them what the fuck is going on! A few heads are going to roll over there! Their job is to shoot down enemy missiles, not to sit on

their ass! Colonel Armstrong, ask them why the hell they're not firing at those missiles."

"Sir, we haven't been able to get through to them. All we get is
static. Something's wrong with the communication system."

"Have you used the back-up system?"

"Yes. All we get is static on that system too!"

"We're in deep shit!" said Sherman.

"Check in with our AWAC control center."

Colonel Armstrong called Colonel Steve Finley at the AWACs
control center. "We've been unable to contact the D.C. Defensive
Control Unit. Do you know what's going on? All we get is static."

"During the past hour, that's all I get, too," he replied. "Something is all screwed up! Missiles are flying all over the place, and nobody knows what the fuck is going on," said Steve. "No one's trying
to shoot them down. I'll contact the outlying units and call you
right back."

He called back two minutes later.

"One of the units reported they received a coded voice message
from General Black, stating they would be test firing starlight missiles off the Maryland shores."

"That's it," said Armstrong. "Either General Black has screwed
up, or someone's taken over the Defensive Control Center for
D.C."

He quickly notified General Sherman.

"Get in touch with the Chief of Staff for that base, and tell him
to get his ass over there. Tell him to take an armed Marine company with him."

"We've got to knock out that ground missile site in Maryland
ourselves," said Mike Sherman. "It's either one of our own mobile
missile units that's fucked up, or it's been taken over by someone.
Either way, it has to go!"

"What kind of weapons are Skipjack's night squadron armed
with?" asked Sherman.

"They're loaded with the latest missiles," said Colonel Armstrong.

"Does he have any air-to-ground missiles?"

"I'm sure the planes do," replied Stuart, a gunnery officer. "Some have high speed anti-radiation missiles, and others have special seeker heads that home in on enemy emitting radars."

"We can't wait for Donovan's Marines to get to Maryland to secure that base. Washington could be destroyed by then."

"Give Skipjack the order to home in and knock out the ground missile site in Maryland," Sherman said. "Notify Donovan."

"Skipjack, this is D.C. Base. Permission to knock out ground-to-air missile site—acknowledge."

"Roger, D.C. Base. We'll knock out one ground-to-air missile site."

Henderson armed and fired his AGM-123A Skylite III, a laser guided bomb with a radar seeker head and rocket motor. To his surprise, his bomb did not explode on the ground, it was blown up in the air by the ground-to-air missile site.

"D.C. Base, this is Skipjack. Ground-to-air missile site has turned off their radar, or they have something else going on. They knocked out our missile. It also looks like they're jamming our radar with some new type of advanced radar jammer."

"We know their location by our satellite's thermal emissions spotting," said Sherman. "If they prevent us from hitting them with their radar jammer, or whatever, we'll hit them with a cluster bomb if necessary."

"If we use a cluster bomb, we could injure quite a few civilians in that area," said Admiral Kane, a member of the Joint Chiefs.

"Not really," said Sherman. "They're on an abandoned Air Force base that supposedly was not occupied."

"We don't have any planes in the air with an attached cluster bomb," said the C.I.C. Chief Gunnery Officer, Stuart. "We didn't anticipate a domestic ground-to-air missile site firing at our planes and at D.C."

"Tell them to load one up at Andrews or Patuxent River, pronto.

Have Skipjack do a flyover using his infrared camera to precisely locate and photograph that ground missile site. Do we have any new advanced non radar-detecting air-to-ground missiles in the air . . . any planes with Phoenix missiles . . . any Starlight missiles?" asked Sherman.

"Yes, we do," said Stuart. "The plane just joined up with Skipjack. It's an advanced F-211 stealth bomber."

"Use it, then," said Sherman.

About three minutes later, there was a massive explosion in Maryland that lit up the night sky and shook quite a few rafters in Baltimore and Washington.

"Scratch one ground missile site," reported the pilot, Major Pete Goode, III.

Suddenly, it became very quiet around the Baltimore-Washington area.

Fortunately, the missile fired at D.C., in the direction of the White House, missed. It hit the State Department Building, which was almost completely empty at the time. The senior officers at the Pentagon, monitoring the action in the Central Intelligence Control Center, didn't know whether to run for cover or start praying. Their defensive missile system was useless. It wasn't functioning. What had gone wrong? On the screen it looked like the missile could be aimed at them or the White House. If the missile missed the State Department Building, it could have hit the Pentagon. The people watching the screen with the missile coming straight at them had a brief moment of anxiety. It was enough to make their hearts skip a beat and their respiratory rates quicken.

President Diamond's helicopter sat in the center of the eighteenth fairway at the Chevy Chase Country Club. Colonel Atwood was still worried that someone at the surface-to-air missile site had used a laser designator on the President's plane and that it could still be fired upon.

He decided to maintain radio silence except to inform the Pentagon that they were okay and to tell them to send the President's limousine.

"I'm not going back to the White House," said President Diamond. "Once that limousine gets out here, we'll head to Camp David."

It took approximately 90 minutes for a contingent of Marines to arrive from Quantico and the limousine to arrive from the White House. Two heavy-lift Marine military helicopters with 150 Marine infantry preceded them. The President and his wife headed for Camp David. No more missiles were fired. They would be safe there.

Camp David had recently been installed with state-of-the-art electronic surveillance systems protected by a Marine Infantry Company and Secret Service Agents. It had an elevator to a command center deep beneath the ground which was encased in hard reinforced concrete, supposedly which could withstand a direct hit by an ICBM bomb.

The Chief of Staff at the White House called the limo and informed the President, as best he could, about what was happening.

"We got'em, right?"

"I think so," replied Fran Kelly, the White House Chief of Staff. "The Air Force has knocked out that ground-to-air missile site. It was at an abandoned air field in Maryland."

"Do we have any more information?"

"Quantico Marines are assaulting that base right now. As soon as I get more information, I'll call you."

"What a mess!" exclaimed the President.

XIII

CAMP DAVID

The Starlight bomb fired by Skipjack's night attack air squadron at the S.A.M. site left a 500-yard hole in the ground and killed most of the intruders. Two special service battalions with helicopters from the Quantico Marine Base, under the command of General Donovan and led by Lieutenant Colonel Daniel Sharp, stormed the abandoned Maryland Airfield Base. They used sophisticated weaponry with night vision apparatus, laser equipment, and some arm held missiles. The Marines captured more than 30 armed militiamen dressed in regular Army camouflaged uniforms, however, seven "crazies", who resisted, were killed. There were eleven Marine casualties. The two hostages, Colonel Brown and Major Stewart, the officers at the control center, survived and were able to help describe what had happened.

As soon as the airfield was secured, General Mike Sherman informed the President that he thought the uprising was the result of domestic terrorists and not an international conspiracy. He announced that the nation would stay on alert for the next 72 hours.

Video phone calls to the White House came in from world leaders in Russia, England, China, France, and Germany. The Russian military was particularly upset because although the cold war had been over for some time, they still maintained their 7000 nuclear bombs in readiness at land-based and mobile sites. The political control of Russia had changed numerous times, but they still had a strong military that was reluctant to give up their nuclear bombs.

The media based at the White House and around the world

wanted to know what was going on, and the members of Congress wanted a prompt explanation from the military. The President decided that the quickest way to allay the anxiety in the country and around the world was to appear on television and give a brief explanation of what had happened without embellishing it with minute details.

All the major networks carried the press conference on prime time the next day.

CAMP DAVID
MARYLAND
WASHINGTON PRESS CORPS IN ATTENDANCE
JULY 6, 2015

President Diamond addressed the nation:

"My fellow Americans, last night some members of a militia group attempted to shoot my helicopter down and fired a missile at the White House with S.A.M. ground-to-air missiles from an abandoned air base in Maryland. The White House was not hit, but the cruise missile destroyed the State Department Building, and a fighter plane was shot down. At this time we still don't know how many casualties there were. We do know there were security personnel and custodial workers in the State Department Building who were killed. We also lost a Major General, one night fighter pilot, eleven Marines, and eight air defense personnel. As you might expect, the missile attacks created great anxiety around the world. We have captured some thirty-odd surviving members of the militia group who perpetrated this attack. As we obtain more information, we will inform the nation. We've also captured the seven militiamen who took over our Washington, D.C. Air Defensive Command unit, and killed eight of our military personnel. They are traitors and will be treated as such. I'm calling a special session of Congress to investigate what happened and to plan ways to prevent anything like this from happening again.

"Now I'll take three or four questions from the press.'

Walter Douglas, dean of the *Washington Press Corps*, asked the first question.

"Mr. President, do we know how these militiamen got one of those surface-to-air installations?"

"We don't know, because the S.A.M. site was destroyed by our planes. Not all the captured militiamen are talking. It will be some time before we learn all the details."

"What do you propose to ask Congress to do?" asked Jack Osborne of the San Francisco Chronicle.

"Congress will be called back into a special session. I've asked that the joint Senate and House Intelligence Committee meet with the chairman of the National Security Council, and the C.I.A., and F.B.I. directors. The Senate Armed Forces Committee will hold hearings to determine exactly what happened and propose legislation to prevent such a thing from happening again."

"How do you plan on punishing these militiamen? Should they receive the death penalty?" asked George Stuart of the *Washington Post*.

"Yes, and promptly!" the President replied. "They need to know we will not tolerate this kind of action against the American government. This is treason."

Sandy Van Patton of the *New York Times* asked the next question.

"I understand that when the missiles started flying, Russia and China tried to contact us but could not receive any information."

"That's true," said the President. "We didn't know what was going on ourselves, so we couldn't tell them anything. This is a problem we must address. Proper early communication is vital for everyone's survival. We must develop international systems to immediately communicate with world powers."

Jack LaSala of the *Chicago Sun Times* was identified next.

"What if that cruise missile had hit the White House with you and the Vice President in it?"

"I've thought about that. We must develop a better Missile Defense System than we had last night. That issue will have to be addressed promptly by the Congress and the military."

Jane Turek from the *Los Angeles Times* asked the next question.

"Mr. President, this crazy militia group could have destroyed civilization in this world. What do you plan to do to control these people in the future?"

"That's one of the most difficult problems we face. This country was founded on freedom of speech and assembly," said the President. "I'm calling for an immediate special session of Congress to address that issue and the other issues that the missile attack presented to our democracy."

Jack Burns of the *St. Louis Post* asked the next question. "Mr. President, the Congress and the executive branch of our government have been debating about a Missile Defensive System for years. Would it have prevented the disaster that we just went through?"

"That's using the retrospective scope," he replied. "We must move forward to prevent this from happening again. That will be all the questions I'll answer at this time."

The gaping five-hundred-yard hole in the ground where the surface-to-air missile site had been destroyed by the night attack aircraft could not be readily seen by the public, but pictures were shown on TV. People could easily see the destruction and havoc created by the missile that hit the State Department Building. There was little left of the building.

"That missile could have just as easily hit the Capitol Building," said Senator Jack Jennings, the President Pro-tempore of the Senate. "If the Senate and House had been in session, just imagine what could have happened to the structure of our government. The commando takeover of our Washington, D.C. Air Defense Center was a well-planned act. It prevented our defensive missiles from destroying that cruise missile. We can't let this happen again! What we have just seen is a screwed-up fire drill in which none of the firemen knew how to put out the fire. The world as it exists today could have been destroyed."

JOINT SESSION OF CONGRESS

Three days later, the joint session of Congress met to discuss the problem. Because of the intense public interest, every representative and senator wanted to speak to the issue, so they could get on television.

"It isn't that simple!" commented Senator Bennett. "We can't snap our fingers and get a Constitutional amendment that affects gun control and militia units. However, we can pass severe penalties for terrorist acts. I, for one, don't plan to let them sit in prison with their habeas corpuses watching television. When you kill your fellow citizens and commit terrorism against your government, justice should be swift and severe!"

"Are you advocating the death penalty?"

"Of course I am!" replied Bennett.

"Hear, hear!" replied the Congress members.

Senator Tom Marshall asked for the floor. "I think we have to think about what happened and why it happened. The people who were captured should be interrogated to see why they were motivated to do this. Were they kooks, or were they law-abiding citizens who were derailed in some way? Do we have any information about this? Will the Senator yield?"

"Yes," replied Bennett.

One of the members of the Joint Intelligence Committee, Senator Maloney, spoke up. "Most of the senior members of their militia unit were killed when the S.A.M. site was destroyed. However, our initial interrogation suggests they really thought our country is going down the tubes."

"They were trying to destroy the people who run this country," replied Senator Bennett. "They weren't playing with toy guns."

"Our litigious society is going to defend them. The American Civil Liberties Union is demanding a fair trial," said Senator Dakin.

"What they did is quite obvious. They tried to destroy our government. Justice should be swift, so we won't have any similar uprisings," replied Senator Maloney.

After much haggling, Congress decided that the best way to investigate the mess was to have the Senate Armed Forces Committee work with the military to determine exactly what happened. Those meetings would be open to the public. Because some information had to be kept from the public for security reasons, the House and

Senate Joint Intelligence Committee would interrogate the F.B.I. director, the C.I.A. director, and the National Security Advisor.

SENATE ARMED SERVICES COMMITTEE
SENATE CAUCUS ROOM
RUSSELL BUILDING
SENATOR ROBERT BALL PRESIDING

There were fourteen senior senators on the Senate Armed Services Committee: eight members from the majority party and six members from the minority.

Most of the committee members were among the most powerful senators in Washington. The Senate Armed Services Committee controlled large sums of money and patronage, allocating billions of dollars for sophisticated equipment for planes, tanks and ships, as well as determining the location of military bases. It was a coveted job; the senators on the committee made sure that some of that money returned to their own states.

Senator Robert Ball, the Presiding Chairman, a Republican from Virginia, would facilitate the interrogation. All of the major participants in the missile attack debacle had been subpoenaed to appear before the committee, including the telephone operator who first received the call at the White House.

The Senate Caucus room was packed. The media were present in force, and it was standing room only.

Senator Ball hit the gavel and called the meeting to order: "This Armed Forces Committee has been asked to have in-depth hearings about the missile attack on the President's plane and the White House. We have agreed to have open hearings in order to inform the media and public as best as possible. However, there are a few aspects of the attack which will remain secret to maintain security. I'm sure that the public and media understand this. We will try not to hide any pertinent material. Our first witness is Dahlia Greene, the telephone operator who was on duty when she received the phone call threatening the White House."

Greene was a middle-aged black woman who had worked as a telephone operator at the White House for twenty years. She raised her right hand and was sworn in.

Senator Ball: "Ms. Greene, I want you to tell us in your own words what happened around 2:00 A.M. on July 4, 2015."

"My switchboard wasn't very busy that evening, so I was relaxing when the phone rang at 2:00 A.M. It was from a John McKittrich. He sounded quite nervous and wanted to talk to the President. I told him to state his business. He hesitated and then blurted out:

'My business is to give you a warning!' He sounded like he was upset about something. I didn't like what I heard, so I had a Secret Service Agent listen in, and we got a fix on the call. It came from a public phone in downtown St. Louis. When he told me he was going to blow up the White House, the Secret Service Agent advised me to keep him talking. He was obviously mad at our government and used some foul words that you wouldn't like to hear. I felt the guy was nuts, but it was not my job to determine why. The Secret Service Agent got nervous and called the President who thought it was a 'crazy call'. He wasn't about to get out of bed. The agent was scared and didn't know if it was for real, so he convinced the President to fly out in a helicopter."

"Ms. Greene, how often do you get calls like that?"

"Not often, but there are a few nuts and crazies who call asking to talk to the President. It usually happens when there is some big issue being debated in the Congress."

"What made you think that this call was for real?"

"The man sounded desperate. He scared me, and I wasn't about to take any responsibility for evaluating the call."

"After hearing what the man said, what did you think about the President flying off in his helicopter?"

"I wished I were in that helicopter," she said . . . there was an outburst of loud laughter in the committee room. Senator Ball hit the gavel.

"When that missile hit the State Department Building, the White House shook. I felt it was the end of the world" . . . suddenly there was silence in the Senate Caucus Room . . . it no longer was a laughing matter.

"What did you do?" Senator Ball finally asked.

"The telephone switchboard was lighting up all over the place, so I kept directing the calls, doing my job. Where could I run to? . . . Calls from the media and all over the world came in . . . Calls from big shots in Russia and China. Some of those calls were directed to the President and to the White House because they couldn't get answers anywhere else. It was unbelievable! I listened to those calls. They were quite interesting."

Senator Ball interrupted, "I don't think the public needs to hear about those calls. That will be all, Ms. Greene. Thank you for your testimony."

The next witness was the Chief White House Secret Service Agent William Clark, who was on call that evening. Mr. Clark was a former police detective from Los Angeles who had served at the White House for sixteen years. He had been decorated in the past for bravery.

"Mr. Clark, when you were alerted by Ms. Greene, what did you think was going on?"

"I didn't know. That was the scary part. I really didn't think it was for real. Where could a citizen get a missile to fire at the White House? I thought the guy was nuts!"

"Then why did you have the President awakened and send him off in his helicopter?"

"I don't know why. Maybe because my job has a great responsibility. Probably because I wanted to be safe rather then sorry. I suppose you can say that it was because I had a hunch that something was wrong. Honestly, I didn't feel it was a real threat."

After Mr. Clark gave the details of the President's escape, Senator Ball asked if any of the committee members had any further questions.

"I do," said Senator Kelli Palmer. "Mr. Clark, are you telling us that a hunch was what caused you to have the President fly off from the helicopter pad?"

"That's right!" he replied.

"How do you think we should screen calls like that in the future?"

"I can't answer that."

"No further questions," replied Kelli.

The Senate Committee recessed for lunch and then came back in the afternoon.

Sgt. Bill Beard, the Marine guard on duty at the gate at the Washington D.C. National Defense Center, was sworn in.

"Sergeant Beard, how do you determine who gets inside your gate? What credentials are necessary?" Senator Ball asked.

"Practically everyone has to have a photo ID."

"Are there any exceptions?"

"Yes, Sir."

"What are they?"

"If a Major General, such as my boss, General Black, arrives in his car with two stars on the license in front of the vehicle, you look inside, recognize the individual, salute, and let him pass."

"In other words, an exception is made?"

"Yes, Sir, that's right."

"Is that considered really tight security?"

"No, Sir."

"Why do you do it then?"

"It's a courtesy to rank."

"What happened that night?"

"General Black arrived in his car. He looked like he was supposed to look, and he was dressed in his General's uniform with two stars. I looked inside . . . gave him a snappy salute and passed him through."

"Did you talk to him or ask for his photo ID?"

"No, Sir."

"Why?"

"Everything seemed to be in order, Sir. He looked just like General Black. I didn't know he was wearing a mask. I think any gate guard would have passed him through."

Senator Ball: "You're excused. Call Lieutenant Colonel Brown to the stand. Colonel Brown is the man who was in control at the Washington, D.C. Defense Control Center."

"Colonel Brown, would you briefly describe what happened?"

"Yes, Sir."

"Around 1:00 A.M., the door to the Control Center suddenly burst open, and there was rapid fire aimed at killing most of my men. Actually, we were not armed and were working the console and screen. It had been a quiet night like it always was. We felt secure with armed sentries outside. Suddenly, there was bedlam. The terrorists worked very fast and precisely. I must admit I was impressed. It was over in seconds. They had complete control of the D.C. Defensive Control Center, and six of my men were dead.

"I didn't know who they were. They all wore masks, including the impostor, Major General Black. Then I was blindfolded, my mouth was taped shut, and my arms were tied behind by back."

"Could this have been prevented?"

"I can't answer that. When you deal with professional terrorists, and they're your own citizens . . . you have a big problem."

Senator White from Oregon spoke up. "Colonel Brown, why weren't you wearing a sidearm?"

"Because we had armed guards posted outside."

"Is that standard procedure?"

"Yes.

"Do you have any suggestions to prevent this from happening?" Senator Ball asked.

"Yes. I believe you have to go to the source of the problem. Why did these American citizens want to destroy our government? How could they become so well organized when no one knew about them?"

"I agree with that," said the Senator. "We have to do something to prevent this from happening again."

The next witness was Marine Colonel Albert Atwood, President Diamond's helicopter pilot.

"Colonel Atwood, would you briefly describe what happened the night of July 4th?"

"When I was alerted that President Diamond and his wife would be leaving the White House because of an emergency, I rushed to the helicopter pad area to check out the plane. Being a military pilot, when we were airborne, I did not like the altitude assigned and requested a change to a lower altitude. The request was granted. When we got to the lower altitude, my plane's radar screen got fuzzy and looked like it was being jammed. I quickly set the helicopter on the ground and turned off all the radio-radar gear. Missiles started flying all over the place. The rest is history. I was really scared. I thought that it was the start of World War III because of the way the missiles were being thrown around as well as one of the fighter planes getting shot down. I knew that the President had to be kept safe. He would have to decide what the country's response would be. I couldn't believe it when I later heard that some Rambo-militiamen in this country caused all the trouble."

"How can we handle this in the future?" asked Senator Dakin.

"There has to be a better way of evacuating the President from the White House. Maybe a secret underground tunnel or underground rapid transit train. Shoulder-held missile launchers can easily shoot helicopters out of the air."

Senator Hunt from Texas spoke up. "Why did you shut off the radio and radar equipment?"

"So that the missiles could not home in on the President's plane."

"If you turned off the radio, how could the President know what was going on? What if he had to press the button to retaliate with ICBM's?"

"We were out of contact only for a short while," replied Atwood.

"Exactly how long?" asked the Senator.

"Maybe five minutes."

"A lot can happened in five minutes."

"Are there any other questions?" asked Senator Ball.

Senator Kelli Palmer replied, "Yes, I have a few. Why didn't you use your chaff or other counter measure devices when your screen was knocked out?"

"I felt that getting down on the ground was more important. That would make the President's plane harder to hit."

"You could have done both," remarked Kelli.

"That's right," Colonel Atwood replied. "I guess I was a little nervous."

"I have one more very important question. If this was the start of a major war, do you feel that the President was properly prepared and capable of determining the proper response?"

"I can't answer that. How do you tell that? The President appeared quite nervous during the whole affair. He didn't make sense all the time. He was shook-up and quite agitated. You could tell he was under great stress and was having difficulty understanding what was going on. We all were! He was sweating profusely, and he kept saying, 'I don't understand! How could this happen?' I overheard him say to his wife, 'I'm all alone. What should I do? Please help me! . . .' You'd have to ask him that question......"

"Did you notice anything else?" Kelli asked.

"He had gotten the football and was clutching it in his arms. I heard his wife tell him to start praying. I saw him put his hands over his face, and he was either praying or crying. I really didn't know what he was doing. All I know is that I wouldn't want to make that decision about retaliating with nuclear bombs all by myself. That's too much responsibility for one person. In some ways, he looked like a basket case. I would've too!"

Senator Ball stood up. He appeared angry. "Colonel Atwood, I'd like you to clarify your response to Senator Palmer's last question. You didn't imply that President Diamond was incapable of making a proper decision, did you?"

"No. But how do you know? I said I didn't know what was going on in his mind, but he did appear quite nervous and agitated. We were all nervous. . . . After all, we were shot at by a missile and could have been blown up and killed. We really didn't know what was happening. It was one hellava mess!"

That evening, a *New York Times* editorial criticized Kelli Palmer for asking embarrassing questions about the President's response to the attack. They questioned her motive, and berated her for trying to gain political points for her party while Congress was trying to unite the country behind the President. "Would she have been so brazen if President Diamond was not about to run for re-election next year?" They asked . . . "After all, she's inexperienced and only a junior senator. . . ." Not all the papers agreed with the *Times* editorial. The *Chicago Sun Times* and the *San Francisco Examiner* felt she had raised legitimate questions. "In a combat situation a President must keep his cool and not be a loose cannon, the *Examiner* stated. "Did President Diamond keep his cool . . . that's the big question!" said the *Chicago Sun*. "Colonel Atwood gave the country important information about the President's reaction. Now it's up to the public to decide."

The next day, the press and TV people besieged Kelli when she arrived at the Senate Office Building.

"Why did you want to know about the President's reaction to the missile attack?"

"I felt that it was a very important question," replied Kelli. "In combat not everyone has the same reaction, and some people actually cannot handle the stress. Sometimes the shock is so great that they just do nothing. Some actually turn tail and run, others get mad and fight harder. I wanted to know how he reacted. After all, he's the Commander-in-Chief."

"Were you looking ahead to next year's Presidential race?" asked a reporter.

"No, not at all. But I'm glad I'm not running in his shoes."

"Would you consider running against him?"

"I'm not interested in that job. I represent California, and I like doing it."

"What would you do to prevent another missile attack?"

"I would definitely put up a Defensive Missile System. It should have been done a long time ago."

"What do you mean?"

"It's obvious what I mean. The seat of our national government has to be protected better, and so do the borders of our country. Sorry, I've got to get to the committee meeting. No more questions." Because she was asked so many questions by the media, Kelli was late. Senator Ball couldn't help but make a comment about her tardiness when she took her seat at the Armed Forces Committee meeting:

"Senator Palmer, we expect all members of the committee to be on time for these hearings."

"I'm sorry, Senator Ball. I was delayed by the media. I had to clarify a point I made yesterday."

"Until this committee hearing is completed, I suggest you limit your remarks and make sure they stay within the confines of this chamber."

Kelli couldn't believe what he said . . . She had to respond.

"These committee meetings were purposely opened to the public, that includes the press and the media. The people are demanding that they know what happened." Kelli tried to keep her voice even as she spoke, but she had had it. Her Irish was up. "Freedom of speech and freedom of the press is necessary in a Democratic government. That's in the Constitution."

The media and press in the chambers stood up and cheered.

Senator Ball hit the gavel and stood up. He was mad. In a loud voice he said, "If there are anymore outbursts like that from the audience, these meetings will not be open to the public, and it will be Senator Palmer's responsibility for having that happen!"

After the noise and commotion died down, Senator Ball called Marine Major General Paul Donovan to the stand.

"General Donovan," he asked, "when you attacked the so-called terrorists at the missile sight, was there much resistance?"

"No, very little. Most of the S.A.M. personnel were killed, and only those people around the boundaries of the old airfield survived."

"How many did you capture?"

"Thirty."

"Did you have any trouble with their interrogation?"

"None whatsoever. They were proud of what they had done and talked freely about their accomplishment. They thought they were really helping the country."

"What were they like?"

"The members of the terrorist group were ordinary citizens. Some had previously been in the military. Most were anti-government. A few demanded legal representation."

"Did they get it?"

"They were told that they had created treason against their own government and therefore, they came under military law jurisdiction. If it had been wartime, they would have been taken out in the backfield and shot."

"How would you punish these people?"

"I'd give them to the people, and see what they'd do. I don't think it would be pretty."

"You don't mean that, do you General?"

"Yes, I do. This could have been the start of a war that destroyed the world."

That evening, Kelli Palmer, rather than Paul Donovan, made the newspaper headlines. In addition to covering the entire gamut of her dialogue with Senator Ball, most of the major newspapers featured her remarks on the front page. Others were in the headlines. 'Junior Senator Challenges President's Capabilities Under Fire' . . . 'Is President Diamond A Wimp?' . . . 'Stress at the White House' . . . 'Who's in Control' . . . 'Missile Debacle Hits the White House.'

The shit hit the fan for President Diamond. Was the media out to get him? How could a no-name junior senator from California stick a knife into his re-election campaign? He called in his Chief of Staff.

"That female senator will kill me if she goes unchecked. We've got to do something to stop that bitch!"

The next day Kelli received calls from the morning and evening TV shows, requesting interviews. The number of media contacts was overwhelming. Senator James Welch, the Senate Minority Leader in her party, and Bob Mitchell, the National Chairman, called for a meeting.

*   *   *

President Diamond met with Senator Ball; the Republican National Chairman, Jack Ford; and his Chief of Staff, Bob White, in the oval office.

"How are we going to stop this fucking broad from California? She's destroying me in your Armed Forces Committee meeting, Senator Ball."

"I don't know. She certainly has gotten the attention of the news media. I'm worried. They want a copy of all the tapes in your conversations with the Pentagon during the missile crisis. Do you remember what you said?"

"Frankly, I don't know. We better review those tapes, and if there's a problem, we'll claim national security."

"Can we do that?" asked Senator Ball.

"I don't know, but the President does have executive privileges," said White.

"Not for those Pentagon tapes," said Ford. "Maybe they should disappear. They could be misfiled."

"With the public clamoring to know just how you reacted, we're in big trouble," said White. "That Colonel Atwood certainly didn't help. He may have saved your life by putting that helicopter on the ground, but he may have destroyed your future by raising the image of your nervousness under fire."

"Why don't we get the Chairman of the Joint Chief of Staff to call Colonel Atwood into his office and advise him to retract his statements. A little arm wrestling here might help. He might subtly suggest an early promotion."

"If Colonel Atwood is called back into the Senate chambers and changes his testimony, he could perjure himself," said Senator Ball. "There's got to be a better solution."

"Since it's an open forum, why not tell Atwood to go on the talk shows and say that the President was a cool customer under fire. It wouldn't be sworn testimony," said Ford, the National Chairman, "and he wouldn't go to jail."

"Colonel Atwood may not be willing to cooperate," said Ball.

"The Chairman of the Joint Chiefs will have to make it work. I'm sure Atwood will cooperate."

"The President can play no role in this if we decide to try," said White. "He must know nothing further about it!"

"Mr. President, I don't think we should do that," said Ford, the party's chairman. "If the media ever found out, you'd be finished."

"I'm not so sure . . . might be a good idea. We could all be sworn to secrecy," the President replied. "After all, if I'm put out of a job, the Joint Chiefs may be replaced. We're playing for big chips here!"

"We should think about that," said Senator Ball.

"I don't like being called a wimp by a female senator. Just imagine what the history books would say."

"Forget history. Think about now. We've got to make some constructive decisions," said Ford.

Senator Ball spoke up. "There's one thing that I can do. I won't let her speak or ask questions in the remaining committee meetings. I'll ignore her."

"That could be difficult," said Ford. "We've got to get some senior senators in both parties to criticize her questioning and motives. We've got to restructure the President's image."

"Should I have a press conference?"

"No. Not right now. That would only increase Senator Palmer's image. We've got to break it down."

Kelli met with the Senate Minority Leader, John Cannon, and her party's chairman, Bob Mitchell, that evening.

"I guess I hit a buzz saw when I asked that question about the President's reaction under stress. I didn't realize what a ruckus I created."

"You were doing your job. You were doing what your people who elected you would want you to do," said Mitchell.

"I have a feeling that I'm going to be blasted by the opposition, as soon as they collect their wits about them," replied Kelli.

"Play it cool," said Welch. "The Democrats on the committee will support you."

"That won't be easy," replied Kelli.

"They may try to ace you out in those Senate chambers. Just wait and see."

On Monday, so many press people surrounded Kelli when she arrived outside the Russell Senate Office Building that she had difficulty climbing up the steps. She had decided not to make any more off-the-cuff statements and slowly made her way to the Senate Caucus Room, refusing to answer any questions. Senator Ball was waiting for her, cornered her inside, and asked to speak with her in private. They walked together to a side room and when they were alone, Senator Ball looked her straight in the eye and said, "Kelli, these hearings that we're holding were supposed to be bipartisan hearings to inform the public about what transpired when our government was attacked. They are not a political forum to attack the President. Your questions and remarks are not worthy of a U.S. Senator. I want you to desist from further derogatory questions."

Kelli looked at Ball quizzically, hesitated, measured her words, and responded.

"Bob, I respect you highly. I thought that these hearings were to inform the public exactly what took place when that missile attack could have destroyed our country. Americans want to know just how President Diamond reacted to that unpredictable situation. I did not answer the question, Colonel Atwood did! It was his testimony that put doubts into the minds of all Americans. The President, who answers to no one, has to be able to handle stress and remain cool. If he makes the wrong decisions and retaliates, all living things on this earth could be destroyed—that includes you and me. Would you want President Diamond to make that decision for you?"

Senator Ball sputtered, got red in the face and said, "Of course I would."

Kelli looked at him right in the eye again and didn't flinch. "Well, I wouldn't!" she replied and then walked out of the room.

*   *   *

When Kelli arrived for the hearings the next day, Senator Robert Ball was waiting for her again. As he came up to her, all Kelli could think about was 'here comes trouble'.

"Kelli, you were disrespectful to a senior senator, yesterday. I had not completed my conversation with you when you blew your stack and walked off."

"I'm sorry about that. You weren't exactly very polite and endearing with your remarks."

"I was trying to make sure you understood that for national unity, we all should support the President."

"Not if he doesn't do his job right. He carries the football that can unleash a nuclear response."

"Hell, you'd be wetting your pants if you were in that position."

"I don't think so," replied Kelli.

"For Christ sake, why don't you keep your mouth shut and cooperate," said Ball, as he got red in the face and raised his voice.

"Because I have a moral responsibility to get at the truth," replied Kelli.

"Bullshit. That's a bunch of hogwash—you know that as well as I do! You're making the hearings into a political arena."

"The hell I am! You're the one whose blowing your stack and being disrespectful now. If you were flying in my squadron in combat, I'd give you a squirt!"

"I don't understand what you're saying."

"You wouldn't. You've never been in the service."

"Oh, that's what it is."

"No, it's not. However, so you understand, I'll explain it to you. A squirt in the air, means that I'd get you in my gun sights and put a bunch of bullet holes up your ass. That's exactly what you deserve. If you'd like, you can quote me on that in the press."

"I'll get you for those comments," replied Senator Ball. "Where did you learn all that dirty talk?"

"From someone just like you," replied Kelli.

TESTIMONY OF LIEUTENANT GENERAL
MIKE SHERMAN
SENATE CAUCUS ROOM—THE NEXT MORNING
RUSSELL BUILDING

Sherman had been recognized as a true hero in managing the crisis, and the public could hardly wait to hear his testimony. The Senate room was packed with a standing-room-only crowd. The TV cameras were ready to roll.

The minute Senator Ball called the committee meeting to order, network executives expected ratings to go as high as the Super Bowl. As General Sherman came into the room, all the occupants stood up and applauded.

Sherman was a tall man with a pronounced military bearing. His back was rigid, he had a cropped haircut, and steely green-grey eyes that penetrated. He looked resplendent in his uniform with his Navy Marine gold wings and a chest full of ribbons. A former head of the Marine Corp, Sherman was Chief of Staff to the Joint Chiefs. It was obvious that he had testified before Congress, and he knew most of the senators on the committee. He raised his right hand and was administered the oath.

"General Sherman, our country owes a big debt to you and to your courage and intelligence in defining the cause of the missile attack . . . " He paused and then continued. "Your quick and effective response saved this country from a great disaster."

All the people in the room stood up again and applauded.

Senator Ball continued, "General Sherman, did the military have any advance warnings of trouble?"

"We did know that there were some anti-government crazies around the country, but we did not anticipate the possibility of a midwestern militia group obtaining a surface-to-air missile launcher that could shoot down one of our own night fighter planes and then launch a cruise missile at the White House."

"What's even more baffling is that cruise missiles are usually controlled by satellites, and this cruise missile must have had a guidance system that wasn't controlled by satellite. My guess is that this group bought this missile from Russia, North Korea, China, or some other foreign country. It probably engages targets at low, medium, and high levels, and uses a radar-radio-altimeter and a sophisticated anterior television guidance system. We don't know exactly how the guidance system worked since it was blown up. The most upsetting part of this whole thing is that those militiamen captured the Washington, D.C. Defensive Control Center and screwed up our communications system, so our defensive missiles could not be launched to shoot that cruise missile down. Some of the weapons we were fighting against had excellent accuracy and radar jamming and aiming capabilities. It looked like they were our own weapons."

"Why was there so much confusion right after the first missiles were fired?" asked Senator Welch.

"Because of the close proximity of the terrorist weapons system in Maryland, we couldn't rapidly deploy a defense. We weren't sure if our own defensive system had screwed up and had misfired some missiles. However, this will shock you. We have no defense against long range missiles. We also didn't know whether this might be a large scale conspiracy in conjunction with a foreign power. The complexity of the problem that we faced that night was incomprehensible."

"Did the other major nuclear powers know what was going on?"

"The major nuclear powers—China, Russia, France and Great Britain have their own spy satellites. Most of them knew that missiles had been fired within the boundaries or within close proximity of our country. Their new photo-reconnaissance satellites can see through cloud cover and darkness. Any heat emissions caused by the firing of missiles are recorded and relayed immediately to their military command centers by the use of sophisticated lasers. Fortunately, contact was made through emergency communication systems, and there weren't any trigger happy Generals firing their own missiles at us—at least that's what they told us."

"Why did you keep the country on alert after the attack?"

"We maintained an emergency military status for a few days until we were sure we were dealing with our own regional problem.

This attack points out that you can't trust anyone in this world today, even your next door neighbor."

"How can our country be more prepared? Are there a few confidential things that you can tell us without giving away any secrets that might be damaging to our country?" asked Senator Dakin from Pennsylvania.

"Believe it or not, I think it's a good thing that this happened now before a bigger calamity. The world is still learning how to control these catastrophic nuclear bombs, and accidents and mistakes can happen. Unfortunately, too many countries have them. Our spy satellite system knew immediately when the first missile was fired and could pinpoint accurately where it came from. We were shocked that it was fired in Maryland and not from an enemy submarine or some offshore site. The big problem is that we didn't know whether it was our own missile or an enemy's. The terrorists were clever in setting this up. They completely fouled up our Military Communication System.

"Colonel Atwood made a smart decision when he realized that the surface-to-air missile was locking its radar in on the President's plane. In fact, they may have put a laser designator on it. He promptly turned his radio and radar equipment off and put the helicopter on the ground before the first missile was fired.

"Unfortunately, a night fighter plane took the brunt of that attack, and a pilot was lost. There was a slight delay in the Command Center, while it was determined whether to knock out that S.A.M. site or have the marines take it by land forces. At that time, we still didn't know whether it was our own forces that screwed up and fired the missiles. But when they fired the cruise missile at Washington and our air defensive system was not working properly, the night fighter planes were given the order to knock it out. We had to destroy the S.A.M. site no matter who had caused the firing. Fortunately, we had some sophisticated planes in the area with smart bombs.

"Some of the captured terrorists who survived that attack talked freely to our intelligence interrogators. They still think that our government is all screwed up and what they did is good for our country."

"What can we do about these fringe groups?" asked Senator Goldberg from Ohio.

"We have to monitor many of the fringe groups in this country better than we have. Controlling domestic violence and militia groups or radical groups must be a top priority. All of our patriotic citizens must become aware of what is happening around them. Even our allies have to be watched and reported if major violent acts are anticipated. Each of us is in this together. That applies to countries we don't like, too! If we want to survive, we have to work together as a team not like a bunch of jackasses pulling in opposite directions. My apologies for using that descriptive term."

"Does the military play any role in controlling domestic terrorist activities?" asked Senator Jones.

"Only if we are asked to by the President," replied General Sherman. "I believe the F.B.I. is supposed to handle that. However, this was different. Missiles were being fired at our airplanes and at Washington. A military attack required a military response."

"General Sherman, I wonder if you would be willing to answer some questions by the members of our Armed Forces Committee?" asked Ball.

"Certainly," he replied.

"I'd like to ask a question," said Senator John Cannon, the Senate Minority Leader. "Everything happened so quickly. The phone call warning came in at 2:00 A.M., missiles were fired at the President's helicopter around 2:30 A.M., and a missile was fired at the White House at 3:00 A.M. How can the military make decisions and communicate with each other and respond in such a short period of time?"

"That's one of our biggest problems," replied Sherman. "The military has means of rapid communications with lasers and the use of computers, but you don't want a programmed computer deciding how you're going to respond. The human military element should decide."

"Senator Ball, I'd like a follow-up to Senator Cannon's question," said Kelli.

"Sorry," said Senator Ball as he cut her off. "Senator Palmer, you've had your share of questions. The other members of our committee should be allowed to ask first. Why don't you listen for awhile?"

John Cannon, the Senate Minority Leader who was the senior member of Kelli's party on the committee and knew the parliamentary laws, spoke up: "Point of order, Senator Ball. I have five minutes of my time still left. She can use that to ask her question. I'll yield to Senator Palmer."

Senator Ball got red behind the ears and was frustrated by the parliamentary maneuvering and blurted out: "So be it, but make it brief, Senator Palmer."

"I'd like to ask what I consider the most important question, General. What do you consider is this country's biggest military weakness now and in the future? What did we learn from this debacle?"

"That's an excellent question, Senator Palmer. We learned that the military's biggest problem is its ability to evaluate a catastrophic situation quickly. I alluded to that in response to Senator Welch's question. We did not anticipate missiles being fired within our own boundaries. We did not know if we were at war with a foreign country. There was a lot of ambiguity out there. The communication systems through our space spy satellites and computers told our military command centers that there was something wrong. We did not know that our communications system had been invaded by outside intruders. Communication and its rapid military interpretation are extremely important. An intelligent, experienced person has to decide quickly how to respond. I repeat: we cannot rely on military automated response systems. They could destroy the world."

"I agree with that," remarked Kelli.

"Fortunately, we eventually interpreted what was happening perfectly. As for the future, who knows what weaponry will be developed. I hope it's never used. I do know that if another major war develops, our military communications systems will be the enemy's first target. They'll be going after our command and central control centers as well as operation units, and we'll be going after theirs if we know where they are. They may also try to interfere with our military operational communications by introducing false information into the system, as they did this time. One of our biggest problems is developing a totally secretive communcation system that can't be invaded by outside intruders. Computer hackers are already invading our government computer systems. The major superpowers do not currently want to destroy the world any more than we do. Countries with intercontinental missile capabilities contacted us promptly and accepted our explanation. That may not happen in the future."

Senator Ball spoke up, "No more questions, Kelli!"

Senator Ball then asked if there were any more questions, and there were none.

"Thank you, General Sherman."

Senator Ball hit the gavel and announced, "The Senate Armed Forces Committee meetings on the missile crisis are now completed."

JOINT SELECT COMMITTEE ON INTELLIGENCE
HOUSE OF REPRESENTATIVES AND THE SENATE
CHAIRMAN: SENATOR SHERWOOD WALTMAN,
TENNESSEE
MEETINGS CLOSED TO THE PUBLIC AND MEDIA
JULY 17, 2015 A.D.

Senator Sherwood Waltman opened the proceedings: "Our job today is to determine what caused missiles to be fired at the President's helicopter and the White House. Henry Watson, head of the F.B.I., Brooke Cole, head of the C.I.A., and Frank Noll, head of the National Security Council, have agreed to meet with our committee to try to come up with some answers as to why this happened and what to do about it. I know you have all reviewed the tapes of the Senate Armed Forces Committee meeting. Our committee's role is to determine the underlying causes of this attack and to develop preventative mechanisms so this will never happen again. Our first witness will be Henry Watson, head of the F.B.I.

"Mr. Watson, was the F.B.I. aware that militia groups might attempt to take over our country or initiate terrorist acts like the one we just had?" asked Senator Waltman.

"We knew that some of the militia groups in this country opposed the political policies of our President and Congress more than others. The F.B.I. has a counter terrorism section that covers both domestic and international terrorists. We certainly did not anticipate they would get their hands on a surface-to-air missile unit, particularly one of our own."

"Someone had to steal that mobile surface-to-air missile equipment, either at the factory where it was made or from a military installation, which suggests that military security was lax. How the terrorist militia was able to set up that installation and make it work has to be investigated further. It was a smooth undetected job. I will say that they picked an ideal spot—a closed air force base close to Washington, D.C. Supposedly the base was up for sale."

"Have you found out how they were able to accomplish this?" asked Senator Waltman.

"Not completely. I don't plan to announce what we know in these chambers."

"Shouldn't the F.B.I. or the C.I.A. have known that the militia groups were big trouble?" asked Senator Jack Kilpatrick from New York. "Shouldn't they have come under closer scrutiny?"

"They have been under scrutiny," said Watson. "But there are so many of them, and we have limited resources. The militia aren't the only source of terrorists. Terrorist attacks occur all over the world practically every day. Look at the World Trade Center bombing, the destruction of Pan Am flight 103, the bombing in Oklahoma City and Saudi Arabia, Kenya, and many others."

"How does the F.B.I. evaluate the potential danger of some of these groups?"

"We have a special C.I.A. office that supplies security-cleared psychiatrists to help us evaluate paranoid and potential psychotic groups. There are a number of our citizens who sound paranoid— some have good intentions but wrong motivations. Some have grandiose ideas. Unfortunately, they can cause big trouble."

Senator Bill Jones asked, "Where do you look for terrorists?"

"They exist all over the world . . . sometimes in your own back-yard. Some are motivated by religious idealism. Others hate us because of the leadership role we play in the world and our stand on democracy and freedom for all people to choose their own form of government."

"How can you catch them after they have committed a terrorist act?"

"That's the big problem," replied Watson. "Most of them use some kind of explosives. We're trying to develop a way of marking all explosives, so a marker will tell us where they came from. That would give us some lead. Believe it or not, some people are opposed to putting markers on explosives. In this case, the terrorists got a mobile S.A.M. missile set-up and also got the missiles to fire. This was a highly intelligent planned attack. It's almost unbelievable what they accomplished."

"What do you suggest we do to prevent this from happening again?"

"We have to have better control over our rapid firing weapons and weapons of massive destruction. We may have to pass new laws or amend the Constitution."

"Any other suggestions?"

"Treason against the government should automatically include the death penalty. I agree with Senator Bennett on that score."

"Are there any more questions for Mr. Watson?"

There were no more questions.

"Director Watson, please stand by for further questions later."

Brooke Cole, the Director of the C.I.A., a career government employee who served under three Presidents, was asked to step forward.

"Director Cole, did your agency have any inkling that domestic missiles might be fired at our planes or at Washington?" asked Senator Waltman.

"We are not involved with law enforcement or police powers in the United States," he replied. "But since we are involved with counter-intelligence and counter-terrorist activities, we were aware that some of the fringe groups within the United States were acting more aggressively. Some were trying to get help from terrorist groups overseas.

"Our main role involves espionage in other countries and seeking classified information as well as surveillance and counter surveillance. We also get involved in covert activities. What happened the other night must be addressed rapidly. I feel that the biggest danger today to the integrity of our democratic government is from within, not from outside. The sophistication of our modern weapons, and the nuclear potential of many countries with increasing proliferation, also has to be watched."

"Is there anything we should be doing now to prevent what happened the other night?" asked Senator Goldberg.

"The shit hit the fan the other night. It could have lit the fuse that caused the end of civilization," replied Cole. "We were in a panic state then, and we are in a panic state now. Our people and our Congress are deeply disturbed."

"Do you have any suggestions?"

"Our laws are too lax with regard to penalties for terrorist activities. It takes forever to litigate terrorists. Lawyers are getting rich defending terrorists. Our taxes are paying the lawyers. The longer the trial, the more money they make, and some of our best lawyers are being paid big bucks. Our society is too litigious. We have to change that. If you commit a terrorist act in China or Russia, you'd be hung in the streets, so the populace could see the penalty. It would be taken care of promptly and is very effective."

"How could the C.I.A. act jointly with the F.B.I. to prevent this kind of thing from happening?"

"We have in the past, and with what has just happened, I believe that military intelligence, the F.B.I. and the C.I.A. have to work together to prevent this from ever happening again."

"We on the select intelligence committee agree with you completely," said Senator Waltman. "I've asked Frank Noll, the Chairman of the National Security Council, to join us to help answer any questions. We'll now go to open questioning by the senators."

"I have a question for all of you three gentlemen," said Senator Bennett from South Carolina. "What happens the next time we get a call that a missile is going to be fired at the capitol building in Washington, D.C., while Congress is in session?"

Frank Noll responded, "We have to create a defensive screen that prevents the missile from getting into the target that would take a big hit. Some kind of a shelter or rapid evacuation system also has to be developed."

"Maybe we need some underground tunnels that will get us all out of town in a hurry," said Bennett. He had a smile on his face, but he sounded serious.

"We can't all become underground moles in order for our government to survive," said Senator Hale. "Besides, how do you know when it's going to happen?"

"There are enough fringe groups out there, just like those militiamen, who oppose all forms of government. They think they're do-gooders," said Bennett. "We've got our share of paranoid personalities out there, too. Those people have to be recognized before they do damage."

"How are you going to keep track of them?" asked Jackson.

"We could put microchips behind their ears like they're doing to animals, I suppose."

"The liberals in our country would not allow that. It would be an invasion of their privacy."

"I always thought our system of democracy had some weaknesses. I never thought it might be destroyed from within. I always thought it would come from an intercontinental conflict," said Bennett.

"A combination of the two would be even more dangerous," said Frank Noll. "Destructive political elements from within working in tandem with elements outside, could be a versatile foe."

"That's sort of like a self destruct, isn't it . . . with outside help?"

"Right!" said Noll. "That's the biggest threat to our country. We were aware of some risks, but we didn't anticipate a missile attack on the President's plane and the White House by some crazy militia. The President's helicopter does carry chaff to divert missile attacks. It also has some antimissile defenses. Who knows what new sophisticated weapons will be developed? Also, when the President flies in the helicopter, there are usually two other helicopters in the air. That's to confuse anyone using a shoulder-held short-range missile."

Senator Hale from Connecticut interrupted. "Ten years ago, when I was a member of the intelligence committee, we considered the question of putting up an anti-missile defense system for the country. I believe we were going to use high intensity laser beams or laser designators to destroy enemy missiles that were fired at us. What ever happened to that idea?"

"We didn't do it. We stopped because Russia and China objected. They felt it would be an aggressive act because they didn't have the knowledge or money to develop their own system," replied Noll. "China has often rebuked us for continuing to develop nuclear and outer space weapons, including guided missile defense systems, while they continue to develop their own."

"I think the time is ripe right now to set up a Star Wars Missile Defense System. When we had a confrontation with China over Taiwan 15 years ago, they threatened to drop a missile on Los Angeles if we came to Taiwan's defense. A defensive missile system in this country would have defused that threat."

"A system like that would not have prevented what happened the other night," said Senator Bennett. "The surface-to-air missile that shot down the plane—and the cruise missile fired at the White House—came from within our own country."

"How are we going to prevent that?" asked Senator Jackson from Oregon.

"That's a good question," replied Noll. "I suppose we need to develop a new system to protect the President, the White House, and other key government areas such as the Capitol. We also need to pass some stringent new laws in a hurry. It's obvious that we have a big problem on our hands."

"Mr. Noll," said Senator Waltman, "what you're telling us in this secret Congressional meeting is that if this country is to really survive, there must be some changes made to the Constitution. Our mechanism of making those changes may be too slow to help us with multi-varied confrontations that are unpredictable."

"That's just the tip of the iceberg," said Noll. "Just think what might have happened to this country if a missile had hit the White House and the Capitol with all our elected individuals inside. Our constitution doesn't cover that debacle."

"Just one more question," said Senator Waltman. "How do you think we should punish the perpetrators of this missile attack?"

"This is treason, causing multiple deaths that could have started World War III. The world is watching to see how we handle these traitors. Justice should be swift."

Justice was swift. Two leaders in the Montana and Wyoming militia, along with the bogus Major General Black, were given the death penalty and hung.

The other militia involved in the attack were all given life imprisonment. A few supporters of the militia, who were involved with planning the operation, but did not participate in the attack, received three to five years at hard labor in a Georgia military prison.

The F.B.I. and C.I.A. determined that the mobile S.A.M. (surface-to-air) unit used by the militia had been stolen when it was returned to ordinance for repairs. The cruise missile that hit the State Department Building had been purchased through arms dealers identified as members of the Islamic Alliance from Afghanistan, Iran, Iraq, or Pakistan. The new missile was of Chinese, North Korean, Russian, or other Middle East origin. It had its visual controls in the nose and did not rely on satellite direction.

2016

XIV
DIAMOND'S RE-ELECTION BID

The missile attack couldn't have come at a worse time for President Diamond. In one year, he would be running for re-election. Despite the swift actions of the judiciary and legislative branches, he was unable to convince the public that the government had tightened security enough to prevent such a thing from happening again.

The American people had a good memory, and if they didn't, they were reminded frequently on TV about President Diamond's rigid stand against a Missile Defensive System. There were photo clips showing Kelli when she was a Representative speaking to Congress and warning about a possible missile attack. The clips showed the President at his press conference blasting Kelli and calling her a junior member of Congress, unduly alarming the public, and telling her to select her words more carefully when speaking on the national pulpit.

The clips also showed Diamond advocating a reduction in the Defense Department's budget, standing with Senator Farber in her unsuccessful primary fight against Kelli.

Senator Palmer's question concerning his ability to respond properly under stress kept surfacing. It was a nightmare to haunt him continuously in his attempt to be re-elected. No matter what his party did trying to refurbish his image, it wasn't working.

Jack Ford, the Chairman of the Republican Party, said it was 'dirty politics' to keep bringing up the past because no one anticipated what happened—not even the military. Of course, that wasn't true because Kelli had brought it up in Congress on more than one occasion.

When Colonel Atwood refused to change his testimony before the cameras, he was drummed out of the service by the senior military. That was another one of Diamond's mistakes. As a frequent visitor on talk shows, Atwood now had nothing to lose by publicly criticizing President Diamond. He openly stated that he wouldn't vote for him; he had no confidence in his ability to stand stress.

Ford suggested that President Diamond leave Washington and go visit the heartland. The press might be easier on him out there. It would be a respite from his mounting political troubles.

"I'll do anything to get out of this hornet's nest of irresponsible journalists," he replied.

They decided to hold their first countryside conference in Des Moines, Iowa. In preparation for the conferences, Jack Ford, the Republican National Chairman, told Diamond, "This state is full of a bunch of farm hicks. Tell them that you're going to increase the farm subsidies, and you'll have them eating out of your hand."

"I hope you're right," replied the President.

The next day, in front of a large Iowan crowd, the President announced that he was all for increasing farm subsidies and said that he would fight any efforts to reduce the subsidies in Congress.

"I'll veto any bill that comes on my desk that reduces farm subsidies."

There was a big cheer from the audience . . . he had the crowd eating out of his hands. There was a big smile on his face.

Everything was going well until Jim Means from the *Des Moines Register* stood up and asked, "Mr. President, the people in Iowa would like to hear more about how you felt and how you were going to respond when your helicopter was about to be shot down? Were you going to retaliate with nuclear bombs? Were you nervous? How are we going to prevent this in the future?"

The President became agitated, flustered, visibly disturbed, and pounded on the podium, almost knocking it over. He hollered. "Why does the press keep bringing up this question? It's history! When I came out here to Iowa, I thought we could discuss the real issues. I thought that Iowans were intelligent thoughtful American citizens, not like that unruly lambasting Washington Beltway crowd. I guess I was wrong! Was I nervous? Of course I was nervous! Wouldn't you be? I acted responsibly and didn't pull the trigger."

Jim Means was persistent. "Mr. President, you haven't answered my question! How do you plan to prevent it from happening in the future?"

"I told you that I don't want to hear about this anymore! Can't you listen?" He pounded on the podium again. "I've answered that question a hundred times! Haven't you read about our press conferences and seen them on television? Use your head! We have all the best brains in the country helping us resolve that problem."

Diamond was fuming and flushed with anger and showed it. The TV cameras were rolling and recording the entire event. He lost his cool, and he was exasperated. . . . He shouted, "Let's discuss the real issues for God sakes! No further questions about the missile crisis!"

The crowd became very quiet watching the President become unraveled, and then there was complete silence.

They didn't ask anymore questions. That evening his comments were on TV's evening news, and the Iowans were not happy about what they had seen. The President had gotten rattled and looked bad. Diamond had imploded his own re-election campaign. He showed a part of his personality that should have stayed in the closet. The meeting in Iowa was cut short, and the President left the next day.

The Midwestern press tour did little to improve President Diamond's image. Maybe the President had lost his cool in that missile crisis and had difficulty in handling stress. Maybe he shouldn't be the individual to make that most important decision of retaliating with I.C.B.M.'s. Rather than allay the fears of the Iowans . . . he had increased their fears, and this was reflected in the national polls which continued to drop. The Republican Party leaders realized that they were in deep trouble and were going to lose big. Many of the local candidates up for re-election were voicing their anxieties, and panic was beginning to set in.

Opposition to Diamond became more vocal and aggressive

around the country. Communications had improved universally with TV, computers, and radio, so that the level of political intelligence of the people was improving. At least they were better informed. The tolerance for ineptitude in government was definitely limited. Millions of people staged a march on Washington. There was a real fear that the President might be successfully assassinated. It prevented him from mingling with the crowds during his re-election bid. He had to rely on pre-arranged press conferences in safe places.

"You're putting me in a glass cage, so I can't meet the people!" he argued. "It's a conspiracy to defeat me for re-election. You're interfering with my rights, which are clearly stated in the Constitution."

"We're trying to protect you, so that some crazy jerk doesn't try to bump you off," said the party's chairman.

"I'm willing to take my chances. I'd rather be shot at and win, then not be shot at and lose the Presidency."

"The party doesn't agree, Mr. President. A shot could kill you. Your political enemies would celebrate. I think we've got to figure out some way to blame that missile crisis on somebody else. Maybe you should fire the Chairman of the Joint Chiefs of Staff. Blame the military for what happened."

"I can't do that! General Jonathan Walker is one of my best friends."

"If he's such a good friend, we could talk to him. Maybe he'd take all the static and get the heat off of you. We can pay him off in some way. He could retire with a good pension."

General Jonathan Walker was fired the next day, with a White House statement implying that he was responsible for the military's inability to prevent the stealing of the S.A.M. equipment and that he didn't respond adequately to the crisis. But getting rid of the Chairman of the Joint Chiefs of Staff didn't help. At President Diamond's next press conference, a member of the New York Times asked: "Why did you relieve General Jonathan Walker? Aren't you the Commander-In-Chief of the Armed Forces?"

"Yes, I am!" he replied. "The Armed Forces goofed when they allowed the equipment for a mobile S.A.M. site to be stolen. You don't compliment them for allowing that to happen . . . that's why I fired him!"

While President Diamond was firing members of his cabinet and stating that the Press was out to get him, he continued to go down in the polls.

The Democratic Party was enjoying the President's trials and tribulations, yet knowing whoever ran would be a shoe-in. A number of candidates entered the ring: Senator Sam Johnson, a popular black from Ohio; Governor Allen from California; Strong from Kansas; and the House Speaker, Representative Jack Glicksteen from Illinois. Kelli's name was brought up but because she was a woman, it was dropped from consideration. At the party's convention in Chicago, it was a crap shoot. Senator George Whitehead, a dark horse from Missouri, finally got the nomination. Whitehead was a tall, 66 year-old, dark haired, handsome, athletic-type, whose image projected well on television. He was a tremendous orator, a centrist, and a shrewd parliamentarian.

President Diamond tried to focus on other issues. California had a large Hispanic population and quite a few Asians. Diamond needed the California vote, if he wanted to win. The Republican Party decided to select Representative Peter Gonzales from Los Angeles to be President Diamond's Vice Presidential running mate. Gonzales was a rising Hispanic star in the Congress. He was good looking, dressed immaculately, and was well educated, having graduated from Stanford. The Hispanic population would back him enthusiastically, and because of the State's large Hispanic population, President Diamond would dramatically increase his chances of carrying California.

Senator Whitehead tried to choose a Democratic Senate colleague as his running mate—Senator Ted Rogers from Texas. But the power in his party and the strong unions overruled his choice. Rogers was too old. They selected Richard P. Kennedy, a representative from California to counter the Republican's choice. Kennedy, 15 years younger than Senator Whitehead, was very popular out West with the younger generation.

There were four presidential debates—one during each of the four months before the election—between the selected candidate of each major party and one top independent candidate.

The four presidential debates were spread geographically throughout the country: Portland, Oregon; Jacksonville, Florida; Chicago, Illinois; and Boston, Massachusetts. Senator Whitehead did surprisingly well in the first three debates, began to gain in the polls, and easily passed Diamond prior to the last debate in Boston. Sixty-five percent of the people said that they were going to vote for Whitehead.

The media described the last presidential debate in Boston as Diamond's last chance to turn things around. The format was somewhat different from previous debates in that, in addition to selected journalists and the audience asking questions, the candidates would be allowed to ask two questions of their opponents. The public and the media were looking forward to a battle royal.

When it came time for Senator Whitehead to ask his two questions, he first read an excerpt from a speech made by Diamond in his previous election campaign.

"My fellow Americans, we have the best of all worlds ahead of us if I am elected President—the world is at peace, our economy is robust, and we have no fears about facing the future. No nation will challenge us because of our formidable Army, Navy, and Air Force. Unemployment is down, and our citizens are all happy. I promise to maintain peace and happiness for all Americans and for our children and grandchildren. A vote for me is a vote for stability and progress."

There was a long pause . . . and then Senator Whitehead asked the question.

"After what happened with the missile crisis, Mr. President, how will you explain to our children and grandchildren the role you played in trying to prevent what happened?"

Diamond sputtered, got red in the face, and blurted out an answer.

"I refuse to answer that question! Some things that happen are unpredictable."

The audience howled and walked out of the hall.

Soon after the polls closed in November 2016, President Diamond conceded defeat. It was a landslide victory for the Democrats. Whitehead and Kennedy carried 41 states, including all the big ones. Senators, Representatives, and Governors were carried on their coattails into the office. The Democrats gained control of the House of Representatives but the Republicans still had a slight majority in the Senate.

Diamond said in the concession speech:

"It was an act of unpredicted violence that did me in. I don't think any President could have predicted that domestic Rambo cowboys would shoot missiles at my plane and then at the White House. All I can say is that I wish my successor the best. There's no doubt it's a tough job, and the buck stops with him."

DICK KENNEDY—THE VICE PRESIDENT

After George Whitehead's inauguration, several senior members of his party met with him and suggested that he make Dave King his Chief of Staff. A "hard nut" and shrewd politician, King had served in the cabinets of two presidents and knew the ropes. He accepted the President's invitation and quickly took on the task of helping the President select a cabinet of diversified ethnic and gender-specific intellectuals, most of whom were quickly approved by the Senate.

President Whitehead immediately made major changes in the Pentagon. He fired all the current members of the Joint Chiefs of Staff, personally interviewed more than thirty military candidates, made his selections, and bypassed most of the senior members. Lt. General Mike Sherman, who performed efficiently and capably when the missile attack occurred, was promoted to full General and made Chairman of the Joint Chiefs. In response to public pressure, Whitehead dismissed the director of the F.B.I. and C.I.A. These were both seen as positive moves by the media.

After being in office for six weeks, the President held his first press conference and made the following opening statement:

"The recent missile attack on President Diamond's helicopter and the White House was the greatest threat to our nation's existence in this century and to the delicate balance of power in the world. Most disturbing was our vulnerability to major global conflict. We can thank only God that other world powers didn't launch their missiles or assume we were attacking them. Through that incident, we recognized how susceptible our communications systems are to enemy attack. No one knew what was going on, and we were extremely lucky that the world powers accepted our weak explanations. To prevent this from happening again, I am charging the new Congress to set up a bipartisan committee to review what happened and to come up with some realistic answers. This will be a formidable challenge because of the sophistication of the weaponry and its capability of massive destruction.

"We are facing other serious problems in this country besides missiles. There is a global economy, and all labor costs are competitive. Some of our major corporations seek out the cheapest labor around the world, and if they are capable of producing the product, use it. Some are using automated robots while people are starving. This has a profound effect on the use of labor in this country. Our labor force must have a good healthy wage. If we wish to survive we must continue to be innovative and creative. However, we cannot allow greed to be our main motivation in life. Our wealth must be shared and used for the betterment of all mankind.

"Our political system must also be improved. Congress and the Executive Branch have been in a quagmire of political obstructionism for years. This has to stop! We must work together, be progressive, and accept change."

Marjorie Cook, the Dean of the Washington White House Press Corps stood up.

"Mr. President, how do you plan to finance all these speculative defense systems for Washington, D.C.? What about the other cities such as New York, Chicago, or Los Angeles?"

"I don't have the answer," replied the President. "We don't know how to do it! We don't have any money to pay for them in our present budget. It will cost trillions. Congress and the scientific community will have to come up with the answers. Any defensive system will have to be inclusive so that it can be used for all major cities. We have a big job on our hands to work something out. Next question."

"I'd like a follow-up question," Marjorie replied.

"Go ahead," said the President.

"Do you think that diplomacy, arms control treaties, intelligence gathering, or military action could solve the problem without a new missile defense system?"

"It didn't do it this time! That's the question we all have to answer. Next question."

Mark Gross from the *Associated Press* was next.

"I'm concerned about the disability of the President, whether it's due to an assassin's bullet, a missile attack, or for medical reasons, such as a stroke or massive heart attack. The 25th amendment is not clear on succession. How do you plan to get the 25th amendment changed?"

"I've already spoken to the House Speaker and Senate Majority Leader about that. They've promised to have a new amendment passed within three months."

"It will take ten years to ratify it," said Mark.

"I've asked them to address that issue also. Next."

George Isaacs from *Reuter's*.

"Illegal immigration from Mexico, Cuba, Haiti, Asia, and Central America is choking the social services in some of our states and seems to be worsening. What measures do you intend to propose?"

"I'm not opposed to legal immigration, but I am opposed to illegal immigration. This is still a country of opportunity. It was founded by immigrants. We'll improve protection of our borders. Next."

Judy Smart, a young new reporter from the *Atlanta Constitution* stood up.

"Are you planning to hire more women for your White House staff?"

"Where appropriate, we will hire more women."

"Why didn't you select a woman to be your Vice President?"

"There are many women who qualify to be Vice President, just as there are women who qualify for my job. I selected Kennedy because he is young and progressive, and we see eye to eye on key issues. He is also from California. Gender did not play a role in my selection process."

Paul Richards from the *British Broadcasting Corporation* was called on next.

"In your opinion, how is your new health care system working?"

"Fine, so far. The single payer system in each state has reduced duplication of administrative costs, and I'm all for it. It also controls excess profits by the insurance industry. Good health is a public right and should not be a business for big profits by administrators. In some H.M.O.'s there seem to be more administrators than there are doctors. The doctors should be well paid because of their prolonged education process. I think that when Congress passed the law that allows each person to have freedom of choice of their doctor or specialist, it allowed our health system to get back to normal. After all, I can pick and choose my doctor and so can the members of Congress. It's a freedom that should be preserved for all Americans. The ability to sue H.M.O.s for negligence, just like the doctors, has leveled the playing field also. Next."

Kevin Stone, from *NBC* was next.

"How do you plan to get the rainbow coalition and minorities to vote for your candidates in the future?"

"They'll play a big part in the make-up of my administration. You'll see."

"Last question," the White House press secretary called out.

Dr. Kevin Stahl, from the *Harvard University Press* stood up.

"Mr. President, returning to the question of health, do you plan to have periodic health check-ups, and do you plan to release the results to the press?"

"Absolutely. I believe the public should know, not only about the health of the President, but the members of the Supreme Court and all the Congressmen. That data should be released. The health of our nation requires this information be made available. Healthy, vibrant Americans should run our government! Good day."

During his first year, President Whitehead's approval rating stayed steady at 58%. He had his problems with Congress like every President, but he prevailed because the Democrats controlled the House. Because of his forceful leadership and frequent press conferences delivered in what was becoming known as "Whitehead's laconic style," he got the people behind him and was able to accomplish some projects but not all.

In the beginning of his second year, when he gave his State of the Union address, President Whitehead cajoled Congress for not passing more progressive legislation. There were still loop-holes in campaign financing; public schooling was always in a crisis; health care and its cost was prohibitive; and many Congressmen were pushing for national health care. Countries around the globe were again doing nuclear testing, and it was only a matter of time before an accident might occur and someone may start shooting with a nuclear bomb. Terrorism was a constant threat.

He briefly mentioned a missile defensive system, but its cost would be prohibitive. He stated that a feasibility study suggested that a missile defensive system wouldn't work. A Star Wars System had been recommended many years before by President Reagan.

In March of his second year, President Whitehead gave a political speech to a large veterans' gathering in Los Angeles. While attending a cocktail party after the speech, he developed a severe headache and the sudden onset of nausea and vomiting. He was immediately taken to the E.R. at U.C.L.A Hospital where his blood pressure was high, and he had a slight slurring of his speech. An electrocardiogram of his heart was done which was normal; Dopler studies of his two carotid arteries in his neck showed a slight narrowing of his left carotid artery with an extremely small plaque. An MRI of his brain and other studies suggested the possibility of some slight change in the left frontal lobe, but there was no evidence of ruptured blood vessels. Neurologists and neurosurgeons were called in, and it was felt that he had developed a vascular spasm with impending thrombosis formation in an artery in his brain.

He was given special medication and intravenous blood thinners to prevent damage. His headache rapidly disappeared, and he was allowed to leave the hospital five days later. The press release stated that he had had an episode of food poisoning. There was no mention of the possibility of a small stroke.

Because President Whitehead was heavily sedated and "out of touch", Vice President Kennedy suddenly was put in the lime-light with the news media. He relished the opportunity to express his opinions on many of the multifaceted problems facing the nation. He quickly pointed out that not all of his opinions agreed with Whitehead. Some of his comments made the headlines.

When Whitehead got out of the hospital and read some of his Vice President's press releases and comments, he almost had another stroke.

"God help this country if I drop dead!" he told his Chief of Staff. "Did you read some of that bullshit that Kennedy came out with when I was sick?"

"Relax, Mr. President. We didn't let him sign anything."

"Thank God for that! You have my permission to tell him to keep his mouth shut if anything like this happens again."

"Yes, Sir!" he replied.

Near the end of his second year, the stress of the oval office started to show quite a bit on President Whitehead. He was gradually losing weight, and his Chief of Staff insisted he take some time off. Whitehead would have no part of a vacation—he was a workaholic.

"I'm staying in Washington, so I can tell what's going on. Somebody's got to watch the store, and it can't be Kennedy. I'll vacation when I'm out of office."

"Your TV image will project better if you get some rest and look healthy," said his Chief of Staff.

Besides dealing with armed conflicts and terrorism around the world, the President had a disgruntled Vice President, who was very outspoken in opposition to the President's programs. Kennedy was bitter about the minor role he played in the administration and openly expressed his feelings. Whitehead had difficulty controlling Kennedy, who did not always agree with some of his policy decisions and let the press know it. Kennedy was quoted in one newspaper saying that Whitehead was "somewhat out of touch with the needs of the people."

When the President heard this, he blew his stack. He summoned Kennedy to his office, and suggested that Kennedy keep his mouth shut or he would send him to the Congo or some other distant area. The story leaked. And when the press announced that the Vice President was gagged because of his remarks, Kennedy became livid. He called the press to his office and told them, "I regret any suggestion the media made that the President is out of touch. Clearly he and I both need to improve our communications. This is a democracy, and I still plan to express my opinions openly."

For about six months there was a cold truce between Whitehead and Kennedy.

In the beginning of Whitehead's third year of his presidency, the Supreme Court came under attack by the media for its inability to respond rapidly to the complicated changes occurring in American society. Everything was global now: communications, industrial corporations, banks, cyberspace, computer research, and crime. Computer hackers were causing computer terrorism that was hard to control.

The court had a group of older jurists who were having difficulty coming up with laws to control all these changes—and there was concern that the laws they passed would not be accepted by other sovereign countries.

One afternoon, after Vice President Kennedy finished a golf game at the Congressional Country Club, a *Washington Times* reporter asked him if he would be willing to answer a few questions.

"Fire away," he said.

"What do you think about the inaction of the Supreme Court in passing laws to control cyberspace, computer theft, and the information highway?"

"Please define what you mean? Are you also talking about software pirating and electronic plagiarism?"

"Yes," replied the reporter.

"Well," replied the Vice President, "if they don't understand cyberspace or the computer world, my daughter would be happy to explain it to them. If they still don't understand, they ought to resign from the Court."

"Are you serious?" replied the reporter.

Kennedy simply continued. "I vaguely remember former President Truman saying, 'if you can't stand the heat, get out of the kitchen.' Why shouldn't that apply to the Supreme Court members, too?"

"Sir, as you know, the justices are appointed for life."

"I know that."

"Are you challenging the Constitution?"

"No. I'm questioning their mental capacities. We had a recent Supreme Court justice who had two strokes with severe brain damage demonstrated on a CAT scan and MRI, and he refused to resign from the Court. One of his clerks wrote all his opinions for him. I think he's still on the court."

The reporter was aghast. The VP had walked out on a wire before, but this was unprecedented.

"Oliver Wendell Holmes," said the reporter, "had a pretty sharp mind at the age of ninety."

"An exception to the rule," said Kennedy. "Holmes also said the nine Supreme Court justices were 'nine scorpions in a bottle.' I think a more cogent description today is 'nine blind men teaching driver's education.'"

"You don't mean that, do you?" asked the reporter.

"Yes, I do!" replied Kennedy.

The next day the *Times* ran a six-column headline: "VICE PRESIDENT CHALLENGES SUPREME COURT CAPABILITIES."

Under the headline was a description of the conversation with the reporter.

One of the Presidential aides saw the article in the newspaper and showed it to President Whitehead.

"Is he nuts?" the President railed. "Who does he think he is? I've been working on the executive-judiciary relationship for two years. Call Kennedy and tell him to get his ass over here!"

When Kennedy arrived with his Chief of Staff, he entered the oval office alone. This, he knew, was personal.

"Dick, you're shooting your mouth off again. This time you shot yourself in the foot! You can think what you want, but keep your mouth shut. The Chief Justice called me and wanted to know what the hell was going on in the White House. I apologized and told him you were misquoted."

"I wasn't," said Kennedy, standing stiffly.

"I don't care if you were or you weren't," said the President. "But if you're going to stab me in the back every time I turn around, you'd better start thinking of what you'll do after government service."

"I'm not leaving."

"That matter is not entirely in your control."

"Sure it is," said Kennedy.

Whitehead glared at the VP. He took some flak from his staff. They were encouraged to challenge his thinking. That's what they were paid for. But they didn't do it publicly. This was different. Kennedy was challenging his will.

"Are you saying," Whitehead spoke slowly, "that you want to go toe to toe with me in front of the American people? You'll lose, Dick, and you will lose forever."

"What I'm saying, Mr. President,"—there was a capricious disrespect in his tone, as if he held all the power—"is that the devil finds work for idle hands."

"You're blackmailing me into a more prominent role in this administration! You're insane."

"No," said Kennedy, growing more comfortable. "I'm the next man in line for your job, and I think you're sick!" And with that, he left.

XV

SCUBA DIVING

The heat in the kitchen (the oval office) became too hot for Kennedy, so he decided to take a short vacation. He went scuba diving with his wife in the Cayman Islands. Before diving he was briefed by the Secret Service Agents who were to dive with him.

"Mr. Vice President, if you have any breathing difficulties, you're to signal and then we'll surface immediately."

"Listen, Jim, I've done this so many times it isn't anything anymore. Relax."

The agents checked the tanks and the valves, and Navy Seals searched the water. A Coast Guard cutter was nearby. The Vice President and his wife gently descended into the waters in their wet suits, and the agents accompanied them down to 35 feet. Things went well for the first hour.

The unlikely group of six armed underwater guards and two protectorates swam through coral caves, flirted with fish, and even allowed a manta ray to mingle with the couple. No terrorist divers launched a spear gun assault, and no sharks threatened them. They descended deeper to 70 feet, nearly at the bottom of the waters off the reef. Kennedy and his wife were having a great time frolicking around, although the visibility had decreased somewhat in the deeper waters, and it was colder. The Secret Service Agents turned up their portable lights. After another hour, Kennedy started to act strangely.

Although there were Secret Service personnel in the water with him, they were not aware of what was going on. He was trying to spear fish when he almost speared his wife. The agents swam to him and recognized that something was drastically wrong, so he was immediately brought to the surface. On board, Kennedy couldn't speak and had trouble breathing. His skin had a distinct bluish-green color. The paramedic in the diving group feared Kennedy might have had a stroke, heart attack, or a possible embolism.

He was immediately administered oxygen from one of the Secret Service's oxygen tanks, but he did not respond. They shook him and shouted at him. He was hyperventilating, his heartbeat was rapid, and he had a severe choking cough.

The only hospital on the island was put on alert before the Vice President's trip. A standby medical helicopter was called. By the time the helicopter arrived, the paramedic had passed an endotracheal tube down the Vice President's throat to deliver a high concentration of oxygen to his brain and started an intravenous. Still, Kennedy continued to fade. He became flaccid and unresponsive, and it looked like he was going into cardiopulmonary collapse.

"For God's sake, do something!" his wife cried. "Help him!"

"We're trying, lady," said one of the paramedics.

He was transported to the Cayman Hospital where they had a hyperbaric pressure chamber, which for some unknown reason, did not work properly. A doctor in the E.R. did have scuba-diving injury experience, so the VP was put in a head-down position and administered 100% oxygen. IV fluids were continued, and he was given steroids. He started to develop swelling around the neck—the E.R. doctor pressed his fingers there, and it caused a crackling sound. A stat chest x-ray showed that his right lung had collapsed, and there was air in the chest cavity. A chest tube was immediately put in to suction out the air. This helped somewhat. His lung expanded, and his respiratory rate slowed down. His blood pressure got better, but his state of consciousness did not. The Secret Service Agents issued a flurry of phone calls to specialists from the States who advised an immediate transfer to a hospital in Miami, Florida, where there was a functioning hyperbaric pressure chamber.

Kennedy was flown in an air ambulance to Miami where he was

put into the hyperbaric pressure chamber and examined by neurologists, radiologists, and rehabilitation specialists, all to no avail. He maintained a blank stare and did not speak or recognize anyone. Tests confirmed severe brain damage, probably due to an air embolism.

Nobody knew what had happened. The Secret Service Agents were dead-eyed. Doctors hypothesized that the VP held his breath, and nitrogen built up in his system which caused him to become confused. The Secret Service personnel panicked and brought him to the surface too quickly, causing the dissolved nitrogen in his blood to come out of solution and form air bubbles in his blood and tissues. His lungs over expanded and caused a rupture of the air sacs, causing the air to collect in the tissues of his neck and collapsing his lung. This could have caused the development of an embolism to his brain.

The President and senior members of Congress were immediately informed of Kennedy's accident. The President's reaction was unpredictable and unprecedented.

"I can't believe that anyone with brains would go scuba diving when he's Vice President. Of course, I never did think he was too smart. What an immature pompous ass! We're better off without him. God rest his soul."

"Sir," said his Chief of Staff. "He's still alive!" The President ignored him.

"I never did like the bastard! I never trusted him. He was always shooting his mouth off. He wanted me dead, so he could be President. Now who's next in line if I drop dead or goof up?"

"The Speaker of the House."

"He's not in our party," replied the President.

"That's right!" replied King.

"Well, so be it," said the President. "Maybe God's trying to straighten out this mess in Washington. Let the Republicans fuck it up if I drop dead."

"Sir, you don't really mean that."

"Yes, I do."

"You're not thinking rationally," said King. "Think of the party!"

"The hell with the party! He's brain dead and may be in a coma forever," replied the President. "What a mess! I knew that guy was bad news. Does brain dead mean there's a vacancy in the office of the Vice President?"

"I think some period of time has to pass before he's declared totally disabled. What really happens is you get to nominate the new Vice President," said King, "but your candidate has to be confirmed by a majority vote of both houses of Congress."

"Good! I know who I want right now."

That evening Dave King met with two senior members of the Senate and two members of the House of Representatives. He told them about his conversation with the President.

"That guy's flipped his lid," said Senator Kelly. "We've got to watch him like a hawk. He's lost his marbles."

"The President," said King, "is fully in control of his marbles."

"He's useless to us right now," said Representative Wilson, the Speaker of the House. "The job has gotten to him, and he doesn't look too good. I noticed that six months ago. I wonder about his health. I never believe those six month reports by that old fogy physician of his. I felt that he was lying all the time."

"The President," said King, "has a 55 percent approval rating."

"The media thinks he's off his rocker and that he's got Alzheimer's disease," said Senator Hanks. "There should be a test to determine that."

"The President is firmly in control," said King.

"Our party's in big trouble," said Hanks.

"That's not true!" replied King, trying to calm the group down.

"We could have a President with Alzheimer's disease and a Vice President who's brain dead. Who decides when the Chief can't command?" asked Kelly.

"We have to abide by the 25th Amendment," said King. "It's very specific in its guidelines on determining a President's disability and the time when the Vice President should take over. We've had a few assassination attempts and serious Presidential illnesses, so we finally had hearings to determine when the 25th Amendment should be invoked."

"Don't you remember the hearings on the subject?" said Wilson. "The Institute of Medicine of the National Academy of Sciences was asked to develop medical guidelines as to how and when to determine the President's physical and mental competence."

"Yes. The Congress was unable to agree on when to blow the whistle on the President," said Senator Hanks.

King was visibly upset about the discussion. He could lose his job if the President was disabled. He had to squelch what was going on.

"Gentlemen, President Whitehead is in perfect health, and he's doing a great job. I see and work with him every day. I suggest we drop all this conversation about disability."

"I don't think we should drop it!" said Senator Kelly. "We have a big difference of opinion here! Bill Jones from the *Chicago Sun-Times* spoke to me the other day and inquired about his health. He said that the President's job was certainly making him look like an old man. He's either in poor health, or he needs to get more sleep. He suggested that we get a new make-up man for him before he goes on television."

"If you were under the pressure that the President has, you'd look a lot older too!" said King.

"You don't think that I'm not under pressure as a Senator?" asked Hanks.

"Not as much as the President."

"We can solve the argument about the President's health by having lunch with the President's personal physician next week," said Hanks. "How does that sound?"

All the members in the group nodded their heads in approval.

MEETING WITH DR. DAVID WILLARD

Before the Presidential advisors were to meet with his personal physician, King arranged for a private meeting. He wanted to be sure that the President really was in good health . . . he was aware of the fact that the President probably had a small stroke in the past.

"Dave, I want an honest opinion about the President's health."

"Why are you asking this question?"

"Because the media and some of the members on the hill think that he may be seriously ill."

"He's not in top shape," replied Willard, "but he's capable of handling the job."

"Can you be more specific?"

"No. He doesn't have Alzheimers Disease, but his brain has slowed down somewhat. It's part of the aging process."

"I don't like what you're telling me . . . the media and the people on the hill may be right."

"If you were President and had to deal with all those vultures out there, you'd look tired and sick too!"

"Dave, you're going to be approached next week by some of the party's top advisors. They want to know about the President's health. I don't want you to be candid about it and tell them too much."

"I don't understand," replied Dr. Willard.

"Some of the senior members of Congress feel that he's losing it," said King.

"I plan to tell the truth."

"I want you to tell them that he's in excellent health!"

"I'd be lying," he replied.

"Yes, but you'd still be keeping your job."

During the next three months, President Whitehead came under the intense and scrupulous visual dissection of the Washington press. They noticed that he had lost quite a bit of weight, had bags under his eyes, and did not project well on television. He was also more obstreperous in his remarks to the Press Corps and didn't seem to care. The fact that Vice President Kennedy was brain dead didn't help either. It was like a noose around his neck. The President and Congress were taking their time in resolving the dilemma. Whitehead's approval rating was down to 42 percent—an all time low for his administration.

At his next press conference, President Whitehead was asked who his choice for Vice President was.

"It's my decision, and I'm taking my time. Nobody's going to tell me who to pick! I want you to know that I didn't select Kennedy. The party did."

"Would you be kind enough to tell us who your possible choices are? Will it be a black, Hispanic, or a woman?"

"Are you kidding? That doesn't come into the picture at all. My choice will be a solid American who has served in the government for many years . . . someone like Senator Ted Rogers from Texas."

There was a big groan from the press . . . Whitehead heard the groan and was taken aback.

"What's wrong with Ted? He's served for years in the Senate with me. He's politically savvy and thinks like me. If I dropped dead, there would be no loss of continuity in the government."

"What are some of your other choices?" he was asked.

"I have none. That's enough for today. No more questions, gentlemen."

In the morning, *The Times, The Post*, and numerous other national papers had editorials and articles by leading journalists suggesting that Congress pass an amendment to improve the method of selecting the Vice President. It was felt that the selection method had been too casual in the past, and the position was not given the respect it needed. Some even suggested a separate national election which was considered a radical approach, but would not be starting a new precedent . . . it had happened before in the history of our republic. The second President of the United States was John Adams, who was elected President in 1796 . . . he ran as a Federalist candidate. He edged out Thomas Jefferson, leader of the Democratic Republicans. According to the laws of that time, Jefferson became Vice President even though he belonged to the opposing political party.

Finally, as a rare proactive measure, the Congress agreed to undertake a review to clarify just what the 25th Amendment meant.

The main fight that developed over invoking the 25th Amendment was a discussion that took place on the floor of the Senate between the Minority Leader, Senator John Cannon (D-NY), and the Majority Leader, Senator Preston Adams.

Senator John Cannon spoke. "I don't like the way the 25th Amendment is written. If the President feels he's disabled, he has to give a written declaration to the President pro tempore of the Senate and the Speaker of the House. What if he has a stroke and can't write anything? What if he's temporarily incapacitated? What if he has an infection or viral disease with a high temperature and is out of it? What if he's in an airplane crash and has a brain injury? What if he has Alzheimer's disease?"

"All good questions," replied Senator Adams. "That amendment is not as inclusive as it should be. There is a clause that may help, but it should be clarified. It states that principle officers of the Executive Department, or of such other body as Congress, may, by law, provide by written declaration, a determination as to whether the President is able or unable to discharge the powers and duties of his office."

"That's ambiguous," declared Senator Cannon. "Who are the principle officers of the Executive Department and what is the other body as Congress, may, by law, provide?"

"Clear as mud," replied Adams. "What if both of them are destroyed at the same time—the President and Vice President? What if the cruise missile that hit the State Department Building had hit the White House instead, and the President and Vice President were in there? They'd both be dead."

"Looks like we have to change the amendment or make a new one."

"Troublesome on both counts," said Adams. "I think the 25th Amendment should be scrapped and a modern amendment determining succession of the President, Vice President and other important members of the Executive Branch be drawn up."

"That may take years for ratification. The whole country would be in limbo until it was ratified," said Cannon.

But Adams was ready. "Our forefathers meant it to be that way. They did not want the Constitution to be amended for insignificant reasons. When the 12th Amendment was adopted in 1804, it took sixty years before another passed. The 15th and 16th Amendments were separated by forty-three years. It takes three-fourths of the states to ratify an amendment after it has been proposed and passed by Congress. It's a long tedious process because it's supposed to be."

"What do you do when an amendment is adopted but doesn't function properly?" asked Cannon.

"You're talking about if a major catastrophe occurs. Is that right?"

"Right. Weaponry is so sophisticated now that many members of the Executive Branch of government and important members of the Senate or House of Representatives could all be destroyed at once. We have a situation right now that's going to be hard to fix."

"Gonna take some good old bipartisan haggling," said Adams."

"That's correct," said Cannon. "And if there's difficulty in determining command, definitive responsible action could be delayed. It could mean the military leadership, rather than civilian leadership, would make all the definitive decisions. I don't believe our forefathers wanted that."

XVI

V.P. CANDIDATES

The political big shots in the Democratic party decided to have a secret meeting to discuss Kennedy's replacement. However, before his replacement could be named, Kennedy had to be declared legally disabled and unable to perform the functions of the office. The Kennedy family was vehemently opposed to the idea and obtained legal counsel to prevent it.

The neurologists taking care of Kennedy presented evidence to a closed Congressional subcommittee that there was no electrical energy in his brain. He had a straight line electroencephalogram and no response to external stimuli. His wife testified that he blinked his eyelids at her, but privately, doctors confided that was wishful thinking; he had fixed dilated pupils and eye drops had to be used to prevent them from getting damaged from dryness. He had no response to light or darkness, and he had to be fed through a tube. Some insiders said that his heart, kidneys, and other healthy organs would be ideal for transplantation and would provide noble political capital, but the family would not give consent.

After legal haggling all the way to the Supreme Court, Dick Kennedy was finally declared disabled. This meant that President Whitehead could name his replacement, and the Senate and House would have to confirm the new Vice President.

Because of what was happening, a secret meeting of the leaders of the Democratic party was set up at the Washington Hilton.

Former Governor Kevin Powers, the Chairman of the Democratic party, moderated the discussion.

"Distinguished guests, you all know why we are here. Unfortunately, our President is not doing well in the polls and is showing signs of chronic illness. Vice President Kennedy is essentially brain dead and needs to be replaced. The implication of both these tragedies is that in our next Presidential election we will be looking for a new candidate. The person selected to replace Kennedy will have an excellent opportunity to run for that position. It's our duty to suggest to the President who that individual should be. I personally believe that this country hungers for youth, and that our candidate should be in excellent health, have political experience, and must appeal to both young and old Americans."

"How can you be sure that President Whitehead won't run? Do you think that he may have Alzheimer's disease?" asked the media mogul.

"That's a good question," said Powers. "Sometimes it's hard to distinguish between normal aging and Alzheimer's disease. It's obvious the President's brain is showing deterioration. He doesn't remember names, and he's lost his aggressiveness. Recently, he announced that he didn't want to give press conferences because he can't remember the questions. The White House physician denies all these problems, but he does admit the President's health has changed. That's why we have to be sure that whoever he selects for his VP is capable of running this country."

Senator Brian Webster from Missouri spoke up. "How wide is the net? Are we going to consider all the ethnic and racial groups — male and female genders?"

"Yes," replied Powers.

"Good. I'd like to recommend Governor Dale Strong from Kansas. He may be a liberal, but he certainly knows what's going on in this world."

"I agree with Brian," said Jack Payson, a black representative from Dallas, Texas. "Strong would be an excellent choice."

"I'll put his name on the blackboard we have here. First we'll brainstorm. Later we'll try to narrow it down to two or three names," replied the moderator.

"What about Kelli Palmer from California," asked Payson. "She's got the credentials: Navy background, four years in the house, now a senator, and great TV projection. Every jock in the country will vote for her."

"Okay," said Powers. "The questions have to come up. Are we ready for a woman President?"

Webster spoke up. "We've seen Thatcher, Bhutto, and Schroeder. Why not? The female vote is a way to stay in power. I think this country is ready for a smart female."

A few in the audience shouted, "Here, here!"

"But . . . she's awfully young," said Senator Webster.

"That might be to her advantage," said Powers.

"And ours," muttered Payson.

"What about Senator Sam Johnson from Ohio?" asked Jack Gibbons, the United Auto Workers Union Chief. "He's a former baseball star, a liberal, and all for the disadvantaged. He's a smart cookie, and he'd get the labor vote."

"He certainly ought to be put on the list," replied Willett.

"What about Jack Barnett, former Senator Barnett's great-grandson from Oregon? He's a sharp Rep. He's going up the West Coast political ladder, and he looks great," said Payson.

"He's another good one," said Powers. "Are there any more names we should put on the board?"

Senator Willett raised his hand. "Before we vote on the prospective candidates who may become President, shouldn't we ask them if they have any skeletons in the closet that might exclude them from running?"

"Why don't we vote first and see who the top candidate is?" said Powers. "That way, we only have to ask one person and won't have to delve into too many candidates' personal lives."

"That's a good idea," said Willett. "We might be poking a stick into a hornet's nest."

"I'm going to pass out ballots, and then we'll all write down our choices and discuss the two top candidates."

When the ballots were counted, Kelli Palmer got the most votes, followed surprisingly by Senator Sam Johnson.

"This ought to make for an interesting debate," said Powers. "We have a young woman senator from California and a brilliant black senator from Ohio. Who wants to fire away first?"

The billionaire software CEO from the West Coast got up.

"I think this country is ready for a black President," he said. "He's had an outstanding record in the Senate, and he's color blind. He'd make a good chief."

Jack Barnett got up.

"I'd like to put a vote in for Kelli. She's tough. She's charismatic. And with her achievements, she's definitely qualified."

Almost all the members of the audience got up and spoke for Sam Johnson or Kelli Palmer. The arguments were dramatic, and the meeting dragged on past midnight. Finally, the moderator spoke up.

"We've had enough discussion. We'll take one more secret vote, and then we'll have to convince the President about our choice."

KELLI RELENTS

At the Capitol in Washington, D.C., President Whitehead was waging his usual battle regarding the Defense Department budget.

The President thought that the House was allocating too much money for defense purposes. He believed in defense but not in what he perceived to be massive duplication of services. This was just a knee-jerk reaction to the missile attack. Terrorism seemed to be under control now. He wanted to cut the budget by one-third.

Kelli, who was on the Armed Forces Committee, was leading the fight against the reduction of funds. President Whitehead put in a personal call to her to try to change her mind.

"Mr. President, there are too many conflicts going on around the world and too many countries have nuclear warheads. We try to aid our allies and end up creating enemies. We have to be totally prepared."

"Ms. Palmer, you're mistaken. The people of the world are better educated today. Telecommunications reach everywhere. The leaders of the major nations know that a big war like World War II would destroy us all."

"I disagree," replied Kelli. "You're talking just like President Diamond did. In the past, when a threat of war developed, our nation had time to mobilize our Army and Navy. Today, there can be no lag time. Our response has to be immediate. We have to maintain a strong Army and Navy and the personnel to run it."

"You've been misinformed," said President Whitehead. "And like a lot of hawks, you're wasting money that could be used for better purposes."

"No, Sir, you're mistaken," she said. "You can't reduce funding for the active services without increasing funding for the Reserves in case you need them. It takes time to train people."

"We are clearly at an impasse," replied the President. "I suppose you want to spend billions for a missile defense system that won't work."

"Yes, I do!" replied Kelli. "You've forgotten already about the missile attack on the White House."

"No. I have not! That's stupid! You're not using your head!" he replied as he hung up.

That did it, as far as Kelli was concerned. She was a member of his party, but he had flipped his lid. She wouldn't support him on the issue. She knew about loyalty, and she knew about closing ranks. But Whitehead was out of it.

That evening, Kelli received a phone call from Kevin Powers, the Chairman of the Democratic party. He was cordial but to the point.

"I'd like to talk to you about a very important subject."

Kelli thought for a minute. Powers had probably heard about her conversation with the President. I bet he wants me to lay off criticizing the President . . . she tried to preempt him.

"I'll cut back on criticizing the President," she replied. "But Kevin, the man has lost it. He's not only sick physically but also mentally."

"Our meeting has nothing and everything to do with that," he remarked. "How about meeting me for dinner at about 7:00 P.M. at Le Beige Fleur or the Capitol Grille, your choice?"

"Le Beige Fleur on Connecticut Avenue," she replied. "There are too many politicians hanging around the Capitol Grille, drinking and smoking cigars. I've had enough second-hand smoke."

Kelli had no idea what the meeting was about, but she knew it would be all business, so she didn't ask if she could bring her husband. Palmer hated meetings like this, anyway.

She took a cab to the restaurant and was greeted by Powers as she got inside the doorway. Bill Bronson, a senior senator from Texas, and Senator Claude Willett from Arizona was with him.

"Kelli, you're the most beautiful senator we've ever had in Washington," he said, as he kissed her cheek.

"Ah, sweet flattery," she replied with a smile. Then after a short wait, looked him straight in the eyes and added, "You want something, or you wouldn't be here!" Directness had always served Kelli well.

"I always knew you had brains," he replied.

The maitre d' escorted them to a private table in a corner. The restaurant setting felt like being inside a shell—pale peach and beige with shimmering gold mesh curtains, etched glass dividers, and hand-tinted wallpaper from Italy. The food was always incredible, and the difficulty in getting reservations equally so.

"What will you have to drink?" he asked.

"Chardonnay," she replied.

"Bourbon, rocks," said Bronson. "Wild Turkey if you have it."

They chatted until drinks arrived. Then Powers got right to the point. "Kelli, I'm sure you're aware of the Vice President's disability, but I'm not sure you're aware of the President's."

"Oh, I'm aware," she replied. "How couldn't you be? Something has happened to him. And something must be done."

"Quite a few members of the party feel exactly the same as you," he replied. "I'm one of them, and that's why we're here. The President gets to choose Kennedy's replacement. Many members of our party feel you would be the ideal candidate. We're here to ask you if you will be willing to serve as Vice President of the United States?"

This was not what Kelli had expected. Her jaw dropped and her eyebrows raised. Their proposition took her completely by surprise . . . she was shocked. There was a long pause. Kelli drained an inch of her wine . . . she hesitated and then took a deep breath . . . "Whitehead won't choose me! I had a big fight with him recently . . . anyway, I'm not sure I would want to serve with him."

"You don't understand," said Senator Bronson. "We feel President Whitehead is sick, and his mind is degenerating . . . maybe it's Alzheimer's, maybe not. It's obvious that he's losing weight. He may not finish out his term, and this would put you in an ideal position to replace him, with re-election coming up next year. We're handing you a candidacy for his job."

"You must be kidding!" said Kelli.

"We're not," said the Senator. "We've given it a lot of thought."

"Wait a minute. What about Johnson?"

"His name came up. I won't deny it. But we feel you can draw more votes. We're serious, Kelli. We need your acceptance in order to pursue this with the President."

"You caught me completely by surprise. I have to think about this. I can't make a quick judgment call on something as important as this."

"Don't take too long. Johnson's probably considering his position right now. He may even try to fight you for the job."

When she got home, she told Mark.

"I'm opposed. Vehemently!" he said. "You've done well. You've had a great career going. You're a prominent senator, but this is different."

"Palmer," she said emphatically, trying to reason with him. "I don't like what President Whitehead's doing, and I feel I could do a better job. This is about public service."

"Public service is a pseudonym for power. You'd be on another ego trip. Haven't you had enough of being number one in everything you do?"

"Being Vice President is number two, not number one. Not very many people get that opportunity. If I get selected, I would be the first woman Vice President of the United States. Not a bad distinction."

"Okay," he said. "You've never listened to me in the past and always done just fine. What are you going to do?"

"I'm going to go for it. I'll call them in the morning."

At six the next morning, she called Kevin Powers. "I'm willing to go for it, if you can convince the President."

"That will be my job," he replied.

Kevin Powers called King, the White House Chief of Staff, and requested a meeting with President Whitehead, indicating he and several senior members of Congress wanted to discuss the selection of the new Vice President.

When the Chief of Staff talked to President Whitehead about the meeting, his only comment was, "I'll pick my own Vice President. No one's going to tell me what to do!"

"I think you should meet with them," replied King.

"All right, but no promises. None. I've been screwed in the past, and I don't plan to get screwed this time."

The meeting was held in the oval office two days later. Kevin Powers introduced the subject to be discussed.

"President Whitehead, we feel it might be appropriate to present some candidates to replace Vice President Kennedy."

"I've already given it a lot of thought, " said Whitehead, "and I've picked my man. It's Senator Ted Rogers from Texas. He's a personal friend and can take the heat. I wanted him in the first place, but no one would listen to me. Now I get to pick and choose."

"That's what we want to talk to you about."

"The decision has been made. I'll listen, but my mind's made up!"

"We'd like to suggest a couple of names, and also we'd like to comment on your choice."

"What's the matter with my choice? Ted's been one of the outstanding senators for the past thirty years. He's always voted with the party. He's a brick."

"Polls show the nation wants youth. They've even gone so far as to say that it should be a black or a woman."

"We've never had a woman Vice President. That's crazy!"

"This might be a good time to make history," said Powers. "Besides, Ted Roger's a year or two older than you, and your own health has come into question. The ticket needs legs going into re-election."

"I'm concerned about now," said the President. "Ted would be a good fill in, and he could intelligently advise about our current problems. I'm sure I'm healthy enough to live another year and a half if that Congress doesn't screw up too much and drive me out of my mind."

Senator Claude Willett from Arizona spoke up. "President Whitehead, we have to be realistic. Our position requires a response to the people's mood. They're tired of illness and tragedy. They want a comer, a colt, someone with blood."

"Hold on! I'll have you know," said Whitehead evenly, "that my personal physician says I'm in good health. My ticker's in perfect shape."

"The media would question that," said Powers. "If they have a chance, they may want to know when you're going to have another press conference."

"I'll have one when I'm damned good and ready to have one! No one's going to tell me what to do! I hate press conferences. All the White House media wants to do is ask hypothetical questions I can't answer. I'd like to see some of them get up in front and answer some of their own questions." He paused, his bluster quickly gone. "Who do you think I should consider for the Vice Presidency?"

"We have two names to discuss with you: Senator Sam Johnson from Ohio, and Senator Kelli Palmer from California."

"That's a black male senator and a white female senator."

"Correct," said Kevin.

"Presidential politics have really changed in this country, haven't they?"

"Yes, Mr. President. Sam Johnson is a brilliant senator. I wonder if the American people are really ready for a black President? How do you feel about it?"

"This is probably a good time to see if they are. As for that horrible female senator from California, you can cross Palmer right off the list," he snapped. "She's a good looking woman, but she's a bitch, and she's been causing all sorts of trouble for me in the Senate. Besides, she's too young to be Vice President."

"I don't think you understand," said Powers patiently. "She's a smart woman. The media likes her. And she'd get a lot of female voters back into the party. She would be less controversial than Sam Johnson."

"I couldn't get along with her. She's too damn opinionated!"

"The process of governing always comes down to compromise," said Senator Claude Willett. "You should consider compromising on the selection of your Vice President. Will you meet with her?"

"I'm willing to meet with her, but I won't make any promises."

After leaving the White House, Powers and Senator Willett talked about what should be done.

"Claude, you've got to get as many people as you can to contact President Whitehead and tell him what a terrific gal Kelli is and how she'd make a great Vice President."

"I can do that."

"I've got to work on Kelli and tell her to be sweet and noncommittal on issues, because Whitehead's going to try to destroy her candidacy."

"You've got to convince her that she can get more bees with honey than with cow manure," said Claude.

"That will be a tough sell. She's a redheaded Irish lass, and she's stubborn."

"If she can see beyond the tunnel, she'll make it," he replied. "Only one other woman has been given the chance to become Vice President of this country, and she didn't make it."

"Wrong candidate, wrong time. This is different," said Powers.

"Kelli may realize the legacy, change her mind, and not take the nomination, after talking with the President," said the senator.

"I don't think so. She's been number one in everything she's done.

This is her opportunity to become the number one person in this country, someday. Maybe as soon as two years."

"If we do our jobs right, she'll jump at the opportunity. And she'll have us to thank. She'll definitely owe us something and will put us on her team."

The following week, a dinner meeting was set up at the White House. There would be approximately 15 people invited. The only woman, besides Kelli, would be the President's wife, Ethel. The President insisted his wife be present.

Kelli went to her favorite beauty salon and had her hair washed and fashioned into a French braid. After, she bought a designer forest green suit.

Palmer was upset with all the preparations she was going through.

"Holy cow!" he said, shaking his head. "You'd think you were going to meet a new boyfriend. He's just an old goat."

"Palmer, relax, would you? You're just a little bit jealous, aren't you?" she said with a broad smile.

"I hope you realize what you're doing."

"I do—completely."

Kevin Powers and Senator Claude Willett picked her up in a limo.

The driver had been told to drive slowly to the White House because they wanted to prepare Kelli for the evening's festivities. They felt that President Whitehead would be like a bull in a china closet and would attempt to destroy Kelli's candidacy in front of the assembled influential guests . . . this had to be avoided at all costs.

Kelli looked beautiful and relaxed when she entered the limo. Kevin Powers sat next to her, and Senator Willett sat in a chair facing her.

Kevin started the conversation. "Kelli, we feel that the President is going to blast your stand on the Missile Defense System and the

defense budget. He's going to pick a fight with you tonight to em-
barrass you. He plans to kill your candidacy. We want you to reconsider."

"No way!" replied Kelli.

Senator Willett, seated across from her, looked her in the eye and
in a stern voice said, "Kelli, you're sitting in the 'cat-bird' seat.
Sometimes you have to give up something to get something. If you
play your cards right tonight, you will be selected to become the
Vice President of the United States. If President Whitehead dies in
office, you will become President. I don't think you realize what that
means. If he doesn't die, you will become the top candidate to take
his place."

Kelli was surprised by his comments.

"I feel strongly about this issue, Claude. It is morally wrong to reduce the Defense Department budget, particularly in regards to the
Defensive Missile System. Look what happened because we didn't
have one. It's long overdue."

"Hogwash," replied Claude. "We don't even know if it will work.
It will take years to build. Just think and put everything into proper
prospective. If you become President, you will become the leader
of the world's greatest and most powerful nation. You can advocate
and direct anything your little heart desires. I think that with your
charming smile, intelligence, and political savvy, you can convince
President Whitehead that you would make a great Vice President.
However, you have to compromise, be humble, and convince him."

Kelli looked at Kevin for support. It wasn't forthcoming.

"I agree with Claude. You have to give up something sometimes
to get what you want."

Kelli was astounded and taken aback by their agreement and aggressive attitude. She was having difficulty in responding to their
arguments. She knew that she was with two of the recognized top
politicians in the country.

"What should I do?" she asked meekly.

"The President's going to isolate you tonight and go one-on-one
with you. In a subtle way you've got to compromise your position
on the budget. Read his mind and stay ahead of him. Be humble.

Be the opposite of what he expects," said Kevin. "We'll be close by and will help you."

"Thanks," she replied.

President Whitehead had made up his mind before the meeting. He did not want Kelli to be his Vice President under any circumstances. He felt that they were too far apart on the important issues. He also knew she had a temper and would be hard to deal with. He was prepared to blast her for her stand on the budget. No woman was going to tell him what to do.

The cocktails and dinner were to be held in the Green Room. It was smaller than the East Room and better for a small group. When she entered, all eyes were on her. Her bright red hair, smile, and demeanor commanded their attention. She shook hands with the President. He was quite awkward at first and tried to be deferential and gruff . . . his demeanor in contrast to hers, seemed forced. They had a drink together, and he suggested that they walk off to one side.

"I'd like to talk to you privately, Senator."

"Fine," replied Kelli, as she took his arm and walked with him away from the guests into the East Room. When they got into the East Room, he stopped suddenly and faced her.

"I don't agree with your stand on the defense budget," he remarked abruptly.

"I've changed my opinion about that," replied Kelli. "Perhaps I haven't looked at the big picture properly."

"Really?" he replied. "You were so vehement when we talked on the phone the other day."

"I know. I had lost my contact with reality. I almost called you back to apologize. I was wrong!"

The President was taken aback by Kelli's answer . . . he didn't know what to say.

Finally, he collected his thoughts and spoke up. "It's good that you have an open mind. In the top job, you have to learn to compromise." He obviously was trying to regain his composure.

"I'm learning that right now," said Kelli, as she smiled and grabbed his arm again. "You've had lots of experience, and you're an excellent teacher."

"I'll drink to that!" he said, as they walked back into the Green Room. He called the waiter over. "Two champagnes, please."

The waiter brought the champagne, and they clinked their glasses together. Kelli kissed him on the side of the cheek. President Whitehead blushed and then smiled. He realized that he had evaluated Kelli improperly. Suddenly he relaxed and became quite jovial. His conversation had a different tone to it.

"I understand you play a good game of tennis, and you're not a bad golfer," he remarked.

"I enjoy being competitive in sports. I believe in getting lots of exercise."

His eyes looked her over and then remarked, "Yes, yes. I can see it's working. Imagine, a sense of charm still alive in politics."

"Thank you, Mr. President. That's very nice of you."

"I think it's time to sit down for dinner. Why don't you sit at the table next to me?"

"I would be honored to," she replied.

The evening was enjoyable for Kelli. Kevin Powers, who was sitting on the opposite side of her, was taking in all the action. He noted that she had the President eating out of her hand. They discussed quite a few controversial political issues, and he overheard her say, "Right on, Mr. President. I agree wholeheartedly."

Just before midnight, the President stood up and approached a microphone that had been quickly set up.

"Fellow Democrats," he remarked in a slow measured statement. "I've some very important news to announce to you this evening. After consultation with members of the Democratic party and many of you seated at this dinner table, I have decided to ask Senator Kelli Palmer to become Vice President of this beloved country of ours. I hope she will accept. Kelli, will you stand up and come to the microphone and give us your answer?" It was a set piece, but D.C. thrived on ceremony.

Everyone stood up and started to clap. Kelli stood up, red hair shining, her green eyes flashing, and a broad smile on her face. She waited for the applause to stop, then she spoke into the microphone as if addressing a drill parade.

"Mr. President, it would be a great honor to be your Vice President."

After she spoke, she put her right arm around him and gave him a hug. The President, looking like a proud grandfather, blushed, and stuck out his chest.

"I think we'll make a great team," she said. "I'll be willing to do anything you want me to do—anything to help the party."

Powers then stood up, and champagne glasses were raised.

"Here's to Kelli Palmer, our new Vice President."

"Here, here!" was the loud unanimous reply.

XVII

THE GLASS CAGE

In the morning, Kevin Powers called Senator Willett. "We did it, Claude!"

"Yes, we did! I'm glad we talked to Kelli in the limo."

"I was impressed by the way Kelli handled the President. Weren't you?"

"Yes. She's learning politics in a hurry . . . she compromised, didn't she?"

"What's next on the agenda?"

"Her past has to be checked out by the F.B.I."

"Anything else?"

"I suppose the party has to make sure that she doesn't have any skeletons in the closet that could come back to haunt us."

"How are we gonna do that?" asked Claude. "Who's going to question her? Who's going to be the prosecutor and whose going to be the judge, now that Whitehead wants her?"

"We're gonna have to get three or four prominent members of the party to ask her pertinent questions about her past."

"Why don't you ask Senator Webster, Dakin, and Bernett . . . add you and me. We'll get together and quiz her," said Willett.

"She may not like the idea of someone delving into her past personal life."

"The past of anyone who runs to become President or Vice President of the United States should be an open book."

"What kind of questions are we gonna ask her?"

"Anything that might disqualify her from serving."

"Such as what?"

"Crime, illegal campaign funding, illicit sex . . . you know what I mean . . . the ones that have gotten our past Presidents into trouble."

Kevin laughed. Senator Willett spoke up. "You mean the ones that they got caught with. Don't you?"

KELLI AND THE EVALUATION COMMITTEE

The committee met with Kelli in a private room at the Willard InterContinental Hotel on Pennsylvania Avenue. Kevin Powers, the Democratic Party Chairman, was to moderate the session. It was agreed that the questioning would be candid, and no notes or recordings would be allowed.

Kelli had been forewarned about the session by Powers.

"Kelli, since you have now been honored by President Whitehead to be his choice for Vice President, it is necessary for the party to ask you if there might be something in your past that would disqualify you for the job. There will be a routine check on your past by the F.B.I., also. Do you object to this?"

"No. Not at all. I have one condition, however, and that is that the answers I give tonight are strictly confidential and will not leave this room."

"We agree to that."

"Do you have any skeletons in the closet that might hurt the party?"

"I don't think so," she replied. "What kind of skeletons?"

"You spent over twenty years in the Navy, most in the Naval Air Corps. I'm sure you've had some sexual harassment. Have you had any problems with it?"

"How specific do you want to get?"

"As specific as you want to get. Have you had any abortions, sexual escapades, or affairs with anyone while you were in the service?"

"Do you mean with any of my senior officers?"

"Well . . . yes."

"How high a rank do you want to go?" Kelli replied with a smile.

"We're serious," said Powers.

"So am I! When I was an Ensign, I was propositioned by a Commander. When I was a Lieutenant Commander, I was approached by a Vice Admiral. Is that good enough?"

"I can't believe that!" replied Kevin. "However, you are quite attractive. How did you handle it?"

"Are you asking me whether I had sex with them?"

"No . . . well . . . yes. What I mean is, only if you had to."

"What you're asking is whether I used sex to gain a promotion— if I read you right. My answer is no. I also feel that you're delving too deep into my personal life with these questions. If I become President, I don't plan to be in a glass cage."

"We have to do it," said Kevin. "Because not all of our past presidents were choir boys."

"I realize that, and I would like to make a statement about my past. Becoming a Navy jet carrier pilot wasn't easy. The best and the most elite Navy pilots are the carrier pilots, and I was thrown into the lions' den with them . . . all that male pulchritude and one attractive athletic female . . . I did succumb . . . wouldn't you? I had the choice of the cream of the crop . . . the top athletes and top pilots of the world . . . but I was selective. You can count the number of my intimate sexual encounters or affairs on one hand, and two of those were with the man that I married."

"What about those three affairs that you had other than with your husband?" asked Kevin.

"One was what I call an indoctrination into womanhood, at the Academy . . . it was nothing. It turned me off on sex. The other was with a pilot at Pensacola. That, I must admit was more interesting. He's happily married and a Rear Admiral now. We're good friends. The third was with a Commander, a pilot I met after I thought that I was dumped by my future husband. He died in an airplane crash . . . If I get into the White House, I repeat . . . I don't expect to be thrown into a glass cage concerning my personal life, and that includes my family! If that's what the party wants, count me out.

I'd like to hear some of you in this room answer questions that I have just answered. What's good for the goose is good for the gander . . . and that applies to the congressmen, too."

Before the group broke up, they all stood up and Kevin proposed a toast. "To Vice President Palmer. May you have great success as our first woman Vice President. Good luck to you!"

"I'll drink to that!" replied Kelli.

WOMEN IN POLITICS . . .
A RISING TIDE AND RISKS

At a joint meeting of Congress, Kelli Palmer's name was placed in nomination to become the first woman Vice President of the United States of America.

The Senate Majority Leader read her background, and there was little discussion about Kelli's qualifications for the job. Once she received a three-fourths majority vote, a motion was made and passed to make the vote unanimous.

Chief Supreme Court Justice Thomas Gregory Evans conducted the swearing in ceremony in front of the painting of George Washington in the East Room, the largest room in the White House. She placed her right hand on her grandfather's Bible and among close family, friends, and senior members of Congress, she promised to uphold the Constitution of the United States of America. She felt confident and happy, but she couldn't prevent a few small tears. Following the ceremony, drinks and hors d' oeuvres were served in the Green Room at the White House, also known as the Thomas Jefferson Room.

Kelli's lifestyle changed almost immediately. After dinner, an official black armored limousine took her to her home. Secret Service Agents would be with her constantly. She was informed that, in the near future, she would be moving to the official residence of the Vice President and would be allowed to make changes and add new furnishings.

Her husband wasn't happy about what was going on, and it

didn't take him long to express his feelings. "Okay, now we'll have a bigger house with guys in shades who talk into their lapels. We're going to be isolated. There will be no privacy. We won't be able to have any private family fights anymore! I predict you'll regret the day you became Vice President."

"We have to give it a chance," said Kelli. "I want you to be supportive."

"Well, I hope you won't forget me," he said, "because I love you."

"I won't," she replied, "as long as you realize we may have some tough times ahead."

"What about the children?" he asked.

"We'll have to work out some arrangements for them," she replied.

It didn't take Kelli long to find out that being Vice President was not just pomp and circumstance. She had to fill in for the President at official visits from heads of states and foreign dignitaries, and travel extensively for speaking engagements. She made a point of continuing her physical exercise of lifting weights and jogging, although her day was much longer now and more exhausting. She hardly saw Mark at all, except for late nights at home when she crawled into bed, exhausted.

Her kids, Anne and Paul, were fourteen and thirteen now. Kelli usually saw them at breakfast before they went to school. She was almost a stranger to her children and didn't like it. Kelli Anne told her mother that she didn't like those men in black suits following her all around the school.

"They're weird," she said. "I don't have any privacy."

"They're to protect you, sweetheart," she replied.

Once President Whitehead realized he made the proper choice in selecting her, he began to demand more of her time. She substituted for him when he wasn't feeling well . . . which seemed to be increasing. The media and the press corps were more active when she was with him and, as a team, they got better press coverage. A lot of voters were now looking at Whitehead more favorably. After all . . . he was the one who chose Kelli to be the first woman Vice

President. The female vote had never been more tied to the Democrats.

Even though President Whitehead had lost more weight and projected poorly on TV, he was beginning to talk as though he might run for re-election. It was unrealistic, and the party bosses tried to discourage him. Many of his former senate colleagues advised him to quit. They didn't want him to run . . . he would lose. Whitehead would have no part of it. It was his decision to make . . . not theirs. He finally decided to run for re-election and made a public announcement at one of his press conferences. The reaction by the media was that of surprise and disbelief.

"Is your Vice President going to run with you?" he was asked.

"I haven't asked her, but I'm sure she will."

When Kelli heard about it, she couldn't believe it. It wasn't planned to be that way. She was to be the Presidential candidate. She was upset, but there was nothing that she could do.

The President finally called her and asked her if she would be willing to run on his ticket for re-election. She reluctantly accepted, even though she had little confidence in winning and knew the campaign might ruin her marriage.

"As Vice President, you'll have to travel around the country raising money for the party and eating lots of chicken dinners."

"I'll do my best," replied Kelli. It seemed the only thing to say, although she knew her husband would blow his stack when he found out.

It didn't take her long to find out that the campaign trail is rough. Some people, she discovered, hated her—some because she was a woman, others because she was a Democrat. A few days before a speaking engagement with The League of Women Voters at the St. Francis Hotel in San Francisco, someone wrote a letter to the F.B.I. stating they would take a shot at her if she came to California. The F.B.I. told Kelli about the letter. It wasn't the first threatening letter that they had received about her. She had no intention of being stopped by some sick nut who didn't like women in public office. She worked with the Secret Service to map out her trip carefully, and they beefed up security . . . everyone remembering that former President Ford had been fired upon at that same hotel.

Kelli took Air Force Two out to San Francisco. When her limousine drove up to the front of the St. Francis Hotel, she noted there were placards carried by what looked like student activists reading, "Four years is enough. Time for a change." Others said, "Whitehead is dead above the neck." Another said, "Get women out of politics!" The signs were a wake-up call and confirmed what she had been told. When she got out of the limousine, a crowd of college students and gays screamed epithets at her. "Down with Kelli, the slut!" "Equal sexual rights for gays." More signs were in evidence. "Go back to the kitchen" and "Women belong at home" . . . Kelli was visibly upset. The agents hurried her into the hotel and up to her room.

Kevin Powers, the Democratic Chairman who was with her, remarked, "California has its share of kooks, Kelli. You knew that! Don't let them bother you. We'll carry California in the fall."

"Since when do gays have anything against me? I'm on the right side of just about every issue they have."

"If you're military, you're anti-gay. At least to them. 'Don't ask, don't tell', isn't working."

"I expected more from them."

"More what?" said Powers. "Respect? Intelligence? Sensitivity? Forget it."

"We need their votes just like anyone else," said Kelli. "I've never been anti-gay."

"Don't let it bother you," replied Powers.

There were over 600 prominent Democrats in the banquet hall. She deviated from the prepared speech the party politicians had given her and stated that term limit legislation throughout the country was a must in the next four years. During the question and answer period that followed her talk, she was asked many questions that she'd been prepped for, but one stood out.

"If you were President, what is the one thing you would like to do to correct the problems we have in this country?"

"I don't want my remarks to be misinterpreted because when I was sworn in as Vice President, I promised to uphold the Constitution of the United States of America. However, if I were President, I would try to change parts of that Constitution. I feel it's too difficult to make amendments to that document. Our forefathers didn't want it changed easily, but with a rapidly changing world, some changes are necessary. And sometimes speed is critical. We can't wait ten years to allow three-fourths of the states to ratify an amendment. I'd change the methods that enable us to change the Constitution.

"However, there's one part of that Constitution I won't change, and that's the Bill of Rights. The Bill of Rights, as you know, was added onto the Constitution by a Constitutional Convention. This country may need another Constitutional Convention. That might be a way to bypass Congress, if necessary, and speed up the process.

"The Bill of Rights states that all Americans are endowed with the unalienable rights to life, liberty, and the pursuit of happiness. The part of the Bill of Rights that I see fading away from the American dream is the pursuit of happiness. If I were President, that's the part I would reinstate. And the most important element in the pursuit of happiness is an equal opportunity to obtain a good education, so each individual can compete in the open marketplace."

After her speech, she met with the local politicians in an adjoining room, and shook hands and chatted with most of them. She was told that the people in California really seemed to like her and that she should ignore the placards and threats by the students. When it was time to leave, she took an elevator to the lobby with the Secret Service Agents. Her armored limousine was waiting for her at the main entrance to the hotel. The sun was starting to go down and, sure enough, the placard holders were still outside grumbling sullenly as they paced around. There seemed to be more protesters than when she had entered the hotel.

Her eyes scanned both sides of the exit area rapidly, as she walked towards the limo . . . much like she scanned the skies when she was flying. From behind one of the placards on the left side, she saw a woman pull a shiny object out of her purse. Kelli immediately recognized it and dove towards one of her Secret Service Agents, as the rat-a-tat-tat of an automatic weapon flashed towards her, and the spray and stutter of automatic weapons fire sang off the cars around them.

She and the Agent landed face down on the sidewalk. There were screams behind her. It appeared that more than one person was hit.

An elderly man, who was standing next to the female assassin, did a Karate chop on her wrist, and the Uzi flew out of her hand. Within seconds she was surrounded, pushed to the ground, and handcuffed.

Kelli and the Secret Service Agent got up and scrambled into the armored limo. The driver and motorcade drove away rapidly. Kelli was shaken up by the incident with a few scrapes and bruises but not hurt. She had taken enemy fire before. It was different this time. This was close-up automatic fire. Five people had been hit by the bullets and were taken to the nearby hospital. One was critically injured.

By the time her plane arrived back in Washington, D.C., the assassination attempt had been shown coast to coast on national television. They ran it unedited and flashed back to the attempt on Ford's life. The scenes were remarkably similar.

The woman had stalked Kelli for two months. She was vehemently opposed to women in politics and she was a sick deranged individual who almost succeeded in killing the first woman Vice President.

When Kelli's plane arrived at Reagan National Airport, the press was waiting for her. Mark was in the midst of the crowd, and he was a basket case. Kelli made a statement to the crowd:

"I want to reassure all of you that I am alive and well. This will not deter my efforts to help shape the destiny of this country. Women have a role to play in politics just like men. I have nothing further to say at this time."

She and her husband rushed off in their limo.

"Kelli, I want you to resign," he said quietly.

"Relax, Palmer. I'm okay. That person shooting at me wanted to get rid of me because I'm a woman or else she's just plain crazy! When I was flying those jets at night off the carriers, I was at just as much risk . . . maybe more. Just one small miscalculation at night trying to land your plane on the flight deck, and you're dead. I'm not a quitter, and you should know that by now."

POST TRAUMATIC EVENT

Mark and the two children were quite upset about the assassination attempt on Kelli's life. Kelli tried to brush off the whole episode and not to visibly show that she was disturbed by what happened. The media played up the assassination attempt as a blow to stifle the increasing number of women playing an active role in politics. The talk shows tried to get Kelli to talk about it on their shows, but she refused to get involved. Too much media publicity was taking place. She felt that the less said about it, the better it would be . . . some other crazy nut might try it again.

Mark and the two children had a difficult time adjusting to Kelli's busy schedule. It was like being on a perpetual merry-go-round and not being able to get off. The phone was ringing all the time, and there were frequent cancellations and times of crisis when she didn't see the family for a day or two, and sometimes even longer. Because President Whitehead wasn't well, she had to fill in for him on short notice for campaign speeches around the country that he was scheduled to give. Sometimes she had to fly abroad, but she always tried to call home just to talk to the children and to reassure Mark that she was all right. She made a concerted effort to be present for critical events the children were involved in.

The oldest child, Kelli Anne, was the most difficult to handle. She would stay up late at night just to see her mother. She looked exactly like her mother, and she was so much like her that it was scary. She was a teenager—fourteen years old and a very independent young lady.

"Mom, you have to spend more time with Paul, me and Daddy! I know you're the Vice President, but I want you as a mom!"

Kelli had tears in her eyes when she said that. She knew she was not fulfilling her job as a mother.

"Sweetheart, I love you. Please try to be understanding. I'm trying to do something for all women. Some day you're going to be just like your mom, and you'll be able to understand."

"Well, I don't understand, and I know I'm not going to be just like you! I don't want to be Vice President . . . ever!" she said as she stamped her foot. "I don't like all those Secret Service people either. I feel like I'm in a cage. It's like going to the zoo, and all the people are staring at you."

"They're trying to keep you safe, Sweetheart."

"Why are they trying to keep me safe, when you're the one they shot at?"

"By hurting you, they might drive your mother out of office. That's why!"

"But if you weren't in office, they wouldn't try to hurt either one of us."

"You're right. I don't have a good answer for that. You're really growing up into a smart young lady."

"I want you as a regular Mom, not a Vice President Mom."

"That can't happen," replied Kelli.

"If that can't happen, I'd rather just be alone with you. When can we go shopping, just you and me?"

"I'm afraid that will have to wait."

"Paul hit a home run in the Little League game last week, and you weren't there."

"I know. I'm sorry I missed it."

"One of the boys on the football team asked me to go to a dance with him. Daddy told me I was too young and to ask you."

"How old is the boy?"

"He's eighteen."

"You're how old now?"

"Mom, you know how old I am. I'm fourteen."

"I'll talk to your Daddy about it. I think you should wait awhile."

"A lot of girls in my class are going to the dance."

"That doesn't make it right. It's a little bit too soon for you to be getting involved with a senior in high school."

"When do you think I'll be able to go out alone with a boy?"

"I'll give it some thought and get back to you. Have you talked to your father about this?"

"No. I want to talk to you. When can we have a vacation with just you, Paul, and Daddy with none of those Secret Service people running around?"

"When I get back from a meeting in Russia next week, I'll arrange a vacation for all of us. I'd like a rest, too!"

"You do look tired, Mommy. You definitely need a rest. I've only got one Mommy, and I worry about you . . . more so since that lady tried to shoot you."

"That won't happen again, Anne. Please don't worry so much."

"I pray for you all the time, especially when I don't see you for awhile. I wish I could see you more."

That did it for Kelli. She hugged her daughter and gave her a big kiss. There were tears coming down both of their cheeks. At this moment, she wished that she was not the Vice President.

XVIII

PRESIDENTIAL
CHARACTERISTICS

Senator Preston Adams III relaxed as he pulled an expensive Cuban Monte Cristo out of the inside pocket of his dark blue suit, lit it up, affectionately nursed a glowing coal into life, and took a big drag. The smoke quickly permeated the limousine in layers. Here within the tinted glass limo, he could smoke his cigar and relax for he was constantly aware of his political image and did not smoke or drink in public. He was also a member of the largest Baptist church in Atlanta and had sang in its choir—the Christian coalition supported his political career.

Preston had climbed his way to the top of the political world and had achieved what he thought was the apex of his potential. He was black—half black, but no one made that distinction—a Republican, and the Majority Leader of the United States Senate. It was a long struggle, and he was 61 years of age. His father Cass Adams, had been a pro basketball player who had made millions as an athlete, a spokesperson, pitch man, and commentator. He had married a beautiful white socialite from Cleveland, the daughter of a business tycoon, who later became Governor of Ohio. Preston grew up in Atlanta, a man of privilege, attending the best schools . . . Choate, Yale, and Harvard Law.

When he graduated, he joined a prominent Chicago law firm and, as a trial lawyer, became famous winning high-profile TV cases. He went back to Atlanta and became active in local politics and served in the State Senate of Georgia for six years. With the gradual progressive change in the USA, and increased emergence of the rainbow coalition, it was fashionable to be a member of a mixed racial group. Adams served as a representative to Congress from his Atlanta district for six years, and eventually became a senior senator from Georgia.

Preston's Harvard Law School affiliation did what he expected, opening doors into hidden chambers that were forbidden to many blacks in the past. He went to all of his alumni meetings and made a point of contributing generously to the Harvard Alumni Fund. When he became Majority Leader of the Senate, he was invited to speak to the law school's graduating class. Attending the law school's alumni meetings was always interesting to him because he got to hobnob with the politicians, lawyers, and successful icons of the world as well as many heads of major corporations. Preston's skin was black, but a lighter shade than his ancestors. It was advantageous for him to promote his Black heritage, but he rarely did. Father Cass's perimeter jump shot paved the way. He could also cross the street and gain support, however, because of his white heritage. His wife, Roseana, was a wealthy socialite from Boston's Back Bay society, a Wellesley graduate he met when he was at Harvard. She was white but had some Spanish ancestors and spoke Spanish fluently. They had two children, a boy and a girl. He was now in his third term in the Senate and planned to continue in the Senate as long as his constituents allowed him to. He was also planning to run against President Whitehead and felt that he could beat him. His whole life was devoted to government and politics. The only obstacle to his staying in the Senate was the perennial attempt by the populace to limit the terms of the congressmen.

As Majority Leader, he had continued the facade of supporting term limits, but by political maneuvering and parliamentary trickery, he had prevented the passage of that amendment to the Constitution in the Senate.

One of the perks that Preston received as Majority Leader was the customized black limousine he was now riding in, as he headed from his farm in McLean, Virginia, to Washington, D.C. The limo was fully equipped with communication equipment and security safeguards: reflective bullet-proof windows, heavy metal flooring for bomb protection, and special bullet-proof tires. Security was no longer a laughing matter. One of his Senate party colleagues, Hector Santos from Florida, was blown up in Liberty City three weeks earlier. His tires were shot out, a bomb rolled under the car, and within eight seconds the job was done. The FBI knew the group that was responsible but not the individual culprits.

Preston glanced at his watch which looked like the one worn by the comic strip detective Dick Tracy in the 1950's. But, Preston's watch had a telephone with screen, a computer, a data base, and instrumentation with voice activation that could record words and fax them through satellite communication to any place on earth. It could also be used as a detection device to pinpoint where he was by satellite at anytime of the day or night. That had its advantages and disadvantages. It was worn by all of the congressmen so that they could be contacted at any time. A beeper would go off, and a red light would flash when a call was coming in.

As the limo continued to speed on Route 95 back to Washington, D.C., a light flashed on the large screen facing him. He pressed a button and locked onto the picture. It was the Chairman of the Republican party—former Senator Jack Kensington.

"I'm calling a secret meeting of key members of the Republican party. As you know, President Whitehead has been sick recently, which I feel will be to our advantage in the coming presidential election. We have some new information about his illness. My office has faxed a questionnaire to each of you. Please fill it out promptly and return it immediately. The meeting will be held a week from this Friday at the Mayflower Hotel in Washington, D.C. A large suite has been reserved, and I will moderate the meeting. The main item on the agenda is to discuss all the potential Presidential candidates of the party. Of course, primaries in Iowa and New Hampshire will eventually have an impact on the selection."

The select committee assembled at the Mayflower Hotel. It was made up of the "Who's Who" of prominent Republicans: Adams, the Majority Leader of the Senate; Brent Ferngrich, a former Speaker of the House of Representatives; Tiffany Spencer, a female Senator from Idaho; a former Secretary of State; and a Secretary of the Treasury. There were also three CEOs of television, radio, and the print media; a president of a large trade union, Robin White; and two presidents of major universities. A senator who was a former heart surgeon, and a former doctor, Eliot Whipple, who had received the Nobel Prize in medicine, were also in attendance.

After the meal, Jack Kensington stood up and hit his spoon against a glass to get everyone's attention.

"Gentlemen and ladies, you all know why we are here. My office has received the questionnaires you were asked to fill out listing the characteristics essential to get the presidency back for our party. It is extremely important that we select the right person to run. I plan to summarize your written recommendations and make a few remarks. Then I'll open this meeting, so we can discuss the relative merits of our presidential candidates. Since two of you are in that category, I'll ask everyone to refrain from discussing their merits until the end of our discussion.

"Patrick Henry, in 1775, said, 'I have but one lamp by which my feet are guided and that is the lamp of experience. I know of no way of judging the future but by the past.'"

"The past tells us that we have had forty-six presidents of the United States of America—more than half of them have been lawyers. A few have been self-educated such as Abraham Lincoln, one of our best presidents, if not the best. Almost twenty-five percent have gone to Harvard, Princeton, or Yale. In the early years of our government, Jefferson, Monroe, and Tyler all attended William and Mary College in Virginia.

"Almost one half of our presidents have served as senators or members of the House of Representatives before being elected president. One third have been governors of their states, and at least twenty-five percent served as vice presidents before becoming president. Andrew Jackson, Zachary Taylor, Ulysses S. Grant, and Dwight D. Eisenhower had outstanding careers in the military. Some of our past presidents—Woodrow Wilson, James Garfield, and Lyndon Johnson were school teachers or presidents of universities.

"I'm sure that many of you have given a great deal of thought as to how to select a perfect candidate for president. It's not an easy task, and as one individual wrote in his reply, 'There is no perfect candidate. So let's locate the least imperfect one.'"

"I'll start with *age*. Many of you felt that we should be choosing younger candidates for president. The rigors of the office are substantial, and the potential for incapacity of the president during his time in office is real. A healthy, mentally alert president is demanded by the public. With television and media coverage of daily issues, press conferences and worldwide summits, it's paramount that we present a strong, attractive individual. Some of you have even suggested that the candidate be between the ages of 40 to 60.

"The average age of our forty-six presidents when they entered the office of the presidency was 54.6 years. Historians have stated that some of our best presidents were young: Teddy Roosevelt (43 yrs.); Abraham Lincoln (52 yrs.); Franklin Roosevelt (51 yrs.); John F. Kennedy (44 yrs.); George Washington (57 yrs.); Thomas Jefferson (58 yrs.).

"In addition to presenting a young personal appearance, a president must be able to project an astute mental capacity, so that the public has confidence in his actions. We want someone who can shine in press conferences.

"The *health of the candidate* also has to be considered. Has the candidate had any heart attacks or serious illnesses, such as cancer? As you know, a past candidate had his doctor verify that he was cured of his cancer, and then after the election he was found to have a recurrence. The public wants to know about the health of our candidates. If a president dies in office, the changing of the guard can be traumatic to the country and the world and should be avoided if it is at all possible.

"The *family background of the candidate* is likewise important. Is there a divorce or a personality characteristic in relation to sexual preference or lifestyle? Polls show that divorce is probably not as important. Until recent years, divorce was taboo if you were seeking the office of the presidency. Marrying a widow, however, was considered respectable. In fact, George Washington married Martha Curtis, a widow with two children, who was considered one of the wealthiest women in Virginia.

"Until Ronald Reagan, practically all our presidents had not been divorced. But as more and more Americans are affected by divorce, this may not be as big an issue. However, the religious right is becoming more politically active, and their numbers are not to be ignored. They are an important voting block. That's why abortion issues, right-to-die and assisted suicides, and marriage, too, must be openly discussed by our prospective candidates. We need to be prepared.

"Is the *ethnic group, skin color, and gender* important? Just look at the Congress, and see how it is changing in regards to ethnicity, skin color, and gender. We continue to see more women, blacks, and Hispanics in Congress every year. There is a black caucus and a rainbow coalition constantly getting stronger. This is what democracy is all about—getting everyone involved.

"Another factor that has to be considered is what I call:

SKELETONS IN THE CLOSET

"As you know, the office of the presidency has become a 'glass cage' with the president in the 'cage'. Sex and sexual preferences are now openly discussed in the media and that includes past and present indiscretions with the opposite sex. If any of the party's presidential candidates have any skeletons in the closet that can affect their ability to lead and govern this nation, they have to be disclosed or withdraw their candidacy. The public wants and demands a fair political playing field for both parties and that includes past and present sexual indiscretions.

"There are many other factors that should play a role in our selection of the candidates who wish to run for president . . . but I'll stop here and take your questions."

"Why in hell did Congress ever allow an independent counsel to investigate the personal past and present sex life of any President?

It is beyond comprehension!" said former House Speaker Brent Ferngrich.

"That's a good question," replied Kensington. "Quite a few of
our past Presidents strayed from the home pasture and had sexual
indiscretions . . . some had mistresses, compliant consensual lovers
or hookers . . . different ages, sizes, and shapes . . . just look at the
history books. Thomas Jefferson, Franklin D. Roosevelt, John F.
Kennedy, L. B. Johnson, and Bill Clinton are prime examples."

"Why did Congress do it?" asked Senator Spencer.

"The political parties were sparring for a political advantage . . . that's why," said Ferngrich. "They were either trying to get
even for something that happened in the past or get votes for the
next election."

"We're all living to regret it," replied Kensington. "It's now part
of the political obstacle course for the candidates."

"The media were also the culprits!" said White. "They had to
have some dirt to talk about to entice and capture the TV audience.
Their reporting was not completely honest. The media journalists
should disclose their sexual indiscretions too. Some of them have
had interesting pasts."

"We could debate this issue forever. Let's go on to the discussion."

Immediately, eight hands went up. "Senator Adams?"

"As you know, I'm a candidate for the Presidency, and I don't fall
into the age group you selected. To tell someone they can't run for
the Presidency if they're over 60 years of age is ridiculous. I'm 61
years of age. Some of our greatest statesmen have been much older."

"That's true," replied Kensington. "However, it hasn't applied to
our forty-six elected Presidents. We've had only two who were over
68 years of age, Preston. William Harrison, who died one month
after the inauguration, and Ronald Reagan. What most of the
group is saying, is that the stress and rigors of the office have mul-
tiplied many times over, and a young individual might be better
able to do the job. In your case, 61 years of age should not prevent
you from being a candidate."

"I was told that Reagan used Hollywood make-up and dyed his

hair for his television appearances, that's why he looked so young and vigorous," said one of the media CEOs. "Why can't the other candidates do it?"

"That was thirty years ago," said Senator Durham.

"Well, he certainly looked young and handsome most of the time," the CEO shot back.

"He was a Hollywood movie star. He knew how to use make-up," said Spencer. "There's no doubt the generation gap will be a factor in the coming election. The country's debt burden on the young is getting them politically united, and they don't identify well with older politicians. It strengthens the argument for youth."

"How an individual projects on television is extremely important," said Mike Goldman, the CEO of ABC news. "A youthful, vigorous-appearing individual like Jack Kennedy, for instance, has a much greater appeal, especially to the younger generation and to women who are more likely to vote for that person. The facial expressions and appearance on television also give the public some insight into the personality of the individual running for the presidency. Too many candidates look too stern or too wishy-washy on the tube. They don't project confidence. Voice is important also. We need someone with a resonant voice who can think quickly on his feet and sound like he knows what he's doing. TV is key, my friends. We must make it a top priority."

"How are we going to know about the health of the candidates?" asked Dr. Whipple. "All doctor's notes on patients are personal and confidential."

"That's a good question," said Kensington. "We're going to ask all the candidates to open the book on their health histories. The media is demanding it. The health of the candidate running for the most important job in the world is everyone's business, including the man in the street. One of you stated that all the candidates should have a complete history and physical examination, including blood work, EKG, colonoscopy, stress test, etc., and then release the results to the press and media."

"If you publicize that rule, you'll have an outcry from every disabled person in the country," said Bill Black, a past Secretary of the

Treasury. "Franklin Roosevelt, a Democrat, would never have been elected under those guidelines."

"If you insist on a public history and physical, someone is going to demand a complete mental and personality evaluation by a psychiatrist," said Robin White, the union representative.

"Might not be a bad idea. It could've saved us from some of our weak presidents," said Kensington. Laughter tinged with malice rippled around the room.

"Look," said Kensington, shifting gears, "the President is the only one who can control all the electronic communication devices that activate our nuclear arsenal. That's an argument for a fully disclosed physical and mental evaluation."

"That's what worries me," said White. "I fear that system is obsolete. All you need is a major disaster and poof . . . that system is history. We need an improved system of control if a major disaster strikes."

"Correct, Sir, correct!" said Dr. Eliot Whipple, the Nobel prize winner in medicine and former head of the National Academy of Sciences. "A presidential candidate could get into office as a healthy robust individual and then, because of the stress of the job, experience some mental aberration that could lead us all on to Armageddon."

"How would you prevent that?" said Kensington.

"By close observation by those who come in daily contact with the president . . . also periodic complete health examinations— every six months, probably, with full disclosure to the media and the public."

"How are you going to prevent cheating by the president's personal physician?"

"By having a second opinion by the American Academy of Physicians reviewing the tests, or . . ."

"Isn't that delving too deeply into the President's personal life?" asked Senator Durham.

"Not really," replied Jack Kensington. "Most candidates eagerly seek the job. If full disclosure is one of the ground rules, and I feel it is, then they should abide by it."

XIX

COMMUNICATION CONTROL

Mike Goldman, the CEO of one of the largest mega-conglomerates of the telecommunications industry, was bothered after the meeting. He felt that neither of the major parties were putting up the best candidates. Most of the voters were disenchanted and frustrated with the government, but no one seemed to be doing anything about it. Once someone got into office, as long as they were on the right side of big business, it was almost impossible to get them out. Large corporations gave big bucks to the incumbents. He was afraid that Whitehead would be re-elected. Incumbents had won nearly 88% of all elections since the year 2000. Goldman knew there were no more Abe Lincolns running for office and none on the horizon. He didn't like candidates who were anointed because their past relatives had served in high political offices. All that did was perpetuate the policies of their forebearers . . . some had been voted out of office. Most were rich or had become wealthy while serving on the National Stage. He was for getting rid of career politicians who made a living out of their perennial candidacy. But that meant term limits. And term limits meant getting both parties to agree on the criteria. Catch-22.

Both the Democrats and Republicans feared the emergence of a new independent party. With so much government dissatisfaction, a party could gain power very quickly if the right person stepped forward.

On TV news, commentators often speculated on this possibility, asking political experts their predictions.

"The independent party will be a mixture of conservatives and liberals willing to communicate with each other," one recently retired senator offered. "A candidate who is a moderate leaning towards liberal on social or economic issues, but conservative on defense issues, could have a great impact on the upcoming election."

Goldman told his secretary to contact Dick Collins, another mega-conglomerate television mogul. He also told her to call Bill Rupert, a third television CEO.

"Dick, Mike Goldman. There are some interesting developments coming up in our next presidential election. I'd like to invite you and Bill Rupert to lunch, so we can talk about it."

"Great idea. I'd like to blow off some steam. I got a call from one candidate's campaign manager who wanted to have more TV coverage than his opponent. I told him if he wants increased air time, I want to know his boy's position on telecom reform. It was a short conversation."

"After I talk to Bill, I'll have my secretary contact you, so we can get together. Is that agreeable?"

"That's fine with me, Mike. You name the place. But have it swept for bugs."

Goldman called Bill Rupert, and he was all for it. They agreed to meet at Goldman's summer home on Oyster Bay. Goldman had private security personnel check the large cottage for bugging devices and set up a tight security system. They agreed that their discussion would not be publicized.

A buffet table and a bar were set up, but no bartender. There would be no one else in the room except the three telecommunication CEOs, who all knew how to pour their own drinks.

Goldman started the conversation.

"Fellas, I'm talking out of church, hoping for strict confidentiality."

The other two men nodded their heads in agreement.

"I recently attended a meeting of Republican leaders about what the prerequisites should be for running for the office of the presidency. They talked about age, health, color, religion, past sex experience, and spent a lot of time on how an individual should look and act on television if he seeks the office of the presidency."

"After that meeting, I came to the conclusion that none of the Republicans fulfilled the criteria in my book for becoming president. I can't support the Democratic incumbent, either. Whitehead's too old and sick, and it looks like the Republicans are going to nominate Preston Adams whose in the back pocket of the big corporations."

"Mike," said Dick Collins, "we're all pissed off, but so what? What can we do about it?"

"If things stay as they are, I think we can really get somewhere with an independent party. But we can't wait for the grass roots. It's got to happen from the top down. Somebody has got to have big bucks to finance it."

"You're sounding like a liberal," said Collins.

"Only when I have to be," he replied. "Liberals are for change, and I hate to admit it, but sometimes we have to have change."

"What are you saying?" asked Rupert.

"I'm saying there won't be any convention to select the independent candidate. I think someone will anoint themselves."

"What do you suggest?" asked Rupert.

"Between the three of us, we control most of the television, newspapers, and radio in this country. In an indirect way, we can demand a more equitable way to select the candidates."

"Are you saying," said Collins, "that you think the independent candidate might have a genuine chance to be elected the next President?"

"That's right," said Goldman. "And if we use our power and influence, we can get the right candidate for the job and help the candidate win."

"It's not that simple," said Rupert. "We get a lot of our advertising revenue from big business. They might not like us interfering in the political mainframe."

"They're in it. They own all of us too. But we have front line control."

"What about the on-line networks?" asked Collins. "How are we going to control them?"

"We'll have to invite some of the boys from the West Coast to join us," said Goldman. "They like to make money, just like we do. They need control, too. They're already bundling computers, televisions, fax machines, copy machines, and phones for mass market. They need some new laws out of Congress. So yeah, we need them, but I want the control to stay here."

"Whoever owns and controls that business will control the minds of the people," said Goldman. "Look what the media did about the sex scandal of one of our past presidents."

"It's going to happen faster than you think," said Collins. "Orville's 1984 has come and gone. What's on the horizon is beyond all reason. It's more than an invasion of the human mind— it may be controlling the future of the universe."

"I wonder if the public understands what's happening."

"How about Congress?" replied Collins.

F.B.I. DIRECTOR'S OFFICE
WASHINGTON, D.C.

Mark Lynch, the Director of the F.B.I., listened to the tapes of the secret media meeting at Oyster Bay. He was disturbed by what he heard and decided to have a meeting with the Attorney General, Tom Morris. He called him on the phone and arranged for a meeting.

"Tom, three of the biggest media CEO's had a recent secret meeting to discuss the upcoming Presidential election. They literally have a telecom monopoly."

"So what?" replied Morris. "There's nothing that you can do about that."

"They're planning to use that monopoly to influence who gets elected."

"What are you saying?"

"They don't like the Republican or Democratic candidates and plan to support an Independent candidate."

"How do you know that? Do you have any intelligence checks on these moguls?" asked Morris.

"Yes, but this is strictly confidential, some of Goldman's staff secretly contacted the Police Chief on Oyster Bay in Long Island about testing security at his house. He told them where to get private help, and then asked why they needed to do such a thing. When they wouldn't tell him, the Chief contacted the F.B.I. agent in the area and then the Manhattan F.B.I. office. After much debate, the F.B.I. decided to plant their own listening devices after the people debugging the place had completed their job."

"I can't believe that," said Morris. "Without clearance?"

"Yes," said Lynch. "It is a palatial estate right on the water. Fortunately, we knew exactly what room was going to be used for the meeting, and with a diverting tactic, we were successful in placing the bug. To our surprise, three days later, three of the CEOs of the major media companies arrived in separate limos. We were able to get them ID'd with a telephoto and tape their conversations."

"You're on paper-thin legal ice," said the Attorney General. "You didn't have just cause to listen to their conversations."

"It's only illegal if we try to use it in court, or if we get caught . . . but we didn't."

"Have you listened to the tape?"

"Yes."

"Once I ask you about it, I'll be implicated, too."

"That's right," agreed Lynch.

"Briefly tell me the broadest strokes, and I'll decide whether I should listen to the tape."

"They don't like the political candidates of any of the parties and, in particular, the presidential candidates. It looks like Preston is going to get the Republican nod."

"So that doesn't tell you anything new."

"That's right, but what they're suggesting will have a profound effect on the presidential election."

"You'd better explain that one. Again, general ideas, no details."

"They feel that the time is ripe for a third party candidate, and they're willing to support the Independent party's choice for the presidency. They're looking for a young, healthy candidate who projects well on television and thinks well on his feet. They're looking at Senator George Bradford, the multi-millionaire."

"Here we go again," said Lynch. "If enough of the voters support the Independent party's candidate, Bradford could really get elected this time. Or one of the other two candidates could get elected through the back door by a split vote."

"That's right," said Lynch. "And telecom may just make that happen."

"Should we tell the President?"

"No. He has to be completely left out of it. If he gets implicated, it could do him in."

"What do you plan to do with that information?"

"I don't know. I haven't decided." replied Lynch.

"Perhaps we should wait and see what happens in the early primaries. A lot of things can happen between now and November. For all we know, one could get shot, and the other could have a heart attack."

"I wouldn't wish that on anyone."

"Let's see what happens."

UNPLEASANT SPECTER

Although Whitehead realized he wasn't in the best of health, he was determined to win re-election. Meanwhile, Kelli Palmer was getting kudos wherever she went. Every time she gave a speech, it was money in the bank for the party and worth twice its face value in political capital. She was enjoying competing in the political arena and was beginning to get interested about eventually running for the presidency.

There was one big obstacle however. Whitehead wanted to be in the history books as a two-term president. Yes, he would be 70 years old when he ran for re-election and knew that his energy wasn't great, but he told his close friends that he really wanted that second term.

There was another important problem he had to deal with. Senator Bradford was getting more and more publicity as well as attacking him on key issues. He was beginning to look and sound like a real candidate with weight, and the media was giving him great coverage. The President really wanted just one opponent to deal with. He felt he could beat Senator Preston Adams, but he wasn't sure about Bradford.

The party needed money for the campaign, so he traveled around the country giving speeches. On those trips, the media often remarked that he didn't look well. He appeared to be pale and emaciated, and they noted that he was using more makeup. When they asked questions about his health, his reply was, "I feel as strong as an ox."

A reporter in Kansas City, Steve Ericson, caustically remarked, "I'd like to see that ox. When did you have your last physical exam?"

"I have them every six months at Bethesda Hospital, and the results are verified by the White House physician."

"I'd like to interview him, Mr. President."

"You're welcome to. His name is Dr. David Willard." Whitehead had mastered the situation, but when he glanced at his Chief of Staff, Dave King, his eyes betrayed worry.

Dr. Willard, an elderly internist, who had been a professor of medicine in St. Louis, had been a good friend and golfing partner of President Whitehead for many years. In fact, he was offered his current position when Whitehead became president. He was what one would call a book-learning doctor. If you had a rare disease, the professor might be someone to see. If you had a belly ache—forget it! When Ericson interviewed Dr. Willard, he knew this and went at the doctor with both barrels to hit him hard.

"President Whitehead has a very sallow appearance. What do you think that's due to, Dr. Willard?"

"Probably because he hasn't gotten enough rest and sunshine lately."

"Has he had his blood checked recently?"

"About six weeks ago, and everything checked out normal."

"How's his heart?"

"His electrocardiogram shows the changes you would expect with aging. Other than that, everything seems okay."

"He seems quite forgetful," said the reporter. "He often asks for questions to be repeated."

"That's a political ploy," replied Dr. Willard. "That gives him some time to think about the question and what his answer will be."

But all was not well with President Whitehead. The constant traveling to raise funds for the coming campaign was taking its toll. He had a few bouts of shortness of breath that were checked out with EKGs, chest x-rays, and a stethoscope exam by Dr. Willard, who worried that his heart might be giving him trouble.

"Mr. President, you have to get rest periods in between these campaign swings, or you won't be around for the next four years."

"I feel fine. I just need to get a good night's sleep once in a while."

"That's what I'm trying to tell you."

"I hear you," said the President.

"How are your bowel movements? Are you passing your water okay?"

"Bowels okay, but occasional problems pissing."

"When we get back to Washington, we'll have a urologist take a look at you."

"The media will blow that one up," remarked the President.

"I can arrange it so the media won't know."

"We have just one more stop before heading back to D.C.—Chicago. It's important."

President Whitehead didn't feel well on the plane to Chicago, the last stop of a major swing to the Midwest. He was to address a large group of party faithfuls who paid $5000 a plate. When he got off the plane, he told his personal physician about it.

"Dave, I don't feel too great. I think I must have eaten something lousy in Des Moines, probably that rubber chicken."

"Have you been drinking too much scotch?"

"No."

"Have you had normal bowel movements?"

"Yes."

"I'll give you a couple of pills to cut down on the acid in your stomach. Why don't you take a nap this afternoon. You don't have to give your talk until 8:00 P.M."

"I'll try that," he replied.

The President had a light scotch to help him relax and then took his nap. At about 6:30 he woke up, took a shower, and got dressed. The Secret Service detail took him downstairs to the ballroom. Kevin Powers, the Democratic Party Chairman accompanied him.

"Feels warm in here," commented the President.

"I hope you're not catching a cold."

The President was led to the speaker's platform. The crowd stood up, cheered, and waved flags as he moved to the dais.

President Whitehead had gone over his speech with his speech writer, and he wasn't pleased with it. The speech first addressed the doom and gloom that pervaded the news when he came into office, and then went on to the economic prosperity and peacetime progress under his administration. He thought his speech writer did a lousy job, but because he didn't feel well, he didn't have time to change it.

First, he had to get through the meal—chicken divan, as usual.

"The economy's gotta be bad," he remarked. "At every one of these gatherings they serve rubber chicken, which makes me sick!" He took a few small bites and put down his fork.

"Kevin, you've got to tell the party organizers to serve something besides chicken!"

"We can have them get you something different from the kitchen."

"No. By the time they've checked it out, I will be giving my speech. Besides, I'm not hungry."

His stomach still hurt, and the pills his physician had given him weren't working. He wasn't looking forward to giving the talk. Usually he enjoyed speaking to the party faithful, but not tonight because he was too tired and felt lousy. After sitting through a long introduction by Kevin Powers, he finally got up to speak. There was prolonged applause.

"Fellow Democrats, I'm here tonight in this great city of Chicago to tell you about some of our failures that were due to an uncooperative Congress. Later I plan to talk about some of our great accomplishments." The President paused, and with a self-deprecating smile, added, *"I think I had something to do with that change."*

The audience stood up and enthusiastically applauded for what seemed like forever. When he started to talk again, they continued to interrupt. "God damn it!", he thought. "Why don't they shut up, so I can finish this speech and get the hell out of here!" Finally, they stopped applauding.

"When I came into office, our opponents left us with a huge deficit. I have instituted measures to straighten it out. Our balance of trade with Japan, Germany, and China was a disaster when I came into office, and we are correcting it. Their trade barriers are beginning to crumble."

The crowd cheered louder, and it lasted for a long time. Whitehead took a handkerchief out of his pocket and wiped his forehead. He couldn't believe how bloated he felt. His belly felt like it was loaded with bricks.

He was sweating profusely now and getting more agitated, as his face reddened. He felt awful—worse then he had felt in a long time. He began to fidget . . . his hands were shaking, and he was losing his concentration. He spoke—hesitantly. He started to stutter. He knew something was drastically wrong and started to panic. "I feel—er—ah—it's hard to explain—sick." He put his right hand on his belly and faltered. Suddenly, he couldn't see or read the prompter. He tried to hold onto the podium with his left hand to steady himself but couldn't. His legs felt wobbly as he started to pass out and fall to the floor.

The Secret Service detail rushed to the podium along with Kevin Powers. Suddenly, President Whitehead vomited explosively all over the speaker's platform and collapsed. Kevin caught him and slowly eased him down to the floor. Dr. Willard rushed to his side. The crowd gasped collectively. There was an explosion of flashes from the photographers at the front of the auditorium, and then there was silence . . . suddenly the silence was broken:

"My belly! My belly! It's killing me," shouted the President.

The agents surrounded the President for protection, as well as to shield him from the public eye. Staffers were already doing damage control down front, pressing reporters back, and reassuring everyone that the President was simply ill with the flu.

EMT's came and placed the President on a stretcher. They gave him oxygen, which made him feel worse. He tore the oxygen mask off his face, flailing his arms and thrashing about on the stretcher, almost falling. Quickly, they wheeled him out of the banquet hall, down a rear hallway to an emergency exit, into an ambulance, and transferred him to the standby Northwestern Hospital.

The E.R. personnel rushed to evaluate their distinguished patient who was sweating profusely, his skin cold and clammy. Leads were put on his chest, and an EKG was done. He had a rapid heart rate, but no evidence of a heart attack. Blood was drawn from his arm, sent to the lab and an IV started. The President kept complaining about the pain in his lower abdomen.

"My belly! My belly! The pain's getting worse! For God's sake, help me!"

The chief surgical resident, Ed Scanlon, examined him and felt his abdomen. The President screamed, "Ow . . . watch what you're doing! That really hurts!" The resident thought he felt a large mass in his lower belly.

"Mr. President, I'm going to have to do a rectal exam."

"Do whatever you have to do, but make this pain go away," Whitehead said through clenched teeth.

The doctor put on a glove, lubricated his right forefinger, and told the President to turn on his side.

At the tip of his finger, he felt a large mass on the anterior surface of the rectum.

"We're going to have to catheterize you, Mr. President."

Chief of Staff King and three aides were in the E.R., despite the hospital staff's insistence that they remain outside. Secret Service agents had sealed the E.R. entrance.

The hospital's Chief of Surgery, Bob Martin, pushed his way through them and approached Scanlon.

"What have you found, Ed?"

"He's got a large tender mass in his lower abdomen. I think it's his bladder. Also, he's got a large prostate, 4+, and I think we ought to catheterize him."

"Don't you think we ought to take a flat plate and erect x-ray of the abdomen first? Use your portable ultrasound, too."

"Yeah, we can take a quick shot."

"Do it."

The x-ray and ultrasound showed a large opaque mass in the mid-lower abdomen with no free air. It was not a pulsatile mass. More blood was taken, and electrodes were again placed on his chest with a monitor attached. His electrocardiogram was still essentially normal, but showed some old damage to his heart muscle.

"Go ahead and catheterize him. Use some Xylocaine jelly on the tube, so it won't be too painful." Whitehead was exhausted by agony, still writhing but weaker.

"For God's sake, do something," he pleaded.

Scanlon had a little difficulty in getting the catheter tube past the enlarged prostate, but it finally slipped in, and he drew out 1500cc of urine. The President immediately felt better.

"Wow, what a relief!" Whitehead looked at Ed Scanlon. "Young man, if you can't get a job when you finish here, I'll give you a job at the White House!"

Two days later, the President flew back to Washington with a Foley catheter in his bladder. It was inside his pants, so no one could see it. He looked 100% better to the press corps, who wanted to know what was going on. The official response: Exhaustion. The President's physician gave out no details of what had happened. Arrangements were made for the President to check into Bethesda Naval Hospital, and the Chief of Urology from Johns Hopkins was called in for consultation.

He had more extensive blood work done, including a prostate

test (PSA) that was well above the normal range of four. An ultrasound was done of the prostate, which showed a nodule in the left lobe, and biopsies were taken from both lobes. The pathology report showed prostate cancer.

The Chief of Urology wanted to know the time and results of his last rectal exam and last PSA test, and was surprised to find that none had been done recently. After taking CAT scans and MRIs of the pelvis, the doctors recommended a bilateral laparoscopic lymph node biopsy inside the abdomen to see if the cancer had spread.

President Whitehead was reluctant to turn over the reins of the government to Kelli Palmer when he was put under anesthesia.

"I'm only going to be asleep for an hour or two," he remarked.

"You have to do it!" replied Kevin Powers. "Anything else will be viewed as a breach of national security at the highest level."

Reluctantly he signed the papers to be sent to the Speaker of the House and the Senate pro tempore.

When the tissue on the left side inside his abdomen was analyzed, doctors found two lymph glands that were positive for cancer. Because of the spread of his cancer into his abdomen, radical surgery was not recommended; chemotherapy and radiation were offered as alternatives. The President refused chemotherapy and did not want his testicles removed.

"I'll take my druthers," he said. "No one's going to take my family jewels out."

"That's your choice," remarked the Chief of Urology.

"That's right!" he replied. "What's the next best option?"

"There is medicine we can give you."

"Do it. There's just one more thing that you have to promise me."

"What's that, Mr. President?"

"I don't want anyone to discuss these details with the press, or with anyone, not even the Vice President. They can say I have prostate cancer and that it's being taken care of and being controlled with radiation. It's common knowledge that men in my age group can live for years with prostate cancer without any ill effects."

But the media was not satisfied with what they were told. Whitehead was going to be running for re-election in nine months. They demanded that the public had a right to know more details. White-head had advocated full disclosure before running for office. Now, Whitehead refused to release his hospital records. The Chairman of the Democratic party and seven members of Congress, who knew the true story, tried to get him to bow out.

"Sorry, fellas," said Whitehead. "But I'm going to slug this one out."

One week later, the results of the tissue analysis of the President's prostate tumor and the glands in the lower abdomen were on the front page of the Sunday Washington papers. The *Washington Post* claimed they had received a copy of the original report from an anonymous source. They said they could prove that the President's cancer had spread to his glands and that his prognosis was guarded.

The White House denied the report completely when it was first presented to them. The F.B.I. and the Attorney General's office were called in to try to find out how the information was leaked to the newspapers. Confidential information had a way of getting out in the nation's capitol. No one was talking.

When Kelli read the article, she called the Democratic Party Chairman.

"Kevin, what's going on? Whitehead obviously is seriously ill and could be dead before the election."

"We can't do anything rash," said Kevin. "I think you and I should meet with President Whitehead and discuss it with him."

"Fine. But this hurts the party and the ticket. We either resolve it, or I'm out."

"You may need his blessing if you want to run for the top spot on the ticket. You're the likely choice to do that. Hold in the reins for awhile, Kelli. We better talk to Whitehead first."

Arrangements were made for Kelli, Kevin, and a few senior senators and representatives in the Democratic party to meet with President Whitehead later that week.

Kelli received phone calls from senior members of the Democratic party who had read the articles. Across the board, they recommended that she tell Whitehead she wouldn't run on the same ticket with him. She was advised to go for all the marbles.

The next day, when they met in the oval office, the President looked even more sickly, tired, and worn out. He had difficulty standing up to greet them. He was bushed. His hair was disheveled, his tie was out of place, and he obviously wasn't himself. He apologized for his appearance and blamed it on his job. It was obvious he wasn't happy about the medical findings being released to the press. He was visibly depressed.

"Those media buzzards are out to get me! They're all bastards! They stuck a knife into me. They finally got me."

Before Kelli could say anything, Kevin spoke up: "Mr. President, our party is in big trouble. The party will lose many seats in the House and the Senate if you insist on running. For the party's sake, you should either declare you're disabled and allow Kelli to take over the Presidency, or at least let someone else run for the job."

"I am sick," replied the President, "and I know it. But my mental capabilities are fine, and there's nothing wrong with my mind." He paused, his head bowed. "Tomorrow I'll tell the press I won't run for re-election and endorse Kelli to succeed me. But I want to complete my term. I don't believe I'll die during the next nine months."

"If you step down now, she could get more publicity and media coverage. She'd have a better chance to win," said Kevin.

"I think Kelli can win if the party endorses her. And her presidency will be stronger if she wins it in a fair election."

"I agree with the President," said Kelli. "I know I can win."

President Whitehead met with the press the next day with Kelli. He declared his withdrawal, adding that he fully supported her candidacy. He tried to smile but his make-up couldn't cover up the fact that he was seriously ill. President Whitehead shook Kell's hand and TV and news photographers recorded the event.

She confidently stepped forward with exuberance and announced:

"I am now a candidate for the Democratic Presidential nomination."

XX

RUNNING FOR THE TOP JOB

Kelli's husband was very upset when he heard that she had decided to run for the Democratic nomination for President of the United States. He was beside himself and told her about his feelings.

"If I didn't think we had a strong marriage, I wouldn't go for it, Mark."

"I understand that, Kelli, because I love you and I know you love me, but we have to think about our children."

"I know, but we have to think about everybody's children. I'm also thinking about all the women in this country who have been striving for equality. If I become the first woman president, I'll be a role model for every young girl in this country and for many others in the world. The Blacks and Hispanics have felt discriminated against for years, but what about the women? They've been discriminated against for centuries around the world . . . not just in this country. If Preston Adams runs on the Republican ticket and I run on the Democratic ticket, the American people will have a choice between a prominent black senator and a prominent white woman senator. They've never had that before. As for our kids—what about them? They're getting opportunities no other kids will have."

"If you run," said Palmer, "it could be very dangerous for our family. One kook has already taken a pot shot at you. There's lots more out there who would love to kill a president. We could lose you . . . to say nothing of the media. Are you ready for the invasion, because that's what it'll be?"

"Palmer, step outside yourself. What about the American people who helped make this country strong? There are an awful lot of poor people trying to make it who need my help. I want your complete support."

"Kelli, the best thing that happened to me was when I gave that talk to those women in Dallas and met you for the first time. Believe it or not, I may have been a star quarterback, but I was depressed. I was a jock making millions, and that was about it. I wasn't giving anything back for what I was receiving . . . and then I met you. You were a breath of fresh air. You had purpose. You were doing something for your country. When I first saw you in uniform, I knew I wanted you, and to this day, you are the best thing that has ever happened to me." He took her in his arms. Kelli's eyes filled.

"Mark, you're making me cry. Look, my love for you is just as strong as ever. But I feel that I have a chance to do something important. If you believed in me then, stand by me now. This country needs leadership which it has not had for a long time. It needs new ideas and has to become innovative again. Big changes have to be made to compete on the world's stage. We have to bring back respect and honor to the Office of the American Presidency. I feel confident that I can be that person so that we make progress in the 21st century."

"You're not going to solve America's problems overnight, Kelli. You're not a messiah, you're a mortal being. And you're not like any politician I've ever seen. I know you. You're completely honest and that worries me."

"Mark, I want your support!"

"Kelli, you know what my answer is, without asking me. Of course I'll support you. And I know you'll win."

"Mark . . . if I win . . . I promise you it will be only for four years if I can complete my progressive program. Otherwise, it can be for eight and then totally out of politics, no matter what the party wants. I want to make some drastic changes in how our government runs. I'll still be young enough, and you will be too after that, so there will still be plenty of time for us to share our love for each other."

"I sure hope so," he replied.

DEMOCRATIC CONVENTION, CHICAGO, ILLINOIS JULY, 2020 A.D.

At the Democratic convention in Chicago, Kelli easily won the nomination. She endorsed her party's platform completely, gave a solid acceptance speech, and added a few personal items to the party's platform. She announced she was in favor of term limits and that if Congress couldn't figure out a way to speed up approval by the states, she'd find a way. She was also in favor of complete frequent physical examinations for the president and vice president with full disclosure to the press. Vice President Kennedy's accident and Whitehead's illness were still fresh in her mind. Also, she favored a new amendment to the Constitution to determine disability and succession to the presidency. She recommended an age for retirement for all members of the Supreme Court and Congress.

She also stated that like Jefferson, she was a primary advocate of public schools. "I am a product of public schools, and I want the education in public schools to be as good or better than that in private schools. If public schools need better funding and better teachers, our government will provide it!"

One week later, Kelli met with Senator George Bradford, the Independent party candidate. She knew him well, and admired him when he was in the Senate. They had a long talk and discussed all the current issues. She asked him if he would be willing to serve in her cabinet if she was elected. He said yes. When the meeting was over, Senator Bradford announced that he was supporting Kelli for the presidency and told the press that he would not be running for the office. He advised his followers to support her candidacy.

PRESIDENTIAL DEBATES

There were to be three debates mediated by different TV journalists in three major cities. The candidates would not know the questions in advance of the debates, because the press and public sitting in the audience would ask half of the questions. Each session would be 90 minutes long, and each candidate would have an opportunity to answer the question with a follow-up.

The first presidential debates took place in Hartford, Connecticut, on September 15, 2020 A.D. Joyce Cronkite, the first moderator, directed the first question to Preston Adams.

"Senator Adams, what is your feeling about term limits? Are you for or against them and why?"

"I'm against term limits. It takes many years to know and understand the political methods used to pass the laws of this land, and experience is necessary to advise and consent to changes. I've been in the Congress for 23 years, and I learn something new every day. Those men and women who Kelli disparaged as 'career politicians' are chiefly responsible for the steadiness and stability of our government."

"Vice President Palmer, would you please answer the same question."

"Everyone knows I'm for term limits. It would allow more of our citizens to participate in the process of government. Too many of our congressmen make a lifetime career of politicking in Washington, D.C. That's why we have a quagmire down there."

"Ms. Vice President, since Congress has to recommend amendments to the Constitution, and their jobs may be in jeopardy if term limits are passed, how do you plan to get term limits?"

Kelli answered, "If the Congress fails to pass an amendment for term limits, I will lobby all of the state legislators to request that Congress convene a Constitutional Convention for proposing amendments. According to the Constitution, two-thirds of the state legislators can request that. And I will go door to door if I have to in order to get it done."

"Senator Adams?"

"Two-thirds of the state legislators will never request a Constitutional Convention, because they know they don't possess the wisdom to rewrite the Constitution."

"Vice President Palmer, do you have a reply?"

"I think the people are ready for change. I think people know that a document rendered 225 years ago needs to be reviewed and changed to meet the needs of the people living now. And it'll be one of my first priorities to make that change."

"Vice President Palmer, tell us your views on gun laws and gun rights."

"I'm in favor of changing our gun laws. We need a federal registration system for all guns and a one month waiting period before purchase. AK rifles and rapid fire guns, including missile firing devices, should be outlawed. Hunting rifles are okay. Hand guns should be limited to law enforcement officers."

Preston Adams replied, "The Second Amendment states that for the security of the state, the right of the people to keep and bear arms shall not be infringed. I believe that applies to all guns. As for the waiting period, I support it."

Joyce Cronkite recognized a member of the audience who wanted to ask Kelli more about guns. "Why are you so opposed to hand guns?"

"Because they are concealable. Because they circumvent impulse control. And because they account for more than 75% of the homicides in the USA. I'm not opposed to hunting rifles. They are less likely to contribute to violence. I am opposed to the rapid repeating rifles used in the armed forces."

Senator Preston Adams was asked the next question by a black member of the audience.

"Do you feel that affirmative action should be continued, or do you feel that it has completed its useful purpose?"

"When we see more minorities in the high paying jobs, then we should consider stopping affirmative action. Right now, African Americans account for only eight percent of all U.S. management positions."

"What about the Hispanics and other minority groups?" asked the questioner.

"They should also be considered for affirmative action."

Kelli was asked the same question.

"The Declaration of Independence states that all men are created equal. It mentions nothing about skin color or ethnicity. In fact, the Constitution should state that all men *and women* are created equal. Women have been discriminated against for centuries all over the world. If anyone has been discriminated against the most, it's the women. That's one of the main reasons I'm running for President. We can't have quotas for blacks, Hispanics, or women. We must eliminate all discrimination. That will be a principle focus of my run for the presidency."

Joyce Cronkite, the moderator, then announced, "You each have one minute to briefly tell us why you should be the next president of the United States. Senator Adams, you're to go first."

"I feel that I should be the next president of the United States because of my lifetime dedication to helping this country. Thirty years in politics has taught me a great deal. I know what this country needs and how to make it continue to be progressive. I also know how to listen to the wishes of the people.

"I have served in Atlanta and Washington, D.C. for most of my life. As a Majority Leader of the Senate, I have pushed for legislation that has helped point this country in the right direction. I believe that I have more experience than my opponent and can better apply that experience to the wishes of the American people."

"Vice President Palmer, you now have your summation."

"Senator Adams has spent his entire life in politics. I honor his commitment. But we differ. I'm for term limits so that this country can tap into new blood and new leadership. Where you've been is important, but it's where you're going that matters to our people. New ideas, innovation, and the will to help, is more important by far. I believe that I can bring new concepts and ideas that will help create jobs and security for all Americans. And so I urge you to view my candidacy not in terms of my gender or my appearance. We must look beyond appearances and examine ideas. My vision is of a nation driven by a political process that constantly brings forth its best people and lifts up those who have been left out. And it's a vision that will work."

NEGATIVE ADS AND DIRT

One week after the debate on national television, Kelli had a bombshell thrown at her candidacy to become president. On one of the syndicated night news shows, a former Navy pilot stated that he had slept with Kelli on four separate occasions when they were fellow pilots on a carrier in the Middle East.

He said he could have slept with her every night if they didn't have to take night duty once in awhile. When she tried to get rid of him, she accused him of sexual harassment in front of his fellow pilots and superior officers, ruining his Naval career.

"Why are you just coming forward with this information now?" asked the TV commentator.

"Because on television the other day, Kelli Palmer was asked if there was anything in her past that might impede her progress to be elected president. She stated, 'There's nothing in my past that I'm ashamed of.' Kelli Palmer is a liar!"

"Are you saying that you had consensual sex?"

"Yes. In fact, I had to fight her off on several occasions."

"Can you verify this relationship?"

"You can ask the other Navy pilots who flew with us if you like. Four or five other pilots slept with her too."

"What is your full name and rank, and were you her superior officer?"

"I was a full lieutenant, and she was an ensign. I out-ranked her. Yes, I was her superior officer."

"What carrier did this relationship take place on?"

"The U.S.S. Nimitz. I was a replacement pilot."

"What rank did you achieve in the Naval Air Corps?"

"That's another part of the story," he replied.

"Ensign Fitzgerald . . . that was her name then, accused me of sexual harassment in front of the Commander of the Strike Fighter Squadron . . . Commander Mike Jessee. He stuck up for Ensign Kelli Fitzgerald against me. It made me mad, and she also got mad at me . . . so mad that one night she and some thug in Naples, Italy hit me on the head with a baseball bat that fractured my skull ... I was unconscious for quite awhile. After that, I couldn't fly anymore. In fact, I didn't remember what happened until six months later and never got total recall. The attack occurred outside a restaurant in Naples, Italy. I found out later that Ensign Kelli Fitzgerald had dinner in that same restaurant the same evening that I was attacked. You can ask her."

"What was your name and rank when that occurred?"

"Lieutenant (S.G.) George Greeley. My nickname was 'Big Dog'."

"Have you been paid anything to make this statement to the press at this time?"

"No! Nothing whatsoever. I'm coming forward with this information because I'm proud to be an American, and I don't want Kelli Palmer to become President of the United States."

"Would you swear on a stack of Bibles that you're telling the truth?"

"Yes."

Within thirty minutes of that presentation on TV, Kevin Powers was told about the program, and he called Kelli immediately.

"Kelli, did you hear the TV program tonight describing your past scandalous life in the Navy Air Corps?"

"What are you talking about?" she asked. "I didn't have a scandalous life!"

"Tonight on TV, a former Navy pilot stated that he had an affair with you aboard the carrier the U.S.S. Nimitz and that you slept with four or five other Navy pilots. You cut off the romance and accused him of harassing you in front of your commanding officer. His comments on TV made you look like you were a slut! He stated

that you and some thug beat him up at night in an alleyway outside a restaurant in Naples, Italy. You hit him over the head with a
baseball bat and fractured his skull . . . That's how you got rid of
him!"

Kelli couldn't believe what she was hearing. She was speechless.
She didn't know how to respond to Kevin's question. Part of her
past was now out in the open, and what they were saying was a batch
of lies.

"Well, Kelli, is it true or isn't it?"

Kelli was silent for quite a while and measured her response.

"Of course it isn't true . . . but I can see a big mess developing."

"You're going to have to respond to the press tomorrow, and it
better be good! Why do you see a big mess developing?"

"It's a long story," she replied.

"It better be good or your candidacy will be shot in the foot. It
could be dead."

"I need to discuss this with you before I meet the press," she
replied.

"I'll be right over, and I'll bring a couple of our senior political
advisors."

Kevin Powers arrived around 1:00 A.M. with Senator Claude
Willett and Senator Dakin in tow.

"Is there any truth in what Lieutenant Greeley said about you,
Kelli?'

"None whatsoever, but it's going to be hard disproving what he
said."

"What do you mean?"

"I did accuse 'Big Dog Greeley' of harassing me in front of my
superiors, but I never slept with him at any time on board that carrier. I'd jump overboard first. I also did not sleep with any of the
other pilots on that ship."

"Can you be more specific?" asked Willett.

"Commander Jessee, my Commanding Officer, told him to lay
off, and he resented that. I'm sure he decided to get even. One part

of his story is true. I had dinner in that restaurant the night that he claimed he was attacked. The next part of the story you won't believe, but I'll tell you the truth. The two senior officers that I had dinner with went to the opera that night, and we separated when I came out of the restaurant. I went to hail a cab up an alleyway, and suddenly out of the darkness I was attacked by a big man. No one was around. He hit me on the chest and kicked me in the belly, knocking the wind out of me. He meant to kill me . . . I thought I was a goner. What saved me was that my grandfather made me learn how to protect myself when I was young . . . I earned the black belt in Karate.

"The assailant knocked me down twice, and the third time when he ran at me, I turned my back and grabbed his arm as he threw his fist. I threw him over my shoulder. He landed on the concrete cobblestone, and slid and hit his head hard against a wall. There was a big thud and then silence. I got up and ran out of the alleyway as fast as I could, because I felt there might be other villians with the assailant. Luckily, I was able to grab a cab and return to the carrier and logged in.

"The next day, I heard that 'Big Dog' had been beaten up by a couple of thugs and was unconscious in a Naples hospital with a fractured skull. I decided to say nothing because there were no witnesses, and I wasn't sure if it was 'Big Dog' who attacked me, but it could have been. Now I know it was him!"

"We've got big problems!" said Kevin. "We've got to stall for time."

"What should I do?" asked Kelli.

"You can't deny that you knew him, but you can deny that you had sex with him and the other pilots . . . you can state that he harassed you. As for you having thugs beat him up, no one will believe that you beat him up in a fight to the finish, causing his fractured skull. There's no way that he can prove that it was you . . . You can suggest that his fractured skull may have injured his brain so that his memory is gone. Also going back to that carrier and logging in immediately will help prove that he's 'full of beans'. I hope we can get a hold of those ship's logs."

"I'd agree with what you're suggesting," said Senator Willett. "Remind me never to pick a fight with Kelli."

"I wouldn't want a fight with her, either," replied Kevin.

"Is there anything else?" she asked.

"Yes. Find out where Commander Mike Jessee is now through BuPers."

"I think I know where he is," replied Kelli. "He's a Vice Admiral in charge of Aircraft Planning and Development in Washington, D.C."

"Good, we'll talk to him and ask him to support your story."

"There is something weird about this whole mess," said Senator Willett. "Kelli, don't tell your full story to the press. Make the statement that you will reply in due time. I think we ought to try to ferret out the instigators of these allegations. Let's see what our opposing candidate and party's response is. There's something that really stinks here, and it ain't Limburger cheese!"

"That's a good idea!" said Kevin.

Kelli appeared on the 6:00 P.M. TV news and read a statement:

"I have not seen the TV tape of my accuser's statements concerning part of my Naval Air Corps past. To clear the air, I deny ever having sex with that individual or any of the other pilots. I would jump overboard before consenting to having sex with him. I deny all charges and will give out a more complete rebuttal and statement when all the facts are in."

The next day in Congress, members of the Republican party in the House and Senate made statements in their respective chambers asking for Senator Palmer to come forth with the facts if she didn't have anything to hide. One congressman suggested she withdraw her candidacy. Another congressman went so far as to ask:

"Is Senator Palmer trying to hide behind her skirt?"

XXI

DIRTY POLITICS

The Washington press and the national media were quick to jump on the story put out by Lieutenant "Big Dog" Greeley. Their main theme was that Kelli's past looked too squeaky clean to be real . . . now maybe the truth was coming out. In the campaign up until that time, the polls showed that she was creeping ahead of her opponent, Preston Adams. The political campaign for the presidency was unexciting and basically a competition of ideas and interests, and no mud baths had developed . . . now a big sex scandal was thrown into the arena, and Kelli wasn't talking. The campaign had been dull, but the drama was suddenly intensified, and the public awareness was escalated. There no longer was any veneer of civility, and the animosity between the parties was brought to the surface. Sex in the headlines often had a way of catching the attention of both male and female readers, and there it was, the story was introduced to the public on the front pages of most of the national papers.

TV quickly picked it up, and Lieutenant "Big Dog" Greeley was seen and interviewed by numerous prime time commentators. He was being paid big bucks to talk. He denied any affiliation with the Republican party, and his juicy sexual comments were downright disgusting.

"We had a good consensual sexual relationship on board the U.S.S. Nimitz, and me and some of my flying buddies were enjoying her hot libido!"

*   *   *

Kelli tried to remain incognito while this was going on, but it was difficult to listen to the filth, slander, and unproven comments being made. Kevin Powers had to restrain her from emotionally blasting the media.

"Let's just wait until we get all the facts, Kelli."

Some of the Republican junior members of Congress spoke up to the press about how there was a strange silence from the Democrats. The environment got progressively tenser as time passed by.

The Chairman of the Republican Party was asked to comment on TV about Greeley's accusations.

"The accusations by Lieutenant George Greeley certainly are impressive. I believe that it will be difficult for Kelli Palmer to refute totally what he has said. It may be an impasse like . . . he said . . . she said. We've had that before. Where there's smoke, there usually is fire."

Kelli was furious when she saw the interview. She was in a presidential race with a nasty land mine in front of her, and she had to get out of it.

"Can't we hurry up and locate all those Navy men who were on the U.S.S. Nimitz with me?" she asked Kevin.

"We're working as fast as we can, Kelli. We can't do anything in damage control until we get all the facts!"

"I know," said Kelli. "But it's frustrating hearing all this bullshit they're putting out about me."

"Don't listen to it," he replied.

Ten days later, Kevin called and told Kelli that they had all the necessary facts to answer the accusations by Lieutenant Greeley. The Democratic National Committee requested thirty minutes of prime time coverage to answer the allegations. They paid for the time, and one of the major TV networks agreed to carry the program at 8:00 P.M. the next evening.

"Kelli, we want you to wear your dress white Navy captain's uniform with the gold Navy wings and ribbon awards. All of Greeley's accusations took place when you were in the Navy as an ensign. You were promoted and progressed upward to become a four-striper in the Navy Air Corps—quite an accomplishment! Now you're running for the Presidency of the United States of America. The Democratic Party wants to project that image. Kelli, we want you to make a live introductory statement."

"I can hardly wait to do it!" she replied.

The prime time program started with her introductory remarks:

"My fellow Americans, approximately ten days ago, my Navy career was tarnished by Lieutenant 'Big Dog' Greeley. The news media requested an immediate response and have been hounding me every day since. It was frustrating for me to have to wait to get all the facts together to answer the blasphemous lies with the truth.

I'm upset that the opposition and the media did not wait for my response, but rather chose to jump on Greeley's bandwagon. I feel that they will eventually regret what they did.

Before I accepted the Democratic nomination to be the first woman to run for the presidency, my past was scrutinized by my peers, and I requested an FBI review. There was nothing in that review that suggested that I shouldn't be a candidate. I've asked the F.B.I. to release their review to the public. I have also asked the Attorney General's Office and the F.B.I. to investigate the past of my accuser. I want the public to know about his past too.

"Kevin Powers, the Democratic National Chairman, and my attorney, Jack Bailey, have uncovered some real facts which they will present in the next thirty minutes for your evaluation. It is my pleasure to introduce to you, my lawyer, Attorney Jack Bailey."

Attorney Jack Bailey: "With the cooperation of the Navy Department and the Attorney General's Office, my office has been able to gather information from pertinent individuals who were present when these so-called critical events occurred in Kelli Palmer's life. We will present the facts and will try to respond to Lieutenant Greeley's accusations in a chronological way.

"The witnesses have been asked to tell the truth and to speak freely about what really happened . . . all have agreed to do this under oath. I have asked Vice Admiral Mike Jessee to be the first witness."

"Ensign Kelli Fitzgerald came under my command when she was a pilot with the Black Diamonds Fighter Squadron on the U.S.S. Nimitz. I was a commander at the time in charge of the pilots. At first, I had some doubts about Kelli's flying ability because she was a woman, but she quickly dispelled those doubts when her name started to appear on the top of the L.S.O.'s list of pilots hitting the #3 wire on landing.

"Because she was the first woman pilot under my command, I had received directions concerning the Navy's transition to a gender negative status. There was no way that I would allow anything unusual to happen to that young lady."

"Do you think she had sexual relations with Lieutenant Greeley?" asked Bailey.

"That's a fantasy of Greeley's imagination. A wishful dream that never came true. Because she was the only female pilot and an attractive one too, she was under close scrutiny and the watchful eye of all her senior officers. Kelli could have had the pick of the crop of the young Navy pilots, but she stayed aloof . . . she was focused on becoming a great pilot. I know that she didn't sleep with any of the pilots. If anyone had tried anything, the whole ship would have known about it.

"Greeley did harass her in front of the other pilots, and I put a stop to that! If you read his fitness report that I made out . . . it's all in there. I thought he was disrespectful to a Co-Navy pilot. His attitude toward women was wrong. It is amazing to me what has transpired here. I can't believe what Lieutenant Greeley is doing. If he got hit by a baseball bat like he said, he must have serious brain damage. What he said, I believe, are all false accusations."

"Thank you, Admiral Jessee," said Bailey.

*　　*　　*

"Our next witness is a Navy officer who had dinner with Kelli the evening that Greeley got his fractured skull. Captain Gregory Allen is a retired Navy captain."

"Captain Allen, do you recall having dinner with Ensign Kelli Fitzgerald in Naples, Italy, when all of these events took place? You were on the crew of the U.S.S. Nimitz."

"I certainly do. She was a young attractive Navy pilot . . . a charming person. It was our first night on R&R in Naples, Italy, after five months at sea, so Bill Perry and I invited her to have dinner with us. We also invited her to go to the opera, but she was just interested in getting off the ship and having a good meal. I was aware of the exact time we left the restaurant that evening because we were told that the opera ushers didn't seat you after the curtain went up. It was exactly 7:30 in the evening when we left the restaurant. We were in a hurry, so we took the first cab, and Kelli was going to get the next cab to go back to the ship. I understand that she checked back aboard at 1825 and that it was recorded in the Navy log which I have here. That's 45 minutes from the time she left the restaurant. It had to be one helluva quick knockout fight to accomplish what Greeley suggested. I don't believe it. I have one question. Where did she get the baseball bat?"

"Thank you, Captain Allen."

"Our next witness is Dr. Nicolas Rossi, a young Italian surgical resident who was on call that evening at the Naples, Italy Hospital. He was listed on the operative procedure as an assistant to decompress Greeley's swollen brain and to remove clots from his ventricles. We were able to locate him. He is now a prominent neurosurgeon practicing in Milan. He remembered the case completely, and we have a video to show his recollections."

"Lieutenant Greeley had extensive brain damage with a large fracture and soft tissue injury involving the back of his head . . . the occipital area. We measured the length of the fracture, and it was eleven centimeters long. Burr holes were put in, clots removed, and medicine was given to help reduce the brain swelling. He was on the critical list and in a coma for six to eight weeks, and we weren't sure whether he was going to make it. His brain was severely damaged with persistent bleeding, and on more than one occasion clots were removed from the ventricles. When he came to, his speech was slurred, and he was slow to recover. He was sent to an American military hospital in Stuttgart, Germany, for rehabilitation, and eventually he was transferred to Walter Reed Hospital in D.C. for a lengthy stay. With the amount of brain damage that he sustained, it's amazing that his memory has returned so astutely. I believe that there's more to this story than meets the eye."

MEDIA REFLUX

All the major newspapers were strangely silent after hearing the program on TV. A few of the conservative papers objected to the format . . . the press said that they could not question the witnesses and therefore, they claimed it was an attempt at window dressing. The media was quick to accuse, but reluctant to retract. The Chairman of the Republican Party was upset and was beginning to become worried about a possible backlash for his party in the upcoming presidential election.

The F.B.I. put two of their top investigators on the project of investigating Greeley's accusations. Greeley obtained a lawyer, trying to stop the investigation when they subpoenaed all of his bank accounts and hospital records. It didn't take the F.B.I. long to ferret out some gross irregularities. The F.B.I. found out that over a period of three months, Greeley had deposited over $90,000 in five separate banks. They were all cash deposits and no checks. Greeley claimed that they were gambling winnings, but when he was asked to produce the people who he had gambled with or played poker with, he was unable to do so. He finally realized that the jig was up but conveniently did not know the name of the man who had furnished the cash in the brown bag. He admitted that he had been rehearsed intensively prior to giving the information to the news-papers and TV.

When it became obvious that Greeley was lying, and the F.B.I. had enough information for a grand jury investigation, his lawyer attempted to plea bargain for his client. Kelli insisted that he go on TV on prime time and tell everything.

Greeley was told that he had to admit that he had lied completely or else legal action would be taken against him. He finally went on TV and admitted that he had lied and was paid $90,000 to try to impede Kelli's presidential bid. He broke down and cried and asked for forgiveness.

The bombshell hit the newspapers and TV, with some editors quickly making retractions about their previous comments about Kelli . . . others were silent. The Republicans were upset and in marked disarray by the strange turn of events . . . no apology was forthcoming, however. They denied that they were involved. The F.B.I. said they would be pursuing all leads about the brown bag-ger who paid off Greeley.

As the campaign entered October, the debates were more heated. Dirt was being slung with negative TV ads, and the bullshit was re-ally flying. It was obvious that gender and color would play a role in the outcome. Preston felt affirmative action should be continued because of the injustices of the past. Kelli thought it violated the constitutional guarantee of equal protection. Greeley's confession obviously helped Kelli, although Adams denied having anything to do with it. Kelli believed Adams, and she stated that she felt it was not his fault but was due to a dishonest overzealous party chairman. There was some evidence to back her up.

Polls showed the public almost equally divided when election night finally came. The results weren't in until the wee hours of the morning.

Kelli took California, nudging her electoral tally up to nearly 197 votes. She had campaigned hard there, despite the fact that it was her home state. Adams' strength through Texas and Arizona gave him those votes easily enough; Georgia, too, was his. But he lost most of the South.

The night wore on. Kelli and Mark watched from their home in San Diego; to have watched from the White House, she thought, would have appeared presumptuous. But at a little after 1:00 A.M., Kelli's total hit 250 electoral votes, and it was almost over.

Finally she went over the top. She had enough electoral votes. She was the first woman President of the United States of America, yet suddenly she became very introspective and humble.

"I'm not so sure that I deserve to be president," she remarked. There were a few tears of happiness in her eyes . . . she gained control of her emotions. She looked at Mark, and he looked at her.

"You've won, Kelli!"

"No. We've won, Mark. Without your love and support, it wouldn't have happened."

"I love you!"

Preston Adams called at 4:00 A.M. after addressing his supporters. His words were courtly and concise.

"President Palmer, I congratulate you, and I concede. A difficult choice has been made by the people, but it has been clearly decided. It has been a fair fight, and the major issues have been discussed. I pray that God will guide you as you lead this wonderful country of ours during the next four years. My best to you and your family."